The Voice of

The Voice of the Sea

Simon Magorian

ISBN: 9781739351700

www.simonmagorian.com

Venetian Palace Books

Chapter One

Burridge by Sea was a seaside resort which had gone into a lengthy decline, becoming what some airily dismissed as *a place where the middle classes go to die.* When David Johnson walked up to the main bar of the Metropole Yacht Club he saw things had changed. He smiled at its new renovation. The building was revealed as an Art Deco masterpiece. For decades it had undergone refurbishments, none of them correct.

The old guard, who had run the club for too long, lived in the past. It was a 1920s building but was previously decorated in the style of the 1820s. A major refit revealed its true elegance. Clearly a fortune had been spent. Chairs in Italian white leather with chrome fittings surrounded glass tables. The windows were stripped bare and framed with discreet curtains allowing the light to flood the cavernous main bar. A summer breeze swept across the room. Large aspidistras were strategically placed, everything was cream and light.

He nodded an acknowledgement as Mary Wintour, the club's new President ushered a party of newcomers into the bar. She was a sprightly, tanned and expensively tailored woman in her forties, gesturing across the room and chattering about the club. Mary was the future of the yacht club, so her group had decided. They had wrested control of the club from the old guard headed by her father, Nigel, who Mary had dislodged from the presidency. As Cassandra-in-chief, he had warned any change would bring disaster. However, Mary had been vindicated, membership was soaring and so was the bank balance.

David walked onto the balcony and watched as the masts of a Russian crewed tall-ship came sweeping into view, its sails engorged, as if they might rip as it tore through the waves. He was mesmerised, only having seen ships like these in old movies. Burridge was hosting a major festival of ships of the sea. Hordes of yacht-club types were scattered beneath the parapet. It was strange these people who were usually conservative dressers wore such gaudy colours when in their yachting togs. The festival had three days before it was launched, and they were arriving in throngs. The clatter of cut-glass accents rose from the quay to the club balcony. Waiters attended tables in gleaming white outfits and were serving food and drink. His appetite sharpened by the sea air, he decided to take advantage of the available provisions. Leaning back enjoying the view he tucked into Parma Ham and chilled Chardonnay. On the quayside below onions were being fried, and children and dogs were scampering.

Mary, having settled her party, went to the bar, which was a second home to her well-upholstered father, who perched on a stool in jacket and club tie was suffering in the heat. Mary knew any attempt to encourage informality would be rebuked.

'Scotch daddy?'

'That would be splendid.'

With a large gin and tonic for herself, and stuffing a whisky in her father's hand, she steered him towards David's table on the balcony.

'How's it going David?'

'We're primed and ready. We're giving all the staff masses of overtime this week.'

She was fond of David as were many of the Yacht club women. He had a striking profile, a sporty body, and with his floppy raven hair was what she called *personable*. He had taken the morning off work. Jennie was in charge. She was focused, diplomatic and a completely reliable assistant. Nigel started grilling him about his stewardship of the Alhambra Hotel.

'That place should be a goldmine. It's perfectly situated and a magnificent structure. If you get the finances sorted out you should be sitting pretty.'

David felt fortunate to be the manager at 29, and although he was updating its calcified image, he feared alienating its older customers. He hoped the investment the festival brought to the town would have an enduring effect. This was *his* town. For years it had been decaying, but now things were changing. He assembled at the Alhambra a good team. The accounts and budgeting were done by Jennie, but now he was hoping to get someone new, who might have a more creative approach.

'This afternoon I'm seeing some guy who lives in one of the houses around the back of the hotel who might be just right. Jennie does a fantastic job but if we can concentrate more on incoming trade, and getting locals to use the function suites for events and special evenings then we can start getting the place back on track. I'm determined this week functions as a kick-start to get things moving again.' David replied.

Nigel, sensing a lull in the conversation decided it was an opportune moment to get a dig in.

'Well, be careful. Since we've had our palace coup here not

everyone's happy with the results. Keep an eye on Jennie. My own daughter did the dirty on me here.'

'Listen, daddy, we're talking about the Metropole Yacht Club at Burridge on Sea. It's hardly King Lear,' Mary said with a glacial smile.

'One of the things which has made a real difference,' Nigel said, 'is clearing away the rubbish from the beach, and I'm not just talking about litter.'

'Oh, let's not go there.' Mary said.

David rubbed his knee nervously and leant forward.

'I'm afraid not everybody is completely relaxed about those security guards the club is using, they seem to be exceeding their brief. I'm not signed up to the idea that they're some sort of quasi-fascist private army, but I think people feel they need to be reined in a bit.' David grimaced as he knew Mary and Nigel were enthusiastic about them.

Mary gave a steely look.

'David, the next ten days, are absolutely critical. You do know that?'

He nodded and stiffened. He was about to be schooled. Mary tightened her shoulders and breathed in deeply. Her pained expression revealed her stricture would be painful, but necessary.

'There is an awful lot riding on this festival, it could get us back on the map. The Seafront Defence Trust is there to defend the patrons and guests of the Yacht Club. You know as well as I do there are a lot of antisocial elements around the beach. They are there to *protect* us. That is all, if there is also the additional bonus of encouraging some of the local undesirables to move on, then all well and good. This is being done in conjunction with the council. I don't want our event to be ruined by drunks, junkies and thieves. This is about taking back our communities. Perhaps it's fair to say the police have gone a bit soft. Some people need to be encouraged to move on. Some people need to be *told* not *liaised.* I think everything is going to work out just fine. You know what George Orwell said: "People sleep peaceably in their beds at night only because rough men stand ready to do violence on their behalf." I think people need to stop being so precious about the whole business. We are taking control. This is all about self-empowerment.'

From her crisp delivery, she clearly felt this closed the book. He felt uncomfortable as her eyes burned into his. The eyes of a believer. David felt it best not to reply and wondered what she meant. It implied an admission the security guards were roughhousing with members of the public; and significantly, she did not see this as a problem. Whatever she meant, it was time to leave.

'Look, I'm afraid I'll have to go. I've masses to do before everything's ready. I'll be popping in again about 8 for 8.30, I'll see you two again then, okay?'

He'd been roped in to compère an event that evening. Saying his goodbyes he paused for one last look from the balcony to savour the view. Looking across the water David knew things were better. The town *was* on the up. Descending the stairs, he thought the yacht club for all its snobbishness and elitism had a level of energy he'd never experienced before. There was a different atmosphere to the Metropole club of old: the heady aroma of new money.

The yacht club was isolated from the rest of the seafront. Leaving its freshly painted façade, gleaming brilliant white and royal blue, he passed an expanse of cobbled walkway leading to a small park whose sole attraction was a flowered clock. This faced an unspoilt piece of seafront. The small park area sheltered the yacht club away from where the restaurants and ice cream parlours commenced, offering a more democratic alternative to the reserve of the yacht club.

Standing on the corner of the Promenade was The Castle on the Cliff. This was a hostelry of a different stripe to the Yacht club. The pink gin and panini set - so much a part of Burridge Yacht club - would not set foot in the Castle. Whilst the Metropole Yacht club was the favoured watering hole of the Pashmina wearing classes, the customer base at the Castle was of a different stripe. It was not one of the roughest pubs in town. Those could be found further down, well past the pier. This was a pub with a shifting clientele of students, punks, hipsters and arty types, and as such, received the opprobrium of the yacht club secretary, Julian St. Hubert. In a letter to the council objecting to its licence renewal he had complained,

'It's so *Bohemian.*'

The Castle had defiantly decided to do nothing to improve its appearance and had displayed garish posters declaring it: *A Festival of the Sea Free Zone*. As David passed he heard Grime blasting through the sound system, crackling and heavily distorted as it was pumped up to maximum volume. He gave a polite nod as Josh from the *Hands off the seafront* campaign, set up in opposition to The Seafront Defence Trust, strolled towards him. He was a friendly community activist and the driving force behind the campaign, wearing retro-mod clothes he stood in front of David in a white Fred Perry shirt and a sharply ironed cream Harrington jacket, the look was finished with classic Ray-Ban sunglasses and blond razor-cropped hair.

'David, any chance of a chat?'

'Sorry, not right now, catch me in the Castle later on. Okay?' David turned and dived into the Morelli Ice Cream parlour. A popular haunt, it was designed in Milanese style by relatives of the proprietor. Chattering children were packed around tables tucking into enormous ice creams and tall frosted glasses of coke and milkshakes. Mrs Morelli was behind the counter with two harried-looking assistants serving a gaggle of French schoolchildren. Surveying the queue he gave a look of mock exasperation and Mrs Morelli laughed and shouted,

'I'll get someone to pop round with a litre of your usual in half an hour if you don't want to wait.'

He smiled and mouthing his thanks eased his way through the mêlée of children onto the street. Sprawling on a bench he lit a cigarette. He mopped the back of his neck with a handkerchief. The congested traffic pumping fumes and the breezeless heat made an enervating atmosphere. Pulling his mobile out to check for messages, he looked up and saw a group of tourists scrambling across the road and into the convenience shop next to Morelli's and decided to buy phone credit.

Happy Mart was staffed by Barry and June who were not the most affable shop assistants in the neighbourhood; the local children had nicknamed them *the gruesome twosome*. As you entered the neon hit you. The lighting was merciless, and presumably intended to encourage a high turnover of customers. Although well stocked it was disorganised and its narrowness gave it a claustrophobic feel. Apart from tourists, it relied upon the families who lived in the narrow Victorian terraces behind the promenade. David had the change placed in his hand by the unsmiling June. As he left, scurrying across the road were a group of the shop's regulars even less welcome than him. Spider Denby was pushing a beaten-up pram across the road. Following close behind him were Ghost, Benny and Ron. They were known as *The Gang of Four* and by local shop keepers by more florid names. Yet to reach their teens, they were accomplished shoplifters. Their plan of action involved what was on offer in Happy Mart. As the pram mounted the kerb he turned it a sharp right and they scuttled along the promenade at great speed. The reason for their hasty detour approached David as he emerged from the shop. Sergeant Jane Okonedo tapped him on the shoulder,

'Hello David, just doing the pre-festival rounds. Any problems?'

'No, everything's fine. No worries.'

David felt at a distinct disadvantage. Her job was the local community liaison and crime prevention officer, and as such he should have attended a meeting that week. He helped draw up their duty roster and timetables. Even though they were roughly the same age he always found her intimidating, knowing if he had problems they would be observed not by any withering comments, but by a clipped remark and a polite smile. She cut an imposing figure, with aristocratic Nigerian good looks and an athletic physique.

'It's only routine. I'll be popping in later. We want to make sure the week isn't marred by visitors being ripped off. These sorts of events attract thieves and pickpockets. You've got the crime prevention flyers to give to your guests. It's important the Hotel management take a pro-active role. But then, of course, you'd know all that had you attended my presentation.'

'Yes. Fine. Point taken.'

He thought he had better move on before her admonishments became more pointed.

'Look I'd love to stop and talk but I've got to get back, I've got people coming for interviews this afternoon,' and he scurried along.

A man came towards her with a shambling gait and lowered himself onto the bench. He was wearing a blouson jacket that was too big for him and red chinos and was unsteady and breathless as he sat. His sandy hair was unkempt and he looked older than his 52 years. He had that careworn look of a man who had mistreated himself or was defeated by life.

'Are you alright, sir? Do you need any help?' she asked.

'Yes, I'm fine. I think I may have had too much sun. I've been mooching on the beach. I'm not drunk,' he sat up smiling, offering his hand.

'Sergeant Okonedo,' she said shaking it.

'Daniel Trent,' he had the low voice of a man broken by circumstance.

'I'm just a little concerned. You seem a bit unsteady on your pins.'

'Oh, I've just overdone it, I'll be okay.' He found her over-solicitous, but reflected it was preferable to the treatment he'd received from other police officers on his travels; where being ordered to move on, or struck round the face was an occupational hazard of homelessness.

'You remind me of someone, sir. I was a high achiever in athletics when I was at school and I had a coach, a Mr Benson who made me all I could be.'

'Ex-Forces, was he?'

'Yes.'

'A real task-master?'

'Oh, yes.'

'Are you still in touch?'

'Actually, we are, and anyway you never forget a good teacher. I know I sound as if I'm interfering. I just wanted to make sure you were okay. There are support structures here. If you need it help is available.'

'No, that's fine. I am getting help. There are people worse off than me. Anyway, I need to be getting on. Thank you for your concern.' He stood and straightened up.

'Oh, one thing, thank you for not saying it.' he smiled.

'Sorry?'

'Thank you for your service. I can't bear it. The ex-military don't need to be thanked or sentimentalised. We occasionally need help- the same as everybody else- we all need a hand-up at times. Don't we Sergeant?'

She nodded as he ambled away.

*

Jenny drained the last mouthful of lukewarm coffee and strode from behind the reception desk through the lobby doors and down the marble staircase. Having spent most of the morning processing piles of paperwork she needed air. It was going to be a busy week at the Alhambra Hotel or *The Ham*, as the locals called it. The town would be groaning with yachting types. All week she had been trying to get the hotel and the staff in optimum shape. The term faded grandeur could have been coined specifically for the Alhambra. The once elegant Edwardian façade was now a pale shadow of the elegant refinement of its heyday. Closer inspection would have revealed the peeling stucco work and the crumbling upper cornices, and the sea air, whilst refreshing for its guests had taken its toll on its overall appearance. The owners were indifferent to requests to invest in any refurbishment, and its appearance whilst not actually seedy was forlorn and run down.

She looked out across the promenade, which had received a major facelift by the council. The painted railings gleamed in the summer sun, and the usual detritus -which had made the seafront so squalid, and at times menacing - had been cleared up. Families were wandering along the beach and vendors were selling hot dogs, ice creams and soft drinks and doing a brisk trade. Jenny liked to think this was how it was during its Edwardian heyday. Twenty years ago, she was one of those children clambering over the sands while her grandmother told her tales of romantic trysts between Aristocrats and Gaiety girls. An elegant time of assignations held in plush hotel rooms quite unlike the appointments made by corpulent businessmen for afternoon fornication now. She smiled and mouthed the word *assignations* and thought about what her grandmother called The Good Old Days.

Along the promenade, major improvements had been made and its prominent advocate, Chairwoman Ivana Bennett-Johnson of the *Posh up the Promenade Campaign* bore down on Jenny with a cry.

'Everything ready for the off then?'

'Yes everything's fine, we're going to be packed to the rafters come Saturday.'

'A word in your shell-like, but are they going to do anything about the drunks and the druggies?'

Jenny didn't want to have this argument again, she had respect for the efforts Ivana had made to improve the look of the area. An unfortunate by-product of the campaign to renovate the seafront had been a rumpus in the local council chamber. This had spilt out onto the pages of *The Echo*, where the letters page was littered with demands that local vagrants, drunks and drug addicts be moved on. Many were becoming concerned at the stridency of the campaign, Jenny was one of those who felt some were advocating a policy which bordered on social cleansing. She had criticised what seemed to be moving a social problem into someone else's neighbourhood. The emergence of The Seafront Defence Trust, organised by Julian St. Hubert the Metropole's Secretary, whose private security guards were harassing *undesirables*, worried some.

'Look, they barely make it up this end. Usually, they only go to the grot bars right down past the clubs. They only make it up here to sleep under the pier for a bit of shelter and I don't think you should begrudge them that, and before you say anything, no, I won't have them in the hotel bar but I think so long as they don't cause problems we should live and let live.'

Ivana shrugged.

'Well perhaps you're right, let's hope there aren't any problems.' She pulled her fingers through her hair and leant on the lamppost.

'This weather is truly glorious. If this lasts we're going to have a fantastic week. I don't need to tell you this could really lift the town up if it goes well.'

Jennie smiled and turned towards the sea and noticed a young man staring at the Hotel. He had piercing blue eyes and corn blond hair and she assumed he was a foreign tourist.

'Can I help you?' she asked.

'No, well not yet. I've got an interview a little later. To be honest I'm just killing time at the moment. My name's John Sykes. I've got an appointment at 2.00.'

His hand offered, Jennie shook it and smiled.

'I'll look forward to meeting you a little later.'

He walked off smiling, and Ivana said,

'Well, he was more than presentable.'

'Yes quite. If all the applicants look like that, I'll be quite happy.'

'On a more serious note,' Ivana said, 'how is David's Aunt Clarissa?'

Clarissa Johnson lived in the well-appointed house on the corner of the promenade. Living almost next door to the Hotel meant David had few excuses not to visit her. As one of her few surviving relatives, he made a point of visiting at frequent intervals.

'Oh, she's soldiering on,' Jenny replied. She was now quite infirm and battling a terminal illness.

She always concealed her dislike of the woman and Miss Johnson's imminent demise made her feel uncomfortable about her true feelings. She wondered if Ivana knew what she was thinking, but concluded, it was unlikely she would say anything to David. She was saved from her awkwardness by the fortuitous arrival of guests.

'Duty calls!'

Shrugging at Ivana she turned and bounded up the stairs.

*

George Miller was in Miss Johnson's garden. The process of weeding and tending the flowers was a task he was inured to, but he was irritated with the non-organic detritus he now had to remove. People threw rubbish into the garden as they passed. He opened the bin bag and threw cuttings into it; pushing them down to join the beer cans, crisp wrappers and discarded newspapers. He ensured everything was cleared before Miss Johnson came down. It meant the removal of any *nasty stuff*. It was unremarkable to find hypos and discarded condoms lying in the gutter there in the morning. The Lady of the House had to be saved from that. She had a restricted future and consequently preferred to live in the past. George and his wife Dennie, therefore, protected her from the seamier side of modern life. He tied the bag up and took it into the house and placed it in the basement for refuse collection day. Hearing Dennie padding down the stairs he walked to the hall to ascertain what the programme was.

'How is she?'

'In pretty good spirits. She wolfed down your Eggs Benedict without any problems, and she's now champing at the bit to get some sea air. She's coming down the stairs under her own steam. I think she's going to have a good day.'

She was somebody with a limited timescale and a good day mattered. Twenty years previously the idea of the pair of them as live-in carers for somebody like Miss Johnson would have appeared to be a failed life. George and Dennie previously had good jobs; he a Lieutenant in the Army, she a nurse at the casualty department in the local hospital. Conflict had visited them in different ways and made them re-evaluate their priorities. In their forties, and in good health, they had decided to get out of their professions and pursue a different life. The experience of seeing active service in Iraq had traumatised George to such a degree he had to leave the army. He was still in counselling but had felt completely unable to talk to anybody about his experiences. He would avoid the subject, but became irritated when people used expressions like *the horrors of war*. As he found it both portentous and meaningless.

George became emotionally enclosed and Dennie felt excluded, and completely helpless that she, as a trained nurse was unable to help as he unravelled before her. An additional problem was Dennie was finding work extremely stressful. The Saturday night shift at the casualty department, which was referred to by the staff as *The substance abuse horror special* had become increasingly wearing. The constant stream of drink and drug-related admissions became impossible for her. The central problem was the ever-present feeling some sort of confrontation was imminent. If people asked her about Saturday nights at A&E she would normally reply *It's a War Zone*.

This was an exaggeration, of course. George had returned from a war zone. It was through Dennie confronting George and discussing how she felt that helped him open up about how he was feeling. This was a process that not only saved their marriage but also as friends pointed out, more importantly, saved themselves. Now freed from their former lives, they were relaxed and contented. Living in one of the grandest houses on the seafront with light duties, they were free to pursue new interests; she retraining as a teacher, he giving private French lessons for a few hours a week. The house they bought three miles down the coast long before the property boom provided a healthy income, and they enjoyed the liberation of being freed from the constraints of ambition. Dennie bustled into the kitchen, followed by George. Rifling through her shoulder bag she checked for her keys.

'I am going to be very late for my class, as usual.'

Dennie had her classes in French Literature to attend to, she found some days trying to service the needs of Miss Johnson, the University and George, problematic. Her long-term ambition was to relocate to France. George was unconvinced, but she was working on him.

'Your lunch m'lady' he said handing her a bag of bacon and Brie sandwiches. Pecking him on the cheek she bolted through the front door.

Returning to the hall he pulled Miss Johnson's chair out of the alcove and positioned it at the foot of the marble staircase in the lobby. It was a large Victorian wheelchair constructed of rosewood and heavily lacquered wickerwork with enormous wheels at the side, it looked like mobile furniture rather than a wheelchair. Once she was ensconced in it with a thick Argyll rug over her knees and reclined against its high sloped back she cut an imposing figure.

George peered up the stairs and saw Miss Johnson outlined against the circular domed skylight, which bathed the hall in a warm yellow glow. She was dressed for outdoors, wearing a light overcoat and a summer hat. Her illness had emaciated her and the coat was now enormous on her, giving her a gamine, almost childlike appearance. With a canvas bag in one hand and the other on the banister she negotiated herself downstairs, one step at a time.

'Does the Lady of the House require assistance?' he asked in a faux posh accent.

'The Lady of the House does not,' she replied, entering into the spirit of things.

He prepared her transport. Collecting her thermos and sandwiches he placed them in the small nook directly under the chair. Piling on several Chinese cushions he proceeded to plump them up.

Checking the mail from the hall table he turned to see Miss Johnson had completed her descent. She took one look at the luxuriant cushion arrangement saying,

'Now that looks most comfortable' and lowering herself, 'and thankfully it is.'

George knew that once down she would be eager to savour the fresh sea air. George opened the front door. Miss Johnson folded the rug onto the cushions behind her declaring,

'It's far too warm for that.'

Easing herself back into the seat she looked up at George

expectantly. Realising this was a command he propelled Miss Johnson towards the bright outdoors.

*

Simret manoeuvred the trolley out of the main door of the Collingwood restaurant. Stevie Norton looked up at her from behind the main desk, and gave her a weak smile as if to say, *rather you than me*. The flustered girl pushed the trolley through the swing doors of the hotel kitchen. Heavily loaded it made a dull clatter as it rolled down the short slope towards the other trolleys. They were piled up with white china and although smeared with the jammy remains of Devonshire cream teas and buttered scones, still gleamed under the fluorescent strip lights like a snow-capped mountain range. The precarious way they were stacked made a statement of managerial indifference to even minimal standards of health and safety. Everything was predicated upon saving money. The next shift due in was the kitchen porters and she wondered if they were now coming from a different agency. These would be what some people referred to as New British, meaning recent immigrants who would be expected to do the sort of badly paid sweated labour the indigenous locals were not prepared to do. This was regarded locally as either shameless exploitation, or people paying their dues. Simret hurriedly removed her hated apron. The dress uniform was a fussy apron with similarly particular caps. It was expected they wear these Edwardian style pinnies whilst serving the hat-wearing harridans who frequented the hotel tea rooms on a daily basis. The hotel dress code was an added humiliation of working there. Management asserted they gave a genuine Edwardian feel to dining there. Stevie Norton, was studying at the University on the Hotel and Catering course as part of a student exchange with an American University and did desk duty much of the week. She pointed out the staff felt it made whoever had to wear them as looking like a French maid out of an ancient Benny Hill sketch, or worse like characters out of some porn movie, but to no avail.

Simret looked up at the clock, it was exactly 1.30. Her shift was over and the kitchen porters were nowhere to be seen. The ungenerous financial rewards did not engender any sort of trouper spirit in the staff and she was not going to remain one more second than her wages required. She smiled at Arrigo the chef, slumped in a chair by the window and pulled on her bomber jacket. She gave a contemptuous look at the trolleys which were sitting there, overloaded, and awaiting the ministrations of the absent porters, and marched out.

Arrigo had done his work for the morning and was relaxing by the window with a plate piled high with almond croissants and a large cappuccino. Organising the meals for the provincial palates of the lunchtime regulars was not something which was particularly challenging. He found the post-lunch ambience in the kitchen particularly relaxing. The warm aroma of bread and butter pudding, vanilla sauce and good coffee combined to make an agreeable atmosphere. He smiled and looked across the empty kitchen- which now, not bustling or noisy, seemed large and cavernous - with a proprietorial air as he wiped croissant crumbs from his moustache. He shuffled menus across the table and scrutinised them whilst gulping coffee, considering them whilst wiping his palms over his rump hindquarters. During his brief tenure as the head chef at the hotel, he had to endure weekly altercations with the manager David Johnson. When he left his parents' restaurant on the Giudecca in Venice he had been warned about British food culture. He had been raised in the tradition of robust Italian cooking and in his first placement had been confronted with the unholy trinity of British middle range cuisine –prawn cocktail, well-done steak and black forest gateaux- and had begun what was to be a familiar round of confrontations with management over the content of menus. The latest dispute concerned the proposed introduction of pasta salad on the house menu. The existence of pasta salad, as far as Arrigo was concerned, was indisputable evidence Satan existed and was active in human affairs. David was just another combatant in the food culture wars Arrigo had vanquished without much difficulty. Now he was looking across at the adjoining worktop at a colourfully labelled ice cream carton. This had been delivered by the staff from Morelli's. Of the disputes he had enjoyed with David- and there had been many- they frequently centred on issues of territory and demarcation. David *knew*, he was saying to himself, this should have been delivered to his office and put in the fridge there. The ice cream, he knew was excellent and the handiwork of his compatriot a few doors away. Even so, this carton of choc-chip ice cream laced with rum he regarded as an interloper. He gave it an accusing stare, trying to quantify the exact level of offence he was entitled to feel. His train of thought was interrupted by the arrival of the guilty party, as David quietly padded into the room.

'This is yours, I believe.' Arrigo said gesturing towards the offending article.

'Many thanks,' David replied with frosty courtesy, picking up the carton and departing quickly before Arrigo had the opportunity to give vent to any other grievance.

*

'How far are we going today Miss Johnson?'

'Oh, let's be a bit adventurous shall we?'

Miss Johnson felt better than usual and wanted to enjoy the sunshine whilst it lasted. Bitter experience had taught her to make the most of the weather before it turned. The promenade was bustling with energy and its newfound effervescence was infectious. George had taken her further along than usual. The central pier gleamed against a clear July sky. It had previously been allowed to fall into severe disrepair, but after the Burridge Victorian and Edwardian Restoration Society had raised funds for its refurbishment it had been triumphantly reopened, and was now shimmering magnolia white, and brimming with its old-world confidence. Miss Johnson smiled and craning her head around at George exclaimed,

'Let's do the Pier!'

George turned the wheelchair a sharp right.

'Hold it! The miracle of the pier has demanded that the lame shall walk!'

She guardedly manoeuvred herself out of her chair and discreetly turned her spine and stretched her legs. The chair was not a universal requirement for her, it functioned as a necessary fallback if her legs, or the rest of her, got overtired and she was unable to walk.

One of her treasured pictures on her dressing table, was a picture of Bette Davis in her later years, holding an embroidered cushion that bore the legend, *Old age ain't no place for sissies*. The constant battles she was now waging with her own body more than bore this out. At the Pier, they were confronted with a garishly confident ice cream kiosk and decided they were entitled to a treat. Progressing down the main concourse they munched on their ices as they negotiated their way through a gaggle of young children.

Further down a string quartet was playing to an attentive crowd. They smiled and clapped as the musicians finished their piece, and swigged from bottles of water they had placed on the floor by their instruments. They were all decked out in matching lemon shirts and shorts and smiled their appreciation to the crowd. After a short break, the cellist moved forward and changed the board that announced each of their offerings. George peered down at the laminated placard and said,

'Mozart divertimento.'

'Ah, lovely. I know you're not a fan of this sort of thing but I'm afraid you're going to have to indulge me.'

The quartet, comprised of students from the university was more than just technically proficient and although she wanted to hear more, what had become of the main hall was of more interest. This was a place of many memories. In her twenties, it was a venue for dancing and live music, but her more cherished memories were of an earlier time. Looking at the outside she thought how it had seemed so much bigger. Reminiscences of her teenage years came rushing back. A Pierrot troupe called the *Fol de Rols* performed there every week one summer, in her childhood. This sort of entertainment was never seen now. It was the relic of a bygone age that had clung on for a while, in seaside towns, long after the demise of the music halls and would be sneered at now. She remembered a production of *Chu Chin Chow*, now a show that would be considered patronising if not culturally insensitive. She remembered the chorus standing against a theatrically imagined version of London's Chinatown in a yellow and ochre glow of lamplights singing plaintively *Chinatown, My Chinatown, when the lights are low*, or something like that. She imagined it was probably from another show, or perhaps another place. Possibly it was a curtain-raiser. She couldn't remember the words but she could hear the tune coming from the small orchestra and visualise the man, encased in Leichner pan stick, peering out from the upright piano, grinning broadly. Withdrawing into memories of her youth was not a way of dealing with the present, but it was an effective form of pain management.

'Look, they had a *Clash* tribute band here last week. I would have liked to have seen that,' George said, breaking the dreamlike state she had entered into. She smiled, it was no bad thing being pulled back from such wool-gathering.

'Rather you than me, I think. Time to move on. I think it would be a good idea to find somewhere nice on the prom to have our lunch.'

After leaving the pier, and a little tired, she announced,

'I think it's time for Queen Boudicca to get back in her chariot.'

They went further down the prom.

‘I want to go down the tacky end,’ she announced, and there they were amidst a panoply of amusement arcades and beach vendors. He wheeled her down to the beach, so she could get the full benefit of the sea air. Along the sand they observed the local council's Sun Awareness workers distributing bottles of sunblock, leaflets and paper hats, whilst giving friendly warnings about the hidden dangers of unprotected exposure to the sun. They tucked into their sandwiches and gulped their coffee,

‘George,’ she said, regarding her cane, ‘if one of those idiots comes near me with one of those bloody leaflets, they're going to get this up the jacksie.’

George smiled at her attitude.

The illness whilst taking a severe toll on her physically hadn't crushed her spirit. She delved into her bag and pulled out a book Rev. Stephens had lent her, a dog-eared copy of the life of Dietrich Bonhoeffer and started reading it. She was now not just hot but troubled by an aching in her legs. She put the book away and looked across the beach at the waves crashing and receding on the sand whilst she rubbed her palms against her treacherous limbs. She was not in the frame of mind for tales of Christian martyrdom. Thoughts of death were never far from her; she needed no reminders. Getting her mirror from her bag she applied a generous coating of brick red lipstick. There was a time she would have thought it improper to put her makeup on in public; but then so many worse things were now tolerated it hardly mattered. The chemotherapy and the medication she took had robbed her of much of her hair, but her makeup confirmed her femininity. Her approaching death was a surprise for her. This was not what she expected. Her gauntness and feebleness she found difficult to contend with. What she feared as a young woman was ending as her dipsomaniac mother had, who she remembered as a bloated and bad-tempered zeppelin encased in mink and astrakhan floating across the Home Counties. Her own death she had imagined as some sort of rail crash, not this inexorable loss of mobility and potency.

George gestured at a woman receiving a Tarot reading a little way in front of them. There was, of course, a fortune teller at the pier, but these were genuine Roma Gypsies and so aroused his interest.

'I know you don't approve of them, but Dennie would love it. You know she loves having her fortune done. Complete rubbish of course, but it's alright for a laugh. I think they're quite clever the way they can get info out of you without you realising, and then feed it back to you like a mystic revelation.'

'I have no use for fortune-tellers,' she replied.

This was true; she knew what her future held. George sensed what she was thinking and his hand hovered over her left shoulder. He contemplated giving it an empathetic squeeze but thought better of it. It would have been ill-received. She still liked playing the dowager and it would have been treated as an unwelcome intrusion.

'George let's go a little further on while the weather lasts. The crowds are getting a bit much here.'

They moved past the busier part of the seafront to an area dominated by retirement flats. At this stretch of the promenade an enormous hotel had been turned into an opulent retirement home. The Imperial was a luxurious boarding school for ageing delinquents, which afforded a dissolute retirement for those who could afford the exorbitant fees. Along the curved wrought iron balcony on the first floor could be seen old buffers lounging in wickerwork chairs quaffing daiquiris whilst reading newspapers and novels, Miss Johnson pointed her stick at them exclaiming,

'Look, George, it's Cirrhosis On Sea.'

'I wouldn't mind booking in there, good food, fine wine, and if you get trashed and make a fool of yourself in the main bar, half the residents can't even remember it the next day.'

'You see it as a holiday camp; I see it as a warning. That's where I'll end up if I'm not careful. It's just an open prison with room service and better catering. That place is just for rich lecherous old drunks. I wouldn't feel safe in there, not for one minute.'

The beach area opposite had been the subject of bitter political controversy. A proposal had been put forward it should become a nudist beach. Many resorts on the south coast had them, people were told. At first, it looked like the proposal would go through on the nod, but it was not to be.

Concerned citizens groups decided this was a Rubicon crossing issue. It was held by those claiming to represent local faith communities it would lead to a surge of social ills. One group, claiming to represent ordinary taxpayers held it would encourage fornication between men and women. A local church group maintained it would encourage general licentiousness. Yet another group headed by the unctuous Julian St. Hubert entered the fray, representing *right-thinking decent folk*, said it would encourage gay sex. The local newspaper then maintained it would probably encourage voyeurism. The plan was finally turned down by

Burridge City Council on the basis it would encourage nudity. Which many felt was unarguable. Some of the residents at the Imperial were a little disappointed, as they were contemplating lounging on the balcony, whilst observing a display of firm young flesh through binoculars as a way of enlivening high tea.

'Well, we've done working-class tacky and upper crust tacky. What's left is fairly dull from now on. I say 10 more minutes of fresh air before we return to *chez* Johnson.'

George concurred.

There was a sharp chill in the wind and he decided it would be better to set back before the weather turned.

Chapter Two

At twenty to two, the prospective candidates for the vacancy at the Alhambra started arriving. The first thing that confronted those who entered was the enormous mahogany reception desk, which imposed a quiet authority upon the capacious entrance, with an impressive lobby, a central staircase and large lifts with brass fittings. It was decorated with a variety of plasterwork characters from classical mythology, Neptune, mermaids and the kraken all jostling for attention, and fitted with thick red carpet with yellow fleur-de-lis throughout. For a visitor, it was a little run down but still with an old world luxury, but to a possible job applicant it could not fail to be intimidating with its air of haughty confidence. The desk imposed its authority with Edwardian arrogance. Stevie greeted them curtly but politely from behind it and gestured them into seats opposite, where they sat browsing through magazines as if awaiting the attention of a dentist. David was in his office doing his paperwork while Stevie was checking on a variety of bookings and fielding enquiries on the telephone. Today, only three had turned up. There was another day of interviews later in the week, but she still thought it odd there was so little response. She leant over the desk.

'Could any of you gentlemen use a coffee?'

This was met with cheery acceptance. They all looked so serious, she thought. She checked on the names David had told her to expect, John Sykes, who she had dubbed the blond bombshell was present, along with Pierre Meilleur, the intense-looking one and

Darren Andrews an athletic-looking type who kept on glancing over at her. However, there was one missing, one Barry Stevenage, who as she was wondering about him, called to absent himself. She phoned through to David and announced they were all present.

As she placed the tray of coffee and ginger snaps on a low wicker table in front of them, she announced,

'David will see the first of you in about ten minutes.'

She returned behind the desk, and as she resumed her paperwork Darren sauntered over.

'Don't I know you from somewhere? I mean, I'm sure we've met,' he said.

Stevie gave a wry smile, but before she ascertained how to react to his approach, she realised she knew him. There then followed a brief moment of social awkwardness as she tried to remember where from. She glanced at his CV on the reception desk and after gleaning the details of his qualifications said,

'The University, it must have been at the University.'

Same course, different years, she thought. The university was extremely cliquey even within departments. Looking at Darren he seemed the football club type, and on one level she was warming towards him. She didn't like heavyset men but Darren had a lithe physique, moved easily and had an engaging manner.

'Do you spend a lot of time in the union bar?' She asked.

Of the aspects of British cultural life which differed from her home town in Michigan, she found most of them pleasing, save one, the seeming indifference the English had to displays of public drunkenness. On the rare occasions she had made it into the main bar on a Wednesday night she had been appalled at the behaviour of the men in the sports clubs. That was the night for clubs and societies, and she had memories of inchoate groups of drunken sportsmen hanging around the main bar singing crude songs and leering at any woman who passed them. Her Lutheran sensibilities were offended by people who regarded getting vomiting drunk as a social accomplishment.

'No more than most'.

Now it was his turn to be ill at ease. He wondered if she had been on the receiving end of one of his clumsier entreaties. Best to change the subject.

'So how long have you been working here?'

It was a dull question. If there was any chance of arranging a date he would have to do better. The glance of desperation he gave her, she found endearing.

'Tell you what, why don't you tell me what your plans are? Hopefully I'll be graduating next year and don't know what I'll be doing. What will you do if you don't get the job here, I mean have you got anything else lined up?' she said, trying to help him out.

'Well, there is the possibility of a job up near Windsor. It's one of those places which puts on those medieval-style banquets. It's a kind of huge Baronial Hall. If this doesn't work out I reckon I've got a good chance of getting that one, as I have certain talents I imagine the other candidates don't have.'

'Really, and what are they?'

Darren smiled and leaning against the counter with a self-satisfied grin, said,

'I can play the lute.'

The way this was announced, he clearly regarded this as grounds for excitement.

'I can play madrigals. Actually, I've won quite a few prizes for my playing. When I was a teenager I competed at a national level. I have some tapes of me performing at the National Lute Championship five years ago. My version of Greensleeves, even my rivals had to confess was outstanding. I have a CD of it at home I could lend you if you like?'

'No, that's okay thanks. Madrigals aren't exactly my thing.'

Her mother frequently remonstrated with her over her indecisiveness, but this was something she was absolutely certain about. She remembered the old bromide that a gentleman is somebody who knows how to play the accordion but doesn't, and firmly felt the lute should also be included in this category. He now seemed the unsexiest man on earth and she wondered what she had been doing for the last ten minutes. She couldn't think of anything more to say to him, and checking the clock she saw an escape strategy.

'Excuse me. Two o clock, time to get things moving.'

She picked up the internal phone and as she prepared to speak to David, he strode across the lobby towards her. Darren hurriedly resumed his seat with the other candidates.

'So only three of them here. I'll see Mr Sykes, first of all, then Mr Meilleur and lastly Mr Andrews. Everything fine with you?' David asked.

Looking over to check Darren was out of earshot she replied,

'Yes, apart from being pursued by the lute world's answer to Jimi Hendrix.'

'What?'

'I will tell you the tragic story of my life later.'

Stevie resumed checking bookings on the computer. She looked up to see David animatedly shaking John Sykes's hand, whilst escorting him in his most courtly manner along the corridor to his office. She smiled, David prided himself on his informality and was a serial backslapper yet here he was reverting to traditional British formality. It was all first name terms and much talk of non-hierarchical management structures. The British upper classes always revert to type she thought.

*

June looked up from the counter of Happy Mart and framed in the window was the diminutive figure of Mrs Armstrong. She turned to Barry saying,

'Look who it isn't. Here comes Mrs Aroma.'

They looked at each other and winced. The lady in question had a certain notoriety, a scruffy, indecorous octogenarian who was inattentive to her personal grooming. Her drop-in carer Valerie, a fresh-faced and compassionate woman in her early twenties had discussed her problems with June the previous month. Valerie had a habit of lowering her head and speaking slowly to emphasise a point as a form of vocal highlighting, and had informed June,

'Mrs Armstrong is a senior confronting the life challenge of living with personal hygiene issues.'

to which June briskly replied,

'That woman smells like a *sewage* outlet.'

The conversation then became increasingly acrimonious until

Barry intervened and calmed things. However, assistance was now being given to Mrs Armstrong and whilst not the most fragrant person in the neighbourhood, even June conceded there had been a significant improvement. She ambled into the shop towards the magazine rack and startled rifling through it. She had made no concessions towards the baking heat and was wearing a thick tartan woollen overcoat and a toque.

As June put cigarettes into the wall unit behind the stained Formica counter Barry served a gentleman known as the Colonel. He had never been in the forces, nor did he pretend he had. A civil servant of some distinction, with a military bearing he had acquired this as an honorific title. Ruddy faced and white-haired he was decked out in open-neck shirt and shorts. He was a cheerful man, and found Barry and June a mystery, as he found many young people. They were young, maybe thirty, and yet so sad and angry. They reserved a special terseness for the elderly.

Mrs Armstrong looked over at them and demanded,

'Where is it?'

June continued with her task and without turning replied,

'It's there, you'll find it if you look.'

Mrs Armstrong continued combing through the assortment of celebrity and lifestyle rags until clenching a brightly coloured journal she gave a gasp of triumph. Her monthly treat was *The Friends Companion*, a brightly hued magazine packed with romantic stories, shortbread recipes and features on stars of stage and screen from the '40s '50s and '60s. Putting it in her steel basket she decided to look at the reduced bay at the back.

Whilst Barry and June were preoccupied with being disagreeable to the Colonel, they hadn't noticed the party trouping through the door. Happy Mart had been targeted for a major criminal enterprise. Not major by the standards of New Scotland Yard, but certainly by the previous criminal endeavours of the perpetrators. The Gang of Four had arrived. They all poured in wearing matching bright scarlet outfits. Ghost and Benny stood behind the Colonel hoping to obscure the actions of Ron, the most diminutive of the group, who was wheeling the pram into the shop and towards the back. Spider, being the Generalissimo took up his position by the till.

Once Ron had strategically positioned the pram at the back of the shop, where it could be loaded up with the desired foodstuffs, he gestured to Benny, who promptly joined him. Ron then cautiously peered from behind the gondola, checking if they were being observed whilst Benny heaved large quantities of cooked chicken pieces and Belgian chocolate into the pram. Barry peered over the counter as he sensed something was afoot. The whole enterprise had been organised like a military operation, or rather how a twelve-year-old perceives a military operation being organised. Ghost positioned himself at the door whilst Spider moved towards the side of the till to cause a distraction.

'Hey knob breath, where are all the footie guides?' he yelled.

This had the desired effect, giving Barry and June someone else on whom to vent their spleen.

'I am not putting up with any of your lip you little shitbag! Now you get out of my shop right now, before you get a smack in the mouth!' June screamed, and while the two shop assistants were suitably distracted, Benny and Ron prised a large box of Stella

Artois from the shelf at the back and dropped it into the pram. Ron darted along the aisle and made a signal to Ghost who was standing expectantly at the door. He pulled the door wide open as this was his task, and with a lurch Ron and Benny lurched forward with the pram, propelling it onto the street outside. Dispensing with any more unpleasantries, Spider sped through the door after them.

In the commotion, Barry and June were unaware of what had occurred. With Mrs Armstrong and the Colonel's clear line of vision in the centre of the shop, they saw everything. Barry and June leapt from behind the counter, and at this point, an inviting prospect opened up for Mrs Armstrong. Standing in front of the chilled section looking at the packs of prime British sirloin steak she decided opportunistic shoplifting should not be the exclusive preserve of the young. Whilst she rammed about twenty pounds of sirloin steak into her oversized handbag, she reassured herself she was not so much stealing, as striking a blow against ageism.

Outside, the Gang of Four were weaving across the road, the pram loaded up with the fruits of their felony, now difficult to manoeuvre, as Barry and June screamed obscenities at them. Ghost's raucous laughter faltered as he turned to see a black hansom cab speeding towards them. Its brakes screamed as it slammed to a halt, the frightened and angry driver leant out the window shouting,

'You *stupid* little shits! You could've been killed!'

They pushed on, mounting the kerb on the other side and hurtled down the pier. Barry and June, who had been rendered mute with terror at the prospect of the children being smashed under the wheels of the taxi, now resumed their chorus of invective.

The Colonel stood there shaking his head and grinning broadly. He turned to see Mrs Armstrong scuttling down the road, her small frame lopsided under the weight of her bag. Barry and June stormed back into the shop seething and muttering oaths until June picked up the phone and called the police.

*

As the last of the candidates walked out the main door Stevie decided to broach the subject of Gary with David.

'Are you going to speak to Gary about the position? He should be considered for the job.'

Gary was the general manager of the Castle on the Cliff and was a qualified graduate in what was rather inelegantly called *Hospitality and Hotel Industry Management.*

'I don't think he'd fit in. I'm sure he's completely competent, but I don't think his ideas about running the place would be the same as mine.'

Stevie thought this was David all over. The post had not been properly advertised, just publicised through some variant of the old boy network. Although the Castle was sneered at by the upper crust yachting types, Gary had a knack for getting people through their doors and spending their money. Under his stewardship it was now a thriving commercial enterprise, whereas The Alhambra was struggling. Stevie thought a blunter approach was required.

'I don't think he would introduce Drag Nights, Karaoke, or Heavy Metal competitions but this place could do with some new ideas, new thinking.'

David liked to think of himself as forward-thinking, but he always erred on the side of tradition and formality. He just stood there turning his head in a noncommittal way.

'David, there isn't any other reason why you don't want him?' she asked cautiously.

'No. You know I'm not prejudiced. He just wouldn't be right for here. What he does down there is fine. He's a brilliant pub manager but he'd be quite lost here. I like him and I like the place. In fact, I'll probably join you for a drink down there after work. But they are totally different venues. He'd fall flat on his face in here and that wouldn't do us, or for that matter himself, any favours.'

'Perhaps you're right,' she said. The phone trilled as soon as David padded his way past the counter to return to his office.

'Hello. Mary Wintour from the Met. Stevie, be a love, when David comes to the thing tonight could you ask him to bring those seascapes? Thanks, bye!' David came out almost immediately.

'Forgot about those paintings, did you?' Stevie asked.

David sighed. A nautical evening had been organised for the foreign visitors at the Metropole and for some inexplicable reason, in Eastern Europe, seascape watercolours, far from being regarded as naff, as they were in England, had quite a following. In fact, the entire evening, in which he had agreed to be the master of ceremonies, would be tiresome. It was to be a night of dancing the hornpipe, third rate sea-based poetry and a quartet playing awful music. If a piece of music had any titular reference to sea or boats it was included in the evening's repertoire, with the exception of *The Flying Dutchman*, on the grounds, it was too German, too Dutch, or too difficult for an amateur string quartet to play.

‘I'll take them along later. That John Sykes left his mobile in the office. You don't want to pop it round to him. He only lives round the back. Actually, it's okay I'll do it.’ Stevie who was taken aback at this uncharacteristic display of selflessness, detected an ulterior motive, and leaning across the counter yelled,

‘Enjoy your cigarette.’

He turned and smirked like a wayward schoolboy as he bounced down the steps.

*

The subject of wayward schoolboys was a primary concern in the conversations being conducted within the confines of the eccentrically named Happy Mart. Sgt. Okonedo had arrived and was endeavouring to find out what had happened. Barry had confidently predicted there would be no sign of the police for at least half an hour after calling them, so Okonedo's arrival within five minutes was a source of particular irritation. He had been anticipating moaning at the tardiness of the police at length in the bar after work, and even that small pleasure had been denied him. Whilst June was serving another customer Barry endeavoured to supply her with all the details.

‘June, would it be possible for you to lock up for a few minutes, so I can get proper statements from you?’ Okonedo said, trying to conceal her irritation.

‘Very well,’ June said as she ushered the customer out of the shop, locking the door.

‘Would you like to put a sign up? This shouldn't take more than ten minutes.'

June shrugged and shook her head. A man came to the door and rapping the glass with his knuckles yelled,

'Are you open or what?'

Without turning, June raised her right arm and gave the man a single fingered salute whilst she continued speaking to Okonedo.

The whole interaction between Okonedo and the retailers was highly ritualised. Even if the police were motivated to do something about thefts like this, the penalties administered by the local bench would make little difference, and fines would be unpaid. Barry and June would make offensive remarks about the police. Okonedo would explain the extensive manpower and technical resources the modern police force had at its disposal could not be prioritised over a case of beer. They would respond they couldn't be bothered to make statements. Okonedo would then remonstrate with them whilst being secretly relieved. After which they would all bemoan what each had to contend with, to anyone who would give them a hearing.

Whilst Okonedo on one side, and Barry and June on the other were circling each other in this adversarial little dance, a radio call came through which extricated her from this ritual. A robbery of a more serious nature had taken place. This made everyone happy. Okonedo could leave the shop and deal with something else, and Barry and June could say the police were indifferent and could feel validated in their victim status.

*

Jennie was now back and preparations were being made for the evening arrivals. Stevie felt reassured it was not all going to be left to her. Two had phoned in sick and David was in his office phoning around for additional staff. The issue of absenteeism due to illness was a perennial problem. Stevie was in no doubt this was a morale issue, that should be addressed by making staff feel more valued, not by managerial platitudes, but by better wages. However, perhaps that this was not a good time to raise it. Jennie seemed to be made of tougher stuff and was cheerful as she booked in a large French group. Stevie admired Jennie. She was a woman who had no advantages in life and had worked hard to get where she was, and part of that experience of starting on ground level was she was scrupulously attentive to detail. If the week went well it would be due to her efforts. Two of the hotel stewards were piling a gigantic quantity of luggage into the lift.
Jennie turned to her,

'Now would be a good time to get yourself a quick coffee. It's going to get really crazy in the next half hour. While you're doing that could you see if those French women in the restaurant are getting what passes for service round here?'

Stevie walked into the Collingwood, and across the deserted restaurant, half a dozen rather soigné women were lounging on sofas by the patio doors. She saw they had coffees, and a well-stocked cake trolley was adjacent to their table and they were enthusiastically tucking in. The remains of a large seed cake was posited on the edge of the table next to some lemon drizzle cakes.

'Is everything satisfactory ladies?' she said, and they smiled and raised their pastries as if proposing a toast.

Stevie felt a level of admiration mixed with envy as she spoke to them. French women always seemed so effortlessly stylish. The wardrobe accessorised and understated as if a sense of chic was a hereditary trait.

'Everything's wonderful,' the woman in the centre said, 'but permit me for asking, but what are the police doing outside, has there been some trouble?'

'I don't know anything about it. I'll be right back. Excuse me, ladies.'

She swept through to the lobby, leant over the desk briskly relaying what she knew to Jennie and scurried down the stairs to discover more. Outside Sgt. Okonedo was talking to George by Miss Johnson's front door.

'More bad news?'

'There's been a theft,' Okonedo said tersely.

George stood there brooding and Stevie knew she would get more information without him present. Clearly the theft had either been from him or Miss Johnson. Stevie believed her house was an Aladdin's cave of collectables, and was curious about what had been stolen.

'Sorry, don't mean to intrude. Look Okie when you're through here why not pop in for a coffee?'

This was an invitation to come in and tell all, over a good cup of Colombian.

'I'm nearly finished here, I'll be over in a couple of minutes,' she said.

Stevie informed Jennie, and she was intrigued.

'I wonder what they nicked from the mad old trout,' she said.

When Colin Markham, one of the evening staff arrived for his shift, he was startled by the enthusiasm with which he was greeted by the two women. They marshalled him behind the reception desk, so they could give Okonedo a comprehensive grilling on her arrival. Five minutes later she was seated with her Colombian coffee coated with a generous sprinkling of chocolate. Jennie started interrogating her.

'So how did they get in and what's been nicked?'

Okonedo cupped her bribe between her hands, blowing on the surface before taking a sip and leaning back in her chair.

'Well as you can imagine, I can't tell you too much. There does seem to be some question how they gained entry. As to the what, an antique clock.'

'A clock?'

'Yes, a rather valuable one. I saw the photos. A really beautiful one, designed by Thomas Armstrong and Brother of Manchester for the Chief Sea Lord of the Admiralty in the 1830s. Absolutely beautiful, covered in pineapples. It was the time when the Victorians went pineapple mad. There's quite a bit of other valuable stuff in there. Some quite exceptional African antiquities, but obviously they would be much more difficult to fence. Even the clock will be problematic, but if Miss Johnson's valuation is correct it's worth between forty and forty-five thousand.'

'Insured?'

'Oh, absolutely. But nothing else appears to have been touched. Which might mean it was stolen to order, and they had a buyer waiting.'

'I'm going to have to tell David. He's going to go ballistic.'

Stevie felt uncomfortable as she discerned an unmistakable glint of pleasure in Jennie's eye. She decided not to enquire as to the reason for her antipathy towards Miss Johnson and put it down to old fashioned class antagonisms.

'I think the sooner you tell him the better. We've got the remainder of the French coming in over the next couple of hours, and frankly I can do without any aggro if it can be possibly avoided. The sooner he throws a fit and gets it all out of his system the better. You can talk to him. I can't. You'd better remind him he's the captain of this leaky ship and he's got to show some leadership.'

Stevie feared it would be impossible to motivate the staff if David was wandering about in a flaming temper.

Jennie nodded.

'No time like the present. I might as well get it over with.'

Once Stevie had Okonedo alone she felt confident to broach the subject.

'So, what exactly is her problem, what is her issue with Miss Johnson?'

'You've never really met her have you, I mean not spoken to her? She is the most dreadful snob and has some pretty bigoted views. David isn't like her at all, I mean he likes banging on about standards and all that stuff but he's pretty open-minded. I think at one point- and don't quote me on this –he and Jennie had something going on. Perhaps she put the kibosh on it; I mean he is very devoted to her.'

Okonedo had just had some rather unpleasant dealings with her, and although she did not wish to confide with Stevie about what had passed between them it had confirmed all the things she had been told. She liked and trusted Stevie; she had an emotional openness she found engaging but she was unsure how much Jennie was aware of what she knew and thought she should be circumspect in her dealings with Stevie. She sensed she had already been indiscreet.

'Ah well, that's families for you. Isn't it?' Stevie said, offering a non-committal way of closing the subject.

The question of how David would react was resolved as he swept from his office and stormed down the steps to the outside. Okonedo stood up and straightened her uniform.

'Time to be moving. Many thanks for the coffee.' and mobile cupped to her ear she was off.

*

Okonedo smiled as she approached the police van parked along the promenade just past the pier. As Sergeant Dalton clambered out of the front she rubbed her hands. He liked Okonedo but he did not want to upset her. She had a fearsome reputation for dressing down officers who she felt had fallen short of her exacting standards.

'I've received a tip-off Fagin's gang are somewhere in the vicinity,' she said.

At least one thing was going to be sorted out, she thought.

'I don't need to tell you this is a pretty pointless exercise,' Dalton volunteered.

'Oh absolutely, but today they've added public drunkenness to their CV. Even Ghosts' parents will realise they've got to wake up now.'

'I wouldn't be too sure about that. I get the impression his father regards anything his brood do short of firebombing the King as youthful high spirits. Anyway, how do you want to do this?'

He had been instructed to bring them in. Community liaison was Okonedo's brief and he didn't want to ruffle any feathers. Dalton was a popular officer and the most notorious canteen gossip at the station, but she admired his relaxed approach.

'This puppy is mine. It might not be much but it's all I've got. Look, give me ten minutes. Okay?' she said.

They were close, and reportedly were not in any condition to move far. She stood on the short wall surveying the beach. People were packing up. Halfway down the sand was a large electric blue canvas windbreak with a family in the foreground massaging coconut butter into each other's vermillion backs. Peering around the side, she saw a flash of scarlet. She felt like a Royal scout in a preamble to some medieval conflict, lurking among the fields and hedgerows for a glimpse of the enemy's brightly coloured ensigns and pennants to identify the whereabouts of their encampment.

Spider and company were sharp-witted regarding authority figures in their vicinity, but alcohol had muddied their wits. As soon as they had staked their patch they had attacked their chicken with raptorial relish and necked down the beers; this combined with the baking sun had so dulled their senses they were unaware of the approaching figure of Sergeant Okonedo.

Spider was in full flow, holding forth in Henry V fashion on how to arrest the decline of England's fortunes on the football field. Ghost, Benny and Ron saw a familiar figure loom up behind him.

Leaning forward she gave a loud stage cough, and as he turned round pronounced,

'Professor Moriarty, I presume.'

They all sat there looking crestfallen at having been rumbled so easily.

'Now let's see. A number of items were stolen from Happy Mart earlier on. Amongst them a large quantity of cooked chicken and some cans of Stella Artois, and my, what do I see here but a large number of chicken bones and some empty Stella cans- Isn't that a coincidence?'

'If I were you, I would find the whole situation distinctly suspicious,' Spider replied, trying to salvage some face by a show of mannered insouciance.

'I am immune to the lovable scamp routine,' she declared.

It dawned upon them a lift down to the police station was inevitable, with a long wait, as the effects of sun and alcohol took its effects on them. The additional realisation that some deeply angry parents would have to collect them cast a cheerless pall upon them. Okonedo leant forward and taking the can of beer out of Spider's hand she turned it upside down emptying its contents over the remains of the chicken announcing,

'Your revels now are ended.'

Taking a step backwards she gestured for them to get up, and as they all slowly stumbled to their feet she added,

'Oh, by the way, if you are going to go around town getting into trouble, what is really, really dumb, is going around in bright scarlet outfits so you can be easily identified.'

Had she remonstrated with them about respect for property or about the dangers of underage drinking, this would have been greeted with smiling indifference, but this was an observation of a complete lack of nous on their part and stung Spider like a mother's slap. They stumbled up the beach in a desultory manner, to find Sergeant Dalton standing there with the police van doors wide open. Spider grimaced and yelled out,

'Please don't say it!'

Dalton gave a courtly bow and replied,

'Anything to oblige-your carriage awaits!'

They clambered into the back more quiet than usual followed by Okonedo and as soon as they were seated she announced,

'Now none of you are to even *think* about vomiting.'

Chapter Three

After the police had been escorted off the premises Clarissa Johnson wanted some peace. She found the robbery disturbing, but the intervention of the two CID officers and Okonedo added to her anxiety. The manner of the men compounded her feelings of distress. They spoke the way she observed many young people did, of being absolutely correct, but with no underlying courtesy. Okonedo, she reflected, had been surprisingly knowledgeable about art.

George was now busying himself downstairs, supposedly upgrading security. Her cocktail of drugs had been provided by him and she swigged them down with cranberry juice as she reclined in her armchair. Tired from the sea air she wanted to relax in a hot bath. She needed no more drama and rebuffed her nephew's attempts at a visit. A light supper and an early night were what she required. Things would look different in the morning. As she sat back in her armchair her eyes kept returning to the space on the mantelshelf. The clock which had dominated the room by its presence now overshadowed the room by its absence. She would find something else to put there. Her lounge was spacious and decked out in the loving clutter of several generations, and whilst the clock was not the only noteworthy item in her collection it was the one that brought her the greatest feelings of pleasure and reassurance.

The room was full of artworks acquired during the age of Empire. Artefacts from Nigeria, hangings from India, two huge Qing dynasty vases framing her French windows leading to the roof garden, and underfoot magnificent rugs from the Middle East. The centrepiece had been the ostentatious clock on the mantel somehow holding sway over the other pieces, at once incongruous and somehow analogous to the whole Imperial attitude of the room. She put her head back as she was now woozy from the medication and decided to try and get some rest. Looking through the French windows she imagined she might even sleep in the roof garden if the weather held up.

*

Jennie walked down the corridor with a tray of glasses and a couple of bottles of Medoc. At six o clock the pretentiously named Alhambra Wine Club would be in the Trafalgar function suite to unwind. It was a narrow room, with dark panelling and walls covered with meretricious oleographs of Napoleonic battles. The Wine Club was an ad hoc assortment of local traders who had an arrangement with David. On certain days of the week, they would congregate in a tiny back room and complain about the general state of the seafront, their customers and everything, whilst polishing off three or four bottles of cheap wine David provided for them at a nominal fee. This was a shrewd bit of local politics. The Trafalgar suite was too small to be used for anything other than tiny groups and was David's way of keeping on favourable terms with the local business community. Jennie uncorked the wine to give it time to breathe before everyone arrived and put out a couple of platters of cashew nuts.

Barry and June piled in first and looked around expectantly. There was much for them to feel indignant about, but it was pointless without an audience. Stevie who had just finished her shift arrived with Doris Markowitz in tow. Doris was the majordomo of the group and was always decked out in masses of loudly coloured shawls, clanking jewellery and exotic headgear. Dressing like a Gypsy Queen from an Ivor Novello operetta was part of her job description, her outré appearance was registered as tax-deductible as she worked as a clairvoyant on the pier. Although she refused to predict anything, she merely gave people possible options.

'Nothing is written, the choice is yours lovey!'

She was in her late fifties, rounded, still beautiful, and a firm believer in all the Tarot and astrological verbiage which was her stock in trade. Her hands were crammed with rings shimmering with semi-precious stones. People had different opinions about Doris and her gifts, but she ensured ignoring her was not an option.

For Barry and June, this constituted an audience, and they could hold forth on the iniquities of their life in Happy Mart. The incident with the children was pored over in exhaustive detail. They then turned their ire on Mrs Armstrong.

'That woman is absolutely unbearable, and she smells like a gorilla's gonads. I'm sure she was on the thieve, the rancid old bag. Everybody thinks it's just the kids, but some of the coffin dodgers we get in are unbelievable.'

June was at her most expansive. When she and Barry were complaining was the only time they seemed happy. Warming to her theme June began complaining about everyone who had annoyed her that day.

'Today's been murder. I've been rushed off my feet all day. I haven't had time to fart. You know that funny bloke who collects all the shells? Well, I've gone out of my way to be especially nice to him 'cos he had special needs. You know, being so slow? It turns out he's not special needs at all. He's just a complete knob.'

Everyone wondered what she meant by being especially nice.

'We're constantly being put in a position where the stock is running out of the shop, and the police don't do a bloody thing. How tradespeople round here are supposed to make a living is anybody's guess, and to top it all we're trying to close down and we have that blond idiot coming in and having a go at me because we don't have the right condoms. I gave him the rough side of my tongue didn't I, Barry?'

'Too bloody right you did,' Barry said. Mrs Morelli walked in and smiled, as she leant over to get a glass of wine. She took a good swig saying:

'This is all very well and good, but if you were the victim of a serious crime, you would expect the police to prioritise that, not shoplifters, correct?'

June frowned.

'Yes, I suppose so.'

June disliked Eva Morelli's getting in the way of a good rant. There were normally six at the wine club, and Stevie wondered where Will, the missing party, had got to, at which point David popped his head around the door.

'Stevie, are you coming?'

She grabbed her coat. She had forgotten they had made a vague arrangement to have a post-work drink down The Castle on the Cliff.

'Stealing her away from us are you?' Doris said smiling. Stevie shrugged and hurried out the door. As they descended the staircase she said,

'Thanks for rescuing me. It was getting a bit tetchy in there. You know what June's like when she's got a moody on.'

'I do indeed.'

The tradition of drinking after work was something Stevie couldn't get used to. She was normally sensible and had a ginger ale. The Castle and its clientele both fascinated and repelled her. The outside had an old-world appeal, even though it had a contemporary feel inside. The sign outside with its Arthurian Castle and crashing electric blue waves was rather romantic. The contrast with the inside was stark. It was a locals pub, and on the occasion when tourists would walk through its doors they usually gave a look of horror as they quickly headed back out. It was decorated inside with panelling with plush Victorian seating, dark wooden flooring and throughout the main bar camouflage netting had been draped across the partitions. At the end of the main bar was a small stage which was used for karaoke and where rock bands and stand up-comedians performed.

David went to the bar and got himself a whisky and a ginger ale for Stevie. She had been advised to avoid mentioning the burglary, as he may explode. It was just after six and many came in for a quiet after-work drink. From eight o clock, it would become raucous, but now it was a good place to unwind. As Stevie leant back she noticed one of the interviewees passing their table.

'Isn't that one of the guys who came for an interview? Shall I ask him over?'

'Not a good idea. He's come in here to relax. I'm a prospective employer. He'd probably feel obliged to be on his best behaviour.'

'I was talking to Jennie and she said a mutual friend had told her he has a chequered history.'

'Chequered? In what way? Professionally or personally?'

'Well knowing Jennie it's sexually. You know how she likes her tea and scandal. Anyway, it's probably just gossip; you know what people around here are like.'

'If it makes you feel any better I'll get him checked out before there's any possibility of giving him a job. I have contacts who can do that sort of thing.'

He looked up and saw Josh descending upon them armed with *Hands off the Seafront* leaflets. David adjusted his posture, as he feared he was about to be lectured.

'Sorry Stevie, just need a quick word with David.' Josh said. She smiled and nodded, she was disinterested in British provincial politics and thought it best to leave them to it.

'David, any more thoughts about supporting our campaign? We could do with a friendly petit bourgeois figure like you taking a stand.' Josh said grinning.

'Yes, but if you had me on board then some of your more Marxist chums would say it had degenerated into a Popular Front.'

'Ooh, using the arguments of the left to avoid taking a stand. You are a smooth customer. Are you getting classes in deviousness from Julian St. Hubert?'

David laughed.

‘Now you're being mean. Josh, I'm aware of what's going on, and I'm not happy about it. I have spoken to various people, and I can't say too much, but people are watching them and action will be taken, if, or rather *when*, they over-reach themselves.’

Josh gave an understanding nod.

‘The quiet word in the ear, well I suppose it's better than nothing. I know you're one of the good ones David. I just hope those bastards don't have to hospitalise somebody, or worse, before something gets done.’ He leant over and put a couple of flyers on the table. He decided he needed a parting shot. Nodding at the flyers in his hand, he gave a broad smile saying:

‘Got to get these out. Just be careful, or you'll end up with splinters up your arse.’ As Josh walked away, Stevie gave David a quizzical look.

‘Splinters up the arse-from sitting on the fence,’ he explained. Stevie smiled and nodded.

Unbeknownst to them, a group of musicians were preparing to perform and started their sound-check. The noise proved too much for them and they grabbed their coats.

‘Good luck with your bash tonight, David. Apparently, there are posters up bearing your name all over the yacht club and beyond. Nervous?’

‘A little.’

At which they went their separate ways.

When Josh had finished flyering the pub he walked to a table and slumped down. It faced the sea. Dirk and his girlfriend Mary were seated drinking cold lagers and chatting. They were both students at the University. Dirk studied Politics and Mary design, she worked part-time behind the bar and had designed the posters for Josh and was wearing her Castle uniform of pub T-shirt and red chinos. Dirk wore his baggy olive cargo pants and matching shirt, he wore little else.

'How's it going?' Dirk asked.

'Oh, I think we're winning. The problem is the yacht club lot have all the power and influence. It makes it more difficult to break through.'

'My senior lecturer Vera put out an online article attacking the yachting junta yesterday. She's American and writes a lot about Democratic party politics in New York. It's very punchy. It refers to them as *a bunch of revanchist assholes.'* Dirk smiled.

'I'll feel able to comment when I've googled revanchist.'

'Ah, revanchist: in this context meaning the old guard, those who feel they were born to rule, attempting to make a comeback, return of the ancien régime, that sort of thing.' Dirk replied.

'Okay. I'm with Vera.' Josh said.

One of the regulars, Will Ferguson approached the table.

'Why is everybody hunched at the window? I can't believe you're all here to watch the boats.'

Mary didn't trust him, she found him shifty. One of those who latched onto others. She looked out the window.

'Well, the goons from the Seafront Defence Trust have been having more fun annoying people on the beach. They were seen along here last night. People are saying we need to keep our eyes peeled. I think this whole business might be coming to a head. That's why we're hanging around here.'

'Perhaps we should mind our own business. It's nothing to do with us.'

'Well I imagine once they've finished socially cleansing the seafront. We will be next on the list.'

There was a commotion as a group entered through the main doors. Half a dozen men stumbled in laughing. They were The Bedlam Brothers, a local band. One smiled and waved at Mary. Dirk leant forward.

'Well, if there are any problems tonight, those guys could be useful. They're good to have around if there's trouble.' Mary nodded and stood up.

'Okay, I think it would be a good idea If we sat out front,' they collected their coats and bags and sat at a table outside.

'Josh, what did David have to say? I imagine you discussed the SDT with him.' Mary asked.

'Oh yeah, but he still thinks the old boy network will work. The quiet word in a receptive ear. I think he has a certain distaste for those thugs but he thinks it can be sorted out through his networks. He needs to address the reality of what sort of person St. Hubert is: a man with the moral empathy of bacteria.'

As Dirk stood to stretch his legs, he heard a disturbance behind him. The sound of shouting.

'You people are fucking vermin! You're not wanted round here!'

Mary leapt up. She knew a moment had arrived. However, it was not her party who were yelled at. A terrified figure in a red jacket came stumbling towards them pursued by figures wearing the royal blue of the SDT.

She recognised the bulky frame of Gavin Lintern, their Chief Steward, but not the other. She charged at the pub doors throwing them open and yelled at the Bedlam Brothers ,

'Guys! outside! You're needed!'

Behind her was the sound of a fist hitting a face. She ran to see Daniel Trent falling to the ground. Blood was pouring from his mouth as he crashed to the pavement. The air had been forced from his lungs as he careered down. He was lifting himself up by his palms and attempting to suck air into his chest when Lintern kicked him in the back. He was booted so hard his body cleared the ground. The group from the pub were now attacking the blueshirts. Mary rushed over to Trent, as she turned she could see a volley of fists being landed on his assailants. Putting her hand around his waist she adjusted her feet to get some purchase. She turned to see the well-built blueshirts running away. When she lifted Trent she became angrier. Clearing his body from the floor was like lifting a hat-stand. His body was so wasted.

The whole thing was over in seconds.

Daniel Trent sat at the table outside shaking. Dirk and Mary were attending him, she told the others not to crowd him and go inside.

'My name's Trent, but please call me Daniel.'

'Are you sure you don't want to come inside, to a private room and we can sort you out.'

'No, no. I really don't want to go inside.' he said dabbing his mouth.

'It's okay, we can patch you up a bit and get you something to eat. Then you can decide what you want to do. Would you like us to get the police?'

'No, I wouldn't, and I don't want an ambulance. I don't think there's any point.'

‘Once we get you sorted, you can decide what you want to do. Okay?’

He was still shaking. Mary didn't know why he was reluctant to have the police involved. Then again, she didn't know his history, and decided not to ask. She turned to Dirk.

‘Could you pop inside and ask them for the first aid kit from behind the bar?’

He nodded.

‘Now Daniel, I can't do anything about your trousers, but your jacket is badly torn and we've got a Six Nations windcheater out the back you could take off our hands, is that okay?’

He gave a smile and nodded.

Jada, the duty barmaid came out with the first aid kit. As Mary went through it she became irritated.

‘It's just plasters and bandages. Nothing appropriate for cleaning a wound. I'll have to use the Opium in my bag.’ Jada looked quizzical.

‘Not that sort of Opium,’ Mary said, ‘Opium, parfum, the alcohol will help clean the wound. And you Daniel, will have the most gorgeous smelling facial gashes in Burridge.’

He smiled as she cleaned his face up. His eyes narrowed, and he frowned rather than winced as she cleaned the cuts on his forehead and mouth. He was examining her; not judging, but sizing her up. Mary wondered if people who helped in the past had betrayed him.

‘Dirk, you've had first aid training. You can take over while I sort out some food.’

‘Oh. I thought it would be better-’ Dirk was hesitant.

‘Being in possession of ovaries doesn't give you superior first aid skills. Does it?'

'No, of course not.' Dirk started unwrapping a plaster.

'Daniel, chicken and chips okay for you?'

'Splendid, that would be lovely.' he nodded.

'Well you two can have a nice chat, while Jana and I sort out some food.'

The two women walked back into the bar. Mary collared Josh.

'Have you contacted the shelter?'

'Yes, I had to beg, they've said they can look after him for a couple of nights. They've cut their beds. I told them what happened, and who was responsible. I can't guarantee they'll do anything.'

'I know, they are dependent on the council for funding and they're the ones giving the nod to those scumbags. Also, who is the premier gobshite on the council?' Mary said.

'Julian St. Hubert. I suppose like the others, this guy won't complain. will he?'

'No, he won't.' Mary sighed.

Jana walked forward with a tray of food.

'Right. We're taking this out to him. When we're done, you're going to take him in a taxi to the shelter. Okay?'

Josh nodded.

Mary sat and chatted about her life while Daniel ate. He was hungry. He didn't want this to appear obvious. It was important for him to eat slowly and methodically, to conceal it. It was a matter of self- respect.

Josh came out and announced the Taxi was parking.

'Thank you for all your kindness.' he said holding Mary's arm.

'Had our roles been reversed you would have done the same. Now if you do decide to do something about this, we'll support you. You know where to find us.' Mary said.

He gave a noncommital smile. Josh escorted him to the taxi. She waved off the Hansom before returning inside.

Mary sipped her orange juice,

'Dirk, did you get anything out of him?'

'It's pretty text book stuff. He is around 50, discharged from the army. Not from round here. Reading between the lines looks like he has PTSD. Evidently no support structures available wherever he was. He went through the usual thing of self-medicating with alcohol and he fell through the cracks.'

'Much as I expected.'

'That Will Ferguson is hovering around somewhere, says he wants to talk to you about something.'

'Yes, he seemed to disappear when it all kicked off. He probably thought it better to be a detached observer so he can make pithy comments about it later.'

Will Ferguson walked over grinning.

'Now the fights over–'

'It wasn't a fight. It was a beating.' Mary said with a hard stare.

'Sorry, you're right. But I've got something that might be useful. I'm pretty sure that Lintern guy is a steroid user. I don't imagine the powers that be would approve. It could be used against him as leverage.'

Mary shrugged.

'I don't know. Perhaps. It's coming up to my shift starting. I need to clean something out the front.'

Dirk was waiting for her outside the pub as she came through with a bucket. On the pavement was the blood splatter from the assault on Daniel Trent. Mary emptied the bucket of hot soapy water onto the pavement. She turned to Dirk.

'Now it's all gone. What happened-has now not happened.' she announced.

Dirk put his arm around her waist and rested his head on her shoulder.

'We did the best we could.' he said.

She stroked his hair.

'I know. I don't know what's going to happen. This can't go on.'

Chapter Four

Miss Johnson padded across her roof garden in her slippers, placing the watering can on a low table. Peering over her wrought iron railings she watered her African violets whilst humming. The fencing around her roof garden barely came up to her thigh giving her a commanding view. The tendrils of tension that had clambered over her shoulders during her encounter with the police had been massaged away by a good soak in the tub.

A lovely day ruined, but perhaps they would retrieve it. After all, it couldn't be sold down the pub, now could it? Reflecting on her good fortune in life would be the best way of dealing with it. She was lucky having a large roof garden with a diversity of plants, and was pleased by the arrival of pots of Kenyan roses that she now admired. Her plants were a gaudy cacophony of colour, and were from around the world. Her sofa bed had been placed in the centre of it, and she would enjoy a night of the smells of the garden and the fresh salty breeze coming off the sea. Her life was good, how awful it must be to live inland and to be deprived of this. It could have been worse; it was pointed out she might have disturbed them. She gave a shudder. She retreated into memories of childhood. Reclining in her bed, her upper body at 45 degrees looking out into the clear night sky she drifted off on a sea of reverie. She was back on the family estate in Kenya. She remembered kneeling at the window and looking out through the veranda and across the plains, studying the sunset as the colours moved from ochre to orange and on to flame red. Britain could not offer such dramatic sights. Why she wondered was Africa blessed with such stunning nature? She remembered the sounds of the animals and enquiring to her parents,

'Were they cheetahs, mummy, were they hyenas?'

Her parents became irritated with her. She loved them, and they her, but they believed the less children knew the better.

'It's only the wind dear, go to sleep.'

They had yet to inculcate in her that the natural world should be treated with suspicion and regarded as thoroughly sinister. It was a charmed life and couldn't last. It was about to change dramatically. Snippets of overheard conversations ending abruptly when she entered a room informed her ten-year-old self something was afoot. Eventually, she discovered there was some group called the Mau-Mau, who didn't like the British. She wasn't told much and her father maintained a harsh silence if questioned about what was going on, pausing to take swigs of scotch and say,

'Nothing for you to worry about my dear.'

She felt some sense of grievance at the time, that she was being kept in ignorance because she was a child. This was in fact a little unfair, as sadly this was exactly the way he spoke to her mother. When it was time to leave she remembered her parents sitting her down and giving her a talk about the *troubles*. Her father gave her a little eulogy.

'When we get back to Britain there will be people who have been told lies about what's happened out here. Some people, mostly Communists, have been spreading the most dreadful lies about the mistreatment of the natives here. It's not true. The British don't torture, and we don't kill defenceless people, even if they are behaving like savages. Remember this, and remind people of the utter bestiality of the Mau-Mau. The civilised world would do well to remember that most of the world would not be civilised were it not for us. It is the people who are now mocking the Empire from fashionable liberal drinking clubs and the like who are probably a greater threat to civilisation than Stalin and his ilk. The greatest threat to the civilised world is the enemy within. Always remember all great Empires rot from inside.'

She remembered the speech. However, she did not remember much of the circumstances that were the background to it. Nor did she remember any of the news reports that emerged in the ensuing years which challenged the veracity of her father's assertions; and she had chosen to believe his version of history. She was happier remembering sunsets, and plains, and shopping trips to Nairobi, and recalling quaking with pleasure in the back of a land rover whilst watching giraffe on the move.

Now she was drifting off, her sleeping memory excising all reference to conflict and political violence. The noises around her made her stir, but not much. Below her, the pubs and clubs of Burridge were turning out, and people were talking loudly; some eating seafood they had purchased from the food wagons along the seafront, others preparing for a night under the pier. The usual noise of drunken revellers and the clatter of bottles at the back of the pub didn't travel up to Miss Johnson's. In the small hours, she was awakened by what she thought was a cry in the night, she turned, wondered what it was, decided it was her imagination and went to sleep.

*

Castlereagh Mews was a small block of 1930s terraced houses a stone's throw behind the Seafront. The house at the southernmost end was distinguished by a sloppy magnolia paint job applied recently. It now had another distinction. The front was festooned with the black and yellow tape marking the house out as a crime scene. Sergeant Penrose smiled with relief. He had difficulties finding it, and now would have to park.

Mrs Lennox had made the discovery two hours before. Having seen off her husband, and enjoyed her breakfast whilst muttering asides to the presenter of the Today programme on Radio 4, she had taken Toby, her King Charles spaniel out for his morning walk.

It was when she arrived at the back of the Mews she saw her neighbours back gate open wide. Unusually for Mews houses they had large gardens. She secured Toby to a wooden post at the back of the garden. Why did people forget to lock things up? The garden was small, and this one had been neglected. Nothing but uneven grass, bleached by the sun and badly tended, and in the middle two cedar trees. An elderly couple had lived there previously and the neglect was theirs. She realised she was being harsh. It was all a bit too much for them. She stopped and wondered what would be the best course of action. She barely knew her neighbour, and if he was in, he might be unpleasant. On the other hand, if he was out, the place might get burgled. Her stomach felt tense and she raised herself upon her calves and peered forward. She was not being nosy, she asserted, good neighbourliness demanded she look inside. As she walked cautiously through the kitchen she felt uneasy.

Stepping through the lounge she could barely see anything and called out,

'Mr Sykes, are you there?'

The curtains were drawn tightly and there was only one dim table lamp in the corner. She could see the hall table with the telephone and a large ashtray on it, next to a small light which was facing the wall. It was practically impossible to see anything through the gloom. There was a stale acrid smell in the room. She felt awkward about going into somebody's house without permission. Mrs Lennox cautiously stood there squinting. As her eyes adjusted to the room, she discerned the outline of a figure lying behind the sofa. Stopping, she questioned what she was seeing. Was he drunk or had he suffered a fall?

As she slowly walked around the sofa she was disabused. John Sykes body was at an awkward angle, the legs turned away to the left, and his arms positioned loosely at his sides. His face clearly drained of what little colour it normally had, the lips shiny in the half-light looking like a fish, and his blond hair cushioned against a crescent of blood now framing his head against the once cream carpet. It was his eyes staring motionless into the back of the sofa that answered all her questions. She ran out of his house and careered through her front door and phoned the police, after which she began to tremble. Two hours later she was still shaking. Her husband was now sitting in their garden trying to give her words of comfort she was too numb to hear.

As Penrose ambled through the front door, of what became known as the murder house, he was confronted by Dr Reid looking through her case on the ground. She was older than his mother but had a habit of looking at young men in a way that made them feel uncomfortable. He had been warned about her and told she was a person who he would be ill-advised to be alone with at social functions where alcohol was available. However, this was the morning and there was a corpse present, so he presumed she would be on her best behaviour. Around the room there were men in white overalls studiously dusting for prints.

'You're late,' she said in a flat disinterested tone. Penrose wondered what her point was, as her voice was devoid of judgment. He glanced in the direction of the body and although the head was obscured he saw a pentagram tattoo on the side of the victim's upper arm, he turned away, he wasn't desensitised to death the way others in the force seemed to take pride in.

Chief Inspector Barclay walked in through the kitchen doorway saying,

'Oh don't be so hard on the poor lad, Reid. Mr Sykes has been dead at least six hours I'm sure Penrose's undeniable first aids skills wouldn't have been much use.'

'It was a little difficult to find, sir, Sorry.'

'Not to worry. I think we'd better walk and talk.'

Penrose had not had many dealings with Barclay and was cautious of him. He had the reputation of being an amiable but private man, who was intolerant of sloppy thinking in others, who however could be lazy towards procedure. He was a heavy-built man with unbiddable chestnut hair who although not fat, tended towards fleshiness.

He was not anxious to impress Barclay, but this would be his first important investigation in Burridge. He was not indifferent to its result but was anxious that whatever transpired if it had an unhappy outcome it would not be due to him. Dr Reid looked up and gestured towards the living room window.

'Could you do something about those kids?'

Whilst going about her duties, she noticed children peering through the net curtains trying to catch a glimpse of the murder scene. As communities went this was one of the safer ones. They were troubled by the odd burglary, a smattering of drug-related thefts, much the same as any other middle-class area. The news of the murder had swept rapidly. The children dissociated it from any human dimension. To them, it was a source of drama and curiosity. Barclay beckoned one of the policemen outside and relayed the request. As the constable moved them along the road they shot him an indignant glance. It was *their* holiday and he was ruining *their* fun.

'Dr Reid, I know I'll have to wait for your report tomorrow, but you can give me the edited version now.'

'Okay, cause of death. As you've no doubt surmised, blunt force trauma. Probably two or three blows to the head.'

She started vigorously miming it for Barclay. She had the rather overenthusiastic delivery of a rather plummy voiced and demented hockey mistress.

'Height of assailant: five foot eight - five foot ten. Right-handed. Could be a man or a woman. This is an equal opportunities homicide. Time of death, I'd say any time between midnight and 3 A.M. Also, we'll have to wait for the tox results, but I'd say he was engaging in recreational drug use.'

'How so?' Barclay said.

With a theatrical flourish, Dr Reid pointed at the table by the sofa.

'You will observe yonder coffee table, and on it a mirror, some white powder and a rolled-up fiver, this suggest anything to you? My evil henchman Steve hasn't arrived yet to check it out. I seem to be the only one who does any bloody work around here.'

'I'd better talk to Mrs Lennox,' Barclay said wearily.

'It'd probably be better if you left the poor woman alone, I'm told she's pretty shaken up and I doubt you'll get much sense out of her.'

'I haven't got much choice, unfortunately; she hasn't touched anything has she?'

'Lindsey asked her, she hasn't. She does have access to television, you know? Any dickhead knows you don't touch a crime scene. Will you be taking your young puppy with you?' Reid said gesturing towards Penrose.

'Sergeant Penrose *will* be accompanying me, and please leave him alone.'

As the pair of them walked next door Barclay confided to Penrose.

'You'd better be careful of Dr Reid. She can be quite predatory you know, and she has an appetite for young flesh.'

Penrose nodded awkwardly and muttered something.

As they were ushered into the Lennox home they saw it was much like any middle-class house in the area, tidy, organised with a sense of pride and with the idea if somebody might visit unexpectedly, there would be no grounds for social embarrassment. It was a home a contemporary interior designer would sneer at, utterly conventional, but done with attention to detail. Walking through they were escorted to the garden area. As Barclay looked across the garden he saw Mrs Lennox sitting hunched over in a wickerwork chair. Alongside her was her husband Luke and Constable Lindsey, who was performing one of the most thankless of tasks; she was on listening duty. Alongside them lay Toby who sensing something terrible had occurred was lying still and looking around warily.

Mrs Lennox was still glassy-eyed and stone limbed from what she had seen. Even when she had locked herself in her home the vision of John Sykes had followed her. It was as if the blood was trapped behind her eyes. She had sat in her front room and had seen the blood on her Sanderson sofa covers, on the walls, against the prints on the wall and behind them. She had run upstairs and thrown water over her face repeatedly, with no effect. It was as if the violence itself was a physical entity which was capable of following her. Now she was sitting in her garden looking vacantly at the bushes at the end of her garden, in a trancelike state.

'It'll be alright Mary,' her husband said attentively.

She felt things would never be alright again. He was slowly beginning to realise he was talking too much and trying too hard, and he was only required to be there. Barclay always felt awkward having to ask questions at such a time. He felt relieved if he was ushered out by angry relatives and could return when people were in better emotional shape. Mrs Lennox looked up at him and realising his purpose gave a tired smile.

'Police?'

'I'm afraid so. Chief Inspector Barclay.'

He offered his hand which she shook unenthusiastically.

'I know you've had a great shock but I have to ask you, did you hear anything, see anything, which might be of any help?'

'I'm afraid not. He was much like a lot of young people. Made a lot of noise. If there wasn't a banging of doors it would be unusual. I honestly can't remember one way or another from last night. Such a good looking boy, it's terrible to see all that promise wiped out. I can't imagine how somebody that young could provoke such hate. He's the same age as my Stephen. He'll be home soon won't he dear?' She said turning to her husband, he nodded.

'Yes, he's on his way. We thought it best we go through this as a family. He's doing Politics at Sussex University.'

Whilst Mr Lennox talked about Stephen's return, his wife looked even more distracted and was swaying like a door in a breeze. It was obvious to Barclay she was in no fit state to be questioned, and he should leave. She was still deeply shocked and needed what Dr Reid called, *a jolly good freak-out,* before she could begin to get over it. He placed a contact card in her husband Luke's hand.

'I think under the circumstances it would be better if I left. If either of you remember anything please don't hesitate to contact me, and I'm sorry, I'm really sorry.'

Barclay turned to Penrose as they sauntered towards the seafront,

'There was no point in tormenting that poor woman. If she has noticed something it'll probably come to her tomorrow. The victim was new to the neighbourhood. Okonedo has made arrangements for an incident room at the Alhambra. Somebody's collecting his computer to see if there's anything relevant on it. I imagine you missed breakfast, I'll treat you to a good feed in the Collingwood. There are a number of things we need to discuss.' They walked to the Alhambra.

Barclay was suspicious of Penrose, his previous partner of two years had transferred to the Greater Manchester force and he wondered how long it would take to train him in his way of doing things. He seemed intelligent and receptive, but Barclay was an unambitious man and didn't much care for it in others. He had seen too many young men in a hurry passing through the force, and he had no desire to be partnered with one.

They sat in the corner of the restaurant, Barclay tapping his fingers expectantly on the table.

'I took the liberty of phoning through an order, Sergeant.'

The waitress arrived and gave Barclay a broad smile exclaiming,

'Here you are Chief Inspector, I know you have a healthy appetite.'

'Ah, magnificent, you always spoil me rotten.' he said pulling the plate towards him and proceeded to enjoy his meal.

It became clear to Penrose that Barclay was a regular at the Collingwood, when he saw the mountainous portions of egg, turkey rashers and mushrooms presented to Barclay. This was no standard order. Barclay saw his junior blinking at the size of it and remarked,

'I don't believe in starving myself, we have quite a day ahead of us.'

Penrose quietly ate a chicken and mayonnaise sandwich whilst Barclay consulted his notes. Barclay leant back and swigged his coffee.

'Before we start, my car is out of circulation this week so for the next few days, you will be the designated driver. What have you got, I didn't notice?'

'It's a Smart car, cherry red. Didn't you see it outside? I don't believe in being flash.'

'A bubble car, nobody who drives one of those things could be accused of being flash.'

'It's very cost-effective and environmentally friendly sir.'

Barclay nodded sagely and returned to more pressing concerns.

'We don't know too much about Mr Sykes. His family live in the country and have three rather successful antique shops. They've just been informed and as you can imagine are in a hell of a state. I'm not going near them until tomorrow. We do know he once worked at a local computer shop so this morning you can pop in and talk to them. Okonedo spoke to them on the phone an hour ago and they'll be expecting you. They inform me he had a steady girlfriend up until about three months ago and we've got a name for her so I'll pay her a visit. We've been allocated foot patrols to ascertain if anybody has seen him in the last twenty-four hours, and somebody must have. They'll be stopping cars and leafleting people along the seafront, something must get turned over.'

'If you don't mind me asking, normally things are painfully slow down here, how come everything is moving so fast?'

'Politics, Penrose, Politics. We have the great and the good arriving by every train, all with oodles of filthy lucre. This matter is regarded as an untidiness by them, as *an unfortunate incident*, if you like. A murder of no importance. They want it cleared up, sharpish. This is going to be all over *The Echo*, along with references to drugs. Our betters have already been on to the Chief Constable, and he phoned me an hour ago, and whilst we are not going to get into a blind panic, if we get a good result on this one, it should make it considerably easier next time when we want to demand more resources.'

'I'm pretty new here, are the local press supportive of the police- I mean in a *genuine* way?'

'*The Burridge Echo* is a loathsome rag. They will be supportive of the police if it sells papers. They frequently run hate campaigns and then blame the police if theory is turned into practice. It's the *Der Stürmer* of the Home Counties. If the editor was walking through Guildhall Square and went to the public lavatories and they'd run out of arse wipe he'd think about it for a couple of minutes and quickly come to a Burridge Echo analysis. This would be that organised gangs of Romanian Gypsy children were stealing toilet paper from public conveniences, so that our own people, our pensioners, the ones who had fought in the war, are having to go around with soiled sphincters. It would demand tough action be taken, and anybody who chose to disagree would be denounced as: out of touch with the public mood, a Trotskyist, obsessed with Wokerama, or some variation of the above. It frequently gives over its pages to the likes of Julian St. Hubert, usually ranting about how the rot set in within the British Criminal Justice system when we abolished Trial by Combat. The Chief Constable thinks it appropriate to cooperate with these people, *I don't.* This is one of the many and varied ways I am not *simpatico* with the powers that be.'

Checking his watch, he rose to his feet,

'I think Okonedo and co should be settled in the function suite by now, I imagine somebody at the station might have turned something up. Once we get the measure of the man we might get some ideas as regards motive. I know we need to keep an open mind, but as a general rule with murder it's usually S and M.'

'S and M, sir?'

'Sex and money. As in all things, two of the great motivators. In Britain anyway.'

As they walked into the function room two officers in uniformed short sleeves were positioning a computer terminal in the corner. Okonedo was leafing through some paperwork.

'Okonedo, something helpful please?'

'I'm afraid you're going to have to make up your own mind on that one. It turns out he had a criminal record. When he worked in an antique shop there was a small matter of selling on repro jobs as the real thing. He had no previous and all he got was probation. However, there was another man, a Grant Maunders, who went down for 12 months for fencing stolen goods, it's possible John Sykes got off a bit lightly. Maunders is now out and lives a couple of miles along the coast. Possibly a man with a grievance? The other thing is yesterday there was a theft from Miss Johnson's. A theft of an antique clock, she's already been on the phone to the Chief as she felt it wasn't dealt with in a satisfactory way. Well sooner or later what I told you will be on local radio. The Chief thinks under the circumstances it might be politic to pop in and speak to her.'

'When you say she wasn't satisfied do you mean she was dealt with insensitively?'

'Well, CID turned up and I attended in my capacity as the local community liaison officer. I think she felt she might have been treated with greater deference.'

'Your talents are wasted here, Okonedo, you should be in the Diplomatic Corps.'

Barclay was clearly irritated, but knew once the media were aware of all the information, the police would be attacked for inactivity, and perhaps there might be a link. Penrose was confused.

'Who is this woman sir and why is she important?'

'Burridge politics. She's old money and once again it's not what you know, but who you know. I think my mother has had the misfortune of sitting on a couple of committees with her. People like her still think they own the town, and that the police are at their beck and call. This clearly applies to our Chief Constable. Well, we had better go and pay homage to the good lady.'

An additional irritation was Barclay feared that they might have to sit whilst she reminisced.

'Right, you ring her and say we'll be there at noon. That will give us time to follow up these other interviews; hopefully, by then, somebody will have come forward with some information to uniform. We'll all three attend, and of course, everybody's to be on their best behaviour.'

*

Penrose was ushered into the manager's office of Computer International and offered a coffee which he declined. It was a business that held since it sold computers, the rooms had to be white and antiseptic, and the place smelt of plastic. Like all British companies which proudly referred to themselves as International, it had a parochial feel to it. He felt whilst Barclay might be happy to wander through this enquiry with little direction, he wasn't, and was unsure how to proceed.

'Sykes, yes he was a bit of an odd one, thoroughly reliable, a good worker. Fastidious in his approach, he would never accept a deal had been done, until the money was paid. People laughed at his over cautious approach, but I rather liked it. I was sorry to lose him, a nice man, but a bit of a mystery.'

Babs Marchant was an attractive woman of thirty-five, smart in a high street way, with a habit of smiling in the middle of sentences without explanation, which gave the impression she was enjoying a private joke. She leant back as she tried to think of something helpful to the police. Penrose sensed there was something hidden behind the smile, some sense of a judgment she might share if the opportunity arose. He decided on a direct approach.

'Miss Marchant, under normal circumstances it isn't good to speak ill of the dead, but as you know this is a murder enquiry, so the normal rules don't apply. Was there anyone who disliked him?'

She leant back in her chair as if deep in contemplation and her face broke into a broad smile.

'John Sykes had a tendency to be a bit promiscuous. He had a girlfriend but he led her a bit of a dance. So I suppose there might be an angry boyfriend or a betrayed woman out there who might hold a grudge, but if you're asking me about someone *I* know who might be angry enough to kill him, I would have to say no. Mind you with John I think you knew what you were getting, I think whenever his girlfriend realised he had been carrying on with other women she knew it wasn't serious, then again they never seemed like a proper couple anyway. Will you be talking to her?'

'My boss will be talking to her at some point. Did he ever mention his family, how did he get on with them?'

'I have no idea, I got the impression they were quite posh. They were immigrants, Polish I think. There's not much else I can help you with. I'm afraid I'm going to have to call it a day. I'm sorry I couldn't have been more helpful.'

*

Barclay thought a quick look over the crime scene might tell him something. He felt it was unlikely to provide him with anything concrete, but he was looking for something intangible that might give him an idea of John Sykes as a social being, rather than as a crime victim. A brief look upstairs was unrewarding. He was intrigued by the state of the bathroom cabinet- half-filled; was it waiting for the contents from a new occupant, a *significant other*? A quick look in the bedroom, revealed the victim's untidiness. There were more clothes on the floor and draped over chairs than there were in the wardrobe. Walking downstairs he saw piles of computer parts stored in corners, clearly, he was doing work *off the cards* to make ends meet.

The living room was sparse, immaculately clean and a little too tidy for comfort and was disturbed by the smell of disinfectant and the coppery aroma of blood still hanging in the air like a fog. He looked for a radio but there didn't appear to be one. The sole entertainment source there appeared to be a large LED screen, with a 4K/Blu-ray player. He pressed the slot to see what Mr Sykes taste in movies was, and inside the slot was a copy of *The Devil Rides Out.*

The call from Penrose told him something of John Sykes's character failings, but nothing that could be called a lead. A large card positioned on the shelf above the fireplace drew his curiosity. The picture of children on the card seemed strangely familiar, and a glance confirmed who they were. *The Miracle of Fatima Society* was emblazoned across the top. He remembered Sister Agnes handing out devotional pictures at the end of term at school and having to sit through an execrable Hollywood film about the Portuguese peasant children who had seen a vision of the Virgin Mary at Fatima. He hadn't seen artwork like that for ages, the same wine and peacock blue coloured clothes and arch positioning of the subjects was specific to a certain type of Roman Catholic popular art. Having fallen from the faith some time ago, he always checked himself from behaving in a superior way when confronted with images he found so comforting in his youth. He scanned the tract and it was all familiar. The story a standard of Roman Catholic Mariology. It was as his eyes reached the foot of the page something leapt out at him. Encircled in yellow highlighter were the words of Lucia dos Santos, one of the Fatima children: *More people go to Hell because of sins of the flesh than for any other reason.*

The scene of crime report would be on his desk later, but everything he was seeing here confused him. When he looked into the kitchen it said little about the man. There was a collection of plants, some pictures of soccer players taped to the wall along with a picture of the Summer Solstice at Stonehenge with a group of druids.

In the middle of the board was a poster for the *Hands off the Seafront campaign* advertising a public meeting. Looking out the window, he felt he was no wiser. He was awkward about interviewing John Sykes's former girlfriend, but she had been insistent on the phone about seeing him, and perhaps she might be helpful.

*

Bernadette Stevens immediately struck him as an intelligent woman, but he was finding it hard reconciling her self assuredness with her seeming tolerance of her former lover's manifold infidelities. She had flame red hair swept back and had adopted a kind of modern version of Joan Crawford hard glamour which completely suited her. She possessed alabaster skin which with heavy black eye makeup and blood-red lipstick completed the severe yet glamorous look, and was wearing well-cut Italian clothes. She ushered him into the offices of Maples Estate Agents who had premises off the high street. The room was decorated in rust and cream colours with a deep pile burgundy carpet. They sat at a small desk in the corner. She was composed, yet clearly unhappy.

'I'm very saddened by his death of course. But we split up quite some time ago, and to be honest I was bitter for a while afterwards. I don't want to go into details but he was terribly unfaithful to me, so clearly I wasn't enough for him. After we split up, I was told he was getting even worse, into sex parties, that sort of thing. I know this makes me sound completely out of the modern world but I didn't really think that sort of thing went on. Well, you know it goes on, but not with people you know. Some time ago I decided that the best way of dealing with the whole thing was to respect the memory. I know it sounds a bit sinister, but it was the best way of dealing with it. So, I remembered all the good times, the cycling holiday in France, love in the afternoon, the Christmas we spent together, even his pathological untidiness, and decided to honour and cherish the wonderful memories. This might sound creepy but he's really been dead to me for quite some time, to consider the stuff he might be up to I found too heartbreaking.'

'I have to ask, did he have any enemies?'

She smiled, she didn't really understand anything Barclay was saying. He wondered if his death had, in her eyes, cleansed him of his character flaws and somehow rehabilitated him in her affections.

'I just can't see it. Having said that, I don't know where he was going with his life. Perhaps he was getting into dangerous stuff. He phoned me this week, completely out of the blue, but I didn't listen to him as I suppose I should have done.'

'What did he say?'

'He was saying he'd made mistakes and was sorry for the pain he'd caused me. I asked him if he was phoning because he wanted us to get back together, but he said no. He was rambling on about starting a new job, and then something about going through a life change, and it sounded as if he was joining some cult, or something, but to be honest I wasn't really listening. I didn't want to hear from him you see, it was spoiling the memory. Now, of course, I wish I'd listened.'

'Had you seen him at all recently?'

'It's quite strange really. A while back I was showing a client over one of those properties down near the Imperial, there are those poky two-room flats that go for two hundred and fifty thousand a throw. Well, I'd just come down and the clients were driving off when I saw him walking along the road with some blonde woman.'

'Would you recognise her if you saw her again?'

'No, I don't think so. You see I didn't recognise him at first, he'd put on a bit of weight. I wasn't happy about seeing him at all. You see it ruined it. Seeing him was like seeing a ghost. I became quite tearful. With hindsight, I wished I'd had a proper look. I wonder if I'd been able to accept the way he was, whether things might have turned out differently. I wonder now what might have been, you know?'

'Do you know anyone else who might know who he was involved with?'

'No, to be honest, he seems to have fallen off the world. I don't know *what* he was up to. He was quite close to his sister as a child, but I think they had some sort of falling out. They might be on better terms now, they might be reconciled, I don't know. I would advise you to talk to her, she might know. If he was going to confide in any member of his family, I would imagine it would be far more likely to be her than his parents. I think he was a little scared of his mother.'

'Do you know what the disagreement was with his parents?'

'No. Not really.'

'Thank you. You've really been most helpful, and I know it's been very difficult for you.'

'Chief Inspector, I have a question. Do you think it was a woman?'

'I honestly couldn't say. We've just started, have to keep an open mind, you know.'

'I was just wondering if he got involved with someone a bit less tolerant than me. He used to tell me I had a bourgeois mentality. But you know what the real killer was? It was when I discovered everybody knew. He was indiscreet about his sexual adventures. It was the slow realisation that everybody was discussing it. I don't think people were laughing at me behind my back, I think they probably felt pity. And you know what? I think that made it even worse. So perhaps, after all, he was right, perhaps if it wasn't for my bourgeois sensibility we'd still be together and he'd still be alive.'

She stood up and was now clearly upset.

'I'm sorry Inspector. I'm going to have to ask you to leave. I hope you find whoever did this.'

Barclay required no further prompting and thanked her for her cooperation and left the building as quickly as courtesy would permit.

*

Penrose bought himself a 99 and joined Barclay on the bench outside Morelli's so they could compare impressions. What they had gleaned from their respective interviews might have given grounds for them to make moral judgments, or even to see how some people had grounds to dislike John Sykes, but it had not identified any suspects.

'Well, the only thing we can be sure of sir,' Penrose said, 'is that he was a sabre-toothed tart.'

'Yes. I'm afraid that without anything else it doesn't really take us anywhere. It might be that this was born out of sexual jealousy. Or possibly betrayal, that is never really defined by the victim is it? We would need a suspect for that. I wonder who the woman Bernadette Stevens saw him with was. I think Mrs Lennox might be a bit of a curtain twitcher, and we might get something more from her tomorrow.'

'Was there very much from his phone records?'

'Practically nothing, it was like he was starting over. There was one London number and a reference on the pad to visiting there on the previous weekend. Nobody's answering that yet. The uniform boys have been over to his former flat in town and the landlord there confirmed what Miss Marchant told us. He said he was a model tenant, paid his rent, a bit of a slob, but nothing untoward. Just because he was a slapper doesn't mean that there weren't other reasons for murdering him. He did a business studies degree at the University of Southeast London and got a 2/ 2, it might be helpful to talk to his course supervisor. I think the most interesting stuff we might get will be from his family, and more importantly his sister.'

'When are we going to talk to them?'

'I think we should give them a break, let's say tomorrow. I'm waiting for uniform to get back to me on that one. Anyway, let's get back to the function suite. I think Okie might have something for us.'

*

Okonedo gave a look of quiet assurance as she greeted the return of Penrose and Barclay.

'A rather mixed bag I'm afraid. As regards the break-in, someone known to us was seen in the vicinity around the time it happened. That needs following up. Also, a bunch of kids known locally as the Gang of Four were in the area at the same time and they might have seen something. The pier manager told one of the beat boys that one of the beach dwellers apparently saw something. There is a problem with that. Most of the lot who live on the beach engage in practically every known form of substance abuse. Also the person in question apparently has certain mental health issues.'

'You mean he's mad as a sack of trolls?' Barclay enquired.

'Yes.'

'Who is he?'

'His name's Harry Stevens. Locally he's known as Mad Harry.'

'The names a bit of a giveaway.'

'On a more hopeful note, John Sykes spent some of the evening down at the Castle on the Cliff. It might have been the last place he went before he was killed.'

'Ah, now that is helpful. We'll have to sort that out a little later. Let's go over and do our duty as regards La Johnson, and Okonedo, you can give us the unexpurgated version as to exactly how badly the boys from CID handled it.'

She smiled remembering how Larkin and Brooks had irritated Miss Johnson. During their brief time there she was made aware every question they asked carried the unspoken subtext; *it's only a bloody clock*. Every enquiry was marked by an indifference to the reply.

An additional burden for Okonedo was Miss Johnson clearly had a problem with a black officer attending. She dealt with racism in a very specific way. As a child she dealt with it with her fists. When it was blatant she took it head on, by verbally flattening the perpetrator. On occasions when she experienced that particular brand of refined unspoken racism she endeavoured to rise above it. She was amused as she looked at the lady's collection of artefacts. Being familiar with the argument that colonialists had sometimes preserved great artworks for future generations she scrutinised the assorted exhibits. It wasn't an argument she subscribed to, and a cursory examination of the room showed Miss Johnson's antecedents clearly had a kitsch sensibility. Amongst the dross, more by accident than design, some interesting pieces had been obtained. She had a brief conversation with her about African art and dropped into the conversation that her uncle was an assistant curator at the main Museum of Antiquities in Lagos. The mood between them changed immediately as racism was trumped by snobbery.

As she confided her experience to Barclay, he gave a pained smile.

'Yes, I'm sorry about that, she lives in Britain's past I'm afraid. We have to do this, and then we can get on with talking to people down the castle, where the company of the punks and drug addicts will be a breath of fresh air. I hope we get something out of this,' Barclay said, as they approached the door.

George escorted the three of them through the large front door and into the cavernous hall.

'I need to ask since there was no sign of a break-in, do you think they entered the premises when you were all in or do you think it was somebody known to the family?'

'I don't really understand the question, Chief Inspector. What do you mean, *known to the family*?'

'There is no record of the alarm going off, so it's more than possible somebody entered through an unsecured door or window and stole the clock when people were actually in. Then left. The only other alternative is somebody who knew the alarm codes took it.'

George gave a comprehending smile.

'Now I get you, about the only regulars we have are David, Doctor Evesham and of course Rev. Stephens. None of them know the codes.'

'If you think back to the morning of the theft, could somebody have crept in and out while you were going about your duties?'

George looked perplexed.

'I suppose it's possible. I don't really know.'

'That's fine, now which part of the house do you and your wife live in?'

George took him through the ground floor and into the kitchen. It was a spacious well-lit kitchen with pine cabinets. The floor was decked out in dark terracotta tiles. In the centre was a large rectangular unit of Arabescato marble beneath a structure with strings of garlic, peppers and herbs hanging down. Something was cooking on the hob and the room filled with the aroma of butter and parsley.

'We have a bedroom through there with our own dining room and lounge. We can take you over it if you like?'

'No that's not necessary. I just need to know if any of the doors or windows could have been an access point.'

'No, we check everything as a rule; this place was as tight as a drum.'

'I think it's more than likely that it was stolen to order. Someone from crime prevention will be coming to see about tightening things up. Try and think if there might have been any unusual characters around, any callers you couldn't vouch for.' George smiled and shook his head.

'I don't know of any, but I'll ask Dennie, she might know.'

As if on cue, Dennie entered laden with shopping bags. Putting the groceries in the cupboard she said,

'No, I can't think of any unaccountable people recently, the whole thing has been extremely disruptive, emotionally I mean. Miss Johnson could well do without this. On that subject, it's almost noon and I believe that's when your appointment was for. She wasn't very happy with those idiots you lot saw fit to send here yesterday. I'm going up to see that she's okay, I suggest you follow me shortly.'

Barclay nodded to her rebuke as she swept past him.

'In case you didn't know, the clock is to be left to us. If it isn't recovered we'll get the insurance money, she's told us that. But it isn't the same. It's nice to be remembered with something, rather than just with money. Dennie's very protective of Miss Johnson, we both are.'

'I understand Dennie is a qualified nurse, why did she leave the profession?'

'Dennie was based in the emergency department, she got sick of it. Nurses and doctors never really leave the profession. They stop practising in hospitals that's all. Ask her she'll tell you.'

'I think we'd better go up. How is Miss Johnson, I mean health-wise?'

George lowered his voice.

'She is not a well lady. It's the C-word, I'm afraid. But she struggles on. But that's what we all do in these circumstances. You just have to struggle on.'

When they arrived in the living room Miss Johnson was seated in a high-backed blond wicker chair. She had obviously put some thought into the meeting. She was wearing a grotesque amount of makeup and had a fuchsia headscarf, tightly knotted at the side of her head and with a straw hat pulled onto the back. The look was finished off with a scarlet summer dress and heavy ivory bangles on her wrists, which made her look even more frail and birdlike.

The sound system was blaring out the pilgrim's chorus from Tannhäuser. The whole thing was thoroughly theatrical, and it was clear to Barclay that he was not so much interviewing a crime victim, as being granted an audience. Barclay turned to George,

'Look, I'm not even going to attempt to compete with that.'

'I'll turn it down for you.'

'No thank you, I want it turned *off.*'

George acceded to his request as Barclay approached Miss Johnson.

'I'm Detective Chief Inspector Barclay and this is Det Sgt.

Penrose; I believe you've had the pleasure of Sgt. Okonedo's company. We've some additional questions to ask you as regards the break-in yesterday.'

He shook her hand in a circumspect manner, fearful a firm handshake might snap it in two.

'I have to inform you that sadly there's been a murder locally, and that's what we are primarily investigating. However, it has been suggested that the two incidents might be linked and that is the line of enquiry we're following at the moment. Having the integrity of your home violated can be a frightening and upsetting experience for anyone. It's been suggested that the officers who attended yesterday might have given the impression that they didn't take the theft as seriously as they should have done. I must assure you that we take it very seriously indeed, and would like to further assure you all steps are being taken to recover the item and track down those responsible.'

It was clear from her face the counterposing of her burglary, with murder put her attitudes about the theft into sharp relief. Her eyes narrowed and she sat upright.

'That's quite dreadful. I heard something on the radio, and I think he was quite young wasn't he?'

'Yes. What would be helpful would be if you could tell me who has the security codes for the alarm system and if there have been any suspicious characters hanging around here.'

'Alarm system. It's only George and Dennie and of course myself, who have the codes. I can't think of anyone suspicious around here, I live a pretty prosaic life, I can't think of anything out of the ordinary occurring here.'

'Miss Johnson, you have a considerable collection here. I'm surprised nothing else was taken. When the insurance people did a valuation on the clock, did they value your other possessions?'

'Yes, Chief Inspector they did. As a whole, the stuff in here is worth many thousands, but most of it isn't worth a great deal if looked at individually. They took the most valuable item in the room. Most of it really belongs in a museum, and Chief Inspector, the witty rejoinder that so does its owner has already been made.'

Barclay smiled.

'This is the problem I'm having. You see to steal something to order, you have to line up a buyer, by knowing what to potentially steal. You've been telling me that no one's been here, so it doesn't make sense. George and Dennie are your live-in companions, so to speak. Can you think of anyone else, cleaner, home help, that sort of thing?'

'Oh, hold on a minute,' Dennie said, 'what about that Willie bloke who used to do the garden?'

George quietly rotated the idea in his head; clearly from his discomfort he felt speaking about him implied an accusation of wrongdoing.

'Sorry,' Barclay quietly intervened, 'but who is this guy, and could we start with a full name please?'

'His name's Will Ferguson, he used to help me out with the garden downstairs, a couple of times a week, put the rubbish out, that sort of thing. I put my back out when I had a fall, it was just a temporary, ad hoc thing, and it was only for a couple of months. He didn't do anything upstairs, so of course, he had no access to the clock.' Okonedo flashed Barclay a look to confirm her familiarity with the name. Barclay nodded at George.

'He was with you at all times, was he?'

'Well no, of course not. But he's a trustworthy type, a local character, certainly not a common thief.'

'You don't know whether he was having a good look over the house, but then, of course, neither do I. However, I would be interested to know how his *being a character* manifests itself?'

'Well, locally I think he does a bit of promoting with the alternative music scene. He goes over to France quite often and sells and buys stuff. You know, posters, clothes, food and wine etc. He's quite an educated, cultured man, he does a bit of this, a bit of that. He cuts a bit of a raffish figure, but he's certainly not a member of the criminal community.'

'Well, we'll check up on that anyway if that's all the same to you.'

'I'm sure the Chief Inspector will do whatever he thinks is right, George. I think it might be a good idea if we all had a cup of tea.' Miss Johnson said.

With that civility offered, George realised he had been talking too much, and hurrying to do her bidding the normal power dynamics of the household had been restored.

'Yes, that would be nice. I'm sure we could all do with a cup,' Barclay said smiling.

'What kind of a host am I? Please, everybody, sit down.'

Miss Johnson made broad gestures to the various chairs and sofas that littered the room. Everybody had been standing awkwardly during the conversation. The tea and an offer of a seat were the first real signs of a thaw in her attitudes, moving her conduct from icy politeness towards what in her value system passed for friendliness. Penrose and Okonedo promptly sat on the large claret coloured sofa by the French windows, whilst Barclay positioned himself in a straight back chair near Miss Johnson. George went to the corner where there was a table with a tea bar. It stood alongside a large roll-top Bureau with an assortment of lavender writing paper and envelopes and a collection of Pearl Buck religious novels. Once everybody had been provided with a good cup of Darjeeling the atmosphere became more relaxed.

'Now, I can remember being on a couple of committees with a Mrs Barclay, your mother by any chance?'

'Guilty as charged, I'm afraid. She does a lot of those things.'

'Yes, I think she's quite active in a number of community projects. You're Catholics, aren't you?'

'I come from a Catholic family, yes.' Barclay replied tactfully.

'Well, I'm Anglican of course. But I was an enormous admirer of Pope John Paul II. At a time when the world seemed to be adrift on a sea of moral relativism, he held the line. As somebody whose health is not as good as I would like it to be, he set a rather wonderful public example. I know many found the sight of him becoming increasingly frail a bit much to bear, but to me, it was a wonderful declaration of faith. It is never for us to question His plan. It was a wonderful public surrender to the will of God.'

'I was wondering, don't you have any other relatives except David round here?'

Miss Johnson made an internal adjustment signalling a sensitive subject had been broached. She gave a pained smile.

'Yes, therein lies a tale. David, I'm quite close to, even though he's decades younger than me, he is my younger brother's boy, by his second marriage and I imagine you know him. Then there is my sister's boy Timothy, who is about fifteen years younger than me. We don't exactly get on, there was a family estrangement. He got hooked into the whole New-Age mystical drug thing, and I'm afraid that's where the breach came. You can find him down on the beach selling his carvings. I think he makes a fairly good living out of it. Married a rather unsuitable cosmopolitan type, they took off to Europe, and she died in rather dreadful circumstances. Drugs, they ruin everything, but I've no need to tell you that Chief Inspector? The door is open as they say, but he doesn't want to get back with his family. I was hoping we'd have some sort of rapprochement before I join the feathered choir, but it's looking increasingly unlikely.'

'Well, let's hope he comes around sometime. All the family disagreements, or at least most of them that I've experienced can be healed if there's enough give and take from both parties. I think we've probably taken up enough of your time, and I'd just like to thank you for the assistance given us, and we'll be getting back to you when there are any developments.'

They exchanged closing formalities and as he stood up to leave, and was standing closer, he could see the perspiration breaking through the thick matte foundation. Her skin had that shiny deathlike translucent quality. He felt more sympathy for her than he had previously.

When the three of them emerged into the fresh air Barclay made his apologies.

'I'm sorry about that, but sometimes a good bit of ass-kissing is the easiest thing in the long run. I don't think we learnt anything very much from that, and I'm sorry.' Turning to Okonedo he enquired,

'I get the impression when Mr Ferguson's name came up, that he might be the person who was known to us.'

'Quite so.'

'We've wasted enough time, I think we need to grab a spot of lunch and work out a bit of demarcation between the three of us.'

Chapter Five.

Will Ferguson's flat was behind the promenade, two streets back from the Imperial, and therefore only a twenty-minute walk from Miss Johnson's. PC Lindsey had been briefed to ask if he had seen anything, and not to appear as if the police saw him as a potential suspect to the burglary. Having spent most of the morning with Mrs Lennox, she wanted to do real policing. Sitting and looking sympathetic whilst being unable to say anything helpful had become wearing.

Parking her police motorbike, she pondered exactly how to conduct herself. As she approached the house frontage she saw the B in 29B Toronto Road didn't stand for basement but a structure out the back. At the rear was a raised wooden hut with the name The Studio. It had the disadvantage of steep uneven oak steps preceding the entrance. The place needed attention and it was with trepidation she rapped on the front door.

The door was answered by an attractive dishevelled woman of twenty-eight who was unhappy at receiving a visit from the police. Lindsey thought her make up had been applied haphazardly until she realised it was the remains of the previous night. The living space she was ushered into was as unkempt as the woman herself, and as she proffered a seat to Lindsey she lit up a cigarette and proceeded to smoke it ostentatiously.

The place had been an artist's studio originally and was now doubling as living accommodation as well. A number of canvases were leaning against threadbare furniture, mostly pop art variations, and these jarred with conventional seascapes on the wall. The oil smattered shirt she wore made it clear she was responsible for the artwork.

'I need to have a word with Willie Ferguson.'

'I'm afraid he's away. He's in France.'

'I'm PC Lindsey. By way of explanation, he was seen in the vicinity of Miss Johnson's, who has the house near the Alhambra on the seafront. Anyway, it was at the time of a break-in and we were hoping he might have seen something.'

'I heard she had something nicked, ah what a pity,' she said smiling.

'And you are?'

'I am Betty Melton, and I'm Will's lover.'

She threw back her head and emphasised the word *lover* as if it were capable of shocking a policewoman five years her junior.

'He does quite a bit of business over there,' Betty continued. 'I can ask him to contact the local plod when he comes back if you like?'

'Yes, that might be helpful. When are you expecting him back?'

'Oh, it might be tomorrow or the next day.'

'He didn't specify when he might be returning then. I mean does he normally not tell you when he's coming back?'

'I'm not really into control games. I know he'll be back when he's finished his business.'

She gave an overhearty laugh, which implied he was possibly the one who exercised control. Lindsey wondered if she knew exactly what her lover got up to, she was clever enough to have surmised that this was just a fishing expedition. It was obvious to Lindsey she found the intrusion of the police to be discomforting. As a defence mechanism, she had decided to portray herself as finding the whole thing vastly amusing. Lindsey felt Miss Melton was probably not as serious an artist as she imagined.

'This your work is it?'

'Yes. Know much about art, do you?'

From the dry delivery, it was clear it was an enquiry she had already pondered and answered in the negative.

'As much as anybody, I suppose.'

Then looking at one of the seascapes which adorned the walls Lindsey said,

'Now that really is exceptional, I do like that. The use of light really is quite stunning.'

'I have work to do. I promise to tell Willie as soon as he gets in to contact you, but I've plenty to get on with. So if you don't mind I'm going to see you out.'

'Thanks for your time. I'll be seeing you.'

As she returned to her motorbike, wondering if she had rattled her and whether there was any point to this, she smiled at the interchange between herself and Miss Melton.

*

Penrose had returned to the station to see if anything useful had been revealed examining the phone pads and computer from the victim's house. He feared he was going to be stuck with all the paperwork and was confused with the events at Miss Johnson's house. She wasn't his type of person but he was perplexed why

Barclay was so unsympathetic towards her. He wanted to make an impression on Barclay but had been advised being a plodder was probably the best way of gaining his trust. The computer boffin in residence, Wilmot, smirked as he discussed the computer.

'This John Sykes has stuff on his computer from a certain Gentleman's club,' he said slyly, '*The Comfort of Strangers.*'

'Yes, and-?'

'It's a Sex Club. I checked up on it. There's a local contact number, at a sex shop in town.'

Penrose thought about how irritated Barclay had been about the local news having information before they had an opportunity to process it.

'I'd appreciate it if you could keep this out of the canteen. The local news media seem to know more of our business than is strictly helpful. If it finds its way outside this building I can promise you Barclay will find you personally responsible.'

'I am *not* a gossip, and I can assure you I will treat this matter with complete discretion. If you are looking for people who are leaking to the press, I suggest you look elsewhere.'

Whilst Wilmot veered off into a torrent of umbrage, Penrose realised hoping to keep a lid on it was a forlorn hope. He had recently transferred from the Cornish Constabulary and found the gossipy nature of the Burridge canteen unnerving. He wasn't certain how Barclay would react to this news, sensing concentrating on sex and drugs might obscure more important issues.

As Barclay and Okonedo approached the pier, they saw the news-stands. The Burridge Echo had *Death at the Seaside* emblazoned on the front page with a small picture of John Sykes's house. Picking up a copy he scanned the front page. It contained one oblique reference to drugs, but nothing lurid enough to cause him anything more than mild irritation. It ran a couple of paragraphs about Sykes brush with the law in London,

'Here's a bit of a shock, apparently he was involved in the antique trade, and had questionable standards. Selling new lamps for old.'

'You don't say, sir,' Okonedo replied.

'Yes, swindling the great British public out of their hard-earned cash. To mangle a quotation *he sold dear what was most cheap*. Actually, this isn't too bad for the Echo. In fact there are some shocking accuracies in the report.'

They looked briefly at the commentary about how the victim was guilty of mis-selling goods.

The weather was holding up and they wondered if the people they needed to interview were there. Okonedo as community liaison Officer hoped something could be utilised from this meeting.

The area was home to an assortment of mainly male vagrants.

'I know that none of these guys will be able to give us anything that could conceivably stand up in court. But there might be something that takes us somewhere. Before we do this I think I'd better add that I've had some reports that those private security guards have been picking on them. Assaulting them.'

'I'm sorry, but if they're unwilling to come forward and make a complaint there's not a lot we can do, and once those bastards realise that unfortunately it makes them perfect victims.'

They were known locally as the beach dwellers, the people at the

Yacht club regarded them as a nuisance, others pointed out they were a manifestation there were some victims of the system. *Orphans of the storm* was what Barclay archly called them. Some of the locals saw them as people who had fallen through the cracks, and although sometimes irritated by them when they were clearly drunk, were becoming increasingly concerned at what they saw as the victimisation of the vulnerable.

Uniformed policemen were passing out leaflets to the locals whilst another two were leaning against the railings munching ice creams. The larger of the two,Sgt. Dalton sidled up to Barclay.

'I have some gentlemen who might have something for you,' he said gesturing towards a burger stand. Immediately adjacent to the stand was a long triangle of shadow caused by the structure, and lying in the shade were two scruffily dressed men. Barclay and Dalton were safely out of earshot of the lounging pair. Dalton explained,

'The one on the left who looks like a sack of rubbish is Charlie; he hasn't seen anything but if you give him a tenner he'll tell you anything you want to hear. The slimmer of the two is Mad Harry, I reckon he has seen something, now I don't think you'll get anything out of him but Okonedo might, as I think he is pining with unrequited lust for her.'

Barclay walked over to the burger van.

'Who's for a hot dog, or a burger?' peering around the van he enquired 'can I offer you, gentlemen, anything?' They cautiously accepted his offer and as they each took a half-pounder with onions and ketchup, he and Okonedo took a hot dog each. Barclay now felt uncomfortable and worried he was striking a slightly benignant tone.

'Harry, there was a break-in at Miss Johnson's; I understand you might have seen something?'

'Not talking to you mate. You're no good. Don't trust you. I'm only talking to her.' Harry gave Barclay an unblinking stare.

He turned to Okonedo,

'Well, that put me in my place.'

Barclay went over to Dalton to engage in small talk while she conducted her interview. Charlie feeling neglected shuffled over and slumped against the railings and dozed. When the interview was over, the two of them walked back to the Alhambra.

'Any joy?'

'Yes, sir. It seems he saw Mr Ferguson walking down Marlborough Street which runs down from Miss Johnson's place. He couldn't be sure, but he thinks he might have been carrying something like a rucksack. The ID is very specific; Mr Ferguson wears that uniform of matching camouflage trousers and jacket and doc martens, so it had to be him. He is keeping something back though, but I don't know what.'

'What do we really know about Ferguson?'

'He's a bit of a dodgy character. No convictions. His name is however linked with low-level crime, he's believed to be involved in borderline stuff, I think some of the merchandise that goes back and forth from England to France and vice versa might be a bit iffy, and there are certain questions raised as to him being involved in the supply of drugs. Having said that we've never had him as a guest, so, as they say, he has no form.'

'What drugs?'

'Not heroin, but he has been linked with cannabis, speed and steroids. But I hasten to add this is all conjecture. He seems to be from a pretty comfortable background, his father was something in the British Council in Italy. Boarding school boy and all that.'

'This explains the behaviour earlier on at Miss Johnson's. There's this middle class mentality if you're dealing in drugs and contraband, providing you have a nice accent you stop being a criminal and suddenly become a lovable rogue. What was that comment "not a member of the criminal community"? Presumably he doesn't play chequers down at the local *Criminal Community Centre*. I wonder how much pain Miss Johnson is in. It could be she's receiving some help in pain management not normally available on the NHS.'

Returning to the Alhambra they found Penrose poring over pages of foolscap. He recounted his conversation with Wilmot, and Barclay nodded vigorously.

'That was absolutely the right thing to say, but sadly futile. The contact at the sex shop, do we have a name?'

'Nigel Daventree. I think he practically runs the place.'

'And the name of this establishment?'

'Intimate Distractions,' Penrose replied wearily.

For the first time that day Barclay laughed.

'Priceless! Only in Burridge could you have a porn shop with such a piss-elegant name, and run by somebody who sounds like a character from a Terence Rattigan play. We'll have to honour Mr Daventree with a visit tomorrow. I think for the time being it would be a good idea for you and I to pop into the Castle and see if anything has come up there. It might even be worth me popping in briefly this evening, just to put in an appearance. People like to cooperate with the police but not when they're faceless. Hopefully we might have some useful statements by tomorrow.'

Okonedo, phone pressed to ear was sitting in the corner.

'I think you'd better take this sir,'

she passed the phone to Barclay.

Penrose wandered out for some fresh air followed by Okonedo. She was curious as to how he was settling in. He tried to be as relaxed as possible, but clearly wasn't, and she was unsure whether he was tensed up by the situation of having a new working partner or felt awkward about being asked about it. He looked a little lost to her, and was probably desperate for advice but was too self-protective to ask.

'There really isn't any side to him. He's fine to work with, slightly snobbish. Don't try and impress him and don't cut corners. If you really want to get on his right side, volunteer to do all the paperwork. It'd be a good move because you'll end up doing it anyway.'

'Do you know him well?'

'Know him well?'

She furrowed her brow and considered her words.

'I have known him a long time. But well? No. Barclay is a deeply private person, good at his job and a good man. But I don't know what's going on inside, there is simply no way into him. You may end up having a good working relationship; you may end up as friends. But I advise you don't try and get matey-matey with him.'

He wasn't sure if he was any wiser. It occurred to her Penrose was lonely, and unhappy about it, whereas Barclay was a man who had accepted his own loneliness.

‘Oh, if he really approves of you, then you might get to be taken to visit the Sibyl today.’

‘Who is the Sibyl?’

‘Oh, you'll find out soon enough,’ she said.

When they wandered back in Barclay was sitting, playing with the phone.

‘That was the Chief Constable. Leon Sikorski, the victim's father has been in touch. He's arriving tomorrow morning; he has volunteered to do the official identification of the body. Whilst he's here he wants to speak to me.’

‘Identification? I'm sensing a subtext.’ said Penrose.

‘I don't think it's his son's body he wants to scrutinise.’

‘You don't seem very happy about this.’

‘Well, frankly I'm not. I don't like these things being organised over my head. There is also some question of some sort of family meeting in the afternoon I'm expected to attend. That of course might be useful. I'm just not very happy about Mr Sikorski giving me the once over. Having said that I really can't blame him. I'll just have to make the best of it.’

Okenodo re-entered the room.

‘There's somebody to see you.’

There was a mirthless smile on her face which made him uncomfortable.

‘And who is it?’

‘Gavin Lintern, the Reichsführer of the Seafront Defence Trust. I get the impression he wants to help with the investigation. He's waiting outside the function suite. Do you want me to clear a place on the desk for the poisoned chalice?'

Barclay gave a deflated look.

'Oh God, that's all we need. I wonder what the bastards are up to. I imagine you'll be happy to sit in on this?'

'I would be *delighted.* Perhaps they want to annex the Sudetenland.'

'Behave.'

They wandered over to the function suite. Gavin Lintern was standing awkwardly outside. He was a heavily built man with cropped ginger hair, looking too warm for comfort. As he walked in he had a deferential manner. He behaved with the graciousness of someone not used to being polite, but felt he had to be. He enthusiastically shook hands and smiled broadly at Okenodo before sitting.

'What can I do for you Mr. Lintern?'

'Well, obviously myself and other members of the Trust are out and about in the community, and we felt we might be of some help in your investigation.'

'That's very public spirited of you. We would be obliged if any of your group saw or heard anything if they came forward to one of our team. We are, as always, dependent on the good will of the public to provide us with any information.'

Barclay noticed that after his over-polished opening Lintern had made a point of slouching back in his chair and was leaning on one side.

'Well I think we can be of some help. I'm going to send an email around to everyone to contact me with any info, of anything they might have seen, or reported to them, so that I can liaise with the police regarding-'

'I don't think that would be appropriate.' Okenodo interrupted, 'we don't really need you as a conduit to people coming forward. I think Chief Inspector Barclay would be happier if they came to us directly. Isn't that so?'

She gave Barclay a steely smile.

'Yes Sergeant. Quite true. There will be an incident room here for people to pop into.' Barclay realised what Okonedo's concerns were. The man looked irritated. As Barclay looked at Lintern his backside halfway down the chair, he could hear his mother's voice inside saying, *sit up straight, stop slouching*! Clearly the wanted to become a significant figure in the investigation, Barclay didn't like the idea of a shadow police force and he certainly didn't want a parallel investigation.

'Well, we're here for you to use however you see fit.'

'From what I understand your role is around the yacht club. It doesn't extend to wandering across the beach and around it. There have been reports of some of your members attempting to police the behaviour of people around here. Also there have been reports of some, how shall I put it, heavy-handed conduct by some of your group. I can't tolerate this.'

'You seem to be a bit hostile to my group. You do see we're both on the same side. We're here to empower the community. I will of course do as requested. However, I think I'll report to Mr. St. Hubert that you weren't quite as supportive of our offer of help as we had hoped you'd be.'

As Barclay looked at Lintern, he reflected that this was a man who could swagger whilst seated.

'I am grateful to any reports from members of your group of anything they may have seen, as I am from any members of the public. I am, however, hearing reports of aggressive behaviour from some of them. Be so kind as to report this to Mr. St. Hubert, that there have been no formal complaints thus far, if however somebody does complain and there is any evidence of violence by members of the Seafront Defence Trust that I will be down on the lot of you like a *ton of bricks*.'

'We're just taking our streets back, that's all,' he said with a grin.

'Well, we don't want to keep you, now do we?'

Lintern stood up.

'Thank you, I'll be seeing you.' he smiled and ambled his way out.

'I'll do the coffees, you get the chocolate orange out of your desk.' Okenodo said.

He placed it in front of her.

'I'm having half,' she announced putting several segments by her cup. He gave a look of exaggerated horror.

'I've never known such cruelty.'

'Well frankly, you shouldn't be eating it at all. If your mother knew she'd put you on special measures. Perhaps I should grass you up.'

'You wouldn't.' he said.

'Don't you believe it. Anyway, what did you make of that lump?'

Barclay leant back and smiled.

'Fairly ghastly. You were quite right to pitch in and put him in his place. He's trying to elbow his little bunch into the investigation. He also had an opportunity to defend his group, and say they would never resort to violence. The fact he didn't is revealing.'

'He's vile. Did you see the way he shook my hand and grinned at me. I was grateful he didn't pat me on the head. That comment about taking the streets back. What an asshole.'

'Yes, I got that. Or alternatively *taking our country back,* where have we heard that one before? Take back the country from whom? Not necessarily from you of course-'

'Just people who look like me. Yes, it was people like him who put shit through my grandparents letter box when they arrived here.'

Okenodo put another two chocolate segments in her mouth, Barclay promptly bettered her by inserting five in his.

'Another thing, did you get that awful comment : *we're on the same side*. Dreadful. The battle cry of the suburban fascist. Every idiot setting up a private army has come out with that one.'

When they looked down and realised they had scoffed all the chocolate they knew it was time to move.

As they walked into the Castle on the Cliff Barclay started quizzing Okonedo on the staff.

'What's this Gary like, who runs the place, is he likely to be cooperative?'

'He's an absolute darling, camp as a vicar's knickers, but a real sweetie. He will be helpful and if there's any anti-police stuff, he will pour oil on troubled waters. We're firm friends. I know a lot of people regard the community liaison unit a bit of an Aunt Sally, and soppy soft policing, but in situations like this it really comes into its own.'

Okonedo knew her commitment to community policing was dismissed by many of the old guard at the station but she hoped in this situation it would pay dividends. As they entered and looked around, the netting and rather theatrical gothic style in stark daylight looked incongruous to the point of being comical. The barmaid Jana realising their purpose said,

'I'll go and get him. Won't be a sec.'

No sooner had they sat than Gary was upon them. He came thundering towards them, his chubby frame encased in matching yellow trousers and a Fred Perry shirt with the collar turned up. He was one of those people who was blessed with a permanent sense of wonderment. His hair was bleached a yellowy blonde, gelled up, and the overall effect gave him the look of a startled hamster.

'We've had a little comeback from the leaflets. They said they'd probably pop in to make statements. But most of the people who were in last night won't be in until tonight. Your best bet would be to have somebody in tonight.'

'Would an appeal from the stage go down well? I mean would there be a good response?'

Gary nodded vigorously.

'I should say so. Get Okie to do it. She's pretty well-liked locally. You weren't thinking of doing it were you? Sorry but you're a bit too posh and suited aren't you?'

'Thank you. Yes you're probably right.'

It occurred to Barclay both Okonedo and Gary weren't any more proletarian than himself. But if that's what people would respond to, so be it.

'Gary you were here last night. Did you see him, speak to him or have you any impressions of the evening?'

'Oh, absolutely! But I was behind the bar so I barely spoke to him. It was very loud we had a Battle of the Bands thing last night.'

'What can you tell me about John Sykes?'

'Not a lot I'm afraid, he'd only turned up here recently. He'd started to pop in here, but he usually just seemed to drum up a conversation with whoever he was standing next to at the bar. I don't even know what he did for a living. I didn't really notice him much last night, but I was running around. It was a bit mad in here last night, but then it is most nights!'

'What went on last night?'

'We have a long-running thing, a *Battle of the Bands*. It's a talent contest for local rock bands we had three sets last night, it all got a bit too Black Metal for my liking but everybody seemed to have a good time. There were some other people there who shouldn't have been here. The favourites didn't go through to the next round which was a bit of a shock. Everybody said *Satan's Nephilim* would go through but they didn't. It was won by *Baphomet's Satanic Orgy*. We also had someone who usually only comes in for the karaoke on Friday turning up.'

'Who was that?'

'She's known locally as Rita the man-eater. She's got a purple beehive the size of the National Debt and she's as old as God, and normally does covers of old standards. Anyway she turned up and I just asked the audience if they wanted to hear her, and we asked for a show of hands and they all voted yes. So she did a version of *Love for Sale*. When she got to the line *would you like to sample my supplies*, her hand gestures over her body were so gross I think a couple of people had to go out to get some air. In fact, if I hadn't seen it with my own eyes I wouldn't have minded.'

'*Baphomet's Satanic Orgy*? As opposed to *Mother Teresa of Calcutta's Satanic Orgy*. I presume that unlike the purple-haired Rita they don't do Cole Porter covers?'

'Absolutely. Anyway, there were various people drifting in and out. Round here everybody wants to be in a band. I gather John was joining one.'

'How's that?'

'Well he came up to the bar with Willie Ferguson and they were laughing and joking. Willie does a fair bit of promoting and has a lot of fingers in the pies of various rock bands round here. There's a good hard rock/ punk scene in this town and he said something about John joining a group called the *Sons of Belial*. It was very loud so I couldn't really hear a lot.'

'There seems to be a lot of occult overtones, but I presume it's all pretty harmless?'

'Oh yes! It's all just Hammer Horror. All the bands have horror sounding names at least all the Heavy Metal bands.'

'Were they together for the whole evening?'

'No. Willie left before him anyway. He was going off to France; he goes over and gets loaded up with goodies. I think we had put in an order.'

'What for?'

Gary made salivating noises.

'Oh, Brie, Camembert, Parma ham, all sorts of delectable delights. We do wonderful lunches in here, you must check us out.'

'So do you know who he was with?'

'I think he was sitting with Róisín and her party over by the window. But then again I think it was more like sharing a table than being with them, if you know what I mean?'

Barclay thought they were getting somewhere; he was hoping he would have some pointer, some revelation, of what he was like as a social being.

'Now who is Róisín, and who was with her?'

'Róisín is a student, does Fine Art at the University. Nice girl, she's the head honcho of the *Socialist Worker* lot at the Students Union. Comes in with three other guys. She's normally holding court from about nine onwards, most nights. She'll be in tonight anyway.'

'Did anybody see him leave?' Barclay said hopefully.

'Sorry!' Gary said, with a pained expression. 'I've asked the other members of staff and they say he left alone. The CCTV recordings are sitting in the office and you're welcome to go through them, but I'm pretty sure you're in for a disappointment.'

'Thanks for that Gary. I'll see you a little later. Is there to be any live entertainment tonight?'

'No, you will be able to talk to people.'

'I think we'd better be making tracks. If we could have that CCTV stuff?'

As they left Barclay turned to Penrose.

'You return to the station with those tapes and quickly go through them with Wilmot, and see if he did indeed leave alone. At least we'll know one way or the other. It's a shame because if he did leave with somebody, it's likely they would have returned home with him. It would give us a real breakthrough because even if they turned out not to be the killer, he might have said to them he was expecting somebody. Anyway, get Wilmot to see if he can get them computer-enhanced, in any event, it'll keep the gossipy little tart out of the canteen. I'll see you back at the Hotel at 4.15.'

Chapter Six.

Timothy heard someone knocking on the window.

'Timothy, Timothy. Are you alright?'

Doris Markowitz was concerned.

Timothy Johnson staggered out of bed, or rather off his bed. He had not so much undressed for bed as disrobed. Too drunk to get under the covers- he had fallen across them. Pulling on a jersey and some jeans he staggered out of his bedroom towards his front door. As soon as he opened it the harsh sunlight blinded him as he tried discerning who it was. He saw the outline of her massive red hair. Without waiting for an invitation she swaggered her way onboard exclaiming,

'You naughty man what have you been up to?'

But of course she knew.

She had popped into the off licence near the yacht club and been told of his visit the previous night. Purchasing a bottle of Morgan's rum, Jessie, the shop manager wondered exactly what he was up to. Once a month he would come in for the same order and blandly inform her he was going to get drunk.

She asked him,

'What's going on with you then love? Some drink to remember. Some drink to forget. Which is it with you then?'

'I drink to remember,' he said smiling.

When he had got back on the houseboat he had dinner and placed an oil lamp on the large oak table, he got several biscuit tins from the cupboard in his bedroom and proceeded to go through the pictures in them. Him and Rachel in France, in Italy, in Morocco and always in love. They were both so young and beautiful. It took him to about halfway through the bottle before he would get tearful, and then he would luxuriate in his grief. He now found it almost impossible to cry under other circumstances, but he would end sobbing uncontrollably. He wondered if it was his feelings of guilt at her death that had closed up his nerve endings.

Doris looked at him. She knew his story and understood. He cleared his throat,

'And what do I owe the honour of this visit for?'

'Hungover are you?'

'A bit,' he said weakly.

'Fancy a bit of breakfast Timothy?'

'I don't think I've got anything in.'

She gave an inane grin and pointed to her bag.

'I've brought stuff. You are going to have a couple of painkillers, and have a shower whilst I have a quick clear up and cook us a good late brunch.'

He leant forward and stuck out his tongue, she placed a couple of pills on his tongue and gave him some orange juice to swig. He downed the pills, smiled and turned around to get cleaned up.

It was a comfortable houseboat, well situated, close to the promenade, on the other side of the yacht club. The interior was all laid out in warm-toned oak and with comfortable red velvet furnishings. He worked at the back on his paintings and sculptures, but when the weather permitted he would take all his materials onto the beach and work there. He was well known as one of the characters of the seafront; always to be seen in a battered Panama working away on his canvases. Occasionally he had exhibitions if he could find an appropriate space, and supported himself with the money he made from his sea sculptures. In artistic terms they were sentimental trash, but they provided him with a living and gave great pleasure. Therefore, he was unembarrassed about the income from them.

Doris bounced into the living room opened the window and changed the air. She cleared up the debris of the previous night's debauch. Although fond of Timothy she knew her feelings for him were always going to be greater than his for her. Rachel was his great love, and she felt it was impossible to compete with somebody who had died so tragically and so young. Doris was reconciled to her inability to crack his isolation; which was not to say her relationship with him was never a physical one, but there would always be something between them. It would never be that grand passion she was hoping for. He was always honest, so she never fell into the trap of judging him because he could not measure up to her expectations. They were not really having a love affair but occasionally would make love. She decided until somebody offered that grand passion, that half a loaf was better than none. He stumbled in and sat, the main room they were in had a large window he peered through and gazed at the beach.

'How's the head then?'

'Not so bad, all things considered.'

She paced back from the galley which was now rich with the aroma of freshly filtered coffee. This had the effect of priming Timothy's taste buds. Placing a large mug of coffee and a copy of *The Guardian* in front of him, she announced,

'Five Minutes.'

Even with a hangover, he looked handsome. The one love that had remained as constant as his love for Rachel was his love affair with the elements. This had given him a rather weather-beaten look which with his trimmed hair, beard and lean physique made him attractive. As she arrived with plates of scrambled eggs, bacon and mushrooms, he perked up.

'What are you wearing today?'

As she sat opposite him he noticed her wardrobe.

'Oh, I'm wearing Egyptian, that's my theme for today. It's all Egyptian silks and scarabs I'm afraid.'

Doris wasn't sure whether he was genuinely curious, or whether he was merely extending gentlemanly courtesies.

'I have a piece of news for you,' she said taking a large gulp of coffee. 'Your aunt has been turned over.'

'Turned over, what do you mean?'

'Burgled. Somebody came in and nicked some stuff, a clock from what I hear and apparently a quite valuable one.'

'She must be going spare,' he said, trying to suppress a smile. 'When did this happen and how is the poor old girl?'

'Oh she's very much in her element; from what I've heard she's enjoying the whole thing enormously. Are you going to run round and cheer up the demented old Nazi?'

'No, I'm sure David will be screaming enough for the whole family. It'll really get her where she lives. It might even get her to question her obsession with possessions.'

'Tim darling, don't give me any of that New-Age crap. Unlike you I've never had enough wealth to be contemptuous of it.'

'Well people do change. We're all evolving, without knowing it, in spite of ourselves, aren't we? She might change.'

'She might at that. On a different tack, I hear those security guards have been hassling people again. Something ought to be done about them, they're going too far, perhaps we should become anti-vigilante-vigilantes,' she said.

'I saw them bothering someone last night,' Timothy said, 'there are loads of people who don't like what's happening. We need some righteous anger. I know they've had meetings down the front but I'm getting worried it's going to take somebody getting seriously hurt before anything gets done. I spoke to that black policewoman down the front. She didn't seem to be very happy about the situation. Her hands are tied. Perhaps others will have to take action.'

'What happened?'

'They were hassling some wino. One of those goons had him by the scruff of the neck. Some guy was shouting at him, and I saw Jennie from the Alhambra coming out and having a go. This is serious; it's about the local bourgeoisie flexing their muscles. The beach is everyone's, not the Yacht clubs. The beach doesn't belong to anyone, it's like the sea and the sun and the wind. People have to stand up and do something.'

Doris clapped and leant forward and planted a kiss.

'Thank you, comrade Timothy,' she smiled, 'you know I'll be with you on the barricades.'

'I know you will, pumpkin.'

*

Barclay and Okonedo walked up the stairs of Palmerstone House, a block of flats on the council estate situated to the back of the promenade. This was one of the better housing estates and had escaped some of the more severe social problems that had afflicted the larger ones on the other side of town. These flats dated from the 1930s and the tenants there saw themselves as slightly better than those stuck in the high rise '60s tower blocks tucked behind the high street. As they walked along the gangway they looked down at a group of youngsters playing football in the small park opposite.

'I refuse to call him Spider, what's his proper name?'

'Peter.' Okonedo replied, ringing the bell. After a couple of minutes a flustered looking Mrs Denby answered the door.

'Hello Okie, you'd better come in.'

As she ushered the pair of them in, Barclay peered around the place. There were piles of laundry in her utility room she was pulling out of the washer-dryer, and the smell of warm clothes permeated the place. Mrs Denby was a lone parent trying to bring her son up in straitened circumstances and doing her best. The hallway was full of boy's things, football kits and piles of comic books set in mythical Imperial regimes in far-flung galaxies. The whole place had the feeling of a child's world where adults were permitted to live.

'We know he was round the back of the hotel around the time a robbery might have taken place and wondered if he had seen anything.'

'I thought you were coming about the business with Happy Mart and the alcohol.'

'I'm afraid that's out of my hands, you do appreciate there is a reckoning to be had on that score. I'm afraid underage drinking is something they take very seriously these days. The days when it could be shrugged off as a rite of passage are well and truly over.'

Peter's mother nodded grimly.

'He's in the front room, come on,' she said, leading them in.

He was slumped on the sofa, elbows on knees staring at the TV. He had entered the world of Rafael Sabatini, a writer of lurid high adventure novels which were made into Hollywood blockbusters of the forties and fifties and shot in eye lacerating Technicolor. Barclay remembered how he would watch them on the BBC on Saturday afternoons if his mother had forbidden him from playing in the garden due to poor weather. Now, Peter's mother was keeping him indoors for quite different reasons. He looked over at the screen as an assortment of Screen Actors Guild members dressed as pirates waved rubber swords and swung from naval rigging whilst singing homicidal sea shanties.

'Peter, Chief Inspector Barclay is here, and needs to ask you some questions.'

'I understand you were round the back of the Alhambra around lunchtime yesterday. I need to know did you see anybody or anything?'

The boy had developed a way of answering any question from any authority figure, with a fixed expression which was midway between pain and indifference.

'Don't think so.'

'You saw nobody?'

'Just some old bloke putting some stuff in the back of his white van.'

'When you say old, how old?'

'35.'

'Ah, could you give me a description of him?'

'Well, s'pose I could, but it might be easier if I just told you his name.'

'Thank you, his name please?'

'Willie Ferguson, he helps organise those crappy rock things down at the bandstand, with all those creepy old farts.'

'Now how big was the stuff he was putting into his van?'

Peter extended his arms to an approximation slightly larger than the clock. The boy ambled to his feet and inclining his head asked casually.

'Drugs is it?'

Barclay shook his head and smiling replied,

'Not so far as we know, and while we're on the subject you are hardly in a position to take a high moral tone on the subject of substance abuse.'

His mother immediately spoke up.

'Peter has been very foolish, he felt terrible this morning and I know he's got to take responsibility for what he's done but he's already been punished with a shocking hangover.'

'I've had worse,' he interjected.

'You are not helping matters!'

Peter had gone too far, and as he began apologising he went from looking a bit older, to much younger than his years.

As Barclay gave his thanks and moved towards the door Okonedo said,

'I just need to have a quick word, I'll see you outside.'

Barclay thought he might have possibly overstepped the mark, Okonedo maintained a studied silence as they proceeded back to the promenade.

'What exactly is the story there?' he said.

'Well, the father got up and left without so much as a *by your leave*, so I don't know whether the boy blames himself or his mother. We don't even know why he left, whether it was for another woman or no reason at all, he didn't say. That's very difficult for any boy to deal with. This is the first time he appears to have got involved with alcohol, as you can imagine the mother is terrified of social services.'

'Does the boy realise he's drinking in the last chance saloon?'

'A rather unfortunate turn of phrase, under the circumstances. I've given her the contact for a local parents group for the umpteenth time. That might help, but frankly, I don't know.'

Okonedo was irritated at her own impotence in these situations. The mother had no real plan how to deal with it, and the police couldn't do much. His mother just hoped things would change by wishing it. Okonedo had attended on enough occasions when his mother didn't know where he was and reacted with relief when he walked through the door. They were basically a good family who could work things out. She had seen how good people got chewed up and spat out by the system, whereas the mendacious always worked it to their best advantage. When they returned to the incident room Penrose was already there. As Barclay entered, he slowly shook his head.

'I didn't think it would be much use. But it was worth a try.'

'Do you think the family will be any help tomorrow?'

'God only knows. Anyway, something might come up tonight. On which subject Okonedo, if we can meet down the castle at eight, okay'

She nodded in agreement.

'Right Penrose I think we need some refreshment lets go.'

Okonedo gave Penrose a knowing smile.

*

When Penrose parked his car they walked to the house on the corner. Their destination was the last house in a Victorian cul de sac. An elderly gentleman was tending to some wild roses in the garden next door and smiled.

'Hello Richard, I think, it's safe. I think most of the coven departed to the four winds at least an hour ago.'

Barclay led Penrose along the side of the house to a well-tended back garden. It was as broad as it was long with an assortment of rose bushes and a large hawthorn bush that was threatening to take over the entire garden. As they approached the back door Barclay turned to his junior.

'If we are fortunate there might be excellent provisions available.'

He quietly opened the back door and they entered the large farmhouse type kitchen. Once inside, Penrose saw a well-stocked oak table with plates of cake positioned at neat two-foot intervals. There was a pile of dirty cups and saucers and plates on the side. Clearly, there had been a recent tea party. As they sat at the table

Penrose noticed there were two clean cups and saucers in front of them. Barclay poured the tea, he looked up as a sprightly, yet plump woman with salt and pepper hair entered the room in a well-cut floral dress. Barclay turned to her and said,

'You should be careful madam; anybody could just walk in and start guzzling your tea and goodies.'

'Hello, Richard.'

'Hello, mother.'

She leant over and he planted a kiss on both cheeks.

'Introductions please.'

'This is my sainted mother; and this is my soon to be, long-suffering partner,Sgt. Stephen Penrose.'

She leant over and shaking his hand said,

'You poor boy, my heart goes out to you. Promise me you won't take any nonsense from him. Now Richard, your purpose for being here?'

'Demanding coffee walnut cake with menaces. I know you have some, so kindly bring it hither, so we may partake of it.'

Mary Barclay turned and brought a huge cake which was sitting on the side.

'Austrian coffee walnut cake with a cream coffee sauce. Stephen, can I interest you in a slice?'

'Yes please, that's very nice Mrs Barclay.'

She presented the pair of them with large portions of cake and sat opposite them. She immediately warmed to Penrose, with his chubby face and ready grin, and his tufts of sandy blond hair; he had an appearance to her which invited mothering.

'Before you go off for your two weeks in Canada, I trust you're going to see somebody is keeping an eye on the place?' Barclay enquired.

She nodded.

'So what are you up to, the seaside murder?'

'That's the one.'

'On the radio it sounded quite horrible, head smashed in. You know how they tend to go in for far more detail than anyone could possibly need. Any ideas?'

'No not really, but as you say considerable force was used, which most people would presume was anger. Although it could be premeditated, we don't really know. I felt we might be in the presence of a great deal of hate.'

'Or great love.'

'Yes, that's very true.'

Barclay took a swig of tea. He remembered the meeting with Miss Johnson.

'We hooked up with one of your cronies today. Dear old Miss Johnson.'

'Oh her,' she said with a barely repressed shudder.

'Tell me, was her makeup as subtle as always?' she added.

'Oh yes.'

'Now there is a woman who doesn't understand the concept *less is more*. This is not a new development, her makeup has always been a bit *de trop*. I can remember sitting on some committee for some earthquake appeal and she made Bette Davis's slap job in *Whatever Happened to Baby Jane?* look positively understated. Mind you with the wheels she's got now she could probably play the Joan Crawford role as well.'

Penrose began to feel uncomfortable

'Oh dear, your sargent is looking at me most reproachfully. He's giving me a look as if to say *how can you be so cruel to a woman that is clearly heading towards the departure lounge?* Well, Stephen, she's not a very nice woman.'

'I'm sorry, I know she's a bit stuck up, but I can't understand why people seem to be so down on her.' Penrose said.

Barclay smiled and nodding at his mother explained.

'Sorry, but I don't think you got the coded language when we were there. She wants to make it up to her nephew, Timothy. They fell out over his choice of wife. Now she's dead and she still can't give her approval. So he can come back into the fold presumably if he rejects the memory of her love. There are certain phrases that ring alarm bells with me, and being a few good years your senior, I'm probably more familiar with them. Did you hear her refer to Rachel as a *cosmopolitan type*, do you know what she meant by that?'

'No, I don't.'

Penrose was now uneasy.

'The term cosmopolitan is used by the British upper classes, to engage in antisemitism and simultaneous denial of that antisemitism. So she disapproved of his marriage, and still to an extent does, due to his wife being Jewish. Now, how do you feel about Miss Johnson?'

'Not so good.'

'Good man. Now, mother, I think you have been given a permission slip to be as monstrously bitchy about her as you like.'

'That's nice dear. Where do you come from originally Stephen?'

she asked.

'Penzance in Cornwall.'

Barclay sensed his mother was gearing up for a more pointed cross-examination. He didn't know why he had moved to Burridge, but being a private person himself, he felt since Penrose hadn't provided the information of his own volition, he should be protected from his mother's interrogation.

'Her antisemitism, It's a religious thing with her, is it?' Barclay asked.

'Yes, she's fairly nutty with her religion; it's odd because Anglicans aren't normally too bad on that score. I can remember having a couple of run-ins with her over the Vatican.'

'How come?'

'She was banging on about how she couldn't understand how anyone could countenance Papal Infallibility. It was really all down to her being a single woman.'

Penrose gave her a confused look.

'Look Darling, all men think they're infallible, it's part of their charm. When men are off on one women tend to say "yes dear, of course, you're absolutely right!" and get on with things. The idea of men being infallible is fine in theory, but certainly not in practice. Papal Infallibility is only an issue for non Catholics. Most Catholics are completely indifferent to any of the Pope's pronouncements. In fact, on matters of sexual morality, nobody gives a stuff what the Vatican line is. The only person I know who adheres to the line on sexual morality is a woman of 92.'

Barclay had long been bemused by his mother's particular version of Roman Catholicism. His late father had been raised Catholic whereas his mother converted some years before she met him. She enjoyed the social life Catholicism afforded her. He had come to the conclusion since he couldn't find any profound religious reasons for her converting it was largely for social reasons, and because it provided her with almost inexhaustible baking opportunities. Thinking his mother's social contacts might prove useful he asked:

'Mother, while we're here what do you know about the two Johnson boys?'

'Well, David as you know runs the hotel. He's quite a nice lad, young and hardworking. He's nothing like his aunt, pillar of the establishment, but not traditional in a backward looking way. Pretty open-minded and certainly no bigot. Keeps an eye on her. Knows everything which goes on around there. He could probably be a big help to you. Timothy is much older than him. He must be in his late sixties, or older. So, cousins with about thirty years or more of an age gap between them. Timothy got involved in the whole hippy alternative religion thing. Certainly got involved in the whole drugs thing. His other half died in strange circumstances, I think they got in over their head with organised drug dealers. He came back a long time ago but only returned to Burridge sometime in the last six years. He has some houseboat along the beach, there's a mooring place past the yacht club, and he still likes to see himself as some sort of artist. I think he survives with those carvings and things, but I believe he still paints. She was a painter you know. I think she was a good one. Before she died I think she had a notable exhibition, in Milan, I think. Italy, of course, was a big thing for her, being an artist they spent a lot of time doing the museums and galleries. Italy is of course the place to be. I think it has something like 60% of all the world's art treasures there. As for him, when she died he had some sort of breakdown and I think he was looked after in someplace in France. I'm certain the Sûreté could help you out on that score.'

'Where is she buried?' Barclay asked.

'You know, I have absolutely no idea. But of course, there must be records. Your department I'm afraid, Richard.'

'There are no other relatives?'

'No. They're a pretty miserable lot. You know that thing from *Anna Karenina*, that happy families are happy in much the same way but unhappy families are unhappy in different ways: well that's the Johnsons for you. They have managed to be miserable in all sorts of weird and wonderful ways. All in all they're a family who've come to a miserable end. Once the backbone of the Empire, but nobody's interested in people like them any more. She just sits there being waited on by that couple, peculiar set up, if you ask me. All alone, reading those ridiculous religious tracts, sitting there hideously overdressed with those Nancy Cunard ivory bangles up to her armpits. David lives in the now. That's why he's happy, she could have been happy, but I think made all the wrong choices. Why were you visiting her anyway?'

'She had a burglary and I thought there might be some connection.'

'Now if you want the low down on anything regarding the Johnson family and their grisly interpersonal relationships, you want to talk to Granville Winters. He's the family lawyer. He's *militantly* indiscreet and you'll get more dirt out of him than you know what to do with. Anyway, before I clear everything away would anybody like another slice?'

'Oh I think we could both eat a lot more, we wouldn't wish to offend you, mother.'

'You do need to watch your weight, Richard. What have you eaten today?'

'I've been very good today. I had a late working breakfast which consisted of cereal and grapefruit. Isn't that right Penrose?'

His junior decided it would be prudent to lie.

'Yes sir, absolutely.'

'Oh, really. In that case, I suppose you'd better have another slice.'

Penrose surmised that having been invited to Mrs Barclay's house and having lied to her successfully, he had now crossed a line and wondered if he should regard it as some Faustian pact, and he had now secured a place within Barclay's inner circle as a trusted colleague.

'So what's next on the agenda?' she said.

'I'm going to be seeing the family tomorrow. But, more immediately, I'm going down the Castle tonight, which seems to be the last place he was seen alive and hopefully something will come out of it. Somebody must have seen or heard something. The man is a bit of a mystery, to me anyway. I've spoken to the manager and he gave some overall impression of the evening, I'm hoping somebody might come forward with something which might be illuminating. Even if it's just an impression of him. Sometimes it's just the small stuff of life that takes you somewhere.'

'Isn't that place a little bit seedy; I thought it was a bit of a drug dive?' she said.

'No, not really. Well no more than anywhere else, really. I think they do their best to keep it reasonably clean, but you can't stop people taking drugs before they arrive there, and of course, you can't prevent those discreet deals being done in corners or in the toilets. Not without aggravating your own punters, anyway.'

'Who grieves for him?'

'That's the problem at the moment. His girlfriend seems to be grieving for someone who doesn't exist, somehow it doesn't seem real. People, or at least the people I've spoken to, seem emotionally disengaged from him. They don't seem to know him. You must remember I used to have that John Lennon poster with 'Gimme Some Truth' on it in big letters. I want to say *Gimme Some Grief*. It's the lack of any kind of emotional involvement I'm finding difficult. It's an awful thing to say, but at least I'm going to get some emotion from the family, at least I hope I am.'

'Richard you seem pretty lost as to who or why.'

'Mother,' he said smiling, 'nothing escapes you.'

Chapter Seven.

When Barclay arrived at the Castle on the Cliff, he felt dispirited. He hoped people would come forward, but since there were other aspects to the crime, silence might descend upon the place. He got the cocaine from someone, and he knew in these circumstances the pressure not to incriminate those who had been decided to be innocent, by those in the know, could be acute. This was born not from guilt or indifference but the unwritten commandment: *thou shalt not dump thy mates in it.* After he ordered a large decaf he found a corner by the bar to check his notes before Okonedo arrived.

He exchanged pleasantries with Sgt. Dalton and PC Lindsey who organised a small desk at the back. He was glad Dalton was there, people found him approachable. He had an easy manner and Barclay recognised he was jealous of him. He was wide girthed and it was his almost permanent grin he imagined people warmed to. His smoky blue eyes and relaxed manner seemed to be effective in getting people to open up. As he turned round Dalton smiled up at him, and even though Barclay had nothing to smile about, he couldn't help himself and smiled back. He was contemplating the meeting with the victim's father the following day, and knew little about him, but inevitably he would want to know what progress they were making. He wanted to claim some development or lead, however tenuous, so they wouldn't look completely useless.

'Evening sir, you're looking very relaxed.' Okonedo said, giving him the once over.

He wasn't sure whether she was administering a sly critique of his dress-sense or genuine approval at his attempt at informality, in a pub where the dress code went far beyond informal. It occurred to him he had never been unsuited in her presence, while she had the advantage of looking good in uniform. Sensing he might not have received the comment in its intended spirit she added,

'No, you look really quite different, I mean in a pleasant way. The important thing is you feel more comfortable.'

The uniform of the place was t-shirt, black jeans and spiky hair, flame red or peacock blue and of course black leather. The wearing of a Mohican haircut was reserved for those regulars who were approaching bus pass age. Barclay was socially awkward, and as he glanced around he felt as if he had walked out of a gentlemen's outfitters on Savile Row and into a Hieronymus Bosch painting. At this point, she decided it might be prudent to change the subject as quickly as possible.

'Sir, I've spoken to Gary, he's going to make a brief announcement. Then I'll come out and do an appeal for information. We've got Dalton and Lindsey at the back if needed. I need to ask, how much longer will we have that function room at the Alhambra?'

'Another 48 hours. Tops. We haven't exactly had a flood of information.'

'I think there might be some people who might come forward if it's over a cup of coffee in the function room who might not come forward to uniformed officers in here. We've had some developments, a member of staff there saw him having a contretemps with one of those security guys outside the hotel last night. Bear in mind David Johnson, who's been off at some one-day conference should be back tomorrow, and he might have something of interest. Sykes might have said something about his plans to him.'

Barclay felt more optimistic. He hoped information would start trickling out.

'I've written up what I'm intending to say tonight. Would you like to go over it?'

'No, that won't be necessary. I'm sure it'll be fine. You know what you're doing.'

'I think I'd better go and press the flesh, good PR and all that,' Okonedo said as she walked off.

As the pub began filling up Barclay sensed an unwholesome atmosphere. There was an ambience of unhealthy excitement. A sense the death was in some way a source of entertainment that was made all the more pleasurable by the fact the victim was an outsider, or somehow unknown. The anonymity of the victim immunised everyone from the feeling they might be held accountable for any perceived ghoulishness. From stool to stool they chattered in a leisurely fashion, if this was a tragedy it certainly wasn't theirs. It was as if an incidental character from a popular soap opera had been despatched in a particularly gruesome manner. The method of his demise was not the primary source of interest, it was the *only* source of interest. After all to them, he didn't really exist. Barclay reflected for all Mrs Lennox's curtain-twitching ways, her display of grief and compassion for a man she barely knew was infinitely preferable to the detachment being displayed here.

At eight-thirty Róisín and her party arrived and were greeted extravagantly at the bar by Gary. It was her regular group, Spike, Bill and Dirk. She was the visual standout in the group, with spiky magenta hair, racing green eye shadow and an enormous aquamarine mohair jumper pulled over yellow tights and Doc Martens. The men, in contrast, observed a rather dour uniform look of slightly messed up hair with army surplus clothes and brogues. They were probably the best-known group in the bar, although not universally popular with some of the heavy metal fraternity when political arguments kicked off. Róisín was a passionate fan of gothic fiction and her favourite book was Matthew Lewis' *The Monk*. She referred to the pub as *The Castle of Otranto*, after the book by Walpole, Gary was not familiar with the book and therefore was unaware she was not being entirely flattering. Had it been made into a movie of the week for the Hallmark channel starring Angela Lansbury he would have been aware of it; but it hadn't, so he wasn't.

The jukebox which had been pumping out a steady diet of '70s rock music abruptly stopped. Barclay presumed the announcements were imminent. In the corner the makeshift stage which was used for live music was suffused in amber light, illuminating a tatty blue canvas background. Gary walked out on the jutting promontory which was decked out in metallic moons and stars and wrestled with the uncooperative microphone stand. As the crackle of the mic echoed around the bar it became clear some sort of proclamation was forthcoming.

'Can you all hear me?' he asked plaintively.

A smattering of voices responded.

‘Can you hear me?’ he asked, the volume increased, and the squeaking of feedback demanded affirmation from those now looking stageward.

A more vocal reply now came from the assorted chairs and tables. Not enthusiastic, but sufficient for Gary to now hold forth. He cleared his throat and angled the microphone.

‘Listen up everybody. I think you all know the local community has experienced a tragedy. It's really important anybody who knows anything comes forward, Sgt. Okonedo will be speaking in a minute. However, I think I need to emphasise a couple of things. The police are requiring the maximum amount of cooperation, and this is a murder investigation. They are more concerned with anybody who has knowledge of any aspects concerning this guy's death than any kind of stuff he might have been into. We really need to come together as a community to sort this out. So it's really important we cooperate, so please listen carefully to what Sgt. Okonedo has to say and show her some respect. Okay?’

Okonedo moved behind the mic and looked out across the room. The crowd in the room had a self-image they were alternative, free-thinking, and a *demimonde*. As she peered at them over the mic she felt a certain level of absurdity at how smug they looked. The general theory in the room was it was the *Prominenti* within the yachting community who were pushing for a swift resolution of this case during their festivities, and if this had been the death of one of the local drunks on the beach little would be done. However, they weren't going to give Okonedo or her colleagues a hard time. After all, as far as they read it, she and her colleagues were merely supine instruments of the establishment, and not the establishment itself. An atmosphere of cultivated insolence hung across the room like an autumn mist.

'Thank you Gary, as everybody here probably knows, John Sykes, also known as John Sikorski was murdered in the early hours of the morning. I presume everybody has seen the photo of him; if you haven't, there are copies at the back.'

She held an A3 photo aloft whilst pointing to the desk at the back.

'He was killed by a blow to the head in his own home, at 12 Castlereagh Mews. A stone's throw round the back. It was a particularly brutal killing and we are anxious to apprehend whoever did this. This pub is probably the last place he was in before he was murdered. He may even have talked to his murderer in here. Perhaps somebody here spoke to him. Perhaps he mentioned he was meeting somebody. Or he was having problems with somebody. He must have said *something* to *somebody*. He had moved here recently and had just started to make friends in the locality. People must have had dealings with him. Somebody in here might even regard him as a friend. It has been reported in *The Echo* he was taking drugs and this might be of some importance. I want to emphasise any information regarding issues of drug use will be dealt with in the strictest of confidence and with sensitivity. This is a murder enquiry and our primary concern is that, and not increasing our clear-up rate for what in comparison we regard as minor offences. If you think you have any information no matter how small, please come forward. We are going to be circulating the room for the next two hours, or you can go to the desk at the far end of the room. There is also an incident room at the Alhambra for the next two days if you would prefer to pop in there, or if something comes to mind later. There is also a phone line on the leaflets. No matter how small a piece of information, it could prove vital. Thank you for your time.'

As she left the stage there was a small clattering of applause which she thought inappropriate, but she was relieved Gary hadn't leapt on to the stage and squealed,

'Give it up for Sgt. Okonedo!'

Barclay gave her the thumbs up as she disembarked from the stage.

'That was just right, very nicely judged.'

'Thank you sir, I hope we get something useful out of this.'

As Barclay surveyed the denizens of The Castle he noticed Gary energetically beckoning them to the table in the corner. Róisín and her party greeted Barclay and Okonedo.

'I suppose you'd better sit down.' Róisín said.

She was not from Burridge originally, she hailed from south London, a third-generation Irish –Englishwoman with a sly grin.

'Since this is a murder enquiry, I suppose we are obliged to collaborate with the forces of the bourgeois state. Sit down the pair of you.'

'Now Róisín, you are going to be nice,' Gary said. 'No bitchiness, I'm not having you calling Okonedo a coconut.'

Barclay shot her a quizzical glance. Okonedo explained.

'A coconut. Dark on the outside white on the inside. A pejorative much used in the black nationalist community, to put down black people who are prepared to exercise their own choices about what they do with *their* lives. Collaborators with the oppressor. It's been co-opted by certain sections of the British left.'

'I wouldn't dream of calling Okie a coconut, after all, you can get a drink out of a coconut.' Róisín said pointedly. She stared theatrically at the empty glasses on the table to reinforce it.

'Okay. Point taken. I'm on it,' Barclay rose and ambled his way to the bar. When he returned carrying a tray with jugs of lager with clean glasses he saw Okonedo and Róisín enjoying banterish conversation and he realised their byplay was based on a ritualised acerbity. When he placed the tray on the table Róisín accepted with a stage Irish accent.

'Oh God bless you sir, it's too good for the loikes of us.' She smiled as she poured the beers out for her party.

'Right this John bloke, he was sitting at the table with us. How much I can tell you about him is another matter, as you've probably gathered from Gary he was getting involved with some rock band. He seemed pleasant enough, quite cute, I'd seen him around, but not really a known quantity. A smiling chatty person, yeah, I liked him. I'm trying to remember. He was talking with some band; I think it was that lot *Bedlam Brothers*, a load of BM rockers who people were complaining about.'

'What's BM rock and what were they complaining about?'

'BM rock: black metal. There's some sort of competition, and they don't want the same bands competing, they had changed their name and other bands were complaining. I think it was all complete bollocks, but some of them take it so seriously.'

'You don't.'

'No they're all complete crap. We only come along for a laugh. The selection of bands here is thoroughly democratic.'

'How so?'

'Because nobody who performs is required to have any talent whatsoever.'

'So these *Bedlam Brothers*, who are they?'

'The same as all the rest of them. Some bunch of Wotan worshipping warlords who hail from Bexhill on Sea. Anyway they're in tonight. You can speak to them. He was yacking with them and then he came over and sat and he was joined by that guy Willie Ferguson.'

'What do you make of him?' Okonedo asked detecting tension in Róisíns voice.

'I don't like him very much. He comes from a posh background and he thinks speaking in London slang all the time will make him more appealing. I'm not an inverted snob but I can't stand posh people who pretend they're not and change their accent, and swagger around in a macho way. It's what my mum used to call the *butchoisie*. I think he's a bit of a shyster and if any of those bands had any talent he'd screw them over big-time.'

'What did he have to say for himself?' Okonedo asked.

'I got the impression they were old mates. He does all these bandstand things; down on the seafront. Got the impression from Gary they were working together, music-wise. He was saying John was a regular Perry Como, or something. It would make a real difference if any of these bands had people with genuine performing ability. The winners last night were a bunch of AS Punks, they've been around forever.'

Okonedo looked confused.

'AS punks?'

Barclay smiled with a glimmer of recognition,

'I think I get this one, AS stands for Anarcho-Syndicalism doesn't it Róisín?'

'Not in this case, Chief Inspector, it stands for Arterio Sclerotic Punks. One of my definitions I'm afraid. Most of them are probably eligible for a bus pass and look like Iggy Pop before rehab.'

'Anything else as regards these two, do you think they arranged to meet?'

'No,' she said cautiously, 'I don't think so. I mean he came to the table sat down and was talking. Then he went to the toilets or the bar or something and came back with this Willie guy. They weren't together long. Willie left before him, I think he was off to France, next day, and John left about twenty minutes later. I'm afraid that's the lot, sorry I couldn't be any more helpful.'

Barclay turned to her companions, who throughout functioned as a Greek chorus, albeit a silent one.

'Have you anything to add?'

They shook their heads. Barclay and Okonedo gave their thanks and moved to the desk at the back of the pub. Dirk turned to Róisín,

'That was the truth, but it wasn't exactly the whole truth, now was it?'

'I'm not going to dump that Willie guy in it, even if he is a complete knob.'

Róisín was defensive.

'I'm sure it wasn't relevant, he'll be back soon anyway. I may be many things, cooperating with the police in a murder enquiry is one thing, but I'm not a grass.'

Okonedo introduced Lash to Barclay. He was a gaunt twenty-something with eyes heavily ringed with kohl, wearing a *Bauhaus* T-shirt.

'This is the guy who was talking to the victim last night.'

'Could you tell me what you were talking about?' Barclay asked.

'He was giving me the thumbs up because I was wearing one of those *Hands off the Seafront* badges. We spoke about that for a couple of minutes and then we were just talking about The Battle of the Bands, and the issue about our name change etcetera.'

'What was the problem?'

'Well we changed our name. Apparently there's some issue about registration in the competition, Okay? Some people thought it should mean we were disqualified but we explained it all to Gary and he was cool about it, right? We were advised to, we got a demo done and we were getting it played on various specialised rock stations here and we were told there was the possibility of it getting played in the U.S.A. A lot of these stations have strong censorship regulation and they said our name was a problem. I wasn't happy because I thought it was an important censorship issue, and you really have to take a stand against the whole issue of censorship, right?'

Barclay nodded sympathetically. Lash was one of those people who turned all opinions into questions.

'Anyway that's all we were really talking about. About how we need to stop those security guys from taking over the pier, right? He seemed like a real easy going bloke. It's a shame what happened to him, right? And that was it; we only really spoke for about five minutes.'

'Well thanks for your help, and good luck with your chosen career. Oh by the way, what was the former name of your band?'

'*Anal Thrush*.'

'*Anal Thrush*? I see how you might have some problems. Having said that, I don't think when James Madison framed the first amendment he had quite this set of circumstances in mind.'

Barclay stood outside the pub with Okonedo.

'They had that Clash tribute band here the other week; I wouldn't have minded seeing that.' Barclay said.

'Apparently, they were more *fromage* than *homage*.'

'Look, I've really had it, and frankly, tonight is getting a bit too *Spinal Tap* for me. I suggest you give it another hour before packing up. I think tomorrow things are going to start coming together. I'm holding off the morning conference until 10.30 after I've spoken to Mr Sikorski; I think we might have a clearer picture by then.'

*

Once Barclay got home he resorted to his crutch of choice. When particularly dispirited only spaghetti carbonara could fill the spiritual gap. After eating, he promptly passed out on his Chesterfield whilst watching a war move on the TV. He lay there drifting in and out of sleep wakening when something exploded on screen. He was dissatisfied with his day and the lack of any reaction other than voyeurism from most of the people he spoke to irritated him. The man's former girlfriend was the only one who showed any grief, even though it had turned it into self-recrimination. He wondered if the essay in tortured nobility she presented was entirely genuine. Perhaps she was a little too virtuous. The clock entered his head. Then looming across came the figure of Miss Johnson, he speculated if there was any genuine goodness behind all her sententiousness.

It was the seeming indifference that bothered him. Were they really that ambivalent, or was it him? He was expected to exercise some detachment. He regarded it as a necessary deviation from emotional norms that was a requirement for the job. The conversations about the victim being in a band had at least personalised him. He had aspirations and that meant he was suddenly human, he had dreams. Nobody even seemed to dislike him particularly. Was he killed because he was greatly hated or greatly loved? Even Penrose was slightly judgmental towards the victim. Were people being indifferent because they disapproved of his morals? The victim died alone and seemingly unloved and this bothered Barclay.

An explosion roused him from his slumber. He sat up and reached for his glass of cognac. As his thoughts about the day receded he decided to give the film five more minutes. On the screen, a group of soldiers were attacking a village and he was confused. Were the villagers the good guys? He realised the soldiers were the good guys because you got to see their faces. Was it the Americans in Vietnam or was it the British in Malaya? The action was getting frenetic. The villagers were being killed at an alarming rate whether they were armed or not. He couldn't work out whether this was an antiwar movie or what his mother referred to as *war porn*. The indiscriminate strafing of both enemy combatants and civilians with indiscriminate firepower left a body count even the Waffen SS would have found excessive. Barclay decided this was not the best way to unwind.

He downed his cognac and turned off the TV. He would be meeting with the victim's father in the morning, and his story would be revealed. That would be where he would find the answers to the questions, or where he would find the questions which would need to be asked. Time for bed, he thought and proceeded to stagger upstairs.

*

At nine o' clock Barclay sat in Dr Reid's office at the Path Lab. As he pored over her report it didn't tell him anything new. Her assumptions about drug use were correct. For the respectable readers of *The Echo*, this might make grimly satisfying reading. The reality was in Burridge cocaine was the drug of choice for everybody from the aspirational working classes, to the upper crust types who inhabited the bars within the yachting fraternity and beyond.

He wandered out to the main entrance of the building. What he had been told about Mr Sikorski implied he was the type of man who would not be merely punctual but early. The Chief Constable had told him he was a successful self-made businessman in the antique trade and was *a pillar of the local community*, which probably meant he was on the golf club committee. Situations like this made him uneasy. The body was waiting for Mr Sikorski's inspection, if indeed that was what he was coming for. He had been informed he did not wish to see his son's remains through a glass partition, but up close. The lights had been lowered in an attempt to make the ordeal less onerous. The lab was some way from police headquarters and was enclosed in a small building adjacent to the local university. Barclay saw a lemon Mark II Jaguar approaching and realised this was him. He took a Kleenex out and wiping the palms of his hands walked down the steps to greet him.

'Mr Sikorski?' He said as the man approached.

'Chief Inspector Barclay?'

They both nodded and exchanged weak smiles. Mr Sikorski was a well-built man wearing a sharply cut suit of Donegal tweed, with the same clear blue eyes as his son although his hair was no longer corn blond but curly grey. He cut a distinguished figure. Shaking his hand he said, 'If you'd like to come this way, sir?'

They walked into the lobby in silence.

'Can I offer you a coffee?'

'No thank you. I'm sorry, I'd appreciate it if I could see my son.'

Barclay nodded and took him into the ante-room. The body was lying on a trolley, a sheet hanging over his chest. The body now cleaned, looking different from Barclay's previous encounter. The gashes on the right temple that had despatched him, were now clean, and looked more like a sporting injury than his cause of death. The father walked over, and Barclay sensing this was a uniquely and horribly private moment for him, kept well back. Mr Sikorski stood there for a few moments swaying slightly with his lips moving in short staccato motions. Barclay was uncertain what he was witnessing, whether he was praying, or whether it was a father sharing a final moment with his son which should have been conducted in life. It wasn't his business. He was an involuntary witness at a father and son's most intimate moment.

After a few minutes, he abruptly turned and walked out, followed by Barclay.

'If I might have that cup of coffee now?'

Barclay nodded and ushered him into Dr Reid's office. After they sat and Mr Sikorski leant back quietly sipping his coffee he said,

'Have you any idea who did this to my boy?'

'Well sir, we're following several lines of enquiry.'

'I'll take that as a *No*,' he said quietly. 'I'm sorry I don't wish to be rude, but my son has been murdered, and I have no desire to engage in Anglo Saxon pleasantries. Can you tell me if you have any hope of finding who was responsible for this?'

Barclay opened and closed his hands awkwardly, he felt wretched as he tried to think of a reply that would not add to this man's pain. His previous concerns about how his department's competency might be perceived now seemed vain and heartless.

'To be honest, we've only just begun the enquiry, I won't insult you by saying we'll find whoever did this. I honestly don't know. As they say, it's early days, and as soon as there are any developments I promise you that you and your family will be informed.'

Sikorski nodded quietly at this.

'We're having a quiet service at the local church, just the family. Afterwards, we're having a get together at the house. I would like you to come along and if necessary bring your junior; I think it would be a good idea if you came along and met the family. You might get a sense of who my son was. I think my daughter might be able to tell you things about my son which I am not privy to. My wife would also like to see you, you understand?'

Barclay nodded, beneath all the courtesy it was clearly a summons, and he wondered if there were things Mr Sikorski knew, he wanted him to find out for himself.

When Barclay arrived at the makeshift incident room at the Alhambra, Okonedo handed him a stack of notes. She took the opportunity of being alone with him to tackle him about something which was bothering her.

'Sir, when Stephenson left, I know you were annoyed that somebody you were used to, went on to bigger things. But that is not Penrose's fault and I would respectfully suggest that you stop taking it out on him.'

Barclay was indignant, when Stephenson had moved on to the Greater Manchester Police he was irritated that ambition had deprived him of his partner, but he was unaware this had manifested itself in churlishness towards his replacement.

'I don't know what you mean. How? I even took him round to mother's.'

'Taking him round to your mother's is all very well and good, but I think you probably did that out of guilt. Apart from anything else, what's that all about? Was that a sign of your approval? This is the police, not the bloody Garrick club. That is no substitute for validation, is it? You've been treating him as if he's some annoying weirdo. He's just moved here from Penzance, he doesn't know anybody and you've been treating him as a sort of semi-detached member of the team. It must be awful for him. I don't think you even realise you're doing it. You make approving comments to me about my work, but nothing to him. How do you think that makes him feel?'

She fixed him with an inescapable stare. He nodded, realising what she was saying was an accurate appraisal. He was aware he could frequently be less than forthcoming in the way he communicated with people.

'You're right, I'll see to it.' He said wearily.

'I'm sorry sir, but it had to be said.'

Once Penrose arrived they moved to a small oak table by the window of the function suite. It was another hot day, but more blustery than the previous one, families were laughing as they negotiated their way through the fierce breeze. Children were giggling as they inclined their bodies against the wind and walked into it. The beach was getting congested again. Once they sat down away from the glare of the windows and started tucking into coffee and croissants Barclay began going through the salient facts.

'What do we really know so far? His name is John Sikorski but he prefers John Sykes, so I think we should call him that from now on. We don't know why he anglicised it. Some people do it for reasons of convenience and some to reinvent themselves, which some of us all do from time to time. However, until we know why I don't think we should read too much into it.

'He was educated in the private sector. Went to a fairly good Independent school in the country. Played a bit of rugby and was a member of the rowing club. He got good grades for GCSE and A levels. Went off to get a degree in business studies at a London University. So far, so what.

'Afterwards he works at an Antiques shop and gets himself into hot water. He then ends up working down here in a computer shop. Seems to be popular amongst the workforce. This is where it starts to get a bit complicated. He has a steady girlfriend. But he appears to have only a passing familiarity with the concept of fidelity. There's no point in beating about the bush. I think it would be difficult to sort out the vagaries of his private life without the use of a flow chart. We need to be careful here. Unless we have some evidence of murderous intent or some jealous ex we would be ill advised to start looking for motive there. It's always a mistake to look for evidence on the basis of conclusions we have jumped to. Due to an absence of any other motivation it is quite tempting. On the other hand we should be open to anything along those lines. I found the way Miss Stevens, his former girlfriend, seemed to be blaming herself, almost unbearable to listen to. It's perfectly possible there is a lot of unresolved anger there. Now there does seem to be the impression he was involved in some sort of sex club. But once again let's not rush to judgment, let's check it all out. She said he might be involved in some sort of cult, but let's see. I think it was probably this Our Lady of Fatima thing, I hope to check that out today or tomorrow. Bear in mind a promiscuous person is someone who's shagged one more person than you, and a cult is a religious group that you don't approve of. Now, are there any questions so far?'

'Well one thing,' Penrose said, 'he doesn't seem to be involved with anyone at the moment, which, with respect is odd, considering his track record. This Bernadette Stevens claimed to have seen him with a woman. Who was she, and more to the point why hasn't she come forward? Why has no one come forward?'

‘Good point. However, just because they haven't come forward doesn't mean they won't. They may not have heard, on the other hand there may be a reason why they might be unwilling to speak out. The one thing is that he obviously went through some sort of life change at this point because he left there. He was signing on but I got the impression from the computers, he was also doing some sort of undeclared work. Also, apparently he was starting a new job. Now we do know he had some scrapes with the law, but nothing too serious. Okonedo, do you have anything on that score?’

‘Well sir, there are two versions to that one. He was guilty of minor misdemeanours for which he received probation. His co-worker Grant Maunders was involved in more serious stuff like fencing stolen goods, for which he went down. That is the court's version. When I spoke to the arresting officer from the Metropolitan Police he took a very different line, saying Sykes was up to his neck in it but got off due to having a smart lawyer and this Maunders guy ended up carrying the can.’

Barclay frowned.

‘There's one problem with that, there's always a tendency, especially at the Met for them to convince themselves they were completely right, and the lack of a conviction is always someone else's fault. However, we need to follow that up, because that is clearly grounds for a grievance. I'm sure it's occurred to everyone here: Antiques trade, antique shop, clock theft. However, all the evidence seems to point to this Will Ferguson guy. There is no specific link and I think if there is a connection it is a coincidental rather than a causal one. I think the crimes might be connected through interpersonal relations and are not *directly* connected. As soon as Mr Ferguson hits *terra firma* we need to have a chat with him.

'I think it would help us all if we went through a timeline. The morning of the Murder he went into the city centre, did some shopping, we've asked Wilmot and co to go through the CCTV footage to see if there's anything of interest like him hooking up with somebody, but I don't hold out much hope. At about 2.00 he went for an interview, after which he went home. According to the notepad by his phone, apart from the appointment at the Alhambra he had a meeting at 3.00 at home but we don't know who with. It just says 3.00 home. There is one interesting entry on the pad it says 5.00 followed by the word Fetley which we presume is a reference to the Fetley Arms.'

There was a murmur across the table. Barclay refilled everyone's coffee cups. Penrose looked around, it was clear the name had a resonance, which as a newcomer he was unfamiliar with.

'Okonedo, I think you must explain to Penrose here what a wonderful place this pub is.'

Okonedo obliged,

'It's Burridge on Sea's answer to The Savoy, the glamour and majesty of the place I can barely do justice to in words. It's situated down a side street just before you get to the Imperial. Don't ever go in there. It's known locally as the Fetid Armpit. It's a shitpit. A notorious rank scrotehole full of druggies and drunks. Inadvisable to visit there under any circumstances, unless you're buying or selling drugs or dealing in stolen goods and certainly not to be visited unless you're wearing vomit retardant clothing.'

'You make it sound like great fun,' Penrose replied.

'In fact it's such a pit of horror,' Okonedo continued, '*Even* off duty policemen won't drink in there.'

'It must be truly terrible.'

Barclay continued,

'What was he doing there? We'll have to put in an appearance there later on. Anyway returning to the victim's movements. The next we see of him he's in the Castle on the Cliff at about 6.30. He strikes up a conversation with Will Ferguson who apparently knew him before, but we don't know how. He chats with some of the heavy metal /punk lot down the pub. He apparently has aspirations to be in a band. The last we hear of him he leaves at about 9.00 PM to go home, we presume. Now did he know his assailant, was it a friend, a lover? What we really need right now is some luck. However, failing that, there are a few things we need to follow up. Firstly, Penrose and I are going to find out if he let anything slip at the interview with David Johnson. Mrs Lennox phoned, she needs to be spoken to again. Okonedo can coordinate things here. Then I think if Penrose and I split up, he can take Grant Maunders and see where he was on the night in question, and I can see if we get any info down at this sex shop. Then I'm afraid the pair of us are going to have to go to this family get together. I think this might prove informative. I get the distinct feeling there's something the father wants me to find out and is unwilling to tell me himself.'

'We don't know too much about the family, do we sir? I mean that might be where it all lies. It might not be sex or drugs or Rock and Roll after all.'

A groan canted across the table at Penrose's intervention.

Chapter Eight.

When they arrived at Mrs Lennox's house she was almost unrecognisable from the woman they had previously seen. The smile which she had proffered last time, so weak and dutiful was now replaced by that of a confident woman accepting people into her home, at her own invitation. Her hair was pulled back into a sailing cap and she was wearing a matching cerise blouse and slacks, with a bit of lipstick and eyeliner she looked breezy and smart.

'You will have a cup won't you?'

In these situations it was always best to accept. Last time she spoke to them she had felt wretched. Offering the small rituals of British civility was her way of wresting back control. She looked years younger and was no longer frightened and tremulous. After all, she had offered some help to the police in a murder case, and that was no small matter. Now, perhaps she might be of even greater assistance.

'I'm not exactly sure of the time, I'd been listening to a play on the radio and I just came out in the garden, and I was down at the end-'

'I think it might be better if you showed us, Mrs Lennox.' Penrose said.

She led them out into her garden, which obviously had time and money lavished on it. Neither Barclay nor Penrose had given much attention to it on their previous visit, but whilst not large, the design made it seem larger. It was laid out with a combination of gravel and intersecting semicircles of bushes with a good two dozen terracotta urns filled with roses. The contrast with the neighbouring garden couldn't have been starker. John Sykes garden had a neatly trimmed lawn, but that was the extent to which any thought had gone into it. Where Mary Lennox had shown thought and flair with hers, it was not neglect which epitomised his garden but disregard. This, of course, was not of his doing, he had been there barely two weeks, but he had done nothing to attempt to arrest, let alone reverse the neglect.

She turned to her son, who was sprawling on a lounger,

'Be a darling and get the Radio Times.'

He arose and slouched into the house reluctantly.

'I was listening to an ancient play, Donald Sinden as some Ambassador, quite funny as it happened. I was sitting in the conservatory, bit of a ritual for me I'm afraid. The afternoon play, feet up and a tumbler of iced tea.'

Stephen padded out and passed her the magazine.

'Ah, here we are. Started at 3.00 ended at 4.00. I remember the news coming on and turning it down. I only have to hear the Prime Minister's voice and I want to start screaming. Anyway, I came down to the garden, and I peered over the wall. If you're thinking I'm a bit of a nosy baggage, then guilty as charged! To tell you the truth I was wondering what would happen when Mr and Mrs Latham moved out. They didn't do anything with the garden, and I thought with a young man there perhaps he might really do something with it. He was normally quite polite and friendly in his own way. When we spoke the previous week he was a little unsure about what his precise plans were. I think he got the place on a peppercorn rent 'cause it's a little run down, I said if he needed any help with the garden I could give him the number of the man who does ours. I noticed when I went inside yesterday it was much tidier, so he must have got himself a cleaner. You have to be so careful these days because if people think you're being funny about their place they'll just tell you to eff off. Anyway, I came down and peered over.'

She beckoned Barclay and Penrose to stand alongside her at the garden fence. Pointing over she exclaimed:

'You see, he hasn't got a conservatory like mine, so you can see straight into his kitchen. That's when I saw her.'

'Saw who?'

'Some woman, I don't know who she was but she was getting a glass of water and John was standing next to her.'

'What did she look like?'

'Blonde, I think. Twenty-something. I mean I only saw her for a moment. Quite attractive I thought.'

'How did he seem?'

'Oh, he looked quite happy. Laughing, you know, he seemed very comfortable.'

'How did they seem together?'

'Ah,' she smiled. 'Now that is a leading question. Now you want to know if they were chummy or intimate. To be honest, I couldn't really say, they could've been old friends or something more serious, but that would be pure guesswork I only glimpsed her for a second. I knew I was being nosy, so I turned and walked back into the house.'

'I was just wondering,' Barclay asked nonchalantly 'did she see you?'

'No, she had her head turned away from me.'

Mary Lennox realised the pertinence of the question.

'Oh God, you mean it might have been her. She might have been the one who killed him?'

The woman they had met the previous day would have been a distressed at this implication but she took it in her stride.

'No, not necessarily.' Barclay said. 'We do however feel it's odd no one has come forward to fill in all the gaps. We have two sets of prints at the house which are not the victims and we need to eliminate them from our enquiries- needless to say we'll need to get yours. I mean most people have a personal life. He appeared to like female company. Did he ever mention anyone to you?'

'To be honest we never had a conversation that personal. It was pretty much day to day stuff. I don't know why, but I assumed he had a girlfriend.'

'Thank you very much for your time Mrs Lennox, but if there isn't anything else-'

'But there most assuredly is.'

'I beg your pardon,' said Barclay politely, 'Please continue.'

'The main reason I rang was not the recollection of what I saw but what I *heard.* About half an hour later I was sitting in the conservatory, feet up having a read when I heard raised voices. Next door they were having quite a ding-dong. I could hear John arguing with someone.'

'Did you hear the other person?'

'I came out here,' she pointed to a cherry tree by the conservatory.

'I was hoping to hear what was being said. He was saying something along the lines that he would keep quiet about something.'

She sat and was trying to recall what happened as accurately as possible.

'The other person, well I can't really be sure if it was a man or a woman was saying something along the lines of somebody could get killed or die if something came out. John sounded as if he was the calm one. But something had to be kept quiet. I mean people say all sorts of things, but I thought with John being murdered you know, it somehow becomes more relevant.'

'Did you hear any more?'

'I only heard a bit of it and then they retreated back into the house. So I didn't hear anymore. I mean I wasn't going to listen through the wall with a beer glass. I'm bad Chief Inspector, but I'm not *that* bad.'

Having thanked her effusively, Barclay and Penrose walked back to the hotel.

'Sir, it's really a pity she didn't listen through the wall with a beer glass.'

'Yes, where would we be without nosey neighbours? If I had my way there would be a section in the New Year's Honours list. *Mary Lennox to be made a Dame Commander of the British Empire, for services above and beyond the call of duty in the field of curtain-twitching*. It would completely restore the integrity of the British Honours system.'

'Interesting theory, who's up next?'

'I think we'll do David and Stevie at the hotel together. You do realise we'll have to keep our wits about us at the Sikorski's this afternoon, and look out for elephant traps. I think if we're not careful we're going to get played like a violin. I get the feeling either he or someone else is up to something. They obviously must realise our attention will inevitably turn to somebody in the family. Perhaps the head of the family who is so skilled at managing his shops is going to try and manage us.'

After returning to the hotel Stevie told him David was still not there. Barclay shrugged at Penrose.

'Tell you what, you talk to Stevie in the staff office and I'll wait in the function room for David Johnson.'

When he returned to the function suite Barclay sat by the window and proceeded to console himself with a large hot chocolate.

'Excuse me.'

Barclay looked up. Framed in the doorway was David Johnson. He rose to greet him.

'Sorry, Mr Johnson please come in. We appear to be constantly missing each other.'

'I've just got off the train. I'm afraid I think I need to throw myself on your mercy. Well, you obviously want to speak to me about the interview the other day. When they were all over I realised he'd left his mobile and I popped it round to him. My prints must be over the door, and I hate to admit it, the ashtray. But that's what you normally do, isn't it? I mean you dust the place for prints don't you? Then you have to eliminate people from your enquiries. So perhaps I should pop down the station and you can take my prints; that is the procedure isn't it?'

'That won't be necessary, we can send somebody over, it'll only take about ten minutes. However, it will be extremely helpful in terms of eliminating extraneous fingerprints. To be honest sir, we haven't recovered the murder weapon so the possibility of bloody fingerprints putting somebody behind bars is a bit of a forlorn hope I'm afraid. But thank you for being so public spirited.'

'This is all such a terrible business. Have you made any progress?'

'Not as yet, but it's early days yet. What would help would be if you could tell me anything about any conversations you had with him, and of course his CV. Anything he'd said about his plans would be helpful and anything about his personal life, you know, girlfriends, family and the like.'

'I'll get Jennie to fish out the CV. At the interview we talked about his education, how he'd done business studies. A lot of it was discussing if he had any ideas about how to turn things round here. He seemed to have some good ideas. I mean the labour costs here aren't particularly high and in the last year bookings have been up but we still don't seem to be taking much more money. I'd met him socially on a couple of occasions. Down the Yacht club that sort of thing, he was with some woman.'

'Can you remember who it was, it may be important?'

'No it was a boozy evening. I was moaning about the hotel as is my wont, and he said he was looking for work and had a business degree but had been doing other stuff, but was interested in the hospitality industry. I gave him my business card. He phoned a couple of times and when I started to arrange for interviews I put his name on the list, and he popped in and got a form. This is going to sound dreadful but in my line of work you have to have people who fit in socially. He would be doing a lot of bookings for private functions at the hotel. I mean, he would have dealings with the rugby club and the old guard in Burridge. You need someone who knows the right things to say.'

'I see.'

'For example we should be getting your lot down from Sussex Constabulary for a cricket match next month. I always make sure I have cordial relations with the police. I occasionally get some assistance from your boys via the sports network. Unofficially of course. Whoever's in charge has to be okay with those sorts of people,' David said smiling.

'Did you find out anything about his background?'

'Well on the CV he mentioned about his family being in the antiques trade, they seem highly respectable.'

'Did he make any reference to his religious views?'

'No, of course not. I would be in trouble if I even asked such a thing. No, that sort of question is strictly off-limits in this day and age.'

'Did he mention anything about any plans he might have, I mean immediate plans? The sort of things he might be doing that evening?'

'No, but I saw him in the Castle and I didn't think it would be fair to talk to him, I mean he had come for an interview and there's a sort of power imbalance. Besides, I was going up the Met for that God awful function.'

'The Yacht Club?'

'That's right.'

'Just out of interest, would you have given him the job?'

‘Oh dear. That's a tough one. To tell you the truth I was impressed with him. We're scheduled for more interviews next week. If the other candidates hadn't been as good I might have considered him for the job. However, Jennie had said something to Stevie about him being questionable, and I value her judgment. She has a habit of being right about these things. So, he would have been checked out. I would had to have him properly vetted. *The Echo* isn't the most reliable of newspapers bless 'em, but if they're right about him selling dodgy goods that would have come out. I'm afraid any kind of conviction for a crime of dishonesty would have ruled him out. I think people sometimes fall down and deserve a second chance, but when you are allowing somebody to handle cash you can't be too careful. When I think about it, he had a look at the books in my office and was saying he could see some things we appeared to be overcharged for and said he had some ideas. Even implied something wasn't quite right. I wonder whether the ideas were good ones or bad ones. I hate to sound callous but perhaps I had a lucky escape.’

‘You've been very helpful.’

Barclay understood more, but was unsure it was helpful. John Sikorski was becoming more fleshed out as a human being and the more he felt he knew him would hopefully take him somewhere closer to a solution.

‘It might not be important but when I left there was a woman outside in an MG sports car, red, I think.’

‘Did you notice anything about her?’

‘No not really. But the car was a classic '60s that I did notice.’

Barclay smiled; the obsession with classic cars was something he shared.

'There is one thing Chief Inspector, I'd like to thank you for the kindness you showed to my aunt.'

Barclay was unsure what he meant.

'She was terribly upset about the theft of the clock, and I know it's insured, and within the great scheme of things, compared with murder etc., is pretty irrelevant. It was enormously kind of you to take the time to go in and show that she mattered.'

Barclay smiled.

'Oh, that's quite alright. I'm glad we might have afforded her some comfort.'

'I'm very fond of her, but I'm not a fool. There are aspects of her personality that are truly ghastly. We all know the L.P.Hartley line, *the past is another country, people do things differently there*, but you have to bear in mind that's where she actually lives. She lives in that other country called the past; a place of deference and intolerance. Most of her idiocies just hurt herself, I've tried to build bridges between Timothy and herself, but she doesn't even realise that she's failing to meet him halfway. But I want to make things as comfortable for her as I can. I know you probably had to bite your lip when you were there, but many thanks.'

'Originally we thought the theft and the murder might be linked, but now I'm unsure.'

'Behind all the imperiousness she does get a bit desperate.'

'What do you mean?'

'Well she made a *mistake* with her medication a while back, so George and Dennie are in control of her drugs now.'

Barclay felt uneasy and wanted to change the subject.

'May I ask what's she going to do with all that stuff?'

'The clock or the insurance money will go to George and Dennie. If you're talking about *the spoils of empire*, we had a meeting some time ago and it's being left to the government to put into museums or whatever. I will get the house- or perhaps not.'

'You won't?'

'To be honest she's becoming less and less mobile. She refuses to have a chair lift. I think she feels having one installed would be tantamount to surrender. You can see sooner or later she's going to need round the clock care, and that means her going into a proper nursing home. Those places, at least the good ones, do not come cheap. I have resigned myself to the fact if she is to be given good quality care there will be very little left afterwards.'

When Barclay left he was a little disturbed at what he had been told. He reflected there were so many people living lives of quiet desperation that could tilt into despair. The reference to the *mistake* over drugs David had obliquely referred to, revealed beneath Miss Johnson's Grande Dame demeanour was a reservoir of pain.

When he returned to the lobby he found Penrose had finished interviewing Stevie. She had returned to standing behind the main desk, and he was talking to her in a relaxed manner.

'Look do you think you can meet back here at three?' Barclay asked.

'Of course.'

'I don't know how much you're going to get out of those two. I think it's the Sikorski clan who will reveal something interesting.'

'I notice how I get the odd couple and you get to do the sex shop.'

'You are far too young and impressionable for such a task. I don't want angry phone calls from your mother about you being corrupted on police time. Anyway, I have the feeling it won't be much fun. It requires someone with nerves of steel. I trust you're suitably impressed by my selflessness.'

'Oh, there is one thing. Jennie Wilkins, David's assistant said something to Okonedo about an incident outside the hotel on the night of the murder. Apparently, Mr Sykes had a bit of argy-bargy with one of those private security guards. There have been a couple of reports of them seriously crossing the line.'

'Follow that up, when you've got a moment. Those guys have got to be spoken to. Tell you what, discuss it with Okie, and then decide how to proceed. She knows better than anyone what's going on around here.'

*

After Penrose had driven two miles up the coast to interview Grant Maunders, he sat in the car and speculated how he was going to approach the interview. He had been given warnings about the girlfriend. Difficult, was the word used, he was unsure whether this meant awkward, or bloody-minded to the point of obstructiveness. He decided presenting a polite and understanding nature was the most effective way to introduce himself in their apparently, very enclosed world. They lived in a small terraced house on the outskirts of Southampton. It was in a back street, lined with small trees and with those fake Victorian lamp posts that were so popular in English suburbs.

The door was opened by a wiry young man, with a severe haircut and wearing baggy clothes,

'Come in, won't you?'

He had a hesitant way of asking as if the police having made this appointment might, in a fit of pique, decline. Penrose was escorted into the front room, where draped over the sofa was Charlotte Ventham.

'Er, this is Charlotte, my girlfriend.'

She looked up at Penrose with a hard stare, which he thought must have taken considerable effort. Clearly, her contribution to the proceedings was to give the police as hard a time as possible.

'Sit down won't you,' Grant said.

On a low table in front of him were three blue mugs and a matching teapot and jug. He had been prompt but he found it odd they were waiting for him with tea things ready. As Grant poured the tea he thought he understood. They didn't want him there. They were however ensuring there would be no circumstance when one of them was out of the room, and the other might be alone and vulnerable. As Penrose took his mug and sat down Charlotte's behaviour made him uneasy. She was wearing a lilac sweater and where Grant was skinny she was stout. No sooner had Grant joined her on the sofa than she started stroking him on his back, and soon her arm was around him. This was no embrace, these were caresses of control. She lit up a Gauloise and exhaled her smoke towards Penrose aggressively.

Penrose sat upright and cleared his throat.

'What can you tell me about John Sykes?'

Grant gave a weak smile.

'We worked together, at Remington's Antiques in South London.

We got on well I suppose. Then of course there was the trouble. I got sent down. He got probation.'

'Exactly how long did you end up serving in prison?'

'Six months.'

At this point, Charlotte dived in.

'Typical. He knew exactly what he was doing. He wasn't less guilty, if anything more so, but he had the nice manners and the clipped speech. So he walked. While Grant rotted in jail.'

In some circumstances, a six-month term of imprisonment might be of small account. Grant, however, came across as a vulnerable person. Penrose imagined him being targeted for physical and psychological abuse as soon as he arrived on the prison landing. He was nervous and damaged, she was angry. Theirs was a symbiotic relationship, her angry resentment feeding on his pain.

'I can't really comment about the trial, but as you know Sykes was murdered this week. Can you think of anyone who might have grounds for being angry or bitter towards him?'

Grant gave a weak smile and was reflecting on the times when they would have called themselves friends.

'No, not really.'

Charlotte spoke in short starts between cigarette drags.

'When Grant came out of jail he did nothing to help. Grant needed help setting up his business. We asked him, he made good money out of all that fencing of stolen gear but did fuck all to help, he could have. Said he couldn't help.'

'Did he make a lot of money out of it?' Penrose asked.

Charlotte was now incandescent.

'He made a fortune out of fencing that stuff,'

‘Charlotte, that's not strictly-’

‘For God's sake Grant, can't you ever stick up for yourself?’

Grant suddenly went quiet and consoled himself by burying his face into his mug. Penrose found the whole thing bizarre. When he arrived the pair of them were the controlled and the controller. Her, with her arms around him. Defining his victim status and permitting him to speak. The pair with their contrasting physiques had the appearance of a creepy ventriloquist act. Yet now he had spoken out of turn, and there was the vibration of impending emotional violence.

‘So,’ Penrose said quietly, ‘You don't really know of anyone who might have had reason to wish him harm?’

‘No, not really,’ Grant whispered.

‘Tell me, what business are you in now, you needed help for?’

‘I wanted to set up a secondhand book-store. I haven't managed that yet but I take stalls to markets and student's unions, that sort of thing, it's beginning to pick up.’

‘I have to ask you this, your whereabouts on the night in question?’

Charlotte intervened promptly.

‘We were together here, and no, there weren't any witnesses,’ she said with a snort.

*

‘Actually Jennie, we could do this in the Collingwood over a coffee. Then I can get it written up and you can give it the once over and sign it. I really need it in writing.’

Okonedo was standing at the main desk at the Alhambra. It was important to get a statement about the actions of the security staff. Their relevance to the murder enquiry she felt was unquantifiable. Her feelings were well known, as the face of the community liaison unit she knew anyone who was a supporter of the security guards was inevitably hostile towards her unit. The Chief Constable was publicly supportive of the yacht club's initiative. She was unhappy with any of the vetting procedures used by the council, but her concerns were ignored. The best option was to play a waiting game, and collate any information that would be useful. The Hands off the Seafront campaign was something she was advised to keep a discreet distance from, but it evidenced the SDT was not universally liked.

'Would coffee and a raid on the cake trolley constitute a bribe?' Jennie said.

'Yes, and I am open to bribery.' Okonedo replied crisply.

They seated themselves in the corner of the Collingwood and Okonedo proceeded to dispatch an enormous slice of Kirsch gateaux.

'Now when would you say this happened?'

'There were two incidents with those guys on Monday night. One of the foreign guests came in and said: "those security guards are pestering somebody." I popped down; it was about 6.30, something like that. From what I can gather one of the beach lot were begging and one of those idiots took exception to it. I went down and told him to go round the back. Masses of food gets thrown out, so a lot of the beach bums know to go round to the kitchen at the rear to get a good meal free and gratis. It's a sin to throw out good food when there's somebody to enjoy it. He must have been new to the area; most of them know not to beg out the front, it's almost an arrangement. Anyway the security bod started to get really arsey with me. I think the guard's name is Wayne Chambers; he informed me that by showing a bit of Christian charity we were, quote, “attracting them like rats.” Well at that point I went ballistic and ordered him off with two well-chosen words and you can probably guess what they were.’

‘I think I can.’

‘As he was doing as requested, that bloke John, the one who got murdered had a go at him. Started pushing him in the chest and offering him out. He was yelling “Nazi wanker” that sort of thing. It didn't go much further. I really wanted to get David out to help but he'd just come in from the pub, and he had some important phone calls to make before going up to the Met, and I know he was a bit nervous about it. He doesn't really like public speaking. David came out of his office about ten minutes later and I said there was something we had to talk about the next day. He had just gone off to the Yacht Club when somebody phoned saying they were from the Met, and I said he was on his way there to give a presentation and the caller didn't seem to understand what I was saying, he was unbelievably stupid, there was all this shouting going on outside. So I had to say “get him on his mobile if it won't wait” and hung up. I went outside and it was the same arsehole arguing with one of those punks and I stood there and shouted: “the police are on their way.” Of course I hadn't phoned, but it seemed to do the trick. It petered out after a few minutes. Later on in the evening there was some incident up the road and I think Timothy Johnson ended up going over and reading him the riot act. Now this is just outside here, God knows what's going on elsewhere.'

'This is getting out of control.'

They both took swigs of coffee. Whilst Okonedo was running her fingers across the plate and licking the last remnants of cream from her fingers something far more interesting was offered to her.

'Oh, there's more, you know the *Socialist Worker* lot who drink in the Castle, apparently Dirk said he recognised one of those security guys from about six months ago. There was an incident when a group of Hooray Henrys were in there and Gary asked them to leave. They pulled a condom machine off the wall of the Gents and threw it across the bar. Well one of them is now one of those security guys. I hasten to add it's unprovable but I happen to believe it's true. I have found out something else quite interesting about those guys. You know they make out they're all ex squaddies who've done their bit for King and Country? Well apparently the nearest most of them have seen of that is playing paintball. Not only that, most of them appear to do their training down at Lucky Johnson's Gym.'

'Also known as the needle exchange. I spoke to somebody who went down there about three months ago. They were offered drugs ten minutes after arriving. It's Steroid Central.'

Okonedo was clearly intrigued by all this.

'Oh, one other thing,' Okonedo continued, 'What did you hear about John Sykes? Apparently you said something to Stevie.'

'Oh, when we got the CVs I did a little ring round. The woman at the computer shop said he was very nice and all that but that he was like a dog with two dicks.'

Jennie was looking smug, she thought the information she had given Okonedo was going to be of some value, she also despised the security guards. The sergeant felt she understood her.

'Are you going to be continuing with those job interviews now?'

'I discussed it with David; we've decided not to bother for the time being. He's also very concerned all this stuff that's going on could be disastrous for business. So, for the time being, they're going to have to put up with me doing the accounts.'

'Are you going to that dinner dance thing up the Metropole on Friday with David?'

'No, he isn't going, I don't think. There's nothing really going on with me and David. I'm fed up with being dragged along to those dreary events,' she paused, 'Okie do you fancy him?'

'No, he is very handsome but no I don't.'

Jennie smiled, 'He's very sweet but he's all gong and no dinner.'

They both laughed, Okonedo said, 'Most of the men round here are pretty useless. I think we're going to have to go online if we want to find anyone half decent.'

'On the subject of useless men have you any further news of Will Ferguson?'

'No I'm afraid not, Jennie. What do you know about him?'

'What I know of him is through the wine club and bumping into him occasionally down the Castle. Not much, a bit of a shyster, keen on showing off with biblical and classical quotations. Like most men who like to show off how well educated and cultured they are, a bit averse to picking up the tab, which I seem to end up doing when he's around. I think if they made a film of his life it would be called *Born Freeloading*.'

Okonedo smiled.

'Much as I would like to spend the day eating cakes and badmouthing men I'm afraid duty calls.'

Chapter Nine.

Barclay felt socially awkward as he arrived at the frontage of Intimate Distractions. He wondered if he *looked* socially awkward. The outside was made up of scrubbed pine and frosted glass. When he walked in there was a buzzing noise to alert the manager a customer was present. The layout inside could have been any high street DVD store or bookshop except the product on offer was far less diverse.

He felt like a stranger in a strange land. The young man at the desk was serving someone. Better leave him to it, he thought. He would stand and peruse the shelves. He felt awkward again, was this the Catholic schoolboy in him, was he worried he would be *caught looking*?

Walking along the aisles the expanse of bare flesh was strangely merged into an amorphous mass of womanhood. Some of the covers were redolent of the forensic photos of naked corpses that had passed across his desk on occasion. It was the same unforgiving glare of flashlight and the denial of tenderness.

He knew he was a sexually repressed man, but what was offered was not complete sexual license, as some critics of the trade thought, but another version of limited possibilities. The eyes looking out from the covers, he felt were supposed to be inviting, but were looking elsewhere. The makeup severe and strangely unfeminine. The same bleached honey blonde hair, silicone enhancement and waxed genitals delivered a militant manifesto denying any concept of diversity or individuality. A large part of it were representations of lesbianism. Or an imagined idea of lesbianism appropriate to the male voyeur.

He remembered being told the problem with porn is it was boring. What staggered him was so much of it looked the same. There was a lack of variety that would have been commented on in any other form of entertainment. Far from being bored people apparently couldn't get enough of the same thing. But then again, that was the case of all entertainment; give the public more of the same. Why indeed should the world of porn be any different? The utter joylessness of it depressed him.

He looked and wondered where the fun had gone, from the traditions of Chaucerian pleasure in rumpy-pumpy all the way through the music hall traditions of Max Miller and co. to the rambunctious *Joie de Vivre* of the Carry On movies. Now it wasn't about sex, the movies seemed to be Olympian contests in physical endurance.

Barclay moved over towards the counter.

'Nigel Daventree I presume.'

The young man behind the counter looked up. He was tall fresh-faced and beamed refulgently with an inner joy, and reminded Barclay of somebody from his schooldays. With a mop of bright ginger hair, toothy grin and matching open-neck white shirt and cotton trousers he looked like he might have been captain of the school cricket team.

'How can I help you?' He said bounding from behind the counter.

'I was wondering if you could help me. I need some information on swingers?'

Thinking this was a request for a specific type of DVD he proceeded to steward Barclay to the appropriate section. The affable way he went about his duties he might have been one of those nice young men in Foyles directing his Auntie Madge to the Daphne du Maurier section. Barclay couldn't help to be struck by the dichotomy of the good-natured bonhomie with which Nigel Daventree went about his business, and the actual business he was going about. He reminded him of one of those Juvenile leads who used to appear in the Burridge Players productions of ancient drawing-room comedies bounding through French windows shouting *Anyone for Tennis*? Barclay discreetly presented him with his credentials.

'Everything's above board here Chief Inspector. There's no inappropriate stuff here. The only stuff we sell is fully certificated. Nothing involving violence or degradation.'

It was clear to Barclay it would be a good idea to let Nigel talk about his business, it was clear he wanted to. After all, any information Nigel would share would be some sort of breach of confidence. It would be best to let him hold forth, and build up some sort of rapport. Barclay let him pontificate about the liberating effects of porn.

'The new acceptability of porn is very important. You have to bear in mind an awful lot of young men get their sex education from porn. It means it's easier to exclude all the unpleasant stuff. You can give them positive messages about stuff like safer sex. It also means you can protect people who work in the industry.'

Barclay had uttered no words of censure. It was clear not all this young man's friends and family regarded his stewardship at

Intimate Distractions as the best career choice. It was a defensive tirade from someone who felt their profession was a beleaguered and persecuted one.

'I need your help Mr Daventree. There is no problem with the license.'

The evangelist promptly relaxed and stepped down from his pulpit.

'You are doubtless aware there has been a murder in town. The victim was I believe familiar to you. One John Sykes, also known as Sikorski. You are also familiar with a private club known as *The Comfort of strangers*, are you not?'

Nigel looked distinctly uncomfortable.

'I am aware of its existence,' he said cautiously. ' but I can't really tell you too much about it.'

'What can you tell me about it?'

'It's a discreet club, chiefly of couples, although there are some single members. Who meet on occasion for their own amusement.'

'I gathered that, where is it based,and are you a member?'

'Me, good God no!' He said laughing. 'I don't know too much about it, but it's an invite-only organisation, and I've never been invited. It's based in London, as far as I know. It's no longer on the Internet, so I can tell you now; you won't get any joy there. No membership lists would be held on a computer for reasons of confidentiality.'

'Any idea who runs it?'

'None whatsoever.'

'So, let's be blunt here, it's basically a wife swappers club?'

'Wife swapping, how seventies! That's such a patriarchal

attitude! I think you've got an idea about these things from way back. Where people left their car keys in the salad bowl. That's an urban myth. People go to these things and have drinks, chat and drift off to rooms when they've negotiated what they want, with whom. The women are very much in control. Part of the whole agenda of these lovers clubs, which is frankly a far preferable expression, is about deconstructing patriarchal power constructs.'

Barclay was becoming increasingly confused. As far as Nigel Daventree was concerned it seemed to be a sex club organised by the deconstructionist wing of the feminist movement, and Barclay was feeling considerably older than his 36 years. He was also smarting from the inference of sexism coming from the proprietor of a pornography shop.

Nigel Daventree smiled at him.

'I'm sorry, but as far as I can work it out this is a bit of a fishing expedition. This John Sykes or Sikorski is not known to me. I don't think you know very much about this club, and I think you want information out of me I am unable to give you.'

'This is a murder enquiry: unable or unwilling to give me?'

'Well, both really. The business I am in requires that I am discreet and I don't share confidences. In any event I can't help you. I can't be accused of withholding information, because you'd have to define which information I was withholding, and frankly I don't think you know what you want.'

Barclay sighed, what he was being told was true. He was hoping to get information which would guide him to ask the right questions, and infuriatingly he didn't know how to get there. He thought perhaps the sex trade hadn't changed much, this young man was much like the brothel madam in the dock, going to jail and refusing to cooperate with the police rather than betraying *her gentlemen*. On this score, he had a certain respect for him; after all, he couldn't give any coherent reason why this man should betray the members of this club. They had every right to live in peace, didn't they?

'Was there anything else I can help you with?' He said smiling. I'd really like to help you but I can't.'

'No, I don't think so.'

'I can offer you a complimentary film; there must be something here that tickles your fancy?'

Barclay was suddenly reminded of a drug pusher in an appallingly acted drugs information film his class were subjected to in his third year at secondary school.

'No they're not really my thing. It's like a foreign language to me. It's all just wall to wall humping isn't it?'

'Oh no,' Nigel's face lit up, now he could revert to being a salesman. 'Some of them actually have plots and play around with cinematic norms.'

'I had no idea people bought these things for their interesting narrative structure.'

'There are all kinds of different movies. Take this one. It's a satire on the War on Terror. It takes some swipes at the limits of American Imperialism.'

'Well Nigel, that's quite possibly true, but I think a lot of people who might be interested in a film with that kind of political approach aren't going to necessarily pick it up due to its title. I mean, no disrespect, but a film with a title like *Anal Apocalypse*, is likely to have an inconsequential attitude to contemporary politics.'

'Yes I know. I'm not going to tempt you am I?'

'No, I don't think so. Perhaps you can answer one question. When did this country become so bottom fixated?'

'Oh, the British have *always* been bumstruck!'

'I really think I'd better be leaving, thank you for your time.'

Nigel beamed at him and as he shook his hand Barclay noticed, as expected, he had a firm dry handshake.

*

When they met back at the hotel the two policemen compared notes and felt strangely relieved that since both had experienced severe disappointment, there was a reassuring mutuality to their ineffectiveness. They clambered into Penrose's car and began their journey to the Sikorski house. It was not far from Burridge geographically but it was in the countryside of West Sussex, so as far as Barclay was concerned it was another world. The house was situated on the outskirts of Denford, a place that seemed to be in a state of permanent autumn. The country surrounding the Sikorski's house was heavily wooded, and was shrouded by verdant hedgerow.

It was an ugly old house, an early Victorian tall Neo-Gothic pile replete with tall latticed windows around its ample façade. Built by a minor shipping magnate- and although well-liked in its time- it was one of the houses of that period whose charm had not advanced with the years. As they shut the car doors and proceeded to check their ties and flies, they were uneasy; this was the type of place they were unfamiliar with and they realised they might be socially tripped up. More to the point, that might be the central purpose of their invitation.

They walked up the four stone steps and rang the bell. A young blonde woman in a tweed jacket escorted them in, and with a half-smile said,

'I presume you are the forces of law and order?'

Barclay nodded and introduced himself and Penrose, the woman barked 'Mary, family friend,' and they entered the main lounge into a throng of about fifty people. Mostly the same age as the victim's parents.

Leon Sikorski came across and greeted them, impeccably dressed in a woollen navy blue suit. He was different from the man Barclay had previously met. He had a polite smile and a diffident manner and seemed genuinely pleased at their presence.

'I'm so pleased you could make it. We had a nice service at the chapel. It was very important for us. I don't think you're very religious, are you? Please don't answer. I'm being rude, but you're a policeman, the things you see, they must rob you of faith.' Barclay smiled politely in a way that denied any answer.

'Mister Sikorski this is Detective Sergeant Penrose; he's assisting me.'

'I'm pleased to meet you Sergeant.'

He looked at him and smiled, he was clearly thinking how young he was, but restrained himself from commenting.

'Now this is an informal gathering and I will be severely chastised if you don't have some coffee and cake. You won't have a sherry will you, after all, you are on duty aren't you? You have to keep your wits about you.'

There was something pointed beneath the surface of the chatter, but both men were at a loss to define precisely what it was.

'I think now would be a good time to introduce you to the women in my life.'

He took them over to the French windows where Mrs Sikorski was working the room, being gracious; doing what was expected of her. She was a large woman who looked older than her years; the circumstances had not made her look any younger. She was wearing a large wine coloured dress and had her hair pulled up in a high Edwardian style. The distress she was in was unquestionable as she moved her head awkwardly as if on sticks like a Chinese marionette. Her face had that bleached look that comes from extreme emotional exhaustion.

'Maria my dear, this is Chief Inspector Barclay and this is Sgt. Penrose.'

He gestured to a young blonde woman sitting nearby wearing a black Chanel suit to join them.

'Cressida, please could you come over?'

Experience had taught Barclay there was little new to say in these circumstances and that some clichés possess a power and majesty that commands respect.

'I am terribly sorry for your sad loss, and I can promise you the police are doing their utmost to bring whoever was responsible to justice.'

'Thank you for being here Chief Inspector, it makes a big difference,' Mrs Sikorski said smiling politely, 'If I might speak to you later?'

'Yes, yes, of course, Mrs Sikorski,' Barclay said.

'Perhaps you might talk to my daughter Cressida a little later,' Mr Sikorski said, 'it might be helpful to you.'

Penrose saw her give him an injured look and he couldn't discern whether she was irritated at being ordered around by her father at such a painful time, or whether she regarded the police as intruders who had no place at a family event.

'Chief Inspector, Sergeant, some coffee and almond cake?'

They were taken by their host and given plates piled high with cake and large coffees and taken to the garden. There was a large patio overlooking several acres of overgrown land.

'If I might introduce you to Father Canelli.'

Seated in an armchair in the patio was a portly man in his mid-sixties in clerical collar and Harris tweeds.

'Good day to you. As you've doubtless surmised, I have the honour to be the family priest. It's good of you to come; this has been a very hard time for the family, we hope that you will bring a resolution of sorts.'

Barclay nodded towards the Priest.

'I think Mr Sikorski thinks I might be of some help about telling you something about his background.' Canelli said.

'Chief Inspector,' Leon Sikorski said, 'in looking to find out who was responsible for Johns death I'm sure at some point you will be wishing to look closer to home,' having made an observation so manifestly true, Barclay said awkwardly,

'Well, obviously we are going to be examining all possibilities.'

Leon Sikorski nodded and gave a broad smile.

'That is reassuring to know. Chief Inspector, when the news

came through of the death I overheard my son in law saying *John's personal life was a mess*, that's what people say about people who have a wholly amoral lifestyle. As a father I have been kept in the dark. Most fathers are. I think the good Priest here can help you, and I'm certain my daughter can. I know that after today we will presumably meet again, you will have more questions. I have been told things on a need to know basis, it has been assumed that as a father I don't need to know anything. As for my own and my wife's ignorance, you have seen my wife; please do not cause her any more pain than you have to.'

He smiled again.

'I have to attend to my guests. Please excuse me.'

When he had walked off, the policemen sat down and Father Canelli smiled at them, although with an Italian name he spoke with an English accent with a slight Cork brogue.

'He is a very good man, but utterly bewildered by what has happened. In case you were unaware it has always been assumed John would take over the family business at some time. There are four shops across the county, which doesn't sound a lot but they have a considerable turnover. Mr Sikorski must be worth 4 or 5 million. John had been doing his own thing for a while, I think he was working in a computer shop. It was felt that it was no bad thing, seeing something of the world you know, but I'm unsure whether he was attempting to completely break free from his family. He appeared to have become a lapsed Catholic, but I'm not entirely sure. Chief Inspector, you're Catholic aren't you?'

'I'm from that background, yes.'

Father Canelli chuckled.

'That's rather evasive. You don't have to worry about my feelings, I will cope. The door will remain open. People like you always come back.'

'It's perfectly possible, I think even W.H Auden reverted at the end. I do need to ask you a question specifically about faith, what do you know about an organisation called *The Miracle of Fatima Society*, would you define it as a cult?'

'Well, sometimes these organisations can become a bit cultish if they attract sufficient numbers of oddballs. However, this lot are not. It's not a weird grouping, fairly traditional, but not one of those Catholic organisations that ends up being run by fascist whackjobs.'

'What about John's personal life?'

Canelli frowned, not with disapproval, but difficulty.

'He was like many young men. This is going to sound terribly hypocritical, probably because it is, but I think it was accepted he was going to sow his wild oats. I think if Cressida had behaved like that, it would have been wholly unacceptable, but being a man, you do know what I mean? He had the advantage his looks afforded him, the opportunity to behave a bit badly. He had the face of a choirboy but not the morals or voice.'

'How aware were his parents of his behaviour?'

'Not very. They knew he wasn't living like a monk, but for the most part they were in the dark, and in case you didn't fully understand what Mr Sikorski said, they do not want the light turned on. They will shortly be making funeral arrangements for their only son. Ignorance is not bliss, but sometimes it makes grief considerably more bearable.'

'How did Cressida feel about all this?'

'Cressida is an enormously sensible girl. She's known since she was a child that as the eldest boy he was going to be spoilt rotten and inherit the bulk of the estate. It's not something that was suddenly thrown at her, so she's always had a pretty sanguine attitude about it. I think she's one of those people who as the eldest child felt it was her duty to be the one with a strong moral sense. She isn't being completely cut out anyway, she's running their Repro Shop, and I think is very successful. She'll get a share, just not the lion's share.'

'Is Cressida quite happy about everything?'

'She married two years ago. They have been trying for a child, but I don't think everything is going smoothly there. All marriages have their ups and downs.'

'Back to religion, father. Are the family very religious?'

Father Canelli smiled and turned so he was leaning on one arm.

'That is a very subjective thing. I would say they were an observant Catholic family, but by contemporary British mores they would probably seem like religious fanatics.'

'But just traditionalists you say?'

'Yes, the family are very devout. Cressida very much so, but Tony her husband, I wouldn't like to say.'

Barclay turned to Penrose and they shared a look, his solicitous restraint about the son in law was they felt revealing in its lack of inclusivity. He may have married into the family, but there was a sense in which he was regarded as semi-detached.

'If you'd excuse us for one minute, Father.'

Barclay rose and beckoned Penrose to accompany him further

down the patio.

'It's my experience in these situations we'll get more from people if we are on our own. If they say something to us together its *blabbing*, if they say something to one of us it's an indiscretion.'

He was aware Mr and Mrs Sikorski were working the room and perhaps it would be appropriate for them to do the same. Barclay heard a voice behind him.

'Chief Inspector, I thought it would be a good idea if we spoke.'

Cressida Sikorski was standing behind Father Canelli. Barclay hadn't noticed her much when they were introduced before, but she cut a slightly intimidating figure in a blue-black tailored collarless suit. It was simply but impeccably cut, made more impressive by her poker-straight back. She was a handsome more than a pretty woman, with strong features and sharing her brother's corn blonde hair pulled up into a French twist. She possessed the kind of lean self-assuredness and tight angular build that would look gracious in practically anything.

Penrose collected their crockery and quietly wandered out towards the main hall.

'Chief Inspector Barclay,' she said, shaking his hand and giving her best air stewardess smile.

'This is a little trying for all of us, and I think I was a little frosty towards you earlier, I'm sorry about that. If there's anything I can do to help?'

'Well, I'll probably make a formal visit to you over the next couple of days. I'll have to talk to your parents too. There are some things it would not be appropriate to raise here. I wonder if you could tell me something about your brother's character, and where as far as you were concerned he was going with his life?'

'John and I were very close. It was always expected he would take over everything at some point. Sooner rather than later, I think dad wants to retire. But he's been doing his own thing. We've all just been waiting for him to sort himself out really.'

'I understand there was some sort of family estrangement and at some point he was questioning his relationship with the church. I imagine with your family that might be problematic.'

'Chief Inspector, I'm not sure what you mean, what have you been told?' she said, as she sat alongside Father Canelli.

'Well, that he had some sort of dispute with the family and he wasn't keen to return to the fold and that he was asking theological questions of some sort. His lifestyle I wouldn't have regarded as completely compatible with religious observance.'

'My brother was a not long out of University, he was young. He was five years my junior, but men are always far younger than women, emotionally anyway. He was having his wild days, women have other responsibilities, anyway this one does. He went through the whole thing of sneering at religion, but people get over that. I wouldn't read too much into that. In terms of his attitude towards his family and his faith, he had gone through a youthful period of minor rebelliousness. There may have been an alienation of affections, but there had been no divorce. Are you suggesting something more? What has been said?'

'Well, I'm following a line of enquiry from somebody he was previously involved with-'

'Who, exactly?'

'Well it's a woman who worked at an Estate Agents locally; I can't give you too much information as you might understand.'

Barclay was at a distinct disadvantage, as this was not an official interview, he couldn't really complain if she was taking control of the conversation. Cressida looked more relaxed.

'That would be Bernadette Stevens, sorry, please continue.'

'She informed me he said something about a change of life, change of direction and about a new job but she didn't get any details. She gave the impression he was involved in some religious group or cult she wasn't sure, he didn't say.'

Cressida's husband Tony walked over and placed a sherry in his wife's hand. Barclay turned to introduce himself, but as quickly as he had arrived she had ushered him away with a glance.

Father Canelli who had been listening to the interchange between the policeman and his parishioner leant forward.

'You implied he had some association with *The Miracle of Fatima Society*, if that's true then it's possible he was reconciling himself with the church. I'm not sure what his falling out was about, but we all of us have at one point had some crisis of faith and have to find our own way back to God; possibly this group was his.'

Cressida straightened herself in her chair.

'Father, I'm sorry but I really need to talk to the Chief Inspector on his own. If you wouldn't mind leaving us?'

'Of course,' he said, as if he'd caused some great offence. 'I'll pop into the main room.'

When he was out of sight Cressida relaxed.

'Chief Inspector, I'm sure you'd like me to be frank. There are some things you'll need to speak to me in private about. Perhaps you'd like to pop into the showroom tomorrow or when it's convenient for you. To meet on neutral ground, if you know what I mean? What I can tell you is that at one point John was going to leave the family business. Turn his back on us. He was also rejecting the faith. How far it went was largely only known to me. I kept in touch with him, and in the last couple of months it was clear he was coming to his senses and was preparing to come back. I would appreciate it if you were very circumspect in the language you use in front of my parents. They were unaware of some of the trouble he had managed to get into; and of his getting into trouble with the police. They were also unaware of his rather promiscuous lifestyle, but I think he'd found a woman he was rather more serious about and was talking about settling down with her.'

'Do you have a name?'

'No, I'm afraid I don't. They know nothing about his drug abuse either, I don't want them to find out. I'm sorry if I seem a little bit driven about these things, but he's dead and I don't want his memory despoiled in their eyes. To be blunt, it's all they have.'

'Thank you for being direct. I'm going to be equally direct. Quite clearly you know him better than anyone else. Can you think of anyone who might hate him sufficiently to want him dead?'

'Well with John it's going to be *cherchez la femme*?'

'Anyone in particular?'

'There was some woman who was practically stalking him. I think it might have been that Bernadette Stevens, but he did talk about some woman who was a bit demented, who was giving him a hard time.'

Her husband walked in.

'Cressida, people are beginning to leave, if you wouldn't mind?'

Getting to her feet, she smiled at Barclay.

'If you could give me a ring, Chief Inspector, and you could pop in, or I could speak to you at the station, if that would help?'

'Yes, of course.'

He followed the pair of them into the main room. He had barely had any conversation with
Cressida's husband Tony. There was a nagging feeling he was barely tolerated by the family, but then again, he thought it probably wasn't relevant. He was athletic and good looking; it was clear why she had married him. Although they behaved in a dutiful way that an older couple behave towards each other, hardly like a young couple.

When he returned to the main hall, it had thinned out considerably. He scanned the room, and noticed what a dull affair it was. It was panelled in dark wood, looking more like a film set of some sort of Ruritanian hunting lodge than anything else.

Why would anyone want to hang on to this without redecorating it? He wondered whether the Sikorski's had that over respectful attitude, of people who wanted to be part of the establishment, for things because they were old fashioned and British, rather than attractive. The place was beautifully furnished in the tools of the Sikorski trade. In furniture which was unobtrusive but perfect. Large William IV cabinets packed with books and Sheraton tables gave the room a luxurious and comfortable feel. He looked over and saw Penrose talking to Maria Sikorski in a deferential yet relaxed manner. He had meant to spend some time speaking to her but Penrose clearly had been more effective than he might have been.

Cressida was doing the duties of thanking people for coming, how thoughtful it was to be there, and to keep in touch. As people began to depart there was the silent murmur which descends upon such gatherings. The unspoken undertone of *it's time for us to leave,* was rolling across the assembled guests. Friends awkwardly trying to think of something comforting to say to the grieving family as they left, that hopefully wouldn't sound crass. Penrose joined Barclay as Maria Sikorski was commandeered into dutifully thanking her condolent guests, and receiving their heartfelt consolations.

Barclay took this lull in proceedings to speak to Tony.

'I haven't really had an opportunity to speak to you, I'm sorry. This must be very difficult for you.'

'I'm only family by marriage. It's a sad business. John's parents barely saw him in the last few months, at least Cressida saw a bit more of him recently.'

'John was of course coming back to take a leading role in things. I suppose that would have changed things?'

'That's news to me. Mind you I'm pretty much surplus to requirements when it comes to decisions round here. You really would have to ask Cressida about that sort of thing.'

'How did you get on with John?'

'On the rare occasions when we met, we got on okay. The papers seem to want to dredge things up, but then they always do. I suppose that's the sort of stuff you're looking for. I think Cressida is trying to protect the family, there was something shown to them in the *Burridge Echo* but Cressida dismissed it with *you can't believe anything in the newspapers*. I don't think there's anything to be gained from trawling up any of the stuff about his private life.'

'Do you know of anyone who might wish him harm?'

'No, from what I gather it was probably drug related. As for the other stuff, I don't see any point about any of that stuff coming out. He liked to put it about a bit. He'd shag anything with a central nervous system. He was a naughty boy, a roué, a slapper, a slut and a bicycle to boot, but that's really not anyone's business.'

'Tony, I don't think we really want to hear any more, do we?'

Cressida had walked over and had issued a command in the form of a question.

'Sorry dearest,' he said smiling. There was clearly some sense of mischief in the way he conducted himself.

'We're just chatting about John, nothing unpleasant meant by it. You were always saying he was a bit of a Peter Pan, but I think on balance he was more like the caterpillar out of *Alice's Adventures in Wonderland*.'

'That really is enough.'

Cressida was clearly unhappy that her controlling conversations with Barclay were being undermined.

'I think I'd better make myself useful. Or scarce.' Tony said, as he gave a smile and wandered off.

Barclay couldn't work out how he really fitted in. Tony certainly stuck out at the gathering, he had an easy way of moving and a cocky manner which gave him an obvious attractiveness, and possibly that was the problem. Barclay had noticed how an affectionate touch on Cressida's shoulder was rebuffed as if it was improper. This was a rather controlled family, which was possibly why John had to reject them even temporarily, to affirm who *he* was.

Barclay and Penrose went over to Mr and Mrs Sikorski. They were now the only non family members there apart from Fr. Canelli. Cressida was now tearing through the room, her jacket hung up, her sleeves rolled. She was at the shelving lifting sympathy cards and finding sherry glasses that had been secreted amongst them. There was ferocity in the way she was clearing through the room with an air of purpose.

'Mr Sikorski, I get the awful feeling this is my fault.'

'I'm sorry Chief Inspector, you've lost me.'

'I think I may have upset your daughter.'

Mr Sikorski laughed.

'Oh no, this is normal. My daughter finds this quite therapeutic. Tony calls her the Hoover queen. If you need to talk to her go ahead.'

Barclay walked over to her with some trepidation.

'I'm sorry; I think I might have upset you.'

Cressida smiled broadly.

'No, not at all. I'm cross with Tony, I don't like being undermined that's all. If you don't have anything else to ask me, if you don't mind I'll carry on. I don't want any mess for mother to clear up.'

'It's just one thing, not particularly important. Your brother called himself Sykes rather than Sikorski. Was this a form of distancing himself from his family or was there another reason?'

She burst out laughing.

'Now you really are losing your marbles. We *all* use Sykes occasionally if I'm phoning for a cab I use Sykes. If you don't it's,

Sikorski how do you spell that? so it's a way of avoiding hassle, the whole family does it. He didn't have it changed by deed poll, did he? No, I'm afraid you're barking up the wrong tree if you think that's remotely significant.'

Barclay was disappointed; he was hoping it had some relevance although he was unable to speculate exactly what. After exchanging the usual formalities with the Sikorski family, they were on their way. Thundering through the country back to Burridge, they attempted to dissect what had happened.

'You any the wiser, sir?'

'Well, we've quite a lot to think about. What did you make of Cressida?'

'A bit intimidating.'

'I think she was being a bit dishonest. The problem of course is the why. She likes to present herself as the keeper of the flame. Is she lying to protect the family?'

'Presumably with the brother out of the way, this will be advantageous to her. I mean the parents aren't going to leave it all to the Battersea Dogs Home. I spent quite a bit of time talking to the mother. I think it is presumed Cressida will take a greater responsibility in running things.'

'Tony, is her trusted lieutenant, so more responsibility will be put on his shoulders.'

'The son in law also rises.'

'Quite.'

Barclay hadn't quite decided what he thought about him. He remembered how Leon Sikorski had initially referred to him as *my son in law*, a formulation which defined his status in relation to the family but robbed him of his own personal identity. Father Canelli also seemed to have a rather dyspeptic attitude towards him. However, he probably wasn't the first parish priest to have absorbed the prejudices of a family towards somebody who had joined it by marriage, and he was unlikely to be the last.

'Penrose, what did you make of Tony?'

'He doesn't seem to be in the loop, no, that's not strictly true, he gives the appearance that he doesn't want to be seen as just another member of the Sikorski clan.'

Barclay's impression was that he enjoyed picking at the fabric of Cressida's beautifully structured narrative of her brother. Regarding, the death not as a joke, but possibly the family's pretensions. Remembering Fr Canelli's comment about the marriage having its ups and downs, he speculated if her marriage was being confronted by problems of infidelity, also if she was a little bit too good to be true. The way she accepted primogeniture with an air of resigned stoicism, might have met with familial approval but could not have endeared her to Tony. Possibly he might find that kind of forbearance wearing after a while. Barclay imagined he had his own ideas about how things should be run. He appeared to be his own man and was unenthusiastic about having his own dreams and aspirations being subordinated to her parent's will.

'Sir, was he deliberately trying to stir it, do you think?'

'Probably not. You have to bear in mind he might have thought Cressida was playing control games. Did you see the way she responded to the way he spoke?'

'I couldn't quite get that. Peter Pan and the caterpillar, what was that all about?'

'Ah, curiouser and curiouser. Well, evidently someone had called him a Peter Pan in the past i.e. he wouldn't grow up, face up to his responsibilities. Tony made reference to his drug abuse. If you remember the caterpillar in Alice, he sits on a giant mushroom whilst smoking from a hookah talking complete bollocks. Lewis Carroll wrote that in the good old days when you could pack masses of fairly upfront drug references into a children's book without any fear of criticism. Halcyon days!'

When they reached the outskirts of town, Barclay was more relaxed. He had been dreading the event, but as far as he was concerned since they had left unscathed he regarded that as a victory. Leon Sikorski had wanted them there because he wanted them to learn something, but he was still at a loss as to know what. Was it just he wanted them to know who their son was, so they might care? Perhaps there was something specific he wanted revealed to them, the more he pondered it, the more it confused him.

Chapter Ten.

Barclay felt more hopeful when they returned. Penrose was more relaxed and Barclay hoped he would receive no further admonishments from Okonedo. He was working better with him and thought he probably had redeemed himself. Penrose was out on a date. The family get together-wake or whatever they called it he was not exactly sure- had reassured him in an emotional sense. He had witnessed grief, dishonesty, resentment, ambition and anger. These were all appropriate and healthy emotions under the circumstances and were a relief from the detachment he had previously witnessed. After a good meal and a soak, he relaxed on the sofa and was contemplating watching a rerun of *Night Train to Munich* on BBC4 to help him unwind when the call came through from Okonedo.

'I know I shouldn't really bother you at home but I simply had to phone you. Oh, before I go off on one, how did you get on at Sikorski villas?'

'It was alright. I can give you all the details later; you didn't phone me up for that did you?'

It was highly unusual for her to ring him at home.

'First the bad news, Mad Harry got attacked by one of those security guards on the beach. He's not badly hurt, just roughed up a bit. The good news is he's agreed to press charges.'

'Obviously that means we can finally do something about those bastards.'

Barclay knew an individual complaint could only do so much. It would depend whether the authorities decided a prosecution was likely to result in a conviction; it was unlikely due to the complainant being under the influence of alcohol or drugs at the time of the assault. There had been rumours circulating for weeks the security firm was functioning as a private army, now things were coming to a head. Okonedo would be adamant for tough action to be taken and he did not want any perceived cynicism on his part being interpreted as undermining her resolve. The slight lull on the other end of the phone was sufficient for her to guess his concerns.

'I know this area sir, and I know these people. Now one person is prepared to come forward I'm sure others will.'

He realised this was true and felt reassured.

There was a pause, she added:

'You have read my statement from Jennie haven't you?'

There was a hesitant noise from Barclay.

'Well sir, I'm going to take that as a no. Then again it's really my own fault. I left it on your desk labelled *very important.* I really should employ a bit of reverse psychology on you. In future, I'll leave it on your desk with a label reading *Chief Inspector Barclay, do not read under any circumstances,* perhaps that will do the trick?'

After apologising, and getting a full report from her about the security guards he said,

'Well, that does put a different perspective on things.'

With a little trepidation he said,

'By the way, I am your senior officer, do you really think you should speak to me like that?'

There was a silence during which he could actually *hear* her raising her eyebrows imperiously. He thought better of the situation; there was no advantage to be pressed.

'Okie,' he said, 'how do you fancy popping down the yacht club for a couple of drinks? Perhaps I could have a word with the Events Organiser there, quite unofficially of course.'

'Oh...kay.' she said cautiously.

'Fine, You get on your glad rags, I'll collect you in a taxi in half an hour.'

When they walked into the yacht club, they were both a little surprised at how quiet it was. They expected it to be livelier. Barclay was wearing a suit and Okonedo was wearing a peacock blue t-shirt with a shiny look collarless scarlet leather bomber jacket with matching trousers. Okonedo looked about and thought smart casual had moved into scruffiness. They took a table out on the terrace.

'Have you been here before?' He asked.

'Not since the renovation. It's a bit too anally retentive for me. As you know athletics are really my thing. You can't argue with that, you're either the fastest or you're not. Also, you can't get messed about in individual sports by people with agendas. In yachting you have to rely on others. I prefer to trust in myself.'

'I always feel a bit odd about places like this. It's a sort of support centre for the over-privileged'

He was wondering how he was going to handle an encounter with the Events Organiser, the driven and self-important spokesperson of the well-heeled residents of Burridge, Julian St. Hubert. He was one of those people who worked on the basis if you did not agree with him on any subject it was a manifestation of a personality defect. If not, he might conclude that you were some sort of political extremist or credulous. St. Hubert had managed to persuade the council that his semi-licensed security firm was essential to the success of the Burridge Festival of the sea, and their role would be *complimentary* to the police, and there were no grounds for any concerns from the civil rights lobby. Everything had gone smoothly, at least in the beginning. They had been looking after the area immediately around the yacht club, giving directions and stern warnings to the easily intimidated about littering the beach.

Soon, they had begun moving down the seafront and turning their attention to people who didn't quite *fit in*, although some wondered whose value judgment was being applied to their conduct. Concern had been building for weeks over what sort of seafront they were going to be left with. The Burridge Yacht club probably didn't just want the drunks and the drug addicts removed. Once they had been moved on perhaps their attention would be turned to the gypsies, doing palm readings, selling lucky charms and providing fire eating displays and juggling to entertain the children. If they had their way it would probably end up with Punch and Judy shows. Barclay questioned if it fitted in with the investigation. He remembered the poster at John's house and whether there was more to his altercation with the security guard.

'That, I believe is Mary Wintour, *El Presidente*. Why I wonder, is she dressed as a pirate?'

Okonedo was being slightly tart, but the Club President was wearing a horizontal striped navy and white shirt with bagged trousers, sharply tapered at the calves with tan leather pumps, which though stylish, did look like fancy dress. As she noticed Barclay and Okonedo sitting at the table she strode over to them.

'What brings you here?'

'Largely a social visit. However, I would like to speak to Mr St. Hubert when he deigns to put in an appearance. Unofficially, of course.'

Mary Wintour raised her eyebrows until her eyes looked like saucers.

'About?'

Barclay smiled politely.

'I'm sure you can guess.'

'Do you mind if I join you?'

Barclay gestured with his hand towards an empty chair.

'I'm sure the security boys are doing a sterling job; I can't imagine it can be that much of a problem. What's the beef?'

'I think since the security issue on the seafront has been very much his baby, I'd better keep my counsel till I speak to him. I'm sure you understand.'

Mary Wintour bridled at not being informed of what was going on, and an additional irritant was his crispness of tone which she knew meant any further entreaty would be rebuffed.

'I'm sure if there are any problems they can be easily ironed out. It was very important for us to have this area of the seafront taken back by the law abiding citizens of Burridge and away from anti-social elements. An awful lot of financial resources have gone into this event, including considerable sums of public money. I think you are aware of how important this is for the town. It's not just the yacht club that is going to benefit. The whole thing is absolutely central to the hospitality and subsidiary industries. An awful lot of jobs for ordinary working people are on the line here. I'd be very careful about how you continue if I were you.'

Barclay smiled politely, he was aware of the implicit threat : *You are dealing with rich, powerful people, proceed with caution, or you could come a cropper*. She was warming to her theme. Her pronouncements had been made before, at sympathetic tables amongst bourgeois sections of the Burridge dinner party circuit. She was talking as if Barclay had to be made to understand. There was an undercurrent of pained irritation in her voice: *he just doesn't get it*.

'The problem with this town, to be blunt about it, is that the police were not responding to people's concerns. Something had to be done. It was really important for us to engage in self empowerment. For too long we've seen a slow decline, and somebody had to step up to the plate. We've taken back the seafront for the ordinary citizen, things have changed and I can assure you things are not going back to the old ways.' As she was speaking, she realised her tone had become hectoring.

'Anyway, I was under the impression the police were supportive of the private sector taking a more proactive role in our own security measures,' she said.

Barclay disliked words like *proactive* almost as much as he disliked vigilantism.

'Miss Wintour, the police have taken a position everyone should take an interest in protecting their own property and themselves, but wearing a uniform does not make you above the criminal law.

Everyone is subject to the full weight of the law. So long as they remain within the law, I think the official attitude of the police has not been one of support but of *tolerance*. I am certainly not one of those who is going to support the control of the seafront being arrogated by a galère of Hooray Henrys.'

She gave a pained smile and continued as if she were explaining something to a child.

'I think you're a bit out of the loop. It's not good enough to leave everything to the police, it's important to take control, to empower yourself.'

She sat back and took a swig of her Martini. She sensed this had not made any inroads with Barclay and the conversation wasn't helping her.

'So you're investigating that chap's death; he was some sort of druggie wasn't he?'

'He wasn't an addict. Miss Wintour, you shouldn't believe everything you read in *The Echo*.' Okonedo interjected.

Mary Wintour didn't like her; she regarded her community liaison group as the worst kind of *do-goodery*. What was needed, as far as she was concerned, was the harsh slap of authority. Barclay thought she was probably one of those people who after clearing away the coffee cups at a dinner party during which everyone had complained about the lawlessness of the lower orders probably offered all her guests a line of cocaine. Her attitude summed up a certain layer of thinking at the yacht club. An interloper, and it appeared, a *foreign* interloper, at that, had died at their party. They would have much preferred the body to have been removed by the council and a discreet veil drawn over the whole thing.

'Well,' she said, 'from what I gather he wasn't from Burridge. I hope the whole thing can be cleared up pretty promptly.'

Barclay was repelled by the dispassion he had seen from many people who perceived themselves as good, even virtuous. Thinking of the Sikorski parents display of grace, under so much pressure, he found that difficult to reconcile with the self-serving platitudes he was now being subjected to.

'I think it might help you to know something about him. His name was John Sikorski; he was born and educated in the country, seemed to do well at school, had some propensity for rowing and rugby and got a good degree in business studies. He had moved into the area recently, he leaves behind a grieving sister, two devastated parents and one self-loathing ex-lover as far as I am aware. He was going to take over a thriving family business and had dreams of a career or at least a hobby in music. He was an important human being to those he left behind, and they are finding it hard to comprehend the utter brutality of his murder. He mattered and he will be *missed*.'

Mary Wintour looked uncomfortable and replied,

'Look I'm not entirely sure why you're telling me all this.'

'You seemed to be confused in some of the things you were saying about his death. I was attempting to assist you. They say knowledge is power, I was hoping that if I gave you some information you might be, well,' he paused and smiled, '*empowered*.'

At this point, she decided it would be best to excuse herself. She extended the curtest of goodbyes before heading into the main bar.

'I think you're off her Christmas card list,' Okonedo opined.

'Probably so.'

'You enjoy upsetting people, don't you?'

'With some people, it's a sacred duty.'

'Do you reckon that Julian St. Hubert is coming tonight? By the way, is that his real name?'

'Yes, he'll be here at some point. Of course that's his real name. No one would have the nerve to make something like that up. Mary Wintour used to be OK you know, I reckon when this little clean up the seafront campaign unravels, which it's going to very shortly, she'll probably come back to her senses.'

'There were a lot of the great and the good backing it. Will they run to Mr St. Hubert's aid?'

Barclay's broad smile answered the question. Past experience had shown him when these things collapsed, the support so effusive when a project had wide public approval disappeared into the ether. If it did collapse, as Barclay hoped, Mr St. Hubert would find friends hard to find and his phone calls would remain unanswered. The security guards would soon be regarded as an unwanted excrescence upon the yacht club. Far from being regarded as supportive of public order, they would be perceived as inimical to it. The man was a politician after all, so Barclay imagined he was savvy enough to understand this. He had noticed over the years the rules which applied to high level politics applied to the less elevated politics of Burridge County Council. In his experience if it was local politics peoples conduct was not equally ruthless but more vicious.

'You know that line about their being nothing lovelier than the sight of the privileged class enjoying its privileges. Well there's nothing lovely about the level of self absorption on display here.'

Okonedo walked up to the bar, avoiding the withering gaze of Mary Wintour who was sitting nearby. As she turned round she was confronted by the attenuated figure of Timothy Johnson.

'Hello, I understand you're here to speak to Julian. Is it alright if I join you?' Okonedo nodded, and he proceeded to get himself large rum. After putting Barclay's ginger beer in front of him and taking a swig out of her tomato juice she relayed this information.

'My, we are popular today. I wonder if he's going to own up to the clock.'

Timothy walked over and slumped himself in the chair opposite them. He affected a look of arty scruffiness and was wearing navy blue chinos and a matching sweater with the collar of a Ben Sherman shirt peeping through the neck and had his hair deliberately tousled.

'I understand you're here to meet Julian. Do you have an appointment, and if so at what time?'

'No appointment,' Barclay said, 'this is a completely unofficial visit. We just popped here on the off chance to speak to him.'

'Right, because I'm here about a painting commission. He did ask me to come in here, and sorry,
I'm first in the taxi rank so I take precedence over you. I imagine you don't feel as socially uncomfortable here as I do.'

'Point taken. You have first dibs.'

'A painting commission,' Okonedo said 'I'm surprised they called you. I know you do those carvings for the tourists, but your paintings are a bit more serious than the stuff they have hanging here. No offence but don't you think a lot of the stuff in here is a bit naff?'

'A bit naff? Are you kidding? Most of the stuff here is into the stratospheric reaches of naffness. This is a colony of planet naff. No, if they want a painting it'll be strictly money upfront and no dictat as to what I do. I'll want complete artistic license to do as I please, if they don't choose to display it that's their problem. But if they want their money back, it ain't gonna happen.'

'When is this for?'

'Oh I imagine Christmastime.'

'On that subject, have either of you seen the Dunkirk picture?' Okonedo asked.

The two men shook their heads.

'Oh, you haven't lived.'

The three of them trooped into the Nelson function suite on the other side of the bar. It was host to an assortment of Russian sailors sitting talking amongst themselves. Along one wall was a sixty-foot long painting of the Dunkirk evacuation, and the mythological status it has within British culture; when many citizens took motorboats or anything seaworthy to get the stranded British troops from Dunkirk and back to Britain, as France fell to the Germans.

It was obvious the painter had used the emotional template of World War II movies like *Mrs Miniver*. It concentrated on a large number of women giving looks of virtuous forbearance as they steered their boats under a sky dark with Luftwaffe bombers.

'Well boys,' Okonedo said, 'what do you make of it?'

Barclay stood back and examined the painting with an impassive stare, asking:

'Do either of you know the artist responsible for this work?'

They shook their heads.

'It's unspeakably dreadful. Staggeringly bad,' Barclay said, 'I'm at a complete loss for words.'

'Well I'm not,' Timothy said. 'It's shite. In fact it's such a pile of crap it's almost worth nicking. There are some paintings that are not great art yet have some sort of emotional truth, this goes one better, it's neither. You know the old maxim about people having to suffer for their art? Well anyone who produces art like this deserves to suffer. If I had my way I'd hand them over to Torquemada. It's the kind of work you'd expect on a fucking jigsaw from the 1950s. As for those women in the headscarves, I'm not sure if women were allowed to take part, only in the movies I think; the expressions don't look so much pained as chronically constipated. They all look as if they need a dose of industrial strength laxatives. The whole thing is a pot of puke thrown in the face of the British public.'

'Don't hold back,' Okonedo said smiling, 'tell us what you really think.'

'Oh enough,' he said, shaking his head in mock despair.

'Let's get back to the terrace,' Barclay said, 'this is making me feel ill.'

When they resumed their seats, Julian St. Hubert arrived and with a look of triumph Timothy got to his feet. As artist and prospective sponsor walked across the main bar Barclay and Okonedo, and for that matter, the rest of the bar, heard Timothy demand,

'How much did you pay for that Dunkirk crap?'

Barclay took a good swig of his drink.

'The money is pouring in Okie, and these people have evidently more of it than sense.'

'Or taste.'

'What do you reckon of Timothy Johnson then, do you think he nicked the clock for the readies, you know, payback time?' he said.

'I can't really see it. At heart he's a bit of a hippy. He's never shown any bitterness towards her. His attitude has been more dismissive than anything else. You know sneering at her values. He has an on-off thing with that nutty Doris woman, who does the Tarot readings down the pier. No, stealing something from her would be distinctly unmellow. What about David, if you want it to be a relative?'

'No, his thing is prestige and status, not money, apart from that he could be doing a lot better out of his aunt financially if he was the grasping type. He doesn't seem to care too much. If people are going to behave like that; there's always some previous indicator.'

'Oh, before I forget, how did your visit to Intimate Distractions go?'

Barclay smiled as he recalled his brief sojourn at the porn shop. He was now able to look at it as a bizarre diversion.

'It went okay, didn't find anything out. However, Okie, I'm sure Nigel Daventree can assist you if you are ever interested in purchasing a post-modern non linear porn movie, or you want someone to explain the interesting anti-imperialist subtexts in *British Prison Anal Gangbang Part 3.* He's quite the believer you know. He's one of those people that if you had a go at him for his chosen profession, would end up making you feel mean and callous for being unkind to him. He has this little spiel about how it's all so liberating, especially for women. I know it's the only profession in which women routinely get paid more than men, but they're still being called sluts and bitches. Perhaps it's the embers of my Catholic upbringing rekindling. I don't think anybody's ever made a porn film where a woman can only achieve sexual gratification by being hit over the head with a shovel, but I fear it's only a matter of time.'

'I get the feeling this was a bit depressing for you.'

'Frankly, yes a little bit.'

'You were going to tell me about the Sikorskis.'

'Well, that was very interesting. The mother is utterly devastated as you would imagine. It's as if she's moving on casters. The father, well I'm not sure what he feels. I think he wanted us to know what people they are, and why they matter. They have their faith to sustain them, which can be enormously supportive in times like this. Leon, I think wanted to put a marker down, to say he has expectations of us. He is not allowed to mourn, well he's allowed to mourn, but not fall apart; as head of the family he has to keep everything together. Like the mother, he has his faith to sustain him that some sort of justice awaits the perpetrator, but I think the father is in need of more temporal assurances.'

'The daughter, I heard she's a bit strange. What's going on with her?'

'She's not strange, but she's incredibly focused. Nothing will crack her image of the family. I'm not sure whether she was lying to me, but I think she's very self-delusional. Her attitude towards her husband is unhealthy, very controlling. I don't think she understands being in control of a relationship is no route to happiness.'

'What do you think she might be hiding?'

'If I knew that, I'd be in a much stronger position. The problem you always get with these cases is people making their own decisions about what is germane to the case. Things are suppressed and sometimes they don't realise they could unwittingly be giving assistance to the murderer. I don't know whether that's the case with Cressida. You get a situation where people are wilfully concealing evidence, because they want to save people from more pain. Of, course there might be another reason; she's protecting someone closer to home, someone she loves, who she believes to have some responsibility. People often make bad choices when they are trying to do what they think is best but are under extreme emotional pressure. Who can say?'

'Do you think you're making progress?'

'Oh yes, I think the whole thing will come to a head soon. Will Ferguson will be back soon. I think he knows something. He's probably unaware of what's happened, I want to talk to him as soon as he hits town.'

Okonedo was about to pursue her enquiries further when the figure of Julian St. Hubert loomed over them.

'I believe you wanted to speak to me?'

The local counsellor and self appointed spokesman of all *right-thinking folk* had finally found time to talk to Barclay. He had a way of talking to people who he assumed were not his supporters, which gave the impression he was in deep pain but handling it with exemplary self discipline. He was a linen suited man in his mid-sixties, with a rather severe haircut, clipped speech and a ready smile which made him popular with well groomed ladies within *law and order* circles in Burridge.

'That's right; I just wanted to have a word about your security guards. It's unofficial at the moment, but there will be communication to you within official channels over the next couple of days. Perhaps you'd better get yourself a drink.'

'I don't know whether I should,' he said stiffly. Barclay smiled,

'Trust me, you'll need one.'

'Perhaps this would be better in the office, on our own'.

He said this in an attempt to exclude Okonedo from the proceedings. He pointedly had not looked at her as he spoke, and it was clear he held the same point of view towards her unit as Mary Wintour.

'No, it's rather important Sgt. Okonedo is here. She has something rather important to tell you.'

'Oh, very well. I'll get that drink.'

When he returned he sat down and put his mammoth gin and tonic in front of him.

'Well my dear,' he said smiling 'I'm all yours, what have you got to tell me? It's quite entrancing being at the mercy of an attractive young woman like you.'

It was clear to Okonedo this kind of oleaginous way of speaking was intended to be disarming. This approach was effective when courting the votes of the elderly matrons of Burridge, but as she gave him a blank look and endeavoured to conceal how repellent she found him, she wondered if this was a man who was ever off duty.

'Before Sgt. Okonedo informs you about the events of today, I think it would be helpful sir if you told us what the pecking order is with the security guards.'

'Well, there isn't really any particular hierarchy. I mean the chief steward is Gavin Lintern. He just organises the rotas.'

'So would you say he's in overall charge of things, I mean have you delegated responsibility to him?'

'Certainly not, I'm in charge of everything.'

'Well with respect sir, it's usual these days to let others take on the responsibility. You have other concerns don't you, what's the expression, avoiding micromanagement? I'm sure with your business interests and your leading role in The Burridge Festival of the Sea, people would feel it was understandable if you deferred responsibility and let others do the work in matters like your security guards.'

'I'm happy to be condemned as a micromanager. I believe in taking responsibility. My whole career has been based upon that. I know the do-gooders don't like the way they have cleared up the beach and had the effect of moving on the anti-social elements. However, when people look back, I'm sure they will be fulsome in giving credit for everything that has occurred to yours truly. I've never thought there was any virtue in false modesty.'

'False modesty sir,' said Okonedo, 'I'm sure no one would accuse you of that.'

He smiled and nodded, like all narcissists she had met he had no sense of his own absurdity.

'Thank you, sir. It was important for me that I have absolute clarity about the circumstances surrounding the security measures here. You have firmly established that any responsibility starts and ends with you.'

Barclay wanted to pin him down on the chain of command.

'Absolutely!'

'Sergeant. If you'd be so kind?'

'Earlier on today we were called to the area just adjacent to the pier. There had been a report that one of the beach dwellers had been assaulted. As you are probably aware there have been complaints before about heavy-handedness by members of your security group. This however is the first time there has been a formal complaint. There is now an arrest warrant issued for one Wayne Chambers, and we will almost certainly be prosecuting.'

'I am obviously very concerned about this and will cooperate with the police to the fullest extent. As you well know, there is always the problem of the individual bad apple in the barrel. You have even had similar problems like that in the police. We can hardly be held accountable for that.'

'I really don't think you understand the gravity of the situation,' Barclay continued. 'There have been grumblings of discontent for weeks; these have been relayed to you and as far as I am aware you've chosen to ignore them. Now somebody has been assaulted. There are some people I'm sure will say *well, he's only a drunken old tramp, who cares?* but I think most people will be a little disgusted at hearing of a man of sixty-eight, little able to defend himself, being beaten up by a much younger man. In situations like that people respond pretty intuitively, and most people will recoil in horror. It's my experience that others will come forward. The pool of potential complainants has been pretty unforthcoming, but pretty soon I imagine the trickle will turn to a flood. Then, of course, there is the *Burridge Echo* who will report it in their usual unrestrained style. Be prepared for some purple prose coming your way.'

'I can hardly be held responsible for the actions of one man now can I?'

'With respect I think that's effectively what you've spent the last ten minutes telling me. If you wish to take credit, you take responsibility, and that's what you just said. Declaring '*don't blame me I'm only the man in charge,'* just won't do, now will it?'

'I had no idea this was going on. I certainly cannot be held responsible for one loose cannon. I know you see this as some sort of private army but I've done the best I could under difficult circumstances.'

'I've never alleged it was some sort of private army. The term private army would imply they were under some sort of system of centralised control and concepts of leadership were being employed. Your one line of defence at the moment seems to be they're some kind of rabble. This is the problem with these sorts of organisations; you have power without accountability.'

It was pretty clear from the secretary's facial reaction he was floundering and was trying to find an appropriate line of defence.

He opted for attack.

'I realise you're in cahoots with those Trotskyites in the *Hands off the Seafront Campaign*. There is a badgering tone to your approach I find frankly offensive. Perhaps it would be better if I spoke to the Chief Constable tomorrow and see what he has to say about it?'

'I really don't think you've got any idea of what's going on here. Your pet project has just fallen apart. It is *over*. You have maintained you are in charge of it, and it is a reflection of your firm leadership. People have been beaten up by people in your employ. When Wayne Chambers is brought in there are other questions about him and other members of your praetorian guard we will require to be answered. They seem to be quick-tempered and to suffer from violent mood swings. This ring any bells? We will also be testing him for steroids. So we will possibly have a situation where your employees have been roughing people up whilst under the influence of drugs. I'm going to go out on a limb here. I don't think your call to the Chief Constable will even be put through, and frankly I don't much care.'

Mr St. Hubert went quiet. He was trying to locate an escape route, but try as he might he couldn't think which way to turn. Under normal circumstances when one of his pet projects fell apart he spluttered about treachery or betrayal and saw himself as a figure of high tragedy.

'I was forgetting you're a skilled detective,' he said quietly, 'all those pointed questions about who was in charge were just to trip me up and trap me. Are you happy now you've trapped me?'

'With respect sir, I think you're being slightly theatrical, if you have indeed been trapped, then you trapped yourself. This is off the record, and I am not in any position to repeat it. What I needed to know was what *you* thought of your role. I don't imagine what you said to me you haven't said to everyone else. I am not your Nemesis; you are more than capable of making your own enemies. There are others who will have reason to rip you to pieces.'

He nodded at Barclay saying,

'What is to be done then?'

'Firstly, all your security staff are to be recalled from the beach front, their duties should be solely around the immediate area of the Yacht club. Since there might be further complaints I don't want their presence around an area where there might be potential witnesses.'

Julian nodded gravely. He looked like a straggler from a defeated army.

'I've been a bit stupid, haven't I? I shouldn't have let it come to this.'

In Barclay's eyes, he had moved from being a pantomime villain to being faintly ridiculous to now being pitiable. He saw how his spirits had quailed under his criticisms.

'Look there might be some way out of this. Before this comes to a head why don't you recall the security men, announce their job will be specifically around the yacht club during the Festival of the Sea and as soon as it is over, due to problems that have recently come to light, they will be disbanded. If you're worried about certain parties preparing to shoot you to ribbons, this will possibly spike their guns, if you'll forgive the clumsy metaphor. But there can be no more of this. This is an end to this particular experiment.'

A look of relief rippled across Julian's face as he began to digest Barclay's proposal.

'Yes, I'll work out a press release,' he got to his feet a little shambolically, 'thank you, Chief Inspector,' he nodded politely at Okonedo, 'Sergeant.'

He smiled weakly and wandered off.

'It's always the same with these characters; they start out as Captain Mainwaring and end up as Captain Queeg. Happy Sergeant?'

'Oh, yes. I bet this will become a personal triumph for him. I don't know how, but the bastard will manage it somehow.'

*

Holed up in the Castle on the Cliff, Róisín was grilled by Dirk about her statement to the police.

'What you said to the police wasn't exactly a lie, was it but it was hardly the truth. Once you decide to speak to the police you can't pick and choose which parts of the truth to tell.'

'Look once Will comes back I think everything will get sorted out. In the meantime, I don't want to get him arrested. He may be a wanker but I'm still not going to dump him in it.'

'Róisín, this is lies by omission. It's what do they call it, *withholding information*? You could get done, you do realise that, end up with a criminal conviction.'

'Not if you shut your yap trap I won't. Anyway I can't really see any relevance to what's happened.'

'How the hell would you know if it's relevant or not. Róisín, think about this. The guy got his brains beaten in. If you go to the police under your own steam there probably won't be any fallout.'

'I'll think about it. No promises. Look we'll meet up tomorrow.'

She got up and put her jacket on. Róisín was tired with Dirk's sermonising. She walked home wondering if she had done the right thing. Her concerns about what she had seen were now beginning to nag her. Perhaps she shouldn't have discussed it with Dirk. He was hysterical about the whole thing. It was not their problem. As she hurried along the promenade to get home, she became certain she was right. Arguments that hadn't surfaced in her mind in the pub, were now crowding in. Within minutes she felt thoroughly vindicated she had been correct. Looking over the road she saw a familiar figure walking in her direction; feeling a little threatened she stopped for a moment, and turned up her collar. It was all right, she hadn't been seen she told herself, and continued walking.

*

When Barclay got home he reflected the short altercation with Julian St. Hubert had gone better than he had anticipated. It had achieved the desired result, the seafront would return to the ownership of those who actually used it, rather than one sectional group.

The next day he and Penrose would be travelling to interview the couple in London. What relationship they had with the victim, the sketchy report had made unclear. He speculated if they would have anything to tell them about John Sikorski, or whether there would be another genteel wall of obfuscation. He turned in early and for the first time in days had a good sleep.

Chapter Eleven.

Barclay awoke and checked his messages. He staggered into the shower. After he ate some porridge and devoured a full English breakfast he considered what potential the day held. Gulping Italian coffee he peered cautiously through the window at the colourless sky. The report he received told him little about the couple but it appeared the victim had used their flat the previous weekend. They spoke to the police, but had been tight lipped about him. He had been told they were from a theatrical background and there behaviour went from being a bit eccentric to way over the top; he was also told they would be offered excellent refreshments, but to be wary of them. Perhaps he could get something out of them, in any case it would be good to get out of Burridge for the day. It might help him think clearly. Penrose would be driving, so it shouldn't be too stressful.

At eight-thirty the phone rang and he was informed Will Ferguson had surfaced. Evidently the previous night he had returned, got roaring drunk, and made a scene in the Castle on the Cliff and not returned home. The police had been called by David Johnson, but he had disappeared. Officers had gone to his flat but received short shrift from his girlfriend; it was clear getting drunk and staying out all night was not unprecedented. This was a minor irritation for Barclay. He knew he would turn up but wanted to interview him. He was certain he knew something and wondered if he and the victim had shared some confidence.

As Barclay and Penrose drove out of Burridge, he started talking about the previous night's encounter with Julian St. Hubert. After fiddling with Penrose's car radio he managed to get the local radio station without it being obscured by crackle.

The first item on Radio Burridge was the announcement the promenades security stewards had been given their marching orders. Julian St. Hubert's richly syllabled voice rang out of the speakers.

'Well, the reality is the whole thing has really been a victim of its own success. It was a remarkable example of how a public-private partnership between the Council and local businesses can bring real dividends. Of course, there have been problems with a certain level of overzealousness amongst a minority of our staff and we have had to confront this issue. As soon as the police made us aware I stepped in and took immediate action. I felt under the circumstances it was appropriate to have the whole thing wound up. I know there are some who think I might have acted precipitously, but I think these situations demand resolute and decisive action. There are circumstances when the mantle of leadership must be grasped, even if it might be unpopular in the short term. I think my record speaks for itself-'

Barclay switched off the radio, exclaiming:

'That man can always speak for himself. My God, on the radio you can actually *hear* that self-satisfied grin,'

'Nobody will buy any of that surely. I'm fairly new to Burridge politics. Surely he must be
finished?'

'The man is a shifty, self-serving, self-obsessed crook. A nasty little Bigot. So he's either going to end up in jail or as Prime

Minister.'

'At least his Hitler Youth has been wound up.'

'They're all too long in the tooth for that particular soubriquet.'

Barclay tuned the radio onto Classic FM.

'That's better, that will help us to think.'

He winced at his comment, and judged himself, it would provide music that would at least let them think about something else. Once they had escaped from the traffic crawling out of Burridge and were on the motorway Barclay knew it would be easier to talk.

'So what did you make of Grant Maunders and his girlfriend?'

'He seems a very damaged person. He's more hurting than anything. He'd clearly be much better off without her. I can't see him killing anyone. She's a very different matter.'

'Do you think she could have done it?'

'She's quite capable of killing, in her imagination anyway. It seems pretty unlikely though. I would be on my guard if she was around. Whoever killed John Sikorski must have been somebody who he felt safe with. There were no defensive wounds on the arms, so presumably, it was someone he trusted. If that woman came to my door at night, I'd call the police, or possibly Van Helsing, she is one seriously scary woman. I certainly wouldn't let her in.'

'There seems to be a woman involved at some level. I'm wondering if there was more than one person involved. The fact his current girlfriend hasn't come forward is indicative, but I'm not sure if it means she's involved or possibly married or in a relationship. Anyway, I think you're right. I can't really see it being those two. On another tack, I'm not very pleased with Will Ferguson slipping through our fingers. I'm sure he knows something.'

Barclay lay back in his seat and proceeded to drift off to sleep until they reached Wembley.

'I think we're nearly there sir.'

Barclay sat up; they were now travelling through what estate agents call a leafy suburb. When they traversed round a large public park, a well-kept block of 1920s apartments rose independently above a more modern conurbation.

'Now I wonder if we'll get anything out of these two. I always feel people are so defensive whenever we ask anything.'

'Do you want to do all the talking?' Penrose enquired innocently.

'Sorry, I tend to hog the conversation in these circumstances. I'm sorry if I haven't given you much leeway. I'm afraid you're going to have to be more assertive. I can be a bit insensitive when I have the bit between the teeth; it's a personal failing of mine.'

Penrose smiled. This was his way of putting a marker down, a fact Barclay was aware of. They approached the building and climbed the semi-circular stone steps to the front entrance. After ringing the bell there was a long pause followed by a crackle. A warm-vowelled Home Counties voice enunciated.

'Yes, can I help you?'

'Chief Inspector Barclay and Sgt. Penrose.'

There was a hum followed by a discreet click as the front door was unlocked. The foyer at the front of the apartments was spacious and gave a feel of muted opulence. It was obvious in its heyday it would have had a suitably magisterial concierge sitting behind the front desk.

'This place must have really been something once,' remarked

Penrose.

Disembarking from the lift on the third floor they were aware of Vivien Deauville standing outside her door.

'You must be the celebrated Chief Inspector Barclay and this I presume is your *divine* assistant, Sgt. Penrose.'

The announcement was made as if they were celebrated performers from the world of show business. She was an excessively theatrical woman wearing a long Chinese print dress with a heavily powdered face, scarlet lipstick and rather violent looking aquamarine eye makeup. She finished the whole look off with a bright red mop of hair which was of such a radiant hue it couldn't even pretend to be natural. Barclay nodded and gave a sideways look to Penrose.

Normally that level of theatricality was reserved for Amateur Dramatic Society divas but that was clearly not the case here. As they were escorted through the flat or what she preferred to call *my humble abode,* along the walls was a plethora of theatrical posters pertaining to her career as a musical comedy star, in everything from light operetta to provincial productions of the works of Jerry Herman and Stephen Sondheim. She was of an indeterminate age, Barclay thought she might be anywhere between mid-sixties to mid-eighties. She was doused in expensive perfume and smelt gorgeous. She kept up a constant patter of nonsense as she gave the pair of them a guided tour through her flat whilst pointing to evidence upon the walls of her theatrical triumphs.

The flat had the benefit of not just large rooms but high ceilings and a proper balcony. The lounge was sufficiently large to accommodate a Bechstein Grand Piano without it dominating the entire room. In the centre of the living room was an enormous cut glass chandelier, and as Penrose looked at it with a sense of awe she exclaimed,

'Oh it's amazing, isn't it? We got that in Rome didn't we Johnny?'

They had been completely unaware of Johnny. He was sitting on the edge of the sofa, and with Vivien holding forth he had been effectively obliterated from view. Where she was light he was shade. He looked a little dark and indistinct in comparison. He was slim and grey and she was full-figured and red-haired. If he hadn't been grey he would have *seemed* grey. There was only room for one star in that marriage, and sensibly he had no desire to compete with the force of nature Vivien was. He had wisely concluded his best way of surviving was by being a completely invaluable supporting player. She cupped his face in her hands and gave him an extravagant kiss, exclaiming,

'You gorgeous man!'

She held him in an impassioned embrace as if she had just had her husband returned to her, after him having spent several years as a hostage of Hezbollah.

She extended her hands towards the dining table in the corner.

'Everybody sit, you must be desperate for refreshments, travelling all the way up from Burridge. I once appeared in *Salad Days* in rep. there.'

The table in the corner was immaculately laid. Barclay began to warm towards her, she was clearly one of those people who tried to make every aspect of her life as aesthetically pleasing as possible. The table had all her best china impeccably positioned, and all the cutlery was the best quality Georgian silver.

'Right Chief Inspector, sit yourself down, now you seem like a gentleman so Darjeeling should be the brew for you, and you young man, would the same be good for you?'

They both acquiesced. As she poured the tea and everyone was now seated it felt more relaxed. She served generous portions of coronation chicken onto everyone's plate, and the four of them proceeded to tuck in.

'Now how can I help you?'

'Well, what we really wanted to know was what you could tell us about John Sykes, sometimes known as John Sikorski?' Penrose said.

'He was an absolute *sweetie*. We were both enormously fond of him, a bit of a little boy lost. We took him under our wing for a while. He was being bullied about going into the family business but was going to strike out on his own. I don't think he ever really resolved it, you know.'

'When was the last time you saw him?' Penrose said.

'Well darling, that would have been about a month ago. He stayed here occasionally, in the spare room. If we weren't going to be here we would leave the keys with the Allington's on the ground floor and he would collect them from them and return them when he left.'

'And that's what happened last weekend?'

'Well yes. We were off at a tribute weekend. There was a thing on in Southampton. *A salute to the great American musical.* They can get a bit mawkish sometimes. I performed two numbers. It's really wonderful to be remembered. A couple of people came up to me afterwards; they'd seen me in *Gypsy* and remembered me from it. It must have been *aeons* ago. My Mama Rose would have knocked your socks off, I can tell you. Anyway, I digress. When we got back the Allington's returned the keys and that was that.'

This much Barclay and Penrose already knew. The Allingtons would be back from visiting the Lake District the following day but it was unlikely they would have anything to add. However, there was a florid vagueness to Vivien's comments and Johnnie was observing a studied silence.

'So how did you meet him?' Barclay asked.

'Oh, I can't really remember. I sometimes go to these musical revivals up and down the country, people like to share memories. I presume it was one of those musical evenings.'

'And I presume not. I think your relationship was more like *Mame*. You know, someone who was supposed to be a responsible figure, but instead was introducing the young man to a dissolute and hedonistic lifestyle? I think that's far more your role in John's life. I think you have an unquenchable love of life and I think you might have been an influence on him in that regard.'

She paused for a moment and collapsed in paroxysms of laughter. After gaining some composure she turned to Barclay.

'I am undone. I throw myself on your mercy!' she exclaimed coquettishly.

'*The Comfort of Strangers*, we need to know your involvement and his. What do you have to tell us?'

'Chief Inspector, you're a good detective I'm sure, but you're not quite as clever as you think you are. We might be in show business but we are not quite as immoral as you may like to think.'

'Come on, then please tell us.'

'Our involvement is strictly in terms of almond slices, Eton mess and sherry trifles.' she said with grande hauteur.

Penrose looked desperately unhappy. He was thinking of the wonderful teas he had with his Aunt Bessie in Penzance. He feared the culinary treats she so lovingly prepared were going to take on an unwholesome connotation after being sexualised by this woman. Vivien sensed what he was thinking and put a hand to her mouth and bellowed with laughter.

'No, it's not what you're thinking. I think you have the image of me writhing around in this food like the scene with Ann-Margret covered in beans in *Ken Russell's Tommy*. It's not like that at all.'

'Please illuminate us.' Barclay said.

'Catering.'

Barclay looked confused.

'Insufficient data. Cannot compute.'

'Well you can imagine with the sort of things that go on at these functions, people get jolly hungry. Ravenous in fact. Well, I have the catering contract.'

'You had the catering contract?'

'Absolutely sweetie. Look, my stage career has been in the dumper for some time. I couldn't even get *arrested*. I run a small catering business to keep body and soul together, and I'm bloody good at it. These are professionally run parties and I do the food, as far as I'm concerned it's just another gig, darling. We don't see anything. This is *Britain*, there's no need to be *obvious*. People turn up, we do the food, and then we leave. What goes on afterwards is *none* of our business. People don't want old bags like me. They just want ugliness. I still have the occasional concert for those who want a bit of glamour and escapism. It'll all come back when they get sick of torture and people being perfectly *beastly* to each other. We'll bang on regardless. All those old musicals, they still stand up.'

The whole situation was sufficiently bizarre to have the ring of truth about it.

'Where did John fit into all this?'

'Well he was at one of these things and he looked so lost, and well I ended up taking him under my wing, he came along to one of my sing-alongs, just for a laugh, wasn't much use, voice like a screech owl, but everybody loved him. I could tell he wasn't really keen on musical theatre. My relationship with him was more of being a courtesy aunt if you know what I mean. I had to keep on telling him life is not a rehearsal! He had business skills and helped me streamline my catering business, he was an absolute Godsend. I mean I hasten to add we serve food at these things and look the other way. He stopped going to those parties, well they weren't really his thing. I think he was getting a bit more focused. The other policemen who came said he was going into the family business. I know he could never have been an entertainer, but possibly a writer or a painter.'

'Did you know any of his girlfriends?'

'I saw a picture of one pretty blonde girl. But no, perhaps he was a bit embarrassed of them. Never saw one of them. Although of course, he talked about them endlessly. I think he may have been getting tired of them.'

Penrose thought it more likely he might be embarrassed by Vivien, most women he knew would have found her a bit of a monster.

'So do you know what he was doing with his life, where he was going?'

'I should hope not! I can't remember who said it, but someone once said: *a life that is planned cannot be lived it can only be endured.* He was young, he had his whole life ahead of him. He was embarking on life's great adventure, discovering himself. He was beginning to discover the mystery of who he was. The poor thing to be struck down like that, Byron said, *Heaven gives its favourites early death*, it was certainly true with him,' she said dabbing the corners of her eyes.

Once the two officers sensed the conversation was veering into total incoherence they felt it wise to say their thank-yous and leave. After hugging them as they left, she gave them tearful exhortations of luck. As they walked towards the lift they heard Johnny hammering the piano keys and Vivien raucously belting out a medley of songs from *Oliver!*

Barclay turned to Penrose, as they both raised their eyebrows in chorus.

'Well, what did you make of that?' Barclay said.

'It was a sort of duet for one, sung in the key of weird.'

'The whole thing was careering towards unacceptable levels of camp. She was like Norma Desmond on mescaline. The problem with this case is my level of understanding is inversely proportional to my increased knowledge. The more I'm told, the less I understand. I think we had better get back to Burridge. It may be macabre but in a much more wholesome way. On many levels that was enormously refreshing but I'm not sure it was particularly illuminating. I wonder what he really made of her. Did he find her entrancing or terrifying?'

Barclay was charmed by Vivien Deauville. He knew there were some people who would regard her as a joke. She was someone who was happy in her own little bubble, a world of hope, colour, love and laughter. If it was a dream it was a good hearted one. She was an unregenerate optimist living in a world of illusions, and he could see how infectious that might be and understand how John would have been fascinated by her. The club she attended to do the catering now came across as almost endearing. In other countries such activities might even be regarded as dark and sinister. In Britain even sex parties were now suitably gentrified with theatrical old ladies securing catering contracts, it was like Arthur Schnitzler's *Dream Story* adapted by Mary Berry. It also seemed Vivien's good-natured heart had robbed these events of their essential carnality. He wondered if at the end of a particularly vigorous night she led them in a rousing medley from Noël Coward's *Cavalcade.*

Perhaps he should introduce her to Nigel Daventree, they'd probably get on famously. As the car crept its way out of London he drifted off into a half sleep. He had a short dream which involved a scene from one of those Cecil B De Mille 1950s biblical epics. Those movies always included an orgy scene which consisted of men and women dancing frenetically but fully clothed. In the corner was Vivien Deauville with a tea tent. She was there with a stall, and upon a large highly embroidered damask tablecloth she was serving out slices of seed cake with a large silver slice. The whole thing had been transformed by her presence from an orgy into a theatrical representation of a Buckingham Palace Garden Party. As the car hit the motorway Barclay stirred from his slumbers.

'Sir, will we have to write all this up in the report, I mean about her involvement with that club?'

Barclay immediately got the point. Burridge constabulary was a gossipy place. He could imagine it finding its way into the papers, *Grande Dame's secret sex shame,* or possibly something far worse. The press weren't interested in her current career, as she said; she couldn't get arrested. *This* they would give her publicity for. It occurred to him she never asked for any discretion on this matter, perhaps she thought it inappropriate to think of her own potential blushes when a case of murder was at hand. That wasn't it, he thought. Vivien had assumed since they were gentlemen the whole thing would be handled with appropriate discretion. Barclay thought they could hold off from writing anything pertaining to her recent business activities until the case was nearing resolution. Even then it could presumably be omitted.

'Tell me, Penrose do you hold to the maxim *a gentleman does not let a lady down*?'

'I think so, under most circumstances. I mean I don't think all that stuff is important, do you?'

'No, probably not. I tell you what, I've got an idea. You're quite keen on protecting *The Madwoman of Chaillot*, aren't you? Okonedo has been telling me, that possibly I haven't been sharing sufficient duties with you and giving you due recognition. Well, I'm going to rectify that, to demonstrate the level of trust I have in your abilities, I'm going to let you do all the paperwork. In fact, I have such total faith in your judgment I'm not even going to check it. I trust you realise what a selfless act this is?'

Penrose had been warned Barclay would try and unload desk work onto him given the opportunity, and was pondering a reply.

'You haven't said anything Penrose you're obviously speechless with gratitude.'

'Yes, I can barely find the appropriate words of thanks; you'd better give me a bit of time.'

'You know Penrose, if I didn't know better, I'd think you weren't besotted with the idea.'

When they finally got out of London Barclay was less tense and wondered if they'd get back before the weather broke. A congregation of pitch-black clouds was moving southwards with persistency.

'Hope we get back before that breaks.'

'Before we do I've got to pick up some flowers. I think it'd be a good idea if we stopped at a petrol station.'

'Who are the flowers for?'

'I'm meeting up with Stevie Norton from the Hotel this evening. Some of us do have personal lives you know?'

Barclay thought the comment a trifle brusque, but then reflected he was probably putting more markers down, telling Barclay there were clear demarcation lines and there was more to his life than Burridge Constabulary, thank you.

'Well a word to the wise, there is nothing more likely to put the mockers on your personal life than getting garage flowers, she'll think you're cheap. We'll go to a proper florist and you can get something decent.'

He remembered during his childhood returning from school after a teacher had chastised him with words he could not understand.

'Mummy, Mr Chatsworth says I'm solipsistic, what does that mean?'

Without looking up from her Rumer Godden Novel she said,

'He's saying you're a self-centred little shit, and you are.'

He had come to terms with the fact he could not just be self-contained but also self-absorbed, and he found it an enormous relief if people were assertive towards him rather than complain about his conduct. Barclay had volunteered to get the flowers for Penrose whilst he waited in the car. As he ran back from the florist to the waiting car, a sombre looking Penrose was taking a call on his mobile.

'Sir, they've found Willie Ferguson.'

'He's dead isn't he?'

'Yes sir, I'm afraid he is.'

Chapter Twelve.

The journey back was conducted in a sullen silence. As the car entered the main sea road into Burridge the rain which had been pebble dashing the windscreen descended in torrents, and the wind buffeted the coast along the beach. After parking the car they trod in a leaden manner towards the crime scene. The van was parked a few feet from a memorial bench. The bench had been placed with support by public subscription. A man in a small schooner had gone out with his two sons in 1952, and he had lost his fear of the sea with fatal consequences. The local community had erected a wrought iron bench to ensure they would be remembered. Walking towards the flapping yellow and black canvas they saw the familiar figure of Sgt. Dalton standing by the road. The awning that had been erected over and around Will Ferguson's van was billowing as the strong sea wind blew in from behind.

'When was it found?' Barclay asked him.

'About an hour ago, by somebody out walking their dog.'

'Tell me it wasn't Mrs Lennox.'

Dalton smiled and shook his head.

'No, young bloke, he's over there, Mr Raymond.'

He pointed to a young man in a green canvas overcoat and jeans with his hair cut into a French crop. He had a small Jack Russell on a lead and was standing twenty feet away and was now wet from the rain. He was smiling more broadly than was appropriate.

'Has he given a statement?'

'Oh, Yes. The dog sniffed around the van, Mr Raymond noticed it was unlocked and opened it up, saw Mr Ferguson. Then he rang us on his mobile. That's it. Body found 11.45 A.M.'

'Then why pray, is he standing around grinning.'

'One difference,' he said smiling, 'between him and the Lennox woman is he is quite obviously not as traumatised as she was. He wants to talk to somebody in charge.'

Barclay exhaled and went over to him.

'Can I help you?'

'I found the body.' he said smiling.

'So I've been told.'

'There was a lot of money there. Will there be a reward?'

'Well thank you for your public-spiritedness. It has been said sir, that virtue is its own reward.'

'Don't take the piss. Will there be a financial reward?'

The man wasn't smiling anymore.

'No sir, I would suggest you leave now. This is a murder scene.'

Mr Raymond stormed off down the seafront, mouthing profanities at the ingratitude of the police.

Barclay turned to Dalton.

'What a little darling. People like that really make the job worthwhile. What have we got from Dr Reid?'

'She's in there, ask her.'

'What frame of mind is she in?'

Dalton grinned,

'She was out on the razz last night so she's like a pit bull with PMT, I'd tread carefully if I were you.'

Barclay ambled up to Penrose.

'She's got a monster hangover, so any danger you face from her today will be physical, not moral. Come on.'

They pulled back the covering and proceeded to awkwardly stand half out, and half in. They were standing only a few feet away from the van, but it was impossible to be unaware of being in the presence of horrific violence. Sometimes at murder scenes Barclay was aware the amount of blood present could be disproportionate to the nature of the assault. This was not the case here. The ferocity of the attack was quite evident. Penrose, far less experienced in these matters decided this would be a good time to play the loyal yet silent lieutenant. It was one of those situations where the usual defence mechanism of gallows humour was inappropriate. It was a shaming, humbling place. The wind outside was so strong it easily penetrated the awning, so it rippled in a rhythmical manner and the van swayed from side to side. There was a bitter wind that came from somewhere deep across the sea that scalded their necks and reinforced their sense of failure.

'Dr Reid,' Barclay said in his softest voice, 'what can you tell us?'

Dr Reid was pale and drawn and had not bothered to put on any makeup and was looking distinctly ropey. She wore tinted glasses, which were not helping, and her speaking voice normally so clear and ringing was croaky and breathy.

'Not a lot. The question I presume is could the assailant be the same person? The answer is possibly. Mr Ferguson had a visit from our old friend, blunt force trauma. He was smashed in the back of the head, repeatedly, while standing at the back of the van facing the open doors. The money was on the floor of the van in front of him. Most of it's soaked in blood, there's a good five hundred pounds at least. All the blood splatter confirms this, so it's a similar M.O. to the other one. After he was dead the blood was still pouring from his head and there's a lot of smearing on the floor as the body was pushed inside the van. The doors presumably were then closed behind him.'

'Thank you. The obvious question, time of death?'

'I would approximate,' she looked into the middle distance chewing her pen, 'sometime between 10 PM and 1 AM. I will have to do a tox screen, but I'd say that boy was having far too much fun last night.'

She was looking tired and Barclay was anxious to get away. The crime scene officers had taken their photos and were crawling around the back of the van. Barclay knew no matter how thorough they were it was unlikely anything helpful would be uncovered.

'Well, he's been bagged and tagged. I'm going to escort Mr Ferguson back to the path lab and then I'm going to have a spot of late breakfast. Good day and good luck.'

As the two men trudged towards the car they decided they would have to discuss these matters when they sat down and had coffee back at the hotel. They kept their own counsel and maintained a studied silence all the way to the incident room at the Alhambra.

Okonedo saw how doleful they were but thought the news she had might lift them.

'Róisín is here, she has some further information as regards the night in the pub. How are you feeling sir?'

'Not so good. I'm just feeling a bit helpless. I'm wondering about the money, and what it means. It could be a pay off he was making or it could be him being paid. If as we were thinking he might have known something about the circumstances of John Sikorski's death then obviously we might be looking at blackmail. Anyway, let's see what young Róisín has to say.'

Róisín came in wearing a voluminous trench coat; the treachery of the British weather had forced everybody to get their winter raingear out of the back of their wardrobes.

'Afternoon Chief Inspector, is it true?' She said as she slumped into a chair.

'Will Ferguson has been murdered, yes, that's true.'

'Head smashed in, like before?'

'Correct.'

He smiled expectantly.

'Right. When we spoke the other day there was stuff I didn't mention,' she grimaced.

'Please continue.'

'John was sitting at the table and started to walk to the toilet, when he turned round and came back and went through his pockets. He was sorting through his money. He then went back to the toilet and when he came back he was with Will. I think the two of them were sorting out a bit of puff or something. Will used to do quite a bit of dealing, just small stuff, I reckon. Normally it's conducted in corners but Gary's been getting quite heavy with people about dealing on the premises. All the staff are keeping an eagle eye on anything suspicious going on in the corners. He's terrified of losing his licence. Those shits up at the yacht club have been trying to get the license pulled for years. I heard about your little spat with that asshole Julian whatsisname, so you know they want to turn the seafront into something out of *Downton Abbey*.

The upshot is, if you want to sort out any gear you do it in the loo. I didn't like that Will guy very much but I didn't want to get him busted: now of course, things are different.'

'Is there anything else?'

'No, except I saw him last night, walking towards the direction of the Met, at about ten. I avoided him, he looked as if he was completely off his face.'

'Drunk or on drugs?'

'I don't know which but he was totally trollied.'

'There's definitely nothing else?'

'No, I know I should have said something earlier. I'm sorry. Am I in a lot of trouble?'

'No, but you know you should have told us earlier, but thanks for coming to us now.'

He turned to Penrose, who was leaning forward, an admonishment teetering on his lips and shook his head.

After she had left the incident room they had coffee.

'I'm sorry, I didn't see any point in getting rancid with her. At least she came forward and did the right thing *eventually*. I think she did it for well-intentioned reasons, after all, she had nothing to gain from it. There are others, who haven't been straight with us for less healthy reasons.'

Okonedo walked over with a note.

'One development that might be useful. They've gone through Ferguson's pockets and found a note, which reads 'Memorial Bench 11.30.'It's written on the back of one of those waxy flyers you get down the Castle.'

'Prints?'

She gave a sad shake of the head.

'Sorry, it's that glossy type of paper that doesn't take prints well. The lab girls and boys are giving it their best shot but I don't hold out much hope.'

'It's something anyway. This tells us he had a prearranged meeting there, and we can assume the person he had the meeting with was the same person who ventilated his head. We're going to have to ascertain whether that was his handwriting or not. On which subject, who told his girlfriend?'

'Lindsey went down and told her, probably not the best of choices.'

'Why's that?'

'When we were looking for him before, she went round to his flat and she took the piss out of her paintings. Apparently, when she was told of his death she didn't react very much which could mean she was in shock or-'

'Didn't give a rat's arse. Well, we're going to have to pay her a visit, aren't we? If he was involved in theft and blackmail or possibly extortion along with petty drug dealing it's beyond credence she didn't know or wasn't involved. What do we know of his movements yesterday?'

'He got off the ferry from France at Portsmouth about 4.00 P.M. That means he hit Burridge about 5.00 or 5.30. From what we gather he parked round the back of the Alhambra like he usually did. He was seen at one of the seafood bars along by the pier stuffing himself. Then we don't really know where he went until he made a bit of a scene in the Castle at about 9.45. There was even a message on my voicemail about it. The word on the street is he spent most of the evening getting stinko in a variety of places. I imagine more information will come to light over the coming hours. That's it I'm afraid.'

'Who was in the Castle who spoke to him?'

'Gary was there obviously, David along with Jennie from the Ham, Timothy and bonkers Doris and some new bloke, Giorgio from the ice cream parlour. Oh, and George from Miss Johnsons place.'

'So what happened, why did they call you?'

'Well apparently David was upset as to how he was behaving so he told Giorgio to phone Police liaison, but he got his wires crossed and phoned me. I'd gone off duty. They don't go through the central switchboard so it just went into the mail, when nobody showed up David phoned through to the main switchboard but it was too late by then.'

'What was Ferguson saying anyway?'

'From what I can gather, he was being a bit aggressive towards Timothy. Now apparently David is annoyed because he felt since the police were looking for him, we should have apprehended him, and he was annoyed about Giorgio mucking up the call. It's just one of those things.'

'Right, I'll visit Betty Melton, and you Penrose, have a word with Timothy Johnson. Sergeant, you can have a word with Doris down the pier. I'm sure with her gifts of clairvoyance she'll have a presentiment you're coming and will have a nice cuppa ready. I want to find out what happened last night. Call Dalton in, he can keep a lid on things here. Phone the station and get them to fax through a copy of the note. Now, before that, I'm really quite hungry, anyone for a spot of lunch? I don't see any virtue in us starving ourselves.'

*

When Barclay arrived at the studio to talk to Betty Melton he felt better. Having polished off a large seafood linguine followed by a Tiramisu with mascarpone he was suitably refreshed and the demoralisation he felt earlier was now diminished. Miss Melton he was unsure of. There was a blankness to her reactions and he was confused as to how to interpret them.

She was standing in the middle of the living room and had moved a canvas so he could sit down. She gave a small smile as she sensed what he was thinking.

'If you think I'm being a little cold over the death of my boyfriend, I'm sorry. I have too many immediate money worries to fall apart. His death means I have to worry about rent, bills and financial survival. I'm not rich enough to start sobbing, I don't have the space in my list of problems to engage in middle class hysterics.'

Clearly she was trying to be clever, but Barclay detected beneath the artifice there was a truth to her financial worries.

'I'm sorry; can you think of anybody who might have some motive to do Will harm?'

'Not really, he was just a modern bohemian, an ageing hipster. A bit of music promoting, selling and buying the odd bit of stuff in Europe. A lot of ducking and diving. He skirted on the edges of criminality but he was no villain.'

'There was a clock that recently went missing from Miss Johnson's do you know anything about that?'

'No, but I do know what being an accessory is.'

'We aren't really concerned with that, but somebody out there has killed twice. Please don't be defensive. We want to find who did this. There is the possibility he might have been involved in blackmail. Think carefully, I don't think you were involved but perhaps he confided some small detail, it could be crucial.'

She gave a joyless smile as she collected her thoughts.

'There was something left on my voicemail the day he went over to France. I can't really remember too well. He had heard something. He said it in a gossipy way as if it was a confidence shared, you know, that might be useful one day.'

Her eyes thinned as she twisted her hands, she looked anxious as what she was unravelling became clearer.

'He said, something like, *this could be a nice little earner.* I took it to mean a good piece of inside knowledge you know, like a good tip. It never occurred to me it could be grounds for blackmail or something that could get the stupid idiot killed.'

For the first time she had a look of genuine distress.

'I'm sorry Miss Melton, was there anything else?'

'No,' she said, 'nothing I'm afraid.'

'One final thing, but could you confirm is this Wills handwriting?'

He showed her the facsimile of the note. She stared at it distractedly.

'Miss Melton?'

'Oh yes, yes. That's right.'

She gave a weak smile and looked away.

*

Okonedo looked up from her desk in the incident room. Dalton told her Barry and June were due in to see her. She wasn't in the mood for being tolerant to them if they were in one of their embittered moods. They had that cold eyed hatred of humanity you only see in members of suicide cults or those who have worked in the low end of retail for more than six months.

Okonedo poured out some coffees.

'Send them in,' she said.

'We need to talk to you.'

Barry and June sat down, and she was doing all the talking.

'We think we might have seen that Will bloke talking to the other bloke, the one who got murdered, in the street.'

'When was this?'

'Monday afternoon about 4.00 in the afternoon. I saw two people who looked like them talking, down the road. I can't be sure, it might have been, but I'm not sure. I feel guilty now I was a bit rude to that John bloke who got killed when he came in late afternoon. I had a bit of a row with him, now I feel a bit sorry.'

Okonedo had some sympathy for June and Barry. They were normally so proud of their aggressive attitude towards their patrons, but now they were unhappy, somebody they had cursed as he left had died. She remembered Stevie's comments when she first arrived:

'Happy Mart, now that's a masterpiece of post-modern British irony. Those two could pick a fight with the Dalai Lama.'

She suddenly saw a side of them she'd not seen before and thought perhaps she had treated them as types and denied them a greater humanity. What would her attitude be if she had to stand all day in that soul crushing job, answering the same questions and trying to stop thefts all the time? June's eyes were now brimming with tears.

'I think you're being a bit hard on yourself June.'

Barry hugged her.

'This is all getting on top of us a bit. I always thought being involved in a murder would be exciting, it's not it's terrible.'

She sat sipping her coffee and sobbing between gulps.

'It's terrible, I mean the idea somebody is going round smashing people's heads in. It's the viciousness. What if we get attacked? This is Burridge for God's sake, you just don't expect it down here. I'm scared.'

It took about ten minutes for her to calm down, but it was clear she had to go home. She went outside to get a breath of fresh air.

'I'll get a cab,' Barry said, 'I don't know what the owners will say if the shop's closed?'

'Well I'm afraid that's too bad,' Okonedo stated baldly, 'I think you need to be away from here for a while and I think she needs you right now. So sod the shop.'

Okonedo looked through the window at the sight of the pair of them arms around each other clambering into the back of a black hansom.

Chapter Thirteen.

When Penrose arrived at the houseboat he was tired, there had been no let up in the weather. The rain lashed the seafront and a chill wind beat his face. Standing outside Timothy's home he saw the memorial bench further down the beach. Where the van had been, a well-wisher had placed primroses on the roadside. Timothy peered through the window and smiled. Penrose was relieved as he clambered inside. He liked Timothy's home, but although cosy, he thought this was something it would be prudent to keep to himself, as he thought it was probably one of those words Timothy would find patronising.

'Sit down my friend. Do you smoke?'

'No Thank you.'

'Do you mind if I do?'

'Certainly not. Your house, your rules.'

Timothy proceeded to fill his pipe and soon the room was filled with the pungent smell of pipe tobacco.

'I was thinking of making some cocoa, the fact I have a guest makes this less self-indulgent. I can make a jug; you'll join me, won't you? It's proper cocoa, not this supermarket stuff.'

This sounded good; the wind swirled around the boat and as he sat there looking at the beach through the windows the rain came down in sheets against the glass. It was that comforting protecting feel, reminiscent of a childhood holiday when he was caravanning in the Lake District with his parents and younger sister. He remembered the bad weather meant they were cooped up in the caravan and spent the afternoon drinking tea and playing board games. With his parent's sense of fun they had turned it into a magical afternoon.

He stood up peering at the books on the shelves above the window; arranged in a chaotic fashion, some of them upright some of them flat. Books on art, a few film books, a couple of books on philosophy by Hannah Arendt, Doors of Perception by Aldous Huxley, some large books on Renaissance art, a book on Caravaggio, a palmistry book, Magick by Aleister Crowley and an assortment of sketchbooks. They didn't tell him too much about Timothy. They reflected a catalogue of diverse taste which had been arrested in his twenties, there was nothing new there. Timothy walked in with a tray which he placed on the table. He sat and poured out mugs of cocoa. Pushing a plate towards Penrose he said:

'Home-baked ginger biscuits, made with real ginger. Enjoy!'

This was one of the most reassuring afternoons Penrose had spent in Burridge. He sipped the cocoa and sunk his teeth into the biscuits that were the handiwork of Doris. They were soft and thick, luxuriantly moist and so drenched with real ginger they made his whole mouth tingle with the flavours.

'I suppose you want to know about last night down the castle?'

Penrose nodded as he munched.

'I was having a nice quiet drink in there with Jennie and David. You know, in the snug out the back? There was one barman on and apart from the three of us there was young Giorgio, he's the new boy at Morelli's Ice cream place and they close up about six. He was in there on orange juice; he's a good lad, just come over from

Milan I think, beautiful manners, like most Italian lads have. He's part of the family, I like the way Italians really look after their families, you know, not in a stuffy dutiful way but in a sharing, loving way. Anyway he was up at the bar and somebody had managed to drag George in, you know who looks after my Aunt Clarissa and it was all pretty relaxed and mellow. That was until Will kicked off.'

Penrose realised that was the first time he had heard anyone mention Miss Johnson's first name, although with her it *would* be more appropriate to refer to it as a Christian name.

'Does George socialise much?'

'Well poor bloke, he's a bit hag-ridden, isn't he? I mean with Dennie who is very nice and all that, but she is very much in charge, and dear Aunt Clarissa, well she *is* the monstrous regiment isn't she? I mean him coming into the pub was a bit of a bolt for freedom, if you know what I mean? Marx wrote about the deadwood of ages bearing down upon us, he was speaking rhetorically but there it's literally true. That house is so full of crap; it bears down on your consciousness. Somebody should burn the whole lot of it.'

'So what happened, I mean what sort of a scene was there?'

'Well we were all pretty relaxed and Will was screaming an awful lot about how everybody was being a phoney. I'll tell you something, I spent an awful lot of time around drug users in my younger days and you can spot it a mile off. You know, this attitude, that *the scales have been lifted from my eyes. I'm the only one with the vision to see it because I've taken a magic pill.* He was clearly completely out of it, putting people down and laughing *at* people. The whole thing was really unpleasant.'

'So what happened?'

'Well I was unaware of what was going on but when we started in there it was Jennie, David and myself sitting round the table. David went up to the bar to get a round in. He brought over drinks for Jennie and yours truly, and got one for himself when Will turned up. He was shouting "who's going to buy me a drink?" and flapping his arms around. Then he was shouting at us and saying "The one with the beard, will you buy me a drink?" David was trying to calm him down. He was pointing at me saying I was a fake, all that sort of thing. It was pretty nasty. I don't know but I'm guessing this was a sort of punk versus hippy thing. I know some people regard me as a bit of a boring old hippy fart, and I think whatever he had taken was egging him on. He was shouting at George as well, something about him being a faithful retainer.'

'So how long did this go on for?'

'Not very long. From what I gather George said to David he thought it'd be a good idea to get the police. I think David asked Giorgio to pop out and phone police liaison but unfortunately he phoned Okonedo, who it turned out was off duty. It was a cock-up. When he finally staggered out David followed him and dialled 999 and told them which direction he was going in, but they never got him. I don't know if he was doing this turn anywhere else. One of the bar staff did mention one thing, although not important in itself, it gives you a rough idea about the state he was in. Apparently earlier on he was outside shouting at one of the Seafront Defence Trust lot across the road: "You fat ginger slag, I bet you're still hitting the roids!" It tells you how far gone he was.'

Timothy smiled, ‘a bit more cocoa?’

‘Yes please, if you could just top me up?’

Timothy opened up the pale blue jug and with a long spoon gave the cocoa a stir and topped up Penrose's mug. He took a deep swig and munched another biscuit.

‘This Will, can you think who might want to kill him?’ Penrose said.

‘I don't know really, as you've probably guessed not really my sort of guy, but be assured old hippies like me have many failings but murdering people is not one of them. I get the impression he was a dealer, drugs you know? They can seem like such fun, but people who make a living out of it aren't really rebels. They like to pose as if they are, but they do the most enormous damage.’

He was looking out the window and his eyes were clouded with a remembrance of enormous sadness. Penrose felt awkward as if somebody's diary had fallen open at his feet and he had inadvertently glimpsed something profoundly private. Timothy suddenly brought himself up sharp.

‘Well Sergeant I'm beginning to ruminate, that's no good now is it?’

They both smiled, and the policeman was reassured at Timothy pulling away from some intimate disclosure. Timothy had withdrawn from some painful half-remembered event. Penrose had no way of knowing but he sensed it was not relevant to the investigation. He wandered back to the Hotel imagining various scenarios for the death of Will with little success. As he ascended the steps he was greeted by David Johnson.

‘Any developments?’

'None that I can discuss sir.'

Or none at all really.

He had made little headway with Timothy; Okonedo had enjoyed a diverting but pointless hour with Doris and Barclay was sitting in the incident room with his feet on the table and his tie loosened poring over notes. As he walked in and sat Barclay said,

'There's something here I know there is, I will find it.'

They heard a polite cough. It was David Johnson again, he stood there awkwardly.

'I think I owe people an apology. I was a bit rude about the police not coming when I wanted last night, I should have just walked out and dialled 999. I should be more aware it's as much the public's responsibility to act as the Police. Apologies.'

Barclay looked up and smiled.

'That's alright sir, just another piece of bad luck.'

David nodded and shuffled out. Barclay turned to the two officers.

'The fates haven't really been with us this week. What was it he knew that got him killed? Were they killed for the same reason, who shared the knowledge? Did John tell him something or could it have been the other way round? Then there's always the possibility they're not related, which might be possible, but seems unlikely.'

He turned to Penrose, 'I think we need to pay another visit to the evasion factory, I think we'd better go back to the Sikorski's.'

It was obvious to Barclay Cressida had been lying to him. He was unsure as to why; it was the reasons for the deception which intrigued him.

It was agreed Penrose should speak to John's mother Maria and

Barclay would speak to Cressida at her shop. Barclay thought he might find her more cooperative on that territory than in the home environment; perhaps the absence of the parents would encourage her to be more forthcoming. Then again he thought, perhaps not. Penrose was remaining tight lipped about how he felt about speaking to the mother. On his previous encounter it had been obvious why she had warmed to him. With his blonde hair and chubby face, he bore a passing resemblance to her dead son. The idea he was in some way exploiting her grief to further the ends of a police enquiry made him feel awkward. He was wondering whether Barclay was aware of this and was being manipulative.

When they arrived in Upper Letchford Barclay was dropped at the shop and Penrose went ahead to speak to the mother and was to collect Barclay later.

Barclay peered through the window of *Pastimes*, nowhere in the listings outside was the word antique used. Everything in the shop was a reproduction of furniture and paintings from the most popular periods. Largely Victorian or Georgian in its theme, it also had a small section of Jacobean style furniture. Along the walls were hung pristine reproductions of the works of lesser-known painters of the Renaissance period. The place was enormous, and though not packed there was a gentle hum of customers through the shop. Cressida strode over to greet Barclay.

'Chief Inspector, how are you?'

She was smiling and looking different from the woman he had met at the family gathering. She was wearing a loose-fitting dress and her hair was hanging around her shoulders. Looking as if she could easily have stepped off the canvas of one of the Pre-

Raphaelite pictures that had such prominence in the shop window she extended a confident hand.

'Very well, I presume you've heard the rather depressing developments.'

'I'm afraid so. Obviously, I don't know who the man was. Are the two things linked?'

'Well, we're working on the premise they are. I promised to keep your family informed, my sergeant is seeing your mother as we speak.'

'If you'd like to come through here?'

They went through to the display room at the back.

'Coffee?'

'Please.'

Cressida summoned a member of staff.

'The stuff out the back is completely undrinkable we'll get some from over the road.'

She gestured across the shop.

'So what do you make of my little emporium then?'

'Very impressive.'

Looking at the item in front of him he commented,

'What a charmingly authentic Regency telephone table.'

She laughed.

'Well, everything here is reproduction. They are not fakes they are copies, or if you like pastiches. Of course, there are some things like that which have a modern purpose but still have a nostalgic feel. For most people if they were to buy genuine antiques from this period they would find it prohibitively expensive. These items are within the price range of most people. I prefer copy rather than reproduction. The whole idea of a copy being a bad thing is really rather modern. There was a time if an Italian nobleman purchased a Titian; it would probably be admired by others, who would contact the studio. They would then get some lesser artist at Titian's studio to run off a copy. Now some of those copies can command quite considerable prices at auction, nothing close to the original of course. However, they are not forgeries, they are copies. It's really no different from people buying prints of that awful Hay Wain thing by Constable that so many people have on their walls.'

'I get the impression that John had a difficulty distinguishing between the two.'

'Yes Chief Inspector,' she said smiling, 'according to him it was a bit of a setup, although as they say *he would say that, wouldn't he?* I don't think there's any point in raking it all up again. I have to be careful, to save myself from any opportunistic civil actions. All the stuff is clearly marked and it's on every till receipt, so as to cover my ass. If you're buying antiques, then the first thing anyone tells you in the antiques racket, and it is a racket, is *Caveat Emptor*. You have to make sure you're buying the right stuff and you can prove its provenance, I'm not excusing him but the customers have a responsibility not to allow themselves to get cheated. If something seems too good to be true, then it probably is. Do you think there might be some connection between that business and his death?'

'We can't be sure quite yet.'

'When do you think you might be?' She said pointedly.

'These things sometimes take time.'

Jackie, Cressida's assistant came in with a cardboard tray and passed two large paper cups of Mocha to Cressida.

'Perhaps we should sit over here.'

She guided Barclay over to the corner and they proceeded to sit down in a Victorian type love seat. The whole situation was a bit comical and awkward.

'To paraphrase the title of a well-known painting, *when did you last see your brother?*'

The question was asked in such a humourless, and direct way Cressida realised that prevarication was not an option. She took a deep breath and gave a polite smile.

'Probably about 4.00 to 4.30 on the afternoon of his death.'

'You really should have told me before, but of course you know that. What can you tell me?'

'Well firstly, I'm sorry I didn't speak to you earlier but I couldn't have told you at the family get together. I hinted I needed to speak to you. I think you'll understand when I explain it all, and I hope you will be discreet. As I think you're probably aware he had gone through a process of cutting himself away from the family. He barely spoke to my parents at one point. I didn't just leave the door open. I demanded he see me. I went around and made him listen. My parents hadn't seen him for some time. If they had been made aware he was still seeing me I think they would have been very hurt, you understand? I don't know if it was student left politics, or what it was, but suddenly our religion was rubbish, the antique trade was rubbish, and he wanted no more of us. His universal pejorative of choice was *bourgeois*. His funny five minutes lasted a few months, if you see what I mean. I get the impression he needed a little more time to sort his head out. He was coming back to us and everything was going to be all right. I think when he returned it was going to be with a prospective wife in tow, that's certainly the impression I got.'

'What time did you get there?'

'Oh, it was about three. I brought some lunch, we sat and had a good lemon chicken dinner with cheesecake. Talked about the family, the business, that sort of thing.'

'Did you know anything about his plans for the day, or what he'd been up to?'

'He was off to meet somebody along the seafront. I don't know who, he didn't say.'

'A man or a woman?'

'I'm afraid he didn't say.'

'Did you have any sort of disagreement with your brother?'

She laughed.

'We always had disagreements, we were siblings. Nothing serious, however.'

'There were reports of a rather heated argument. Was that with you?'

'It was a woman's voice, was it? I'm afraid not, if he had a row with somebody then it wasn't with me. After the meal, I cleaned up, had a bit of a tidy and then left. If he did have a row with a woman it was probably the owner of the lilac coat.'

'Sorry, lilac coat, what's this?'

'There was a woman's coat hanging over the chair in the kitchen. I presume it could have been hers. He did have someone in his life.'

'Can you describe it?'

‘Not really, just a woman's blue coat. When I drove away there was a woman walking up his drive, it might have been hers, your guess is as good as mine.’

‘Did you see her enter?’

‘No. Sorry, for all I know she was just delivering a leaflet.’

‘The new woman in his life, what did he say about her?’

‘He didn't offer any information. I got the distinct impression he didn't want me to pry. It was one of those occasions when I thought it better to respect his privacy. Now, with the luxury of hindsight, I wish I had pursued the matter, but I didn't.’

‘Is there anything else you can tell me?’

‘I don't think so. I'll be straight with you Chief Inspector. I know your primary concern is to charge and convict someone with John's murder, but it's not mine. Nothing you do will bring him back from the dead. If you could reverse time, no one would be happier than me. My concern is that as soon as you can, we have his mortal remains returned to us, so we can give him a good Christian burial and go through a grieving process. As for you finding his killer, I hope you do. However, as you are no doubt aware I'm a devout Catholic and I shall be putting my faith in the condign punishment of a higher authority. I am now going to be taking a far more prominent role in the family business and I am painfully aware that gives me a motive for murder. Certainly, if material concerns were uppermost in my mind, the family business would provide a very handsome motive.’

Barclay swigged his coffee and understood how she felt. He endorsed Cressida's demand for a right to mourn. He had been to so many services which had opened with *we have come to celebrate the life of...* Catholic ceremonies always seemed to have some element of commemoration and validation. He thought on many occasions at services of any denomination, or none, it was almost considered indecent to display grief. You should be at some level a celebrant. He was unsure why this was now the case, but the social unacceptability of grief in some circles, he found unsettling and a little macabre.

'We will, of course, be returning John to you and the family as soon as we can and I promise you he will not be retained one more day than is necessary. I know the delay is painful and I'm sorry. Before I go I do need to ask one question. I think you are someone who wants to do her best to protect her family and their feelings at a very difficult time. I think you also want to protect the integrity and the memory of your brother. Sometimes with the best will in the world, people can inadvertently give succour and protection to the guilty. Please give this some thought, and if you wish to speak to me at some time in the future, please do not hesitate to do so.'

She replied with the blankest of smiles that was impossible to interpret. They both drained the last dregs of the now rather cold coffee. He awkwardly arose from his seat.

'Many thanks,' he said, and as she stood, with no acknowledgement, she turned and disappeared to the back of the shop.

He checked his watch and as he stood feeling irritated at her behaviour a familiar figure sidled up to him.

'Chief Inspector, may I have a brief word?'

Tony Perrot was standing at his elbow smiling. As far as Barclay could surmise, he must have bolted out of a side door; he had clearly been working out the back and was dressed in a French Rugby shirt with well-cut jeans, and smelt of beeswax. Barclay smiled and nodded.

'I presume you've just had a talk with *Catherine de Medici*?' Tony said grinning broadly.

Barclay smiled, Tony was likeable and did not seem to be playing games with him like the rest of the family. He was the most relaxed person in the household and revelled in having a disregard for all the nostrums they held most sacrosanct. Perhaps this is what Cressida had found most attractive about him, and she was now trying to mould him into a version of a husband more appropriate to her. Clearly he was not the type of man who would let any woman treat him as a work in progress.

'I have indeed been talking to your good wife.'

'My wife is rather conflicted over her brother's death. They were very close, perhaps a little too close. I don't know exactly what she's been saying but I'm sure you're a savvy enough guy to know what to take with a pinch of salt.'

'Yes, I believe so.'

'I won't say too much, I do realise the British police force are not *completely* stupid, so I reckon you've managed to filter out all the self-serving crap. Having said that, please bear in mind there is nothing, I repeat, absolutely nothing, my wife won't do to protect her family. I'm sure when you attended that pseudo wake at that mouldy mausoleum they call a home, you managed to work out how obsessed some of the family are with appearances.'

Barclay smiled and nodded. Cressida measured her words out with an apostle spoon. Her conduct was measured and solicitous.

He clearly didn't give a damn.

'We have to develop our own filtration system when we talk to people. Unfortunately we don't always get it right. I know it's a controversial idea but it would be considerably easier if people just told us the truth.'

'I'm sure you'll get there in the end. If I can just give you one piece of advice regarding Cressida. She seems to hold to the view that although John was in some sense lost to the family in life he can be reclaimed in death. Bear that in mind. Good day!'

He turned and bolted back towards the shop. In much the same way he was infuriated by Cressida's conduct he was charmed by Tony's. He walked along the side of the shop, and parked out the back was a rather smart red MG sports car. He turned back and as he stumbled along the anterior of the shop he suddenly stopped short. Through the window he saw Tony standing with his arms encircled around his wife's waist, she facing away from him and he was nuzzling the back of her hair, it was a moment of tenderness and he was shocked by it, probably by the inadvertent wholesomeness of it. Had he become so cynical that he couldn't feel some level of comfort and pleasure from the niceties of marriage? It unsettled him because nothing either of them had said implied they had a healthy relationship.

After Penrose had collected Barclay he talked about his encounter with Cressida.

'I get the impression she's actually quite a good woman, but extremely devious. Everything is dressed up to present things in a light of her approval. Tony, now what do we make of him?'

'Could he or both of them have done the deed do you think?'

'What links either of them with Ferguson though? I mean I was thinking that before. John's murder was very fortuitous for both of them. What is now bugging me is who is the woman the victim was involved with? How was Mrs Sikorski?'

'Much as you would expect.'

Barclay looked at the flowers he had left on the dashboard.

'Ah, those are for us from Mrs Sikorski. I'll tell you all about it.' Penrose said.

Penrose felt anxious when he arrived. He remembered how emotionally drained she was at the family event. The problem was what *not* to say. To ask a victim's mother how they're feeling invites a terse reply. Perhaps being over-cautious would be the best thing.

He was ushered through to the large conservatory at the back of the house. It was a tall Victorian extension, with high iron framed windows and fussy tiling. It was uncomfortably bright and the smell from plants and flowers was almost overwhelming. Mrs Sikorski was busying herself arranging flowers on a metal table. Adele was playing on the audio system in the corner. He wondered if this was a good choice, and then reflected that people grieving don't want to be *cheered up.* It may be distracting, he thought, as it was music about a different kind of loss. She gestured to a woman of her age sitting in a wheelchair.

'This is Patsy Duncan, she's my dearest friend. She's here to support me. You can say anything in front of her. Anyway, she's being collected shortly.'

Penrose nodded politely towards her.

'To save any awkwardness, it was a riding accident.' Mrs Duncan said.

'I'm sorry to hear that.' Penrose offered.

'Oh, it was a good 10 years ago. I've moved on with my life.'

'Mrs Duncan is quite an extraordinary woman. We've been friends since we arrived here in the 1970s. She runs an architectural firm. In fact she's designing a new marina along the coast from Southampton. Along with all that she is constantly out of the road as a motivational speaker.' Mrs Sikorski smiled.

'Yes I learnt a few lessons. Taking one day at the time is all very well, but you have to have plans, you have to look to the future. Even though it might seem quite bleak. I spent quite a bit of time feeling sorry for myself then you have to move on, don't you? Try to see what you've been through can be of some help to others.'

Penrose wasn't sure about her sunny optimism. However, he couldn't help but compare it to Miss Johnson's self-absorption. Mrs Duncan wore her disability lightly, Clarissa Johnson hers like a shroud.

'Let's have some orange juice.' Mrs Sikorski ushered him into a seat next to Patsy Duncan and wheeled over a small trolley and passed around refreshments. She sat opposite him with an expectant look. Penrose made a calculation: a question about how the family were, rather than herself, might elicit a more helpful response.

'How are you all bearing up?'

'Well, under the circumstances not too badly. Leon has been busying himself with one of the shops up north. Cressida and Tony also have responsibilities, and I suppose that is taking their minds off what's happened. I'm sorting out my own emotional support. I have had well-meaning people coming round and informing me that there are 5 stages of grieving. Somebody else told me there are 11, I'm sure in the not too distant future I'll be told there are 15. Not sure where in the checking list I'm actually supposed to be. I looked down amongst the many responses like pain and guilt, anger and bargaining, loss, et cetera and I cannot find *complete and utter bewilderment*, it did not feature on their checklist, which presumably means I'm in error. I'm clearly having an inappropriate emotional response. I know they mean well, but I think some people spend too much time watching daytime television. I intend to grieve in my own way, and at my own pace.'

'I can remember some of the things my mother went through during a bereavement. Some people don't always say the right things. But the support is real.' Penrose said.

Mrs Sikorski smiled and nodded.

Patsy's mobile shuddered on the table.

'I'm afraid that's my driver.' she said.

Mrs Sikorski gathered some flowers for her guest.

'I'll be seeing you in the next couple of days, Maria, you look after yourself. Sgt. Penrose, very nice to meet you.'

As her elegantly dressed driver pushed Mrs Duncan out of the room Penrose thought her absence might be helpful.

'Now what can you to tell me Sargent?'

'I think you've been told about the death of Will Ferguson. Obviously, it seems as if the two are connected. To be honest we don't know exactly how. We have however been enormously busy doing outreach amongst the local community to see if anybody knows anything. It might take a couple of days but we're pretty confident somebody will come forward with something. I'll be honest, I don't like to predict in these situations, but I can promise you we are doing our level best.'

'I'm sure you are Sergeant.'

'To be honest it's very difficult for us to find a motive. I imagine it's the same for the family. This is why it's difficult for us. Chief Inspector Barclay is talking to Cressida as we speak, perhaps she might be able to help.'

'Well, perhaps she might. I trust she is going to be truthful and direct with Mr Barclay. I love my children very much, however occasionally they can be less than honest in their dealings with me and their father. Cressida has been annoying me a little though with this *cherchez la femme* nonsense that she's been throwing around.'

'Sorry-'

'She was going on about *cherchez la femme* when we were talking at the family get-together. I can't bear that expression. Loaded up with all that nonsense about the inherent wickedness of women. Neither of us are what you would call feminists, but she is distinctly unsisterly. I love Cressida, but she thinks I'm a complete fool. John wasn't all he pretended to be, but then neither is she.'

'What do you mean?'

'Well I think John managed to get into a little bit of hot water – I'm not interested in what, so please don't tell me – but so did Cressida. When she was at university she managed to get herself arrested for obstruction at an anti-abortion demo. Utterly stupid. She shouldn't have got involved in things like that. This is not a Catholic country. It's a democracy not a theocracy. I know what the church's teachings are on such matters. It's always a mistake when people start confusing sin with crime. The silly girl got let off, they didn't press charges. But she should never have been there in the first place. Cressida doesn't know that I know about it. There are other things that Cressida doesn't know about.'

'Such as?'

'Well I had a strange visit from John's girlfriend, as was, a Bernadette Stevens, I think her name was. I think he'd moved and she had lost his address. The whole thing was very odd. I could see she was deeply unhappy. I think on one level she'd come to check me out. I think she was having problems, and she wondered if they were rooted in the family. Instead of coming out with it, it was all about addresses. I think she had a couple of books she wanted to return to him. Nothing real was said. I learned a long time ago in this country the British can conduct entire conversations in subtext.'

'What did you think the conversation was about?'

'I think she was seeing things in John she didn't want to see. I think she was desperate, or possibly desperately in love. I'm not entirely sure. She was a woman who was not levelling with herself. I have the impression that John, like many men had problems with fidelity. I think that she was realising that something had come between them that was a greater problem in terms of their relationship, than his unfaithfulness with women. That normally means religion, politics or something too big to ignore.'

'She didn't tell you?'

'No as I said, it was all lurking in the background. She was not direct. However, you could see she was a deeply unhappy woman. She was deeply hurt. Also a little bitter. Cressida doesn't know anything about this meeting.'

'What was her relationship with her brother like?'

'Oh, they were very close. The problem with Cressida is always the same, whether it's with her parents or her brother or Tony for that matter. With her it's always about control issues. This is the problem in her marriage at the moment. She wants to change Tony. I rather like him. He's his own man. It's okay for people to change in a marriage so long as they're changing together. That's healthy, that's a sign of emotional growth. The other problem is if you're controlling others you end up controlling yourself. You end up a bit stolid and frankly, very, very boring.' She gave a wry smile.

'I get the impression Tony feels he is a bit of a spare wheel. That must be difficult.' Penrose said.

'He comes from a rather interesting family. Anglo-French they are. His father had a rather good mechanical toy company in Paris. They produced wonderful things, but they went under. People are too cynical for that sort of thing these days. Children are too cynical.'

Mrs Sikorski had been quite forthcoming, Penrose was unsure why. More to the point, he didn't know if anything he had been told was in any way helpful.

'Well I've spoken quite a bit about us. I would like to know a bit more about you and Chief Inspector Barclay. What can you tell me about him?'

'Actually this is the first case I've worked with him. He has a very good reputation. If anyone can sort this matter out I imagine it would be him.'

'Is there a Mrs Barclay, is he married?'

'No, he isn't. He's a rather private man.'

'Is that because women aren't interested in him, or is he not interested in women.'

'I really don't know,' Penrose felt awkward, 'I would never really ask about such things to be honest.'

'But tell me about yourself than Sgt. I understand you're not from these parts. You must have a family?'

'I'm from Penzance. I'll be honest, I miss it quite a bit. People down south can be a little standoffish. I have two brothers and a sister. I'm quite close to my mum – and before you ask – I ring her every Sunday.' He said with a smile.

'Are you a religious family?'

'Not really. We're sort of low Anglican.'

'During times of trouble it can be a great support.'

Mrs Sikorski stood up and started going through the flowers on the metal table again. Clearly her flower arranging was a form of self-therapy.

'You know Sergeant, you remind me a little of my boy. That's why think it's so easy for me to talk to you. He always wanted to be a good sportsman, rugby and rowing and all that sort of thing. Are you?'

'I was desperate to be a good rugby player, but I wasn't good enough. It was temperament more than anything else. I didn't like being knocked over.'

'I can see how that might be a problem.' she smiled.

Maria Sikorski pointed at the flowers.

'I'm going to make up a couple of offerings for you and your Chief Inspector, and then I'm afraid I will see you out. I'm feeling tired, I think I may have overdone it.'

'That's very kind of you.'

'I'm going to give you some lovely Victor Hugo roses with some sprigs of rosemary. Sir Thomas More said of rosemary '*It is the herb sacred to remembrance and, therefore, to friendship'*. I feel you two need friendship and people to be friendly towards you.'

As he informed Barclay of his discussions he excised all references to her queries about him. Barclay pulled the flowers off the dashboard and sniffed them approvingly.

'Well, I think you might have had a more productive time than I did.'

Barclay was distracted, he wanted to evaluate what Cressida had told him to see what had any meaning. More importantly he had to analyse what she was concealing. As they approached the outskirts of Burridge he turned to Penrose.

'I think we should crash Granville Winters chambers. Mr Ferguson seemed to be picking on the Johnson boys last night; he's the one who might give us some dirt on them. I think we've both had a pretty thankless couple of hours. Also from what I gather I think it might be fun, and right now we need some fun.'

Chapter Fourteen.

When they arrived at the chambers they were greeted by Mrs Caldicot-Rogers the creaky clerk of the firm who had a marked stoop and looked as if she was held together with moth balls. She was immersed in heavily knitted clothes and had the unmistakable aroma of lavender water and urine.

'You wanted to see Mr Winters did you? I'll see if he's in.'

'We phoned ahead, we'll walk through.'

She peered after them suspiciously as they walked through, and returned to her tea and shortbreads. They arrived at a large oak door with Mr Winters name on a large plaque. As soon as Barclay gently tapped, a stentorian voice shouted for them to enter.

'Hello, Chief Inspector, such a pleasure for you to drop in. Always eager to see your lot. After all, you're the provider of the feast. You sir,' he said to Penrose. 'Can't say I've ever seen you before. You must both sit down and make yourselves comfortable.'

'This is Detective Sergeant Penrose,' Barclay said, 'I don't think we've met properly, have we?'

As Granville shook hands with Penrose he said,

'I haven't met either of you, but of course, I've passed Barclay on occasion in the courts. When I've been defending one of the thieves and cutpurses of old Burridge town, I have brushed his broad shoulders although I have never had the pleasure of cross examining him.'

He tipped his head back and scooping some bilberries from the plate on his table he tipped them down his throat. Neither of them knew what to make of him. Clearly, he liked to play the amiable buffoon, which he obviously wasn't. He wouldn't have lasted long if that were the case. He was in his early seventies and looked like a battered and much loved Chesterfield; lumpy, a little past its prime but utterly comfortable and reliable. He gave off the odour of stilton and claret and you got the impression those two things would feature prominently on any prospective DNA test. If Granville Winters was soaked in a vat of patchouli oil he would still smell of stilton and claret. He was comfortably fat and the ashy remains of blonde hair stuck out at awkward angles, and his rubicund complexion was a manifestation of his enthusiastic support of Burridge's plethora of wine bars.

'Now you will sit down won't you?' Barclay and Penrose pulled up chairs to his desk and obliged him. It was a comfortable room with rich wooden panelling and high shelves crammed with leather-bound books. Immediately behind the sprawling figure of the lawyer were large high windows set off with luxuriant floor to ceiling burgundy velvet curtains. The whole ambience of the place muttered comfortable reassurance. Barclay thought if he came in a time of crisis he would leave comforted and unburdened.

Penrose looked around and smiled. Granville leant back,

'Sergeant, you're impressed by this place aren't you? One of the first things I learnt in this game is people want to feel safe and comfortable when they go to a lawyer. Image isn't everything. I still do a massive amount of business here. Reputation you see? I'm good at keeping people out of prison. Best sort of advertising in the business. Now how can I help you two?'

Barclay smiled and sat upright.

‘I understand you are the lawyer who acts on behalf of Miss Johnson. We wanted some information about her family setup and we need some information about the Johnson boys.’

‘Well yes, I do represent her and as the family lawyer of course, I know them. I hardly think you could describe them as boys. Mind you if you ask any of the posh totty in town they will concur that young David is worthy of the appellation *dreamboat*. Obviously there are professional niceties that must be observed, and I'm afraid client confidentiality prevents me from saying too much. I'm sure you understand Chief Inspector.’

‘This is a murder enquiry. I can assure you any confidences shared will be dealt with respectfully. Sgt. Penrose and I are the soul of discretion and anything of an untoward nature will be kept under wraps.’

‘Even so, there are professional imperatives that require me to decline to cooperate if it involves any violation of lawyer-client confidentiality. Also, there are certain pieces of information which I have been privy to as a family friend. I'm sure you wouldn't want me to violate that sacred trust.’

Barclay inclined his head and gave him a reproachful smile.

Granville sat bolt upright in his chair.

‘I see it's like that is it? Clearly, I am to be browbeaten into providing information! Very well. But I think it might be easier if we had some coffee and refreshments. We can get Mrs Caldicot-Rogers to sort something out. Perhaps not such a good idea. She insisted coming back, poor old thing. She's been off sick with a mild dose of dysentery. I'm afraid the mad old fascist has been going through a period of estrangement with bowel continency, so on reflection it probably wouldn't be a good idea to have any foodstuffs that have been near her. I don't really want to be held responsible for you two spending the next month on the lavatory when you should be pursuing felons. I certainly wouldn't want to get on the wrong end of a civil action involving the distinguished Chief Inspector Barclay. Tell you what, Penrose be a good chap and pop down the corridor and get that mad old harridan to send Jocasta in here.'

Penrose trotted out to relay his request.

'Jocasta is the work experience slave. She's better than most of them. If you ask them to do anything, including moving, they think you're exploiting them. I think the last one thought being asked to make the tea was a violation of the Geneva Convention. As we speak I'm certain we're going to find she's lodged a formal complaint against us with Amnesty International.'

Penrose walked in with Jocasta. She was a sprightly teenager in a cotton blouse and jeans.

'Jocasta my angel, I have a task for you,' he passed her a note, 'pop over to Thornton's coffee shop and get three large coffees and an assortment box of their cakes, say it's for Mr Winters they'll know what to do. Afterwards you can go home if you like.'

She beamed and bounced out the door.

'She's not a bad kid. I got her father off for breaking and entering, more years ago than I care to remember. Now Chief Inspector, how can I help you?'

It occurred to Barclay the gap between Granville's robust defence of client confidentiality to collapsing at his insistence could have been measured in nanoseconds.

'You probably know about what's been going on down the front, burglaries, double murder. I don't know whether there's any connection but the second victim seemed to engage in a bit of unpleasantness with the two Johnson boys. What can you tell me about them?'

'The set up down there is very odd. Then again, they're all very peculiar people. Miss Johnson's holed up in that dump with Dennie and George. You'd think they could do something better with their life. He's ex-army you know and I think he saw some pretty shocking things. She was a nurse and I think she got out for obvious reasons.'

'What reasons?' Penrose enquired.

'Nursing is probably the second oldest profession for women. During the Crimean war, Florence Nightingale was wont to point out it was sometimes a combination of the oldest as well. It is an honourable profession but working at the casualty department became a bit much for her. On Saturday nights for example, when the clubs kick out and everybody starts punching lumps out of each other, the ambulances start pouring through the main entrance, do you know what they call the first ambulance in? The vomit comet! She finally had enough of it and I don't blame her. Anyway, they look after old Miss Johnson. She is the primary loonbucket there. My God her make up can be seen from space! I have this image of Dennie backing into an ante-room and applying La Johnson's eye make-up with a slingshot. She normally wears the volume of makeup Dame Maggie Smith would wear if she was playing one of the Von Trapp children in a West End revival of *The Sound of Music*. Why they have sacrificed their lives to looking after the most hellish woman alive is anybody's guess.'

'What about Timothy's relationship with her? What's all that about, I mean why are they still estranged?'

'Timothy doesn't have a relationship with her. I've heard people go round the houses on that one. Are we going to sit here avoiding the core issue, antisemitism? It's no longer a significant part of British society, but amongst certain sections of the upper classes it lingers like a fart in a lift. You do occasionally see some follically challenged members of our community standing on street corners distributing Holocaust denial literature on what looks like recycled toilet paper, but largely it's been eradicated. Miss Johnson I'm afraid has a problem and that's what caused the rift. I'm not religious myself. The God she bent a knee to was a pretty mean spirited one. Rachel was a knockout. Timothy adored her and what happened was incredibly sad. If they hadn't been so young and stupid it would never have happened.'

'So what happened?' Barclay said.

'Timothy was young then, they both fancied themselves as artists. In those days people were absurdly romantic about drugs. In fact they hitched their ride on the Marrakech Express a little bit late. There was a time when the drugs scene was barely penetrated by traditional organised crime in England. It was considered beneath them. It was largely done by middle-class amateurs. It changed long ago but

I'm afraid that image lingered on. That's where Timothy got caught out. How far he got involved I'm not sure, but things were going a bit sour in a number of ways. I think people don't realise when things have changed until long after it's actually happened.'

'What went sour and how?'

'The dream died Barclay. It was that hinge moment when the loved-up atmosphere of Woodstock gave way to the carnage of Altamont. Nothing was the same after that. People attempting to live the hippy dream after that were deluding themselves. I remember Rachel was a big fan of Hannah Arendt, who gave the English language one overused expression, *the banality of evil*, well I'm afraid no evil is more banal than the Mafia.'

'They were involved with the Mafia?'

'No, I'm unsure of what they got up to. I think they might have bought some cannabis or possibly something else and were selling it on. I think they were regarding what they were doing as a bit of small-time supplying, rather than dealing. I think they came to the attention of the Mafia and didn't know how to deal with it. I hasten to add nobody will tell you anything if you contact the Italian police. According to them, it was all just a fire.'

'So what happened?'

'They were running some *Ristorante* Bar thing on the outskirts of Milan. That much we know, the rest is a bit confused. He was out at an exhibition. He came back late and by then it was on fire. He tried to get in to save her but was beaten back by the flames. She died in the blaze. At some point he was questioned by the police, but he wasn't charged or anything. The pair of them had an extremely volatile relationship. There were grounds for believing he might have been knocking her about, like some of the Johnson men he had a violent temper. He had a complete mental collapse and ended up being looked after at a nursing home in the Loire valley in France. I don't know who but somebody locked up their studio in Italy.'

'How much of a mental state was he in?'

'Oh, we're talking about a complete mental collapse. He started doing those carvings as a form of occupational therapy. I think he was there close to a year. Eventually, a couple of friends went over and collected him and went down to Italy and shipped all his and Rachel's artwork.'

'What was she like?'

'She was a beauty, absolutely stunning. A considerable talent as an artist apparently, but of course she never had any success here, but she did have a successful exhibition over there I think. She was quite involved in the occult or alternative religions, I don't know, it was the seventies everybody was into that sort of crap.'

'What about her family, didn't they have anything to say about it?'

'Nobody knows. I think they rejected her or she, them, a lot of that went on in those days. I remember when I was at university somebody claimed to have rejected their rich family but we found out he was still getting an allowance from daddy. But she wasn't from here, I think her family were American or perhaps it was Canadian, I'm not sure.'

There was a polite knock on the door.

'Enter if you have provisions for hungry souls!' Granville exclaimed.

Jocasta cautiously eased herself in and put the coffees and an enormous box of cakes on the table.

'There you go Mr Winters. Can I really go home now? I mean Mrs Caldicot- Rogers might get a bit cross.'

'Pay no heed to her, my dear. If you have any problem with Quasimodo then just come to me, I'll sort her out.'

She shuffled out smiling and quietly shut the door behind her.

'Sargent, would you like to do the honours?'

Penrose stood up and proceeded to apportion the various cakes and pastries around. They had been provided with cream éclairs, macaroons, almond croissants, cream horns and a cornucopia of other cream saturated delights. Granville's method of dispatching a cream horn put Barclay in mind of a sword swallower he had seen at a circus in his youth.

'Now, where were we Chief Inspector?'

'Timothy returned to Britain, then what?'

'He had that tremendously successful exhibition at that gallery in London. What was the name of it? The Bellevue Studios, off Wardour Street. I must say a lot of people were surprised. He was seen by many as technically proficient but that's all. A journeyman painter, but everyone was astonished at the variety and depth of the work there. It really was a *succès d'estime*. It's odd how love can inspire you. It was clear she had positively influenced him. In two senses really, technically, in terms of the way he painted and also in an emotional sense. Great love can inspire great works. It can be that magic spark that takes something to another level. It seemed to have released something within him, but he never repeated an exhibition like that. He was using that heavy *impasto* technique that she used. Building up heavy layers of textured colours, it gives paintings a texture and immediacy like nothing else. Actually, that heavily layered way of building up colour with a palette knife isn't entirely dissimilar to Miss Johnson's way of applying foundation.

You see everything ends up with her.'

'What happened to all the paintings from Milan they were working on?' Barclay enquired.

'I think the bulk of it is upstairs at Miss Johnson's. That surprised you didn't it? She wouldn't take him in when he came back but then he didn't ask. The guy who got Timothy back from France. I can't remember his name, some French guy - he was some big cheese or should that be *Grande Fromage* from The Chelsea Arts Club. He turned up and told her it was her responsibility to lend a hand. Well, she couldn't very well say no. He'd just had his wife killed in a fire and suffered a mental breakdown. Perhaps she did it out of guilt. It's all crated up round at her place in the top two rooms. It's assumed he'll collect it one day, in fact I think some of it has gone to him in dribs and drabs.'

'How does David fit into all this?'

'Oh David. Well, he's a different sort of mess. Of course, he's exempted from most of that rubbish. For one thing, he's a different generation. Which means he wasn't raised with all that nonsense, his mother brought him up at the local school and she had him late in life. The snobberies he is subject to are harmless little things. For the most part, he tries to make sure Miss Johnson is looked after, but don't confuse his sense of familial duty with an endorsement of her views. There is one thing, which did happen there which was a little strange,' he said teasingly.

'Please go on.'

Barclay sensed a greater indiscretion was imminent.

'There was an incident when David went there some time ago. Miss Johnson was very groggy when he arrived and George said she was probably overtired. Anyway, David promptly dialled 999 and when she got to hospital it was pretty clear she'd overdosed on her prescription drugs. She denied deliberately overdosing and of course David was very concerned and has since insisted George and Dennie look after her drugs. There was however more. Later that week an old friend of hers, living over in Antwerp received a letter from her, which was completely rambling and incoherent. It went on at great length about how she couldn't cope and wanted to end it all. I think she even identified herself with Jezebel, for God's sake. It was barely intelligible and the writing was practically unrecognisable and I think the old bird who received it contacted the local vicar over here.'

'So it was a suicide attempt.'

'Apparently so. She couldn't remember writing it, since then David has been very watchful of her. He was due to get the house but he's really let that go. He fully realises that when she gets really ill it's going to get eaten up by the health bills. David's only real fetish is his standing in the community amongst all those yachting and rugby types which can get a bit boring after a while. Then again we can all get a bit snobbish about our own peer group or what we've latched onto. He's another one who should get out and make something of himself. He won't say it but I imagine this murder business has knocked him for six. I think he was relying on the Festival of the Sea thing to help the hotel. It's disastrous publicity. He is wise enough I'm sure not to say anything though.'

'Will Timothy get anything from her at all?'

'Oh yes, David's very friendly with him. I think they spoke some time ago and some of the artwork in the house has been earmarked for him. He really needs to draw a line and move on. He's still a talent of sorts and he would be a lot happier if he was a bit more relaxed about life, he could start by buying a round more often, or even *once*. That man is as tight as a seal's bum! He's got that voluptuous Doris woman chasing after him. She's a bit of a corker from what I remember. Enormously attractive in a sort of Rubenesque way. From what I remember she has norks the size of the National debt. She's Burridge's answer to Madame Arcati and she does have the propensity to talk almost fathomless bullshit. But he could do a lot worse than her, but he's still moping over Rachel. Men are such fools!'

Barclay started making mental notes.

Granville sat up and inclined his head towards Penrose.

'Well, I heard this John Sikorski was a bit of a dark horse, what can you tell me about him? I've heard mutterings of all kinds of dubious practices. What can you tell me?'

'Well, Mr Winters from what we can gather he was a bit of a sexual outlaw.'

'A sexual outlaw,' Granville said laughing, 'It brings to mind someone dressed as Dick Turpin holding up the coach between London and Manchester at pistol point and performing lewd acts upon the startled occupants. Oh, please tell me more!'

It was clear they could be there for hours. Granville had an inexhaustible supply of stories and much as Barclay believed you should never underestimate the importance of gossip, he thought at some point they would have to leave him and now would be an appropriate time. Granville looked suitably wounded as they got up to say their goodbyes and Barclay felt guilty when they got up to leave.

'You will pop in again, now won't you?'

'Absolutely sir.'

As they wandered down the road to the car Barclay reflected on the lawyer's behaviour.

'You know Penrose when I was a kid my father brought me up on the novels of *Alistair MacLean*. They would quite often have the plot device where one member of the British unit sent to save western democracy would be captured by the Gestapo. It would end up with the nasty Nazis getting the evil doctor to pump him full of scopolamine so in spite of being an Officer and Gentleman he would betray the others. If it was Granville Winters they would get an immediate result if they had access to a patisserie. He would be happy to sell his comrades for a franzipan fancy.'

As they got to the car Barclay stopped.

'I have a proposal. I'm going to pop in on the forensic squad for a quick heads up, whilst you go and touch base with Okie. We make a very quick visit to the Fetid Armpit. Then we can sign out. I imagine you have plans for tonight which might involve Stevie. Why don't you two and myself and possibly Okonedo meet up for a bit of seafood down the Met? It's partly work as far as I'm concerned, to put in an appearance after all the nonsense with Julian St. Hubert. I was thinking 7.30, we can be through by 9.00 then you can do whatever you're doing, it'll be my treat.'

'I'll have to check with Stevie, but I'll give a provisional yes.'

*

Barclay walked down the ramp whilst the noise of the electric saw rattled the air. Stephen Jensen was leaning into the back doors of Will Ferguson's van. Barclay heard a shout and saw Meera Devon sitting near the windows. He waved at her, she was wearing white overalls but had removed her mask and was sipping coffee.

'Barclay, you've come just at the right time. The van is surrendering its secrets to us and they are many and varied. We found money. We found drugs. Who could ask for anything more?'

The sawing sound whirred down. Stephen pulled his head from the van.

She gestured to the automatic doors at the back. Barclay walked through followed by Meera and Steve Jensen. There was a large red desk with several forensic bags on it.

'Cocaine', she said pointing at the bag on the desk.

'*She don't lie, she don't lie, cocaine.*' Stephen sang.

Barclay looked confused.

'*Cocaine* , by J J Cale it's an absolute classic. One of the greats from the '70s.'

'Yes,' said Barclay, 'not all of us have your familiarity with dreary drug songs from the 70s.'

'He was in the Velvet Underground, my Gran might have some of their albums.' Meera said.

Stephen shook his head.

'No, that was John Cale. He was the one in the Velvets, I'm pretty sure about that.'

He paused and frowned.

'Hold on, I think that might be John Cage. Or is he the experimental composer? I'm not sure.'

Barclay was getting irritated.

'Enough. Apart from anything, Cage was the one who did 4 minutes 33 seconds of silence, which frankly I would really like to hear right now. Fascinating though this sojourn through the counter-culture of the seventies may be, I'd like to know what you've found. If it isn't too much trouble?'

'Well that was a little brusque.' Stephen looked wounded.

'Sorry,' Barclay said, 'but would you be so kind as to tell me what was in the van? Please.'

Stephen gestured at the table.

'Well so far there is a large amount of cash we found, yet to be counted. The cocaine of course. We also just discovered this item, which is a load of MDMA, we are yet to process fully. I'll email you all the details in the next 90 minutes or so.'

'Thank you.'

As Barclay left he gave them a sheepish look.

'Sorry, I got a bit ratty.'

They smiled and laughed as they waved him out of the building.

Stephen turned to Meera.

'Well he's a moody bugger.' he said.

'Isn't he just.'

Chapter Fifteen.

Penrose had envisioned the Fetley Arms would be something in between Maxim Gorky's *Lower Depths* and an opium den out of a Fu Manchu movie. Since he had such a colourful idea about the place it would inevitably be anticlimactic. It was a provincial kind of drug dive; repellent, but in an understated and dull way. It was situated well back from the sea front near a 1950s conurbation and had been tacked on as an afterthought. It was almost if it had been designed as a drinking unit by a government functionary to fulfil a social need.

It was just a square from the outside, with a large oak door and anachronistic Victoriana fittings. The pub sign bore some heraldic coat of arms with something in Latin. This was obviously fake and had been designed sometime in the late 50s. The tall ersatz Victorian-style windows and plum wooden bordering had not seen attention for decades. The time for a facelift was over, now it required major corrective surgery. It looked shabby rather than malign and had all the personality of a council skip. Since it had little character of its own it had assumed the attitude of its patrons. This meant even when it was largely empty, it had the aura of being ill-disposed, ill-tempered and argumentative.

'Penrose, the main reason I wanted you to along is I'm a little scared of coming in here on my own.'

Although joking, there was a scintilla of truth in this. This was not a pleasant pub to enter alone. There were run-down pubs in Penzance, Penrose thought, they may have been scruffy but they were largely clean. There was no pride here. This place had no self respect. As they walked in there was an acrid smell in the air and they were struck by the shabbiness of the place. It was musty and the pub had the dusty patina of neglect. The furniture in the pub was not broken, but it *looked* broken. The place had the ambience of a bar after a brawl in a John Ford Western.

'I don't imagine you've thought of taking Stevie in here. It's not really celebrated as a centre of haute cuisine in Burridge. Having said that, it would be an unforgettable experience. This is not a very refined place. There are people who come here who think spaghetti is finger food. I promise you we won't be in here any longer than necessary. I wonder if we'll get anything out of Mister Carter, the malodorous maître d'?'

As they approached the bar they became aware there were half a dozen people lounging around by the TV screen watching horse racing. They looked over at the two police officers. They were immediately aware of who they were and what they represented.

'Ever get the feeling we're the ones who are under surveillance,' Penrose said.

Barclay tapped his knuckles on the bar.

'Mr Carter, people to see you.'

After a short pause they noticed the manager secreted in an alcove at the end of the bar, talking on the telephone. He glanced furtively at them, but they couldn't hear what he was saying. It was their conjecture they were the subject of the conversation, and somebody was being advised to delay their visit. As he saw them observing him he turned his back and hurriedly finished his conversation. He sauntered down the bar and stood smiling. The cultivated scruffiness of the middle class rebels who used the Castle was not on display here, this man was a genuine mess. He looked like an unmade bed, and his general déshabillé was analogous to the state of the pub. He had the wiry physique and hollow faced look that was due to either severe and prolonged undernourishment or substance abuse. Clearly, it was more likely to be the latter. Speaking with a scratchy voice and that slightly distracted way of talking that comes from prolonged use of amphetamines he stood there tucking and untucking a lumberjack type shirt from his jeans.

'Can I help you gentlemen?'

As Barclay put his hand in his pocket Carter laughed.

'Oh, I don't need ID from you, I know who you gentleman are.'

'Good, then you'll hopefully not mess us about. I am Chief Inspector Barclay and this is Det. Sgt. Penrose, we want to know who this gentleman was with when he came in here on Monday.'

He passed him a photograph of John Sikorski.

'We'd like to know what he was up to. Before we get off on the wrong foot we know he was in here and the sooner we get some information the sooner we'll get out of your face.'

When the manager realised a certain line of response was closed he knew he would have to give the police something approximating the truth.

'I have some recollection of him coming in and sitting down, but I can't remember who he spoke to.'

'Was he carrying anything?'

'No I don't think he was.'

'Was he looking for drugs?'

‘I couldn't say. This is a clean establishment. We don't allow any drug use on the premises.’

This was said with such a flat delivery it was obvious to Penrose he was being arch, and it was the worst kept secret in town this was a drug dive. Barclay was a little confused whether there was some reason for the seeming official tolerance of this, he was not privy to.

Barclay pursed his lips and paused for a moment as he prepared his next query.

‘Right. Here goes. Is it possible he came in here and met up with someone? They went off to a corner, or the loo, or something and he bought some drugs off this other guy and left. You being a thoroughly respectable fellow would have stepped in and intervened had you known. There is no reflection on you or the possibility of you losing your licence. If of course, this is not the case I will have to spend some time down here with a lot of uniformed officers until we find out the truth. Now, what do you have to say?’

‘You know now you put it like that, it sounds like that's probably the most likely scenario.’

‘Thank you *so* much.’

As they walked back to Penrose's car, there was a sense of relief at leaving the place.

‘No offence sir, but I think that's the first time I've seen you in a place that serves food where you didn't have anything.’

‘I like to live dangerously, but even going through the front door without tetanus shots constitutes high-risk behaviour.’

‘Can you explain to me why that place is still open?’

'I'm not entirely sure. Why hasn't Julian St. Hubert launched a concerned citizen's campaign about It? It's probably that so long as it's there, the powers that be know where all the druggies and thieving scumbags are. Who can say?'

*

After being deposited at the Police Station Barclay walked up to his office on the first floor. He was fortunate to have missed out on the move, which practically everyone else had been obliged to make, into a new building. Most had greeted the move with enthusiasm, but he was happy to be cut adrift in a large Victorian building around the back, finding the large draughty rooms and noisy radiators more conducive to thought. Although perceived to have a rebellious streak this was not entirely true, it was simply his veins did not flow with the type of thinking inherent in big bureaucracies. He was accustomed to the exasperated comments about his apparent semi-detachment from the police.

The wall opposite his desk was dominated by a large Italian coffee machine. He prepared himself a large café latte and began going through the notes on his desk. The email from Stephen, was more informative. Will Ferguson's van had surrendered its secrets but none of them much worth sharing. As he had been told, there were drugs in the van: 100 tabs of ecstasy and 25 grams of cocaine. The only interesting factor was the large amount of cash found secreted under the seat, around 20, 000 Euros. This was not a revelation but a confirmation. He was working on the assumption Ferguson had stolen the clock; it would presumably be the cash from selling it in France. There was a flyer for the market he had attended on the outskirts of Fécamp and a brief report informing him it was a popular event held every other month, where people who were buying and selling antiques, furniture, paintings and collectables would attend in large numbers.

He smiled, as it confirmed what Cressida had told him; there was more than the odd rogue involved in the antique trade. The Sûreté was digging into this and he was certain something would be forthcoming.

His greatest interest was what the Allingtons would say. Perhaps John Sikorski said something to them, and was he alone in London that weekend? As he reclined in his chair there were things nagging him. He knew that probably there were two crimes central to the case, possibly three. He pondered what Ferguson knew and how he learnt it. He was certain it was what got him killed. His girlfriend seemed alienated from his death and it concerned him. Then again she was probably in shock. There was something which he couldn't quite recall Granville Winters had told him about the pictures and the art exhibition which was bothering him. He remembered the brief conversation with Father Canelli. As he swigged back the now cold coffee, he thought he might get more valuable information from another family cleric. They could be relied on to share the odd bit of information if properly prompted. It is doubtful he might be as forthcoming as Granville Winters but he could still be helpful.

He went to the window, the good weather had returned. The dark clouds had been ushered away by light winds. What little clarity beginning to break through was in spite of, rather than because of, the conversations he had with people. Whatever happened he would have to bring people in for questioning. Whilst there may not be enough to charge anyone, he would have to question someone under caution to get some truth.

*

Barclay and Okonedo settled themselves in their seats on the Balcony of the Metropole. As all the implications of drug abuse and violence became clearer, the yachting community were distancing themselves from Mr St. Hubert. The club's President Mary Wintour had been receiving concerned phone calls.

Barclay leant towards Okonedo.

'You have your ear pretty close to the street. Has there been any comeback over the dismantling of Julian's little Junta?'

'Not much directly. Not from the great and the good. Then again the yachting lot I think are all a bit embarrassed about it. Mary Wintour has been detaching herself from Mr St. Hubert. I'll bet good money by tomorrow lunchtime she denies ever having been formally introduced to him, let alone being compadres. You can't really defend assaults on people of pensionable age can you?'

'What about the general community?'

'If you're talking about the people who use the beach as opposed to the people who think they own it, most of them are pretty happy about it. The posse from The Castle on the Cliff is going to be holding a beach party tonight. It's going to be combined with a victory rally. I imagine dear Róisín will be holding forth. I suppose the late Mr Sikorski would have been pleased, he was a supporter of that group. You can't even find any of the small business types saying they supported them. It's odd so many of those people who were slagging off the police and saying private security firms were a necessary development have gone a bit quiet. What is that Hilaire Belloc thing?

Always keep a tight hold of nurse,

For fear of finding something worse.'

'You often get this,' Barclay said thoughtfully. 'People get swept up in things, but once the mask comes off, they turn with a vengeance. I know it's in some ways a crazy comparison but it's a bit like Senator McCarthy in the States. They had a documentary on BBC Four the other day. It was the Army hearings on television that did it for him. When the American people could see him day in, day out, they saw him for the nasty bastard he was. Television can make you, but it can break you. Ah, the power of television; he revealed himself as a bully and a braggart. The Americans aren't stupid or nasty people and they turned on him. These things happen all over the place, it's just here in microcosm, writ small.'

'Do you think Mr St. Hubert can survive this?'

'Sadly yes, but then again that's not our problem is it?'

'When are the others turning up?'

'Oh, I imagine they should be here soon.'

Mary Wintour walked past the table and moved her mouth slightly in a pretence of speech, and offered a smile born out of the obligations of office.

'Ah well sir, at least she's still speaking to us.'

Barclay stood up and walked to the balcony, it was an elegant chrome and marble affair, a product of pre-war elegance. The weather having cleared, the view was stunning. There were boats gliding in, and the Russian manned tall ships which were to be the highlight of Sunday's events had arrived. As some of the more sedate motor launches passed the quayside people were waving frantically. The recent problems as regards the security guards hadn't dulled the spirits of the yachting crowd; so perhaps the *soi-disant* Seafront Defence Trust weren't quite as representative as they pretended. In these cases, it was nearly always a strident minority who were speaking for others who were reluctantly acceding to a campaign they weren't comfortable with.

'I think they're coming sir.'

Okonedo was anxious to start the meal. Penrose and Stevie arrived, he in an open necked white shirt and chinos, she looking relaxed in a lilac summer dress and sandals. The four of them stood around awkwardly shaking hands.

'Has anybody ordered?' Stevie enquired.

'Yes I did,' said Barclay.

'Everybody sit down. I've ordered lobster thermidor, a large seafood platter, side dishes of jersey potatoes done with butter and parsley and a large Mediterranean salad. That Okay?' Everybody nodded.

'Drink?' Penrose mouthed.

'Well, I wasn't sure. So I ordered a couple of bottles of mineral water, a Chablis and a Moselle. The Kitchen god for this week is that guy they got from Benton's restaurant in Torquay. I think he got his training in Dublin. He's got a tremendous reputation. I know that frequently doesn't mean anything, but let's hope it does.'

They all sat down around the large marble topped table.

The waiter came over and proceeded to put out the plates and cutlery. The trolley arrived with the Lobster and an enormous plate with an assortment of freshly sourced seafood with small dollops of sauce interspersed amongst the portions of prawn, shrimp, crab and other seafoods. A side table was provided for the salads, potato portions and chilled wines.

They helped themselves.

'So Chief Inspector,' Stevie said, 'how's it going?'

'This one's an odd one. It's been a confusing situation, due to being unclear about the victim. It's like one of those paintings, a palimpsest I think it's called. Where you have one painting on the surface but there's another one hidden directly underneath. I keep on trying to see the painting that's hidden but every time I try, there's somebody splashing more paint over the top. Under normal circumstances I would only be dealing with one devious person but that's not the case here.'

'There is one thing which is bothering me, well a couple of things,' Penrose said, 'If he was religious, what about the cocaine? The reference Cressida made to his politics, I didn't see much evidence of that. In fact, I didn't see much in the way of books or music, the man seems to be a bit of an empty page. But what we are being told of him is other people's impressions, or rather what they want to see.'

'I had pretty much the same problem,' Barclay said, 'but the way I see it, and I may have got it completely wrong, is people live very contradictory lifestyles. People are religious in public and have a pretty different attitude in private. When you get down to it there's nothing in the Bible about snorting coke, and we never question religious people who abuse alcohol. Some people like to challenge societal norms on sex and drugs as a form of political protest. There was one of the Baader-Meinhof group who did a porn film. Then again perhaps he was having his cake and eating it, good old fashioned British hypocrisy. I think it might be curious but I don't think it's significant. The lack of books or CDs I do find a bit mysterious.'

'Do you think there's any chance he might have been dabbling in the occult?'

'I don't see any evidence of that, with whom?'

Penrose shrugged, and Barclay thought why do people always *dabble* in the occult as if it was not something to be addressed with high seriousness? Any crimes he had come across where there had been any occult connection the problem had not been they had explored it in a dilettantish way, but they had taken the Secret Art too seriously.

Okonedo leant forward.

'What is John Sikorski's mother like? Nobody's told me anything much about her.'

Penrose wiped his mouth and took a swig from his glass of Moselle.

'Well as you'd understand she's absolutely devastated by his death. When I was talking to her at the family event the other day she was speaking about how he was her husband's golden boy. It became quite difficult. She was standing there talking about how he was smashed like a butterfly on a wheel. She did say one thing that was very odd. Something about being wary of her daughter, she said she was an opportunist. It was difficult to understand what she meant. I also feel she knows more than she's letting on.'

'Well it must be difficult for her,' Barclay said. 'This has violated the natural order of things. You're not supposed to bury your children. A mother is there at conception and birth; she doesn't expect to attend their funeral. Even when a child is taken by illness or accident it's devastating, but in these circumstances, you can't even begin to understand the pain. Mothers give so much to their sons, the most giving thing they do is the act of letting go. She had barely let go and he was murdered.'

'She did say one thing which was odd,' Penrose continued, 'it was something about, how there is no well of forgiveness that is deep as a mothers love. I think it was a quote. I wonder what she felt she had to forgive him for.'

'Hold on' Stevie said, 'are you sure she was talking about him?'

Penrose smiled and nodded.

'Good point, I hadn't thought of that.'

'The problem I have,' Barclay said, 'is that if you take all the comings and goings from his house and his complicated private life it starts to resemble a Whitehall farce. There was a gap on his bathroom cabinet shelf, was this gap for someone about to move in, or had possibly someone moved out.'

'I'm sorry Chief Inspector,' Stevie said, 'but this American girl does not know what a Whitehall Farce is, if you wouldn't mind?'

Penrose was relieved at her timely intervention as he had no idea either.

'I'm sorry, there were a series of very popular farces that originated from the Whitehall Theatre in London, they were at their most popular in the sixties, with people hiding under beds and in wardrobes, running in and out of doors, dropping their trousers and speaking at cross purposes. It was the confusing aspects I was alluding to.'

'Many thanks, that's something else I've learnt.'

'Talking at cross purposes, that's probably at the heart of this case you know?' Penrose said. 'Oh before I forget, Dr Reid, did she say anything about the tox results for Will?'

'I only got the edited version,' Barclay replied. 'I'll have to wait for the final one but her prelim was that he'd been taking LSD and MDMA, she said the initial screening report *looked like a bomb at a scrabble convention* as she put it. Which considering his behaviour was no great surprise.'

'You know sir, this is a fabulous meal,' Okonedo said, 'and I could do without all the tox reports.'

'Yes, you're right, too much shop talk. This is one of the best seafood meals I've had in years. What do you make of it?' He said, looking around. Everybody was oily mouthed and nodding.

'I don't know what this guy did, but this is so succulent.' Okonedo said, scooping spoonfuls of lobster into her mouth.

'Look I imagine you two have other plans for this evening, Okonedo and I will be quite happy to stay here stuffing ourselves if you want to run along.'

He thought it would be a good idea to give the two of them an escape route. Penrose and Stevie were happy running along, they'd had more than enough of Barclay's shop talk.

After they left, Okonedo and Barclay relaxed and could give full vent to their gluttony.

'Anybody else had any thoughts on the investigation?'

Okonedo smiled.

'Jennie reckons it might all be Doris.'

'Doris has no motive though.'

'I pointed this out. She said *what if Doris is mad?*'

'But Doris *is* mad. No, I'm afraid that won't do, that won't do at all. Talking of which, what did Doris say about the evening with Will and co down the castle?'

'She seemed a bit confused about the whole thing. She noticed, as everybody else did, that dear Will was on a rocket to the fourth dimension. I'm not sure what went on in there or how relevant it really is.'

It occurred to her they were trying to read something into what happened that wasn't really relevant, due to the incident's proximity to Will's death.

'What was her impression?'

'Well, she was sitting near George; I think she was giving a Tarot reading. Jennie was with David and Timothy. Giorgio was sitting at the bar. David had gone up to the bar. Will came in and was sneering at Doris I think calling her a phoney. Then he turned back to Timothy shouting *the beard'll get me a drink as usual*. She said David found the whole thing quite threatening. The inference was Timothy had bailed him out before. If he was being threatening to Timothy, I can understand David getting angry; I just can't see Timothy being violent can you?'

'David wouldn't arrange an appointment with him to bash his brains in though; he'd just call the police. That scenario barely works at all, and only if you concede both murders are completely unconnected.'

Barclay couldn't see the point of dwelling on it too much.

'Something is bothering Doris though. We'd better talk to her again, I don't think it's about that evening, I'm sure it's something else,' Okonedo said wondering.

'Do you think she knows something or more to the point do you think she's protecting someone?'

'I get the impression it's something she's unaware of, not properly worked out, hopefully, it'll come to her.'

Chapter Sixteen.

Doris struggled along the road with her pushbike, made more difficult by the overpacked Waitrose bags hanging precariously from the handles. She had a small garden flat situated in a street behind the Imperial, and had decided after she had arrived, bathed and fed herself and her co-tenant, she would engage in a little meditation to see if she could discover what was bothering her. As she pushed her bike into the side gate and dumped her bags by the front door she was confronted by two of the occupants of the house next door. Jimmy and Sandy Leighton were peering over the wall, nine and ten years old respectively, they had been having a conversation with friends at school and wanted Doris to enlighten them on certain issues.

'We got a question to ask you, Doris.'

'Oh, really?'

Doris was rather fond of them, they were scruffy, likeable children, who were inquisitive and adventurous and had freethinking parents who had brought them up to be proud of their enquiring nature. They also had not acquired that rather judgmental attitude so many children had towards the adult world, that Doris found tiresome.

She opened the door and was confronted by her co tenant sitting in the hall licking his lips and giving her an indignant stare. The two children climbed over the wall. The conversation at school had focused on various aspects of clairvoyance and the occult and they had been informed any woman involved in Tarot readings and similar disciplines was a whisper away from being Satan's handmaiden.

Jimmy pointed into the hallway at her friend and confidante,

'Doris, is he your familiar?'

'No Jimmy. He's my cat and his name is Smudger.'

He looked at her suspiciously. Doris leant over and picked up her Ginger Tom. Smudger looked at her and gave her the same accusatory stare he always used when she had been away. Holding him out with his face nuzzling Jimmy's, Doris enquired,

'Does Smudger look like he might be an instrument of Satan? Can you imagine the forces of darkness calling upon their servant in Burridge, *Smudger, slave of the dark forces of Hades we have tasks for you to perform, oh Devil cat*, does that sound reasonable?'

Jimmy had been informed that these *familiars* were capable of flying through the trees and committing nefarious acts. However, looking at Smudger, Doris's morbidly obese cat, he doubted whether British Aerospace could get him airborne, let alone Satan, who he wasn't sure existed.

'Nah, alright I'll let you off. We'll call off the exorcism.'

'That's very nice of you,' Doris said as she staggered in with her shopping.

Sandy turned to Jimmy and in a world-weary tone that only a ten-year-old girl can deliver, muttered,

'Boys.'

Having treated Smudger to a generous portion of a salmon terrine and consumed a large mushroom omelette herself, Doris had a good soak in the bath with her usual cocktail of essential oils. She lit several small candles in her living room and placed them on the large oval table where she occasionally gave card readings to visitors. She opened a bottle of Medoc and gave it time to breathe before applying herself to her task.

She stopped in the hall before a picture of her late husband, Stanley, in his Naval uniform. After blowing a kiss, she checked herself and moved on.

She poured a glass of wine and arranged the candles; the darker red ones at the outer edges the more golden and amber ones in the middle. She sat and sipped her wine. Doris wanted to bounce something out of her subconscious. She became focused to discover what was nagging her. If she concentrated she could force out what was hidden. Closing her eyes she channelled her thoughts. She hoped at least to find out what was hiding in the back of her mind.

As she drifted off into a meditative state, half asleep and half awake, she begged questions of herself. There was someone in the shadows who did not want to be revealed. She was muttering *stand up I want you to show yourself*, but it was no use. She awoke in the darkness, shivering. The candles once so warm and reassuring had guttered out. Now cold and nervous, nothing had been revealed but she had felt threatened. The room was in darkness and she sensed a presence near her. Narrowing her eyes she tried to discern if there was anybody there. Somebody was near her, she felt a near and immediate presence. She smiled as she realised it was Smudger.

She got to her feet, extinguished the candles and put the overhead light on. Knowing she was close to her goal she decided the beach would be the best place to go. A good walk with some fresh sea air would do the trick. She put on her three-quarter gold lame jacket with matching turban and downed the remains of the Médoc She applied some lipstick and headed out. She knew the beach would be teaming with people.

When she arrived at the stretch of sand immediately after the pier the beach party was in full force. Fires had been lit and there was a band performing with the aid of a generator, pumping out blues rock. There was a fire eater, jugglers and the entrepreneurially minded had put burger vans along the sea road to feed the large crowds now milling around. It was a carnival atmosphere. For many people there, a dragon had been vanquished and it was time for rejoicing. There was a large bonfire and people were cooking sausages. The smell of sodden driftwood and kerosene filled the air. Doris went along to one of the vans and purchased a chilled mineral water and sauntered to an uncrowded part of the beach.

She sat with her back to the sea, swigging it down. She reflected on Kate Chopin's words, *The Voice of the Sea speaks to the soul,* and smiled and thought, *but will it speak to me?* The sound of the beach revellers was a distant rattle in the background. Come on Doris, she thought, get in the zone. Turning things over in her mind she tried to get back to where she was, but everything had been so amorphous she didn't know where that place was. She shut her eyes and let the changing rhythms of the sea float her mind away to a place more susceptible to the further reaches of her imagination. She was drifting away to a place of greater suggestion, into a somnolent dream-like state. As the waves murmured onto the beach and whispered their withdrawal, she was adrift. The susurrations of the sea seemingly sharing a confidence with her. With a start she sat up. She didn't know what it precisely meant, but something was revealed she knew was important. She got to her feet and staggered along the beach until she reached the promenade. Stumbling up the steps of the Alhambra she cantered in. Gasping for breath she demanded,

'Stevie, where's Stevie? I must talk to her.'

Albert was doing the evening shift. He looked blankly at her.

'She's not here I'm afraid. Can I take a message?'

'No, I don't think so. I need to leave a message for her so she can speak to that nice Sgt. Penrose, they're stepping out together I think. Is David here?'

'No he's at a match in Portsmouth he won't be in till late.'

Doris was flustered.

'You see it was about the other night. That Will bloke, he wasn't threatening Timmy, he was pointing at her you see, and now David could be in danger.'

She was twisting her hands in an agitated state.

'Writing paper, give me some writing paper. I'll leave a note, that's the best thing.'

Stumbling to a corner of the lobby she sat down and started writing furiously.

Albert one of the legion of part-time staff drawn from the local student body was the evening relief. Although dull-witted he compensated for his lack of intellectual acumen by a kindness of spirit. Sliding his copy of *Rugby World* under the counter, he realised by her agitated state she was in need of assistance.

'Can I get you a coffee or something?'

'A decaf lovey, if you would?'

She continued writing furiously, screwing paper up and throwing it in the bin. Albert was both intrigued and alarmed at her behaviour. He brought her decaf. Doris didn't stop writing, and looking up gave him a smile of thanks.

Finally, she sat back, her task apparently concluded and swigged down her coffee. She ambled up to the counter.

'Now Albert, I want you to listen very carefully, you're to see Stevie gets this, it's rather important Penrose and Barclay see this first thing.'

She placed an envelope into his hands and he nodded gravely.

'No one else you understand? I can remember when I was younger I was a carer to an old lady, a Mrs Forbes-Robertson, and her grandson opened one of her letters and she gave him a dressing down, and described looking at somebody else's letters as *an unconscionable incivility*. Please bear this in mind.'

Doris was aware she was rambling, but couldn't stop. She ran down the Hotel steps and hailed a cab. Her behaviour was erratic even by her standards. Doris felt if she got it all down and handed to the relevant authorities that would somehow make everything safe for others. Also she believed it might ensure her own safety.

Chapter Seventeen.

Barclay arrived at The Alhambra at 8.30 AM and had some bacon and eggs. He had slept well but was troubled, he knew something was eluding him and the more he tried pursuing it, the intangibility of it pushed any solution further away, and any disclosure withdrew entirely. Barclay noticed Penrose was happy and focused. His relationship with Stevie appeared to relax him, then again, he didn't know what the nature of it was, and he certainly wouldn't ask. Okonedo was shuffling paperwork, and there was a sense they were waiting, something was imminent. Barclay did not like being subject to events, he didn't see himself as an agent of change, but he felt he was somehow nudging things along.

'Do you know when we'll hear anything from the Allingtons?'

'I think they should be interviewing them anytime. If they have anything to report we should hear within the next half hour.'

'There's going to be a handwriting expert contacting me sometime this morning. If all goes to plan, we should be able to make an arrest for something. When are these idiots going to phone?'

*

Doris entered her kiosk at the pier at 8.45. It was hardly a kiosk; it was more like a living room. However, she preferred kiosk to what the council now called it, which was a unit. How would she reveal anything to her clients if it was a unit? Nothing remarkable could happen in such a place. She couldn't say *please make yourself comfortable, this is my unit*, or *would you like to enter my unit?* No, she thought that would sound thoroughly improper. It was decked out in a variety of styles, Chinese lampshades and cushions, Italian chairs, an oval rosewood table to have tea with her clients whilst doing readings. Not for her one of those gloomy rooms, that was pretentious nonsense. Homely touches would put people at ease. Her mood was defiantly optimistic when she arose, and she was wearing a combination of fuchsia and magenta.

Charlotte, one of her regulars had requested a reading on the phone, when there was a sharp rap on the glass front door. Doris peered through the glass and smiled whilst she gestured to her phone. Unlocking the door she beckoned her visitor in, whilst she put the hand over her phone.

'I'm glad you're here, I need to talk. I'm in the middle of doing a reading. Sit yourself down lovey. I'll only be a few minutes.'

Charlotte was demanding relationship advice. Doris didn't approve of people abrogating responsibility to clairvoyants or lifestyle coaches. In her view, the Tarot merely gave people more information and provided clarity, so people could make informed choices.

'Charlotte, I'm sorry I can't tell you what to do, you've got to make your own choices and live with them. That's all right love. I'm not marrying him petal, you are. Well perhaps your mothers got a point. Look darling you've got to weigh up all the pros and cons.'

She was trying to extricate herself. She maintained the more knowledge you had the better likelihood there was to make the correct choices. What Doris was didn't know was her visitor had knowledge she was unaware they had.

Her visitor, unbeknownst to her had committed an unconscionable incivility.

*

Penrose joined Barclay outside the Alhambra as he tried to collect his thoughts.

'Still no word from London, sir.'

'Somebody once described waiting as masochism in its purest form. Let's get on with other stuff. I've just been told a message was left for us, from Doris via Stevie at reception; I'd appreciate knowing what was in it. Her shift starts at nine, at the risk of offending you, could you prise it from her fingers so we can either dismiss it as the deranged ramblings of bonkers Doris or a lead of some description?'

Penrose turned and hurried to the staff room. Barclay walked out and stood by the grey painted rail and looked out at the sea. It was a sunny crisp day, but with a chilly undertone. An indistinct remark was bothering him, a comment, something undefinable. That was what he was missing, something there on the outer reaches of his peripheral vision, that suddenly disappeared if he turned too quickly. Also, what he couldn't work out was where Cressida fitted in. Was she being dishonest out of cussedness or was she protecting somebody? That was the problem, if he only knew who she was protecting then he would have some sort of solution. He also thought it was possible she was protecting herself.

*

Doris was bringing her reading to a close. Chatting in her usual animated fashion. She always gave her complete attention to who she was talking to, so she was unaware of things going on around her. Her visitor quietly went to the entrance door of the kiosk and bolted the door and turned the closed sign to the outside. The khaki roller blind attached to the top of the door was quietly lowered, but engaged as she was, she was unaware. Her visitor sat in the seat immediately behind her so she could not see a metallic object emerging from an inside pocket and being handled circuitously. She was too busy practising her craft.

'You've got to make your own decision about this guy, even if the judgment call you make is the wrong one and it turns out to be the wrong choice, so be it, but it'll be *your* choice.'

*

Okonedo put the phone down and walked outside.

'I've got some news for you, sir.'

'Finally.'

'The Allingtons have given a brief statement to uniform in London but we need to follow it up. Apparently, when Sikorski left he had a brief chat with Mrs Allington, mentioned how he'd been over a couple of picture galleries in London. As she waved him off she saw some guy who appeared to be with him and they left in a car together.'

'Anything more?'

'Oh yes. Mrs Allington was very specific; she said she would have no difficulty identifying him.'

'What did uniform make of that?'

'Apparently, the Allingtons spent the last few days in the countryside up north, they're twitchers. You know, birdwatchers? She's very sharp eyed. She can identify a bird 200 feet away by the distinctive plumage on its tail feathers. You wanted some luck, well here it is.'

Barclay smiled.

'Thank you, Sergeant, thank you very much.'

He looked out across the water adding,

'I want you to do me a favour, I want you to ring the Sikorskis and find out what John's singing voice was like.'

*

Doris was finishing her reading and was conscious it was approaching nine o'clock and people would expect her to be open.

'Look I've been through this as much as I can dear. You really have to make the journey yourself. The responsibility for any decision is firmly in your hands. I can only take you by the hand to the river, how you wish to cross it is your choice, your responsibility. No dear I don't think another reading will tell me to advise you any differently.'

She pushed the cards away from her, as a way of defining she was not going to be coerced into shifting her ground.

'Your life, your choices sweetie. Okay,' she said laughing. 'Look give me a call when you've made your decision darling and we can meet up for a coffee or a glass of bubbly depending. Cheers. Bye.'

She pursed her lips and exhaled a deep sigh as she lowered the phone. Turning to speak to her guest she gave a broad smile. As she turned she was alarmed by a rushing movement behind and felt the shock of cold metal against her throat.

*

Mary Wintour looked out across the water from the Metropole and reflected things were going pretty well. The business with Julian was an embarrassment, but it could be weathered without too much difficulty. The event was more important than any one man and it would be irresponsible of her to sacrifice the legitimacy of the festival in a rush to defend him. Her duty to the yachting community demanded she should not compromise their standing in vainglorious displays of support for a politician, and a rather self-serving one at that. She would have to stand aloft from him, it was clearly her duty.

The Russian tall ships sweeping across in formation would be the big event. It would be for everyone, not just the yacht club. They would, of course, be watching it from the balcony with haute cuisine and fine wine, but everyone else could share it however they chose to. The whole beach would be thronging with people. All the old reprobates at the Imperial would be raising their gin and tonics as it went past. Everyone could enjoy it in their own way, with picnic baskets along the seafront if they chose. Many of the pubs further down would put on lunches and turn the thing into an event of their own. Since everyone could enjoy it in their own way, there was no reason to open up the yacht club to the general public.

In fact, since it was such an open event it would be *utterly* preposterous suggesting such a thing.

*

The Colonel was worried. He had seen Doris cycling to work a good twenty minutes ago. He regarded Doris as one of those colourful figures who gave joy to the world. Impossible to miss in her bright pink outfit, she had waved frantically at him.

'Come in, I'll give you a reading at nine before the rush, I've got Croissants.'

'You're on girl, I'll see you there!'

Most people didn't turn up before about ten-thirty. In Doris's eyes, she had to be there, as she put it *to show the flag*. When he arrived the blind was down and he was confused. Normally he saw her through the window, pottering around, on the phone or singing along to the radio whilst shuffling her Tarot deck. He had seen her arrive but this didn't look right, it didn't look right at all.

What was it Doris said, *trust your instincts, let's face it why were we given instincts if we're not supposed to act on them?* He walked from the kiosk to the promenade.

His instincts were ringing alarm bells. The comforting figure of Sgt. Dalton was hovering near a tea wagon. After he had dragged him to the kiosk they both positioned their ears against cracks in the door to ascertain what was going on. They shared a sense of social awkwardness. The Colonel heard some movement inside.

'I'm sorry officer something's not quite right there. I think you should break in.'

*

As all the various disparate and contradictory snippets of information started assembling into a coherent whole, Barclay realised Tony, far from being troublesome and quixotic in his dealings with the Police had inadvertently, or possibly deliberately, been the only one who was truthful in what he said. The way Barclay had evaluated the crimes as somehow independent of each other was where he had been idiotic. He suddenly realised the whole enquiry had become mired in deceit. Everything was now more focused, and that gave him greater concern.

Stevie ran down the stairs, followed by Okonedo and Penrose.

'There's no letter for me. I don't know what's happened. I've just rung Albert and he said he put it on the corkboard in the staff room, well it's not there. I've turned over the staff room and the main desk and I can't find it anywhere. I can't get Doris on her mobile and I'm scared.'

Barclay had a cold dank sensation in the pit of his stomach. They had been led around in a little gavotte largely by people not directly involved in any crime at all, whose petty concerns had compromised his enquiry at every turn. Doris had put herself in harm's way because she wanted to be helpful. His sense of revulsion was turning inwards.

'Penrose, Car!'

He turned to Okonedo as they ran down the street.

'See if you can get there any quicker on your bike.'

As the car leapt out of the corner at the side of the Alhambra, they felt the wake from Okonedo's motorbike buffeting the car as it went screaming by.

If only they had taken Doris seriously. He hoped that when they arrived they would find her sitting there in yards of Chinese silk, beaming at them and amused by their concerns. He needed no precognition to tell him this was unlikely, merely the balance of probabilities. He was beset by self-judgment as he imagined what may have happened.

When Okonedo dismounted she thundered over to the Colonel, who was standing near the booth.

He looked at her and said,

'You're a bit late.'

'What do you mean?' She said shaking her head.

'Oh, sorry officer, not that. I'm standing here watching for the ambulance. Myself and your colleague Dalton saved the day about five minutes ago.'

He pointed along the pier. There huddled on the bench was Dalton with a clearly distressed Doris, alive, but bloodied and traumatised. As the other two arrived it became clearer what had happened.

Doris lay there her head resting on his shoulders, her arms wrapped around him. Her head was twisting and shuddering in such a way it was clear no communication was possible with her. Her magenta coat, one of her favourites, was ripped and bloodstained. Doris had been through a horrific ordeal. Her face was streaked and smudged with her own blood and there were angry red weals across her neck.

She lay there sobbing, muttering terrified inanities, rendered incomprehensible due to the damage done to her throat. The attack had been partly successful. Its purpose was to silence Doris, and in that objective, it had achieved its aims, but not permanently. She would have her turn to speak. Now, however she was too terrified to think. Her conscious sense knew the immediate danger had left, but was unable to communicate this to her shattered body. Her head was lolling on his shoulder, and her alabaster skin looked stretched and stressed as if it could tear. She let out large sobs whilst her lungs expanded and contracted to accommodate her erratic gasping as she let out cries of pain.

The scream of the ambulance siren wailed as it rattled down the pier, the paramedics disembarked and sped towards Doris. Barclay turned to the chief paramedic.

'I think it would be a good idea if Sgt. Dalton goes with you. Is that okay?'

'Yes. Not a problem.'

When Barclay walked back Penrose said quietly,

'How bad is it?'

'Physically, of course, I think the neck took the brunt of it but I get the impression she put up a hell of a fight. I think the real damage might be on the inside.'

Dalton helped her up, as the paramedics attended her she held his hand tightly, and stared at him anxiously.

'It's alright angel, I'm coming with you.' He said as they manoeuvred her into a stretcher, but her legs kept failing her and going into spasms.

As they sat together they reminded Barclay of some Victorian lithograph of a shipping disaster with Doris as some shipwrecked wastrel clinging to wreckage. She lay there and even though her eyes were closed rivulets of tears furrowed down her face. As her head rolled back they saw Doris's neck normally so pale and fleshy now bloodied and wreathed in ugly bruises. Barclay approached Dalton and hurriedly scribbled something in his notepad and discreetly showed it to him, he looked back up at Barclay and gave a joyless smile and a nod. The paramedics gingerly ministered to her needs as the ambulance doors closed and the vehicle swept away.

Penrose looked as it moved away and without turning said to Barclay,

'Do you think she'll be alright?'

'I think she'll live.'

Okonedo roused them from their torpor.

'The squad cars will be down here soon, sir. If I might see the name?', she said with some asperity.

He passed the notebook, she glanced at it and without comment turned away.

Moving down towards the promenade clusters of onlookers were hovering around the pier entrance. Okonedo turned towards the Colonel who was peering across the side of the pier.

'Sergeant,' he shouted pointing, 'there he is!'

Running over to the rail she peered over and saw a figure weaving erratically through the holidaymakers on the beach towards the promenade. She ran the length of the pier slamming the window of a waiting police car for attention, as she sprinted down the promenade. After a couple of hundred yards, she paced to a halt. Stopping at a brutalist sculpture erected in the'60s, she leant against it and took out her radio.

'The bastard's along here somewhere, I'd like a squad car down here *now*, please.'

She noticed a figure many yards ahead stumbling up from the beach. Using a hand above her eyes as a visor she peered down the promenade. He staggered for a few steps and broke into a run. She launched herself down the stretch at full pelt. She pounded down the promenade her arms moving in disciplined scissor movements. It took two hundred yards to gain on him and when she judged she was at the appropriate point she launched herself against his midsection flooring him.

Chapter Eighteen.

The Colonel was an astute and deferential gentleman, one of those people who instinctively knew what was helpful when talking to the police. Consequently, his interview was short and helpful. When he emerged from the interview room he saw Okonedo in the corridor and smiling said,

'Your arrest yesterday, quite an impressive flying tackle, we could have done with you at Twickenham last week.'

'Thank you sir, we aim to please.'

'Doris, how is she?'

'Physically they say she'll make a full recovery. The worry is how it will affect her. Everybody likes to take the rise out of her beliefs, but it's the Pollyanna aspect of her personality people like. I'd hate it if she lost that. Having said that when I spoke to one of the nurses on the phone about half an hour ago they said she was sipping beef tea and had managed to raise a smile.'

Barclay sidled up.

'I need a word,' he said. 'Penrose is going to follow up a couple of things, its important he speaks to Cressida to get something confirmed. I trust you will be happy to be my second whilst we interview Mr Johnson?'

'Of course sir,' Okonedo said, 'what is he being charged with?'

'Two lots of premeditated murder and attempted murder, it's all him.'

As Barclay and Okonedo sat in interview room 2 at Burridge police station, it all seemed anticlimactic and they felt numb.

David Johnson had received medical attention after his arrest but he still looked rough and the combination of the crunching tackle from Okonedo and receiving a right hook from Doris during his struggle meant he still looked dishevelled.

He was looking around the room in a distracted way as Barclay began the proceedings.

'..If you wish to have a lawyer present...' was he listening, was he really there?

Barclay took a sip of tea; the station coffee being too acrid for him.

'Tell you what sir, why don't I go through what I think happened and what we can prove and you can respond if you feel like it?'

David declined to respond.

'Very well. Here goes. I don't know when you met John Sikorski. However, at some point you became lovers. I think he fell in love with you, I don't know what your feelings were for him. I think it's fair to say his love for you was greater than yours for him. It's pretty clear you pressured him into being more discreet about the relationship than he would have preferred. Some say lovers shouldn't have secrets; well I think he did, and it was those that got him killed. The plan was you employ him as your assistant, and you could therefore facilitate a personal relationship and a professional one, I think this was sold to him due to not wishing to distress your aunt and he reluctantly went along with it; I also think he wanted to save his family any distress. When I spoke to Bernadette Stevens she said he spoke about starting a new job. This was before the interview. His previous boss went to great lengths to say he was always very cautious about securing contracts, this means the job was in the bag and the interview was a formality. When he came Stevie noticed somebody like you, who enjoyed being tactile and as she put it was a serial back slapper, rather stiffly shook hands with John. This was somebody who you already admitted to knowing socially beforehand; it was all rather over-egging the pudding wasn't it? If it hadn't been for the amount of confusion and downright dishonesty surrounding the circumstances from others, much of your own deceptiveness would have been obvious.

If we go back to the day of the murder it all becomes much clearer. John arrived at the hotel for the non-interview and after you talked, he left and went home, at some point, you popped his mobile round and then left. His sister then came for lunch. I presume he discussed his personal life with her. She has traditional Catholic views on sexuality. They rowed as siblings do. She said that if their parents found out it could kill them and he agreed to remain silent. This conversation was overheard by his neighbour. After the meal, she cleared up. I have had the privilege of seeing his sister clearing up and it is a terrifying sight to behold. She gives a whole new meaning to the word *thorough*. The idea that she would leave a dirty ashtray on the telephone table isn't really on. His ex-girlfriend and his previous Landlord amongst others commented on his untidiness. His neighbour said that when she discovered the body, she presumed he had got a cleaning lady. This implied the tidiness of the place could not be due to his endeavours. No such cleaning lady has come forward. When I arrived there I found the tidiness a little troubling. The only things out were the cocaine and mirror and the ashtray, which bore your fingerprints.

That, I'm afraid places you there much later.

'After Cressida left he went down to the Fetley Arms to score some drugs. He then popped into Happy Mart and had a barney with June over the fact that she didn't have the right condoms. It was a centrepiece of her complaints down the wine club immediately afterwards. A couple of days later she came in and made a statement about it to Okonedo as she felt a little guilty at how she had spoken to him. He arrived at the Castle at around 6.30. This is where the confusion started to set in and I'm afraid we started looking in the wrong direction. He bumped into Will and was unaware of his burglary. When he was sitting with Róisín and her friends she assumed that when he got money out of his coat pocket before going to the toilets it was for drugs, it wasn't, it was to buy condoms, after all, he was already sorted for drugs. He'd gone down the Fetley Arms for that.

'This is the part where I'm afraid I'm going to engage in pure speculation. However, there is some underpinning supporting evidence, based upon what was said later which I think validates my assumptions. He goes into the toilet and buys condoms, and bumps into Will, men being men, they engage in some banter over why he's buying condoms and who they might be used with. They were friends, why shouldn't he tell him after all. When they are up at the bar he speaks to Gary. He told us he could barely hear him but thought Will was talking about John having joined the Sons of Belial, which he assumed was a band. Now he couldn't hear him, but Will apparently liked to show off how erudite he was. The Sons of Belial is a term used I believe by Milton in *Paradise Lost* to describe a group of drunken rioting homosexuals. In, I think it's

Genesis; the Sons of Belial arrive at Lots house and demand to *have knowledge* of his two male guests. Lot promptly offers them his two daughters instead. A contemporary reading of this passage would conclude that Lot was quite clearly mired in the more worrying strands of post-feminist theory, and needs a schooling from the Me Too movement. Actually if Lot was around today he would probably be invited to appear on one of those Incel podcasts, but I digress.

'Gary assumed he was talking about a band. I couldn't quite understand this because it didn't make any sense. In his house, there were no CDs, no sound system, no radio, just a television and DVD player.

It was clear that John had no vocal ability. Vivien Deauville said he had a voice like a screech owl. Father Canelli also observed he had no singing voice. I know that in contemporary Britain having no singing ability is no impediment to a successful career in music, but he clearly had no interest in music whatsoever. It also confused me that he was supposed to have said *he was a regular Perry Como* to Róisín until you remember that she found his blokey slang irritating. He didn't say he sang like Perry Como, or sang in his style, it was rhyming slang, Perry Como: Homo. It was laddish joking between the pair of them.

'The tragedy occurred when you got to hear about John having some question mark over him from Stevie, repeating what Jennie had said. This bothered you and you decided to have him checked out. You phoned some friend of yours in the Metropolitan Police. You take pride in your contacts. He phoned back and spoke to Jennie, when she was having a moment with one of those security guards and she was getting confused because he said he was from the Met, she thought he meant the Metropole but of course he meant the Metropolitan police. She said *he's on his way*; it didn't make any sense because if he was from the Metropole he would have known your whereabouts as your name was on posters all over the place. Incidentally, Sergeant Wilmot is going over your phone records and I imagine when we find out who you spoke to, they will probably be very cooperative if it comes to saving their own skins.

'Whatever you were told is a matter of pure speculation, but I imagine it would have featured him having been dishonest in the antiques trade and this was when you put two and two together to make five. You presumably thought some cold calculation had taken place in his robbing of your aunt. Granville Winters made some comment about the propensity for violence from the Johnson men, and since you two are the only Johnson men this was clearly a reference to you and Timothy. But what happened that night between you, we will only find out if you choose to volunteer the information.

The murder of Will was on the surface much the same, but I imagine much less painful for you. His phone call about finding out something which could be a nice little earner pre-dated the murder of John but his knowledge of your aunt meant he knew how valuable it might be. For all your protestations of having no interest in any inheritance, there is a substantial motive for keeping a lid on things here. I don't know how much the house is worth. When I was talking to Bernadette Stevens she made a reference to sighting John when she was out showing somebody one of those 'poky two-room flats that go for two hundred and fifty thousand a throw.' Well, Aunt Clarissa's residence is an Edwardian townhouse with a substantial roof garden on the main promenade. How much is it worth? If I were to be quite conservative I'd say probably one or two million pounds. That provides a commanding motive for murder. Your aunt holds views which to be frank are pretty loathsome, she's a rabid antisemite and by most people's criteria is a religious fruitcake. If she found out about your dalliance with John you'd be disinherited without a second thought. From what I gathered about Will he probably thought he could touch you for a bit of money now and then. Of course, when it became clear that the object of your affections had been murdered it occurred to him he could dump you in it. I'm guessing here, but I don't think that he imagined you had even done it. However any association with it would cause a minor scandal which under normal circumstances would mean that people would rally round and show some compassion, and give their moral support, but in your circumstances, the ensuing revelations would be financially calamitous.

'Will's arrival in the bar that night was blatantly threatening to you. There was clearly an element of spite that night in the games he was playing. All his references to *the one with the beard* whilst speaking to you was particularly unpleasant. Timothy was sitting with Jennie. The way you used to use Jennie was particularly shabby, dragging her along to social functions at the Rugby and Yacht clubs. As a professional subordinate this was wholly unfair and from what I gather she was getting a little tired of it. Beard, in old English, apart from meaning facial hair, meant to oppose, to defy; now it more frequently means a gay man's female date invited along either for the sake of appearances or for the purposes of concealment. When he said I'll get the beard to buy me a drink as usual it couldn't possibly mean Timothy. As far as I'm aware he never buys a round under any circumstances. The beard was Jennie. She was always picking up the tab for Will. What was it she said, Sergeant?'

'If there was a film of Will's life it would be called *Born Freeloading*. I can remember at the time thinking it was quite funny.' Okonedo said.

'What Will was doing was saying in front of a room full of people was *I know your secret, would you like me to share it.* The whole approach was brutal. There was the possibility of somebody phoning the police, but that was something you didn't want, so rather than let George dial 999 you got Giorgio to phone the police liaison number. These numbers are for working hours and being new he wouldn't know about police officers coming off shift after he had finished. He phoned Okonedo so it went into voice mail, but of course, you'd know that anyway because you are aware of the Police Liaison timetables. You did dial 999 when he left the building, why not do that in the first place? As Timothy said, you followed him out, giving you ample opportunity to arrange a meeting with him later, which he dutifully made a note of on one of the castle flyers. It also gave you the opportunity of pointing the police in the wrong direction. At roughly the same time you were sending the police in the direction of the pier Róisín was passing him going in the direction of the Metropole in the *opposite* direction.

'I think that the combination of the drugs and his arrogance encouraged him to let down his guard if indeed he was guarded at all. As soon as he started counting his money he was a dead man. I think you believed you were home and dry at that point.

'Unfortunately, there was Doris, and she sensed something didn't quite add up. Doris noticed that there was something about the way Will was talking to people that others hadn't seen. She realised that in fact, he wasn't pointing at Timothy, but at Jennie when he made all those beard references. She got the wrong end of the stick and thought Jennie was somehow involved.

'Now I'm presuming you're not denying the attack on Doris. Unless of course, you're suggesting one of Doris's occult rituals caused a tear in the space-time continuum which resulted in a David Johnson emerging from a parallel dimension bent on attacking Doris. I don't think even a Brighton jury would buy that one.

'Clearly you opened the letter from Doris. He realised somebody would find a way to the truth. You have been responding to events and as such you will have made other errors that will come to light. As we speak Dr Reid and her chums are going through your apartment at the Alhambra. I think we're going to find further evidence, blood spatter on clothing, shoes, something like that. I get the impression you're an arrogant man. I think you will have been careless.'

Barclay sat back in his chair, he was hoping for some reaction from David, but he replied with a look of blithe indifference.

After staring into space for an almost interminable period of time he turned to Barclay.

'Chief Inspector, could you get Granville Winters here please?'

'Certainly, sir, is there anything you want to say to me?'

'No,' he said smiling, 'I don't think there is.'

'Any messages need passing on?'

'No I don't think so, do you?'

'Very good.'

Barclay looked over at him and was trying to get the measure of him. He didn't seem upset or angry; the only emotion he sensed was profound disappointment. Barclay could only sense anything through guesswork and intuition, David didn't want to give anything away. His blank incongruous stare implied he was being frowned upon for some imagined slight, some minor inadvertent solecism. He appeared to be cloistered in a universe of indifference. Barclay wondered what his dreams were, and sensed he had a vision of himself standing alone in his richly appointed Edwardian townhouse, looking out through his bay windows at the waves rolling elegantly onto the sands of Burridge beach. A Martini in his hand, but alone.

Certainly, John wasn't there. It was unlikely his long-term plans featured him at all. With such an incommensurate obsession for property and position he wondered if he had room for anybody else. He seemed to feel that John and Will were characters from a film, who had no back story, and once they had become a nuisance, they were clutter that had to be removed. In David's clear unblinking eyes he discerned no evil, just a huge echoing nothingness. If there was any emotion in his crimes it was anger, not passion. Barclay resented the fact he could not even feel some level of pity towards him. Sometimes murderers were figures of heroic tragedy, if only to themselves. He felt he was being confronted by a figure of almost militant social and moral ambivalence.

As Barclay and Okonedo walked down the corridor they maintained an almost religious silence.

When they went outside Okonedo broke the quiet.

'I would have liked him to have said something.'

'There's not a lot he could say, is there? He couldn't have asked us to pass on a *get well soon card* to Doris. I'll have to speak to the Sikorski's, I doubt if they'll be happy but then again no resolution was going to be a happy one.'

'How do you think it's going to affect them?'

'These things change people totally. His parents will never recover, but they may change for the better or worse, but then again that's the nature of life. Others can move on in different ways. It can function as a wake-up call. Doris, if she recovers may stop wasting her life on Timothy. He might realise what he's got. Strangely it can spur you in different directions, sometimes positive ones. If people think they can turn the clock back, well, that way madness lies.'

'What do you think Granville will advise him?'

'Well if he agrees to advise him, I don't know. I think he might advise him to throw in the towel. Johnson may realise it's pointless. Also, a guilty plea might mean a little bit gets knocked off his sentence. Even with that, I can't see him seeing the light of day for about thirty years.'

*

When Barclay and Okonedo arrived at the hospital they were at least reassured by the news Doris was now sitting up and talking. She had apparently had a good night's sleep and was receiving visitors.

'I wonder if Timothy's been to visit,' Okonedo said acidly.

'I should think so, why wouldn't he?'

'Well Doris has committed the ultimate faux pas, she has survived. He can't idealise her and sob himself to sleep over lost love. Now if she'd been strangled he'd be having a whale of a time, he could really get into a crying drunk thing. The dead can never fail and you've no worries about crows feet or cellulite. God, men are such pricks.'

'Thank you for that. Well, he might come to his senses, and so frankly might Doris. I think it might occur to her that she could do better.'

When they arrived on the first floor, they were waved through. Her hospital room looked like a florist's, filled with ribboned flowers. Well-wishers had sent in enormous bouquets and Doris was deeply touched.

She was sitting up in bed wearing a fire red Chinese dressing gown.

'Hello Chief Inspector, nice of you to visit,' Doris said hoarsely.

'How are you feeling?'

'Well under the circumstances, I feel pretty damn good. Will I have to give evidence?'

'I'm working on that, I'm hoping you won't. What are the Doctors saying?'

'All things considered I came out pretty unscathed, physically I mean. There's no real damage to the vocal chords it's mainly surface lesions and cuts and bruises. Mind you, I put up a good account of myself. I spent most of yesterday sobbing and I think that's a good thing. I mean apparently, it makes it easier if you just let your emotions rip, rather than bottling it all up and ending up in therapy for the next ten years. They've offered me counselling but I think I can take myself through it.'

Doris coughed and cautiously added,

'The thing which really worries me is my return to work, you know to where it happened, I don't know what psychic echoes might be there or whether the violence will still be there in some form. That truly frightens me. Do you understand?'

They nodded, they were not co-religionists of Doris but they could understand why she might be fearful about returning.

As they were leaving Timothy arrived at the reception. The nurse was gently interrogating him.

'So, what is your relationship to the patient?'

Timothy looked crestfallen as he didn't know what to say.

'Let him through he's a good friend,' Barclay said.

She smiled and nodded him through. Timothy gave the two police officers a weary smile as he ambled past laden with roses.

Doris took a look at the flowers.

'Oh Timmy, let me relieve you of your burden!'

Chapter Nineteen.

Okonedo was helping herself to some tea from the drinks machine at the station when Granville Winters approached her.

'Barclay around?'

'I'm afraid he's off duty. I'm about to see him for lunch as it happens. We're all meeting up; his mum is just back from Canada. I can take a message if you like?'

'Well firstly,' he said, lowering his voice 'How is Doris?'

'It's over two weeks now, physically she's made a full recovery. She *seems* to be alright. She's going into her consulting booth today, how she copes, is, of course, another matter.'

'I see. Well, I have one piece of news which I think is good for all concerned. I have just had a meeting with Mr Johnson, and of his own volition, he has made a full confession. This will take a considerable burden off Mr Sikorski's family. It will of course mean that Doris will not have to relive the trauma of the attack in the witness box.'

'That is excellent news. It might even put a spring in Doris's step.'

He gave a wry smile and moved his head in a nonchalant way that made her uneasy. His tone changed and he began talking in a conspiratorial tone.

'Of course,' he said 'based on my conversations with Barclay there will be no other charges forthcoming.'

Okonedo was perplexed,

'I'm sure I don't know what you mean. What are you talking

about?'

'Oh nothing, anyway just popped in to tell people. I must rush.'

He promptly turned on his scuffed shoes and thundered out of the building.

When Okonedo arrived at the Pier, the party was already settled. At the far end past the theatre, they were all sitting by the sea waiting to order. As she settled down next to Penrose and opposite Barclay and his mother she pondered how she was going to raise her concerns over what Granville had said. Perhaps it would be best to allow him to volunteer the information.

'Good time in Canada, Mrs Barclay?'

'Wonderful, thanks, Okie.'

'I have good news. Johnson is going to cough to both murders and the attempted murder of Doris. That I believe is going to save a lot of people a great deal of grief.'

Barclay gave an approving nod.

'Well, it's going to save John Sikorski's parents having to go through all the theatre of a trial. I don't believe in *closure*, I don't think people can ever recover from these things, but at least they can *turn a page* as they say. I think however now that to a large extent that part of things is largely out of the way, they are going to have some very hard questions to ask Cressida.'

Penrose leant forward, 'What exactly was she playing at?'

Mrs Barclay smiled,

'Yes, I wouldn't mind having a few blanks filled in. Indulge me.'

'She saw herself as the keeper of the flame. As soon as I met her she started to grill me. It was my own fault really. When she heard what we knew she pushed us in the wrong direction. Her primary concern, no, her *only* concern was protecting what she perceived as the family's self-image. I think *honour* would be pushing it. Every conversation was about a woman having done it, *Cherchez la femme* indeed. She emphasised this to get us moving in the wrong direction. She didn't see a woman's coat, no woman was stalking him. He clearly was not contemplating marriage. I don't know what his religious views were but that thing from the Miracle of Fatima was pure opportunism. I assumed he had put it there but of course, he hadn't. She had.

'Now, remember what Mrs Lennox overheard *somebody could get killed or die if something came out*. That was presumably something along the lines of *if your lifestyle becomes public it will kill mother and father.* When she left just to emphasise the point she left that Miracle of Fatima thing and highlighted, *more people go to hell because of sins of the flesh than for any other reason.* She actually told me that she was indifferent to us bringing John's murderer to Justice. All that business about him returning to the fold was complete crap. If he was returning to the fold why had he just moved into a new flat and was starting a new job? It was obviously nonsense. Incidentally, John didn't mention the job interview to her, presumably because no real interview had taken place. Cressida also said he was returning to Catholicism. When he spoke to Bernadette he said he was moving on with his life, he obviously meant with David. If you return to Catholicism, you normally say you are *reverting*, don't you? Where Cressida was duplicitous, Tony was scrupulously honest. When I said I'd been told David was coming back to the business he said *that's news to me*. He also told me what Cressida didn't want me to know but I wasn't able to hear it.

'He informed me that he was bisexual. He said John was "a naughty boy, a roué, a slapper, a slut and a *bicycle* to boot". He also made a reference to the caterpillar from Alice's adventures in wonderland. A fairly caustic reference when talking about a gay man coming out of his chrysalis to emerge as a butterfly. The reference to cocoons and butterflies used to be pretty standard when people were talking about coming out of the closet. He said there was nothing Cressida wouldn't do to protect the family. When I saw him at the shop he did give me a piece of advice, that although she regarded him as lost to the family in life she would try to reclaim him in death, and of course, that's exactly what she tried to do.'

'Are you going to charge her with wasting police time?'

'No, that family have been through enough, I do think she'll have a reckoning with her parents, though. In the meantime, they can have their full-blown requiem mass and I hope that brings them some comfort. It's worth remembering funerals are not for the dead they're for the living. I also think that Mrs Sikorski knew. If not the absolute truth I'm pretty sure she had some sense of what was going on. The comment she made to Penrose was from Balzac: *The heart of a mother is a deep abyss at the bottom of which you will find forgiveness*. Mothers know their sons, that is their burden. I think anything she had to forgive John has been done, how she judges her daughter is another matter.'

Penrose frowned and shook his head.

'How do you think Mr Sikorski will feel about the whole thing?'

'I've no way of knowing. Let's hope he finds some sort of peace.

Cressida confused everything. You see the comparison with a Whitehall Farce is correct. Once we see the whole thing as a humourless Whitehall Farce with everyone talking at cross purposes it became glaringly obvious.'

'I do have one question to ask,' Okonedo said cautiously, 'Granville Winters said something about further charges not being pressed. I'm at a loss to understand what he meant.'

Barclay smiled, and at that moment the waiter arrived with Caesar salads and bottles of Pellegrini water and glasses.

'The circumstances we investigated started with the murder of John Sikorski, that's the way it might seem to an outsider. It's a little more complex than that. For a start it might seem it was about two murders, right?'

'When it's about three.' Okonedo asked.

'No.'

'Doris, being the third?'

'Oh no, I see what you mean, Doris being the third, it was really potentially about four. When he decided to kill John it's shocking because we can't understand how people make the journey from being a person who doesn't commit murder to someone who does. However, for him, it wasn't as difficult as you might think because he had already made that journey. The whole thing was about him inheriting property. He was prepared to kill his aunt if he had to. We repeatedly got this steady mantra from him that he didn't give a stuff about the money, about how it would probably have to be spent on healthcare. The one thing about Clarissa Johnson which is glaringly obvious is that she's close to death. I saw that when we went there and to be honest it made me feel awkward. When

Penrose and I went to visit, mother, what did you say about her? *Now there's a woman who's heading for the departure lounge.* Correct?'

Mrs Barclay nodded.

'However, he was preparing for any eventuality. If she died of natural causes so be it, but if she needed some assistance from him he would have been more than happy to pitch in. When he spoke to me at the hotel his performance was quite extraordinary. When you talk to people during a murder enquiry people will tell you the most extraordinary things and will share confidences they wouldn't dream of doing normally. However, this was nothing to do with the enquiry, and he suddenly saw fit to share with me that his aunt had attempted suicide. I'm a public servant, admittedly an *enormously* charming one, but that's all, why would anyone want to share that with me. Extraordinary behaviour. When we spoke to Granville Winters the penny began to drop. He described the letter, which was supposed to be a suicide note, as barely intelligible and the writing was *practically unrecognisable.*

I've been to her house, the bureau of her desk is available to anyone, and when I was there I could have swiped some of that revolting lavender writing paper. The other thing is if you write a suicide note you leave it don't you? You don't post it to an old friend in Antwerp, now do you? The other thing is her belief system. Do you remember all that stuff when she was talking about Pope John Paul II? She admired *his public surrender to the will of God*, Speaking for myself I found the public decline and death of the Pope utterly repugnant. He should have been pensioned off to some villa where he could have been waited on hand and foot. An elegant retirement where he could have enjoyed excellent food and fine wine in the company of some good books, being visited by the great and the good. Anyway, that was Clarissa's model, hardly a candidate for suicide. What David was establishing was a pattern of suicidal behaviour, if he needed to stiff her at some time in the future. I imagine he put the pills in her juice and he could be portrayed as the loyal relative saving her life.'

'How do you think he would have killed her?' Penrose asked.

'Well you've got to bear in mind this is all speculation. That roof garden has a rather low wall, and I wouldn't think it was safe if I was worried about somebody attempting suicide. In that letter, she supposedly referred to herself as a Jezebel. Perhaps this was his little joke. People used to call an overpainted woman a Jezebel. Also, Jezebel died by defenestration, being thrown from a balcony. By coincidence and this really is weird, I think amongst the righteous she was known as a Daughter of Belial.'

Everybody went quiet.

'That is really creepy,' Penrose said.

A shiver descended upon the table.

'Could any of this be actioned?' Okonedo asked.

'No, there's basically no evidence, everything I've just said is entirely speculative. I thought somebody might have the letter, I think the cleric who received it from her friend will not be cooperative about producing it, if indeed he still has it, although he did tell me its contents.

'However, I think it is important in understanding how David arrived at the situation of killing his lover. How murder became a form of problem resolution. John endangered the project in his eyes and had to die. That's the real tragedy, John was probably standing there, remonstrating that he really loved him before he had his skull smashed in. It's only when you understand the journey David has taken that it makes any sense. I dislike the term *moral compass* but I think I can be forgiven for using it on this occasion. People ask how people get to the point where they lose their moral compass. Well, David threw his into the Burridge Sea a long time ago.'

'The whole thing is such a mess,' Mrs Barclay added 'they could have been so happy if they'd wanted.'

'If *he'd* wanted.' Barclay said, 'The whole situation emanated from David's obsession with wealth and position, and not upsetting that vile woman. Nowadays he could have had a happy life. They could've got married. These days even down the Rugby club he wouldn't have had that much of a problem. You can be public in places like that so long as you're discreet. I know of two guys down Burridge Rugby club who are clearly an item and *everybody* knows. So long as you don't start rutting like hounds during the loyal toast to the King nobody's much bothered. It's like some middle-aged businessman who decides its cheaper to murder his wife rather than get a divorce to marry a new love. The primary motivation there is selfishness without moral restraint. However, I suppose *Selfish Murderer* doesn't sell newspapers. But then again I suppose selfishness without moral restraint is a good working definition of evil. Poor John, what a terrible waste of love.'

'Is love ever wasted?' his mother said.

'Well, I think it was in this case. Anyway, you're beginning to sound like bonkers Doris. On which subject, what is the latest?'

'I spoke to Stevie earlier on', Penrose said 'she and Jennie popped down to her booth yesterday and cleaned the whole place up. When she goes in there it's going to be full of flowers. They've pushed the boat out. She's going to open it up and see how she feels; nobody knows how she's going to react. I think most people agree that it's important not to put pressure on her. These things take time.'

Barclay nodded, he wondered if Doris's rituals would help her through this period in her life. He felt much the same way towards her belief system as the Sikorski's. He was faithless but he thought how her Tarot, I Ching and her astrological charts were all carapaces against the chill winds of reality.

*

Doris arrived with Stevie for moral support. She stood back as her friend pulled up the metal shutters at the side where there was a large window. Opening up the front doors she turned to Doris, who walked slowly in.

'Cup of Tea?'

'Oh, yes please dear.'

After making a large pot of China tea, Doris sat there holding her cup whilst scanning the room suspiciously.

'I'm very grateful dear, but I really need to be on my own for a bit. You do understand?'

'Sure.'

Stevie arose and proceeded to walk back to the hotel. Doris sat whilst trying to get some sense of the place again, and was trying to discern how she felt about being there. There was a small rap on the door; it was one of Doris's regulars.

'Hello, how are you, Doris? We've all been so worried.'

It was Raine, a retired woman in her late sixties.

'Come in lovey, come in.'

After they had settled down and were on their second cup and third almond slice, she asked her about what had happened.

'I understand it was a leather belt is that right?'

'Oh no, not at all. In the movies when it would be a cyanide pill slipped into a dry martini or a jewel-encrusted dagger used by some Russian assassin. But no it was a bloody lavatory chain, that says it all. That's all that's good enough for Doris.'

She was now shaking with laughter. Her laughter was a little over hearty. Raine looked at her and smiled, she was trying to see if Doris was faking it, whether she was treating the whole thing as a joke, a little too much. She wondered if Doris was behaving this way because she thought it was what was expected of her.

'The reason I'm here Doris- I feel a bit bad after what you've been through- but I need your help, you know, your guidance.'

Raine had no idea what she had said would have such an effect, but it was probably the most helpful thing she could have said. Something internal clicked inside Doris. Although seemingly trite, the idea of being needed was central to the way she dealt with the world.

Doris took out her cards.

'You know you're my first reading for a long time. Let's hope the Tarot is in a good mood.'

As Barclay and his party left their table and ambled down towards the promenade, they peered past her door. She was tapping the cards on the table, and as they turned they heard Doris's pealing laughter ringing down the length of the pier.

THE END

Printed in Great Britain
by Amazon